ONE HOUR

A CHAPEL HILL BOOK

With
a New
Introduction
by
Margaret
Rose
Gladney

ONE HOUR

Lillian Smith

The
University
of North
Carolina
Press
Chapel Hill
and
London

First published by

The University of North Carolina Press

in 1994

Manufactured in the United States of America

Originally published by Harcourt, Brace and Company

Library of Congress Cataloging-in-Publication Data

Smith, Lillian Eugenia, 1897–1966.

One hour / by Lillian Smith.

  p. cm.

"A Chapel Hill book."

Includes bibliographical references.

ISBN 0-8078-2178-0 (cloth : alk. paper). — ISBN 0-8078-4489-6
(pbk. : alk. paper)

1. Malicious accusation—Southern States—Fiction.   2. Sex crimes—Southern
States—Fiction.   I. Title.

PS3537.M56305   1994

813'.52—dc20   94-21668

                                                                    CIP

The paper in this book meets the guidelines for permanence and durability
of the Committee on Production Guidelines for Book Longevity of the
Council on Library Resources.

98   97   96   95   94   5   4   3   2   1

TO DOROTHY NORMAN

liberal and outspoken of mid-twentieth-century white writers on issues of social, and especially racial, injustice. Her writing boldly explored the interrelatedness of her culture's attitudes toward race and sexuality and the ways in which the South's economic, political, and religious institutions perpetuated a dehumanizing existence for all its people.

Such boldness in the 1940s brought both censure and censorship along with fame. First, an unsuccessful attempt was made by the Atlanta postmaster in 1943 to ban *South Today* from the U.S. mails. Then *Strange Fruit*, which chronicled the emotional and social upheaval surrounding a biracial love affair in the 1920s Deep South, was banned in Boston and later temporarily banned from the U.S. mails. More important to Smith, however, was the fact that despite its instant popular and financial success—selling over three million copies and being made into a Broadway play—critics often regarded *Strange Fruit* as a "race" novel rather than as a significant literary achievement. Although *Killers of the Dream* was never overtly banned, it offended too many white southerners, including powerful moderates, to be financially or critically successful. Both its subject matter and innovative style, a combination of personal memoir, allegory, and direct social commentary strongly condemning the white South's deep-seated commitment to racial segregation, were met with hostility, or deliberate silence, by the literary establishment (the New Critics) and the general public of Cold War America.

After the largely hostile response to *Killers*, Smith began to adopt a broadly philosophical approach in her writing, explicitly demonstrating that her concerns extended beyond race relations in the American South to include all aspects of human relationships in the modern world. In the early 1950s she studied contemporary art and "the effect of World War II and the atomic bomb on the creative mind" and became interested in "the anxiety-inducing effect of the body image," especially the latest developments in the field of physical rehabilitation.[1] Smith first developed her thinking on these subjects in *The Journey* (1954), which may be read as a companion volume to *One Hour*. Begun in 1951, it was completed after Smith discovered she had cancer and underwent a radical mastectomy. In its Prologue she wrote, "I went on this journey to find an image of the human being I could be proud of." Writing to her friend Horace Kallen about *Journey*, she explained: "I had to find what I believe, what is meaningful in human experience, for me; what is the creative meaning of ordeal."[2] The theme that life's meaning is to be found in the creative response to ordeal fully informs her second novel, *One Hour*. Indeed, it may be read not only as Smith's analysis of the widespread oppression and censorship associated with the McCarthy era in general, but also quite literally as her own creative response to her personal ordeals involving the effects of mob thinking and mob violence.

In the late fall of 1955, while Smith was teaching for a month at Vassar College, two young white males vandalized her home near Clayton, Georgia. Her bedroom and study were burned, destroying her personal belongings, thousands of letters, and irreplaceable unpublished manuscripts. A few weeks later, as if to add insult to injury, Smith learned that paperback copies of *Now Is the Time* (1955)—the book she wrote specifically to encourage support for the 1954 Supreme Court ruling on school desegregation—were being removed from bookstores and newsstands and that the publisher was not filling orders. As Smith tried to extract an explanation for the book's removal and fought to get it reinstated, white resistance to desegregation escalated into mob violence in the Deep South.

As Smith was arguing in vain for the urgent need for *Now Is the Time* to be available to college students and the public in general, *Life* printed a letter from novelist William Faulkner in which he, claiming to speak for moderate white southerners who opposed racial segregation, pleaded for the North to "stop now for a moment" the efforts to end segregation forcibly.[3] Smith wired *Life* immediately, asking for the opportunity to respond to Faulkner's letter, but her request was denied.

Acutely aware of being spurned or deliberately ignored by the national media, Smith wrote her friend Frank Spencer: "Now, please sir, HOW AM I GOING TO BE HEARD?" Besides questioning "how," she asked, "Why can't I be heard? . . . Is it jealousy? Is it that I am a mere woman and my opinion is not worth anything?"[4] The questions were not merely rhetorical. Refusing to accept the efforts to silence her, Smith wrote many letters to journals, newspapers, and friends seeking assistance in getting her ideas published in larger magazines. Eventually, however, she turned her questions into writing *One Hour*. "When I want to find out something," Smith had written Kallen, "I write a book. It is my way of searching. Not to give the world 'answers' but to find them myself."[5] In writing *One Hour*, Smith was, in effect, addressing her own questions about how she was to be heard and why her ideas about social change and human relationships were so strongly resisted.

Smith's thoughts about the scope and intent of *One Hour* dominate her correspondence from the summer of 1956 through the spring of 1959. To Eleanor Roosevelt, on August 15, 1956, she wrote:

> I am working seven days a week on a novel. Called *One Hour*. It has to do with the silent, invisible mob in men's minds and hearts that is waiting to burst out into spiritual violence and sometimes physical violence. The plot has to do with an eight-year-old girl framing a young scientist on a sex charge. That is a mere plot; it goes on from there into deep places in the human heart and out to the ends of the earth. It is concerned with innocence and guilt; with suspicion; with goodness, too; and knowledge and truth. It has something of the quality of *Journey* in it but is a hard driving, dramatic novel, too.[6]

Similarly, an early outline of *One Hour* indicates that Smith thought of her story as having universal implications:

> *One Hour* is not a story of a culture in microcosm coming to a close—as was *Strange Fruit*. It is, rather, a story of rational man in a cold war with irrational man: the conscious intelligence struggling against the unconscious mind; the creative good dreams and feelings man has found for himself fighting a survival battle with the archaic, primitive drives so long kept behind bars—now let loose in the name of "freedom," in the name of any holy idea: be it segregation, or nationalism, or Hinduism, or "the Church," or the Moslem religion, or communism, or color, or the sanctity of sex normality, or so on.[7]

Her references to "Hinduism" and "the Moslem religion" reflect Smith's long-standing interest in democratic movements for social change throughout the world. She had studied Mohandas Gandhi's writings in the mid-1920s, while teaching music at a girls' school in China; had traveled to India as a member of the American Famine Commission in 1946; and had returned to India for an extended visit from December 1954 to May 1955 under the unofficial auspices of the U.S. State Department. Thus, she knew from her own experiences the many faces of what she called, in a letter to the editor of the journal *Booklover* in Bombay, India, the "new authoritarianisms." Responding to his request for promotional information on her new novel, Smith wrote:

> *One Hour* is, I think, a better novel than was *Strange Fruit*: it goes down into human vision and dream and motivation more profoundly, it appeals to any person who realizes that he is living in 1960 and not the 19th century, that he is a watcher of the cosmic skies and of the vast, chaotic changes taking place in the depths of man. . . . I think *One Hour* may be the first American novel that has dealt directly and on many levels with the problem of the human being caught in his many traps called [science], art, God, freedom, the importance of the masses, and yet the dangers inherent in proletarian rule; the new authoritarianisms, etc. etc.[8]

The novel is dedicated to her friend Dorothy Norman, in whose Long Island home Smith spent several weeks while writing *One Hour* and through whom she met many of the liberal intelligentsia of New York City in the 1940s and 1950s. It was their world, in a way, that Smith was addressing, but the message she sent was a coded one. *One Hour* is set in a small city in the Upper South. Its principle characters, the town's educated elite, read modern authors, European classics, and modern theologians and philosophers, listen to modern music, collect modern painting, and meet in the local bookstore for intellectual discussions. Yet they, like the characters in *Strange Fruit* and *Killers*, are still haunted by their childhood memories. Their unacknowledged fears and anxieties both reflect and render them incapable of dealing with the anti-intellectuals whose actions threaten to destroy their community.

Significantly, "how" Smith attempted to be heard—the "mere plot" through which she framed and analyzed the existential dilemmas of modern America—involved not race but sex. It is no accident that when Smith removed race as the focus of her writing, issues of sex and gender took center stage. As historian Elaine Tyler May observed, "Fears of sexual chaos tend to surface during times of rapid social crisis," and the Cold War crisis provoked urgent efforts to control a number of "explosive issues," including sexuality as well as the bomb.[9]

Yet Smith was bound by the restrictions she was trying to probe. Precisely because she was writing in the 1950s, the explosive issue of sexuality could not be addressed directly. However, issues of sex and gender permeate the novel thematically and structurally, and Smith's analysis of the tyranny of sexual normality is not difficult to uncover. Reflecting Smith's perceived position as a woman writer, the narrator is male and women's voices are relegated to subplots; yet both male and female characters reflect the limitations of their society's rigid gender roles. Priest and scientist are left crippled and silenced by war, the ultimate masculinist act, as well as by their own definitions of masculinity. The most powerful and, therefore, most destructive member of the community is the businessman, and the source of his rage to control is seen to be his jealousy of the friendship between the scientist and the priest and, not surprisingly, his fear of his own homoerotic desires. The male narrator sees women as either mirrors to the men they love (Grace, the artist), manipulative Medea types (Renie, modern southern belle), or ultimately wise but unknowable (Jane, the camp director, who like Smith "knew so much . . . but would it ever be told?"). Significantly, after completing the novel, Smith wrote that she would like to tell the story from Grace's perspective.

Not surprisingly, Smith's willingness to probe and question America's sexual fears did not win her the critical acclaim she sought. A reviewer for *Newsweek* criticized Smith for trying "to make you believe that she is talking about good and evil, but, what she really is talking about is sex."[10] Yet in the multilayered subplots (the stories of eight-year-old Susie, her southern mother, Renie, and the totally silenced grandmother, and the repressed adolescent love affair between Grace and The Woman), we see the interaction of sexuality, gender, class, race, and region from which Smith could not extricate herself. And it is the stories of women in the novel, and especially the stories of those characters whose experiences of gender and sexuality challenge the norm, that call now for a reassessment of Smith as writer. The novel then becomes a study of what happened to the text and voice of a woman who wrote in the 1950s metaphorically and from multiple perspectives about our fear of difference. Its flaws or limitations may be reread as strengths when we see in them the cultural consequences of repression, both for the individual writer and the community to and for whom she speaks.

NOTES

1. Quoted in Margaret Rose Gladney, ed., *How Am I to Be Heard?: Letters of Lillian Smith* (Chapel Hill: University of North Carolina Press, 1993), 115.
2. Smith to Kallen, February 24, 1954, in ibid., 144.
3. Faulkner, "A Letter to the North," *Life*, March 5, 1956, 51–52.
4. Quoted in Gladney, *How Am I to Be Heard?*, 165.
5. Smith to Kallen, February 24, 1954, in ibid., 144.
6. Smith to Eleanor Roosevelt, August 15, 1956, in ibid., 202.
7. "*One Hour*: Resume," p. 4, Literary-Manuscripts Division, Lillian Smith Collection #1283, Box 46, Hargrett Rare Books and Manuscript Library, University of Georgia Libraries, Athens, Georgia.
8. Smith to Sion, July 11, 1960, in Gladney, *How Am I to Be Heard?*, 243–44.
9. Elaine Tyler May, *Homeward Bound: American Families in the Cold War Era* (New York: Basic Books, 1988), 93, quoted in Jane Hunter, "Putting Sex in Its Place," *American Quarterly* 43, no. 3 (September 1991): 531.
10. "It's No 'Strange Fruit,'" *Newsweek*, September 28, 1959, 121.

ONE HOUR

1

The most obvious thing about this hour is that it refuses to stay in its place in time. As I reach for minutes, I find years stretching back endlessly. When I search for its beginning, for that first tick of the first second, I hear only hearts beating.

And yet, for a long time, I felt compelled to keep at it: I must find that elusive beginning, I must find who started it. Surely someone was to blame for what happened! But the beginning only slipped further back each time I grasped it, and the face of the scapegoat kept changing as I formed name after name in my mind.

Baffled by this compulsive search for what could never be found, I turned to that even more futile *what if* business: What if I had never come to Windsor Hills as rector of All Saints? what if my parachute had opened ten seconds earlier when that plane crashed years ago? what if Mark had gone somewhere else to do research? or had chosen another field of work than biochemistry? or what if he had not seen Grace standing in the rain that night in front of the Royale Theater? Or suppose Dewey Snyder, senior warden of All Saints, had not known Charlie long ago? suppose that small paragraph in his life had not been tucked away on a lost page: would he have pushed Mark so hard? Or what if Susan's mother had not been the daughter of old Congressman Addams—what if. . . .

There is no end to this kind of thinking which is not thinking at all, of course, but only a most human try at unraveling stone.

After Mark and Grace left Windsor Hills, after that final up-thrust of mad fury, there were nights when even the wrong questions could not find their way into words: When my mind was no more than a trashpile of faces, things, sounds: when I'd lie there unable to sleep, staring at an empty half-dark store I had never been in, watching two shadows slowly converge . . . hearing Duveen in that beauty shop saying, *Sugar, did the man do something real bad to you?* . . . hearing Miss Mabel's small, percussive feet following S.K. down the corridor at the lab . . . and as happens in a dream, suddenly only Susan was there, nowhere at first, then in my bedroom holding my crutches and saying, *Now, I'll tell you a story once upon a time once upon a time* . . . and as I listened I was emptying the .38 and Charlie was staring at a little schooner and the pages of his opera were sliding from the chair to the floor . . . and old Yellow Cat was sliding, too, back on the lumber pile and a rear door was wide open . . . and superimposed on these broken images and sounds was Grace's desperate *Andy must not be told all of it* . . . then Mark was in my study holding that dead cigarette and Grace and I were listening to what he had decided he must tell us, and snow was falling everywhere—

When the snow began, I'd turn on the light and read whatever happened to be on my bedside table. It didn't matter: Reinhold Niebuhr or Paul Tillich or a novel, or the ads in a magazine—whatever it was, I'd hang on to it, sometimes turning ten, twenty pages before one sentence would stick in my mind. But finally, the words would recover their meaning, my thoughts would somehow focus, and I would begin to think about what I was reading, or about next Sunday's sermon, or the fund-raising campaign or the altar guild's problems or camp for the choirboys—And then, All Saints Church would slowly rise up and surround me and the memories would crouch down behind its unyielding walls—and finally, I would sleep.

Now, two years have passed. The foolish persistent questions have grown almost silent; the trashpile has slowly receded and no longer keeps me awake at night. It would be easy to say, *It is all over. Try to forget it.* And I did say it for a time. Then, one night, I dreamed of Grace. It was more than dream: it was a large charity bestowed on me by an unknown donor: for she was standing in her living room, smiling, and slowly she laid her hand on Mark's shoulder and then, on mine. And I awoke, feeling a deep sense of reconciliation: feeling, There is meaning in it, somewhere. In all this insane chaos there is something that makes sense, something that links on to the next hour—if I can find it.

For the first time, I wanted to think about it: I wanted to bring it back, to set it down in words; that is, as much of it as I could: not in order to confess or to blame or to exonerate or to find lost beginnings; not just to stare, paralyzed, at the unmoving face of evil: but to shape those senseless, broken memories into something I could live with. Or perhaps another way to say it is simpler and closer to the truth: like Susan, I, too, have a story and the time has come when I want to tell it.

My name is David Landrum. I have been rector of All Saints Church for six years. My age is thirty-eight. I am a Virginian and attended the University—it is possible a few old-timers may remember me as the halfback who was called "Preacher." From college, I went to Union Theological Seminary in New York for three years; served as chaplain in the Air Force in World War II, and lost a leg in a plane crash two months before the war ended. Spent a few weeks at a rehabilitation center, then went to Boston for another year of study. From Boston, I went to our mission down in the old Bowery and from there I came to All Saints in Windsor Hills, as assistant to the rector who died a few months after my arrival.

Windsor Hills was once Windsor, a small century-old hamlet surrounded by a few fine estates, some of which had been there long before the Civil War. But as the city grew it reached out and pulled Windsor block by block and acre by acre into its boundaries: spacious homes began to appear in the hills close to All Saints Church, new streets opened up, more and more of them, and smaller houses were built. In recent years, the elaborate and expensive houses have begun drifting down toward the newly developed lake front. It is there, on Lake Shore Drive, that Dewey Snyder and his daughter, Katie, live. Scattered among the contemporary homes are the old landmarks: Miss Hortense's three-storied turreted gray house set back in its pecan grove, and the old Pottle place where Paul Pottle now lives and has his book and record shop. The shop is in the former servants' wing and has become a bit of a Left Bank for those in our town interested in ideas and books and art.

At the time of the trouble—a poor word but I hardly know how else to speak of it—I had temporary quarters in the Parish House on Arlington Road while the new rectory was being built. Across the street, the Mark Channings lived in a small house of great charm which had been designed for them by a friend who had studied with Frank Lloyd Wright. Four long blocks away, toward the west side, is the shopping center where Susan went, that Monday afternoon. Thirty minutes after she skated down our street, my life and the Channings' and other lives too numerous to name had changed direction although few were aware that anything had happened at all. Certainly, I did not know.

The first I heard of any of it was on Thursday morning when Neel came to my study.

It was early. Hardly more than eight o'clock. I was having my coffee and beginning to settle down to an hour's reading before getting into my duties for the day, when he tapped on my door. I was surprised to see him for he rarely comes without calling first. I thought, He has a case he wants to talk over, something urgent, perhaps. I laid aside my book and offered him a cup of coffee.

He had been in the room about ten minutes before I realized his visit was of an extraordinary nature. Neel is casual in his approach, tends to delay getting to what is on his mind—and now sat in the leather chair opposite my desk, and slowly drank the coffee. He commented briefly on weather and the news, asked a question or two about a book by St. John Perse which happened to be on the table near him. Once he looked at me rather a long time, then looked at Ali Baba, the cat I had inherited from the old rector. Ali Baba, lying in the other chair, looked at him. Neel rubbed his thin nose and looked down at the rug. None of this surprised me. It is his way to take his time. Less a personal trait, I think, than simply an old custom of his region—he is from a remote part of the Smoky Mountains—which he has never sloughed off.

Neel is special assistant to the police chief of the city and is in charge of the Juvenile Bureau. As chairman of the city's Youth Committee, I had worked with him on parole cases and on the city-wide program which he was developing for the prevention of teen-age delinquency. Now and then, he dropped by the study when he saw my light on late, and we'd talk an hour or so: about a case, or a book; or he'd tell me about his years on the New York police force after he received his doctorate in clinical psychology from Columbia University; or he'd launch into nostalgic tales about coon hunting and rabbit trapping when he was a kid in the mountains. I talked too, of course, and in process of swapping ideas and books and experiences, and now and then beating our heads against the impenetrable mind of a young delinquent, we had become friends.

After eyeing the rug for quite some time, he looked at me, and laid aside his cup. "I know I should apologize for coming in, like this, when it is the only time of day you have to yourself." I realized that he was deeply embarrassed—but not because of his unannounced visit. I felt, Neel doesn't want to tell me what he is about to say. Then I had a dull warning: this has something to do with me.

He made a quick plunge: "We have run into a puzzling situation, Dave, which concerns several of your parishioners." He stopped. "Have you, by chance, heard about it?"

I told him I had heard nothing of an unusual nature.

"It happened Monday afternoon. But we were not informed of it until early last evening when the mother called me at my apartment and said that an attack had been made on her little girl—an attempted rape. She used that word. She said she could not discuss it over the phone, and asked me to come to her home —her husband was out of the city and she felt quite helpless. When I arrived, I found a distraught woman and a calm, slightly resentful little girl who obviously wanted the story told in a certain way. She corrected her mother a number of times. The child looked all right except for a scratch on her arm. The arm was bandaged."

I was, of course, sorting out all the little girls in my parish—

"She's about eight, I'd say. I didn't ask. I was interested in hearing the story as they wanted to tell it. It seems her mother thought the child was going out to skate on the sidewalk in front of their apartment. Instead, she went to the Arlington Shopping Center, and was enticed by a man—according to the mother's story—into a vacant store which is being remodeled. The workmen had gone home— You know the place, I presume: Toni's old store, she called it."

Yes, I knew it. It is at the corner of the shopping center, next door to Nella's Beauty Shop. I told him the store had been closed for a long time. The shopping center was completed about the time I came to Windsor Hills, four years ago. "I have the impression it has been closed since Toni went away."

"Who is Toni?"

"I don't know. He ran the store for many years, they say, then closed the doors one night and went away. No one has ever heard of him since. The store is being remodeled—but she told you."

"Yes. Well— Now, when the mother used the word *enticed,* the youngster said he didn't entice her, she went in the store because she wanted to. Then she looked at me and pulled down her lips." Neel laughed. "Cool little number. Or extremely scared. I'm not sure which. She has a face that looks four years old one moment, twelve the next."

Susan. That is when it came to me. No child in my parish but Susan who sat with her parents in the fourth pew on the right and had been carrying on a cold war with my sermons since I came here, trying to divert me with her antics, could have. . . .

I said, "Her mother says an attempt was made to rape the child?"

"She said so when she phoned. Later, she admitted she was not sure just what had happened, or what the legal terms were for this kind of thing. Then she told me the man's name. He is on the vestry of your church." Neel's face was expressionless.

I smiled, said, "How about some coffee?" Went over to the cabinet, picked up the coffee urn and poured what was left in his cup. Put the kettle on—we'd need more—

I had instantly lined them up, of course:

Dewey Snyder: of Snyder and Kent, chairman of a half-dozen boards; senior warden; rich; powerful; highly esteemed as a patron of the city's art and music activities; small, barrel-chested, a shade dapper in appearance, although his suits are made by the best tailors in the country. . . . Lee Esteridge: redfaced, paunchy, forehead heavily creased; telling his jokes at which he never laughs; losing his temper over trifles; always slapping at creeping socialism and the integrationists or reaching for a tranquilizer or a glass of bourbon. . . . Dr. Anderson Guthrie: seventy-two years old; poised, cheerful, shrewd, extremely helpful in practical or routine matters, noncommittal in vestry crises. . . . Ben Jordan: eyes quizzical; thin body, wiry; an expert on Plato and quail shooting; often flies his small plane down to his plantation in south Georgia—to have a chance to read, he says; president of First National Bank. . . . Mark:

My mind blurred. When I came to, Neel was saying, "The woman is prominent. It could blow to Kingdom Come."

"Do you think it actually happened?"

"I have grave doubts, of course. That is why I wanted to talk to you. I feel there are things you can tell me, probably. There are several points that puzzle me: one is the fact that they held it back two days before reporting it."

—I could see Susan, thinking it over . . . beadily selecting her victim—

"Another is: the youngster told me she ran from the store into the beauty shop, next door. Now her mother, apparently, had not known this. The two argued it for a minute or so—"

He hesitated, looked at the Marin print on the wall opposite him, looked at the papers on my desk—

I said, "Neel, this is sort of rough on me. Can't you tell me who the child is and who has been accused? To be told a little girl in your parish has been assaulted by one of your vestrymen—"

"You have a right to know. I am finding it difficult because I just don't have enough facts and the few I have cancel each other out rather completely, and yet something did happen, there is little doubt about that." He hesitated, made a quick decision. "The child is Susan, the daughter of the Claud Newells. I am sorry to tell you that her mother is accusing Dr. Mark Channing."

It was incredible. I said so. "I know it does no good to say a certain man couldn't possibly commit a certain crime: you can tell me that no matter how well I know him, I know only an infinitesimal amount about him as he really is. Not enough to make that statement stick. But if it can be said of any man that he wouldn't or couldn't make immoral approaches to a little girl, it can be said of Mark. He's absorbed in his research, deeply in love with his wife—he has values—but you know how I feel about him."

"I know."

"Have you talked with them?"

"Last night. After I left Mrs. Newell. They seemed as shocked as you are."

"Little girls make up these things, one often reads—" I stopped. He knew more about little girls than I did. I asked him if Mark had been arrested. He said no. There were not, in his opinion, sufficient grounds for an arrest. "You know, of course, that this case is not technically in my department. I've handled it up to this point because Mrs. Newell brought it to me—and because I am not sure, as yet, that it isn't my case. It seems Susan wanders into all sorts of places—have you heard of her having trouble before?"

"Nothing big. She's a brat, all right. I mean she has a talent for annoying people but that is hardly delinquency."

Neel said he'd like to talk with the Chief before turning the case over to Andrews's department. "The old man's shrewd. I'd like him to hear the two of them tell their story just as they told it to me."

I went to the cabinet and poured the boiling water in the drip pot. "Have you talked with anyone at the beauty shop? Mrs. Perkins?"

"Last night. Briefly." Neel told her he had picked up a rumor around town, something vague about a little girl who had run into her shop saying a man in a vacant store had hurt her. He went at it carefully, knowing it would trigger off more talk. Nella Perkins gave him Susan's name. When he asked for the man's name, she said Susan had told them she had never seen him before. She also insisted she was not hurt. But she was deathly pale, Mrs. Perkins said. They asked if it was a Negro and she said no. She could describe the man only as tall and thin. Then they saw the scratch on her arm: deep, jagged, about five inches long. Nella asked Susan where she got it. Susan said she didn't know. Nella tried to clean it up: Susan screamed and refused to be touched. This was the only time she showed emotion. Nella then suggested that they call her mother to come for her. Susan said she had her skates, they were just outside the door of that store—and she didn't want her mother to come. Mrs. Perkins went out with her, watched her put on the skates and start down Arlington Road toward home.

A minute or two later, Duveen, one of the shop's operators, ran into the store, herself, and came back looking like she had seen a ghost. She said the back door was wide open but no one was in the place—except old Yellow Cat, who was acting in a most peculiar manner, sliding back on a lumber pile—

"Neel, the cat scratched Susan, of course."

"Probably. But she couldn't have thought a cat was a tall thin man." We stared at each other for quite some time. Neel is tall and thin and I'm tall, six feet two, but my weight of one-eighty-five takes me out of the thin category. Suddenly we both laughed. Neel said, "Mrs. Perkins has developed a theory about Yellow Cat, as she calls him. It seems Duveen—by the way, who is she? I asked only the most necessary questions last night."

I told him she was Johnny Lemon's wife. Johnny worked at the Windsor Hills filling station where I bought gas.

"Duveen, it seems, is fond of cats and has, according to Mrs. Perkins, made a pet of Yellow Cat. He's been around Toni's store, inside and out, since Toni disappeared. Mrs. Perkins thinks Toni's spirit lives in the cat and she thinks Duveen should leave people's spirits strictly alone."

I said, "I've seen the cat. He is usually in the window of the store, asleep."

"When did you last see him?"

I had no idea. "Perhaps a week ago. I just don't know."

"Mrs. Perkins hasn't seen him since Monday. She believes something happened in the store: Yellow Cat witnessed it, was terrified by what he saw, and ran away. She elaborated this at some length. Then, suddenly, began to talk about horoscopes, hers and Duveen's and mine. I got nothing else from her that made much sense."

Why hadn't they called me! Last night, they could have— Susan must have noticed him at church across the aisle only two seats back—

I said, "How can I help?" I thought he would ask me about the Newells and the Channings, their background, character, relationship and so on.

He said, "If you'll give me a run-down of your activities last Monday—say, from noon on? Do you mind?"

I didn't mind, of course; but I was surprised. I told him I had gone to a luncheon of the Cancer Committee at the Yacht Club, at twelve. Our annual drive for funds was about to begin. Dewey Snyder, who is chairman, was there, of course; so was Mark Channing, and about fifteen others. We were planning a special TV program which had been set up: Mark was to speak on recent trends in cancer research and specifically on what the lab, here, is doing. "We must have been there two hours."

"Did you talk to Dr. Channing?"

"Briefly. We walked to my car—his was parked a few yards away. He was telling me he had been analyzing some data on his experiments that have to do with viruses. Very interesting. He seemed almost elated—after all, he's been on this a long time; he was completely absorbed in what he was saying. Then he said he must get back to the lab—and I went to the Windsor Hills Sanitarium to call on two of my parishioners. —You want this sort of thing?"

"If you don't mind."

"Let's see: back here. Then to the church office for thirty minutes, I'd think, with the church secretary—then back here again. I worked on my sermon. Not sure how long. Had the usual number of phone calls. Two or three people came in—the architect with a problem about the kitchen in the new rectory; someone selling magazine subscriptions; then Charlie Owens came by for about five minutes. He is the organist at All Saints. He brought me a Hindemith record we had discussed a few days ago. That's about it, I guess."

"You didn't go to the shopping center?"

"No."

"Did you see Susan at any time during the afternoon? Would she have skated past the Parish House?"

"She does, now and then. Comes up and plays with Ali Baba, the cat, now and then. But ordinarily she skates on the other side of the street. Their apartment is on that side of Arlington Road. I certainly didn't see her. As I remember it, I was at my desk until after five."

"You did not see Dr. Channing after he left you at the Yacht Club?"

Yes. I was remembering it, now. I had called Mrs. Riley—another member of the vestry—to thank her for the bowl of chrysanthemums she had put on my desk, and she had talked twenty minutes about her fourteen grandchildren and five children, especially the one in the State Department who was doing so well —then about her tachycardia and the new drug she was taking— then she said she hoped I was not tired of chrysanthemums, next week her small white ones would be blooming and she would bring over a bowl if I was sure I had not grown tired of chrysanthemums, etc. Listening is an essential part of a clergyman's work but I don't seem to have the stamina for these prolonged telephone bouts. Afterward, I went up to the bathroom and, somehow, knocked a bottle of hair tonic into the tub. It broke into a hundred pieces. I cleaned the mess up, then opened the window of my bedroom which is directly across from the Channings' terrace—

I said, "Yes, I saw him on his front terrace, reading."

Neel walked to the study window. "From here?"

"No. The rhododendron obscures the view from here. I saw him from upstairs."

"What time was this?"

"Five-thirty."

"You are sure about that?"

Now, I am never too sure about time and was on the edge of saying, No, I am not at all sure it was five-thirty; it could have been five-forty or -fifty—when something tense and unreadable in his face stopped me. I heard myself say, "Yes, I am quite sure." And then, I was thrown into sheer agony by the thought that maybe this was the worst possible thing I could have said. I was about to retract it with, Wait—I am not at all sure about this; I'm no good when it comes to time—

At that moment, Neel smiled. Not much of a smile: it hardly left his eyes, crept no farther than the muscles of lids, did not touch his mouth, but I knew my words had been right for Mark. As for Susan: she was no more to me at this moment than an unknown name in the news.

He was saying, "That settles it, then. If you saw him on his terrace at five-thirty he couldn't have been in the store for Susan ran out of the store and into the beauty shop at exactly five-thirty. Mrs. Perkins says everyone in the shop made a note of the time."

I lit a cigarette, went over to the cabinet to see how the coffee was doing. Brought the urn to Neel's table and filled his cup; forgot to fill mine. "It was exactly five-thirty when I saw him there," I repeated, somewhat redundantly.

Neel drank the coffee slowly. He picked up the book near him. "I have never read *Anabasis*. In fact, very little of Perse."

"Would you like to take it along with you?"

He opened the book, turned a few pages, read a few lines here and there, said, "Yes, I would." Laid it back on the table.

"You know Mrs. Newell well?"

"We are not personal friends in the sense that the Channings and I are. But I see quite a bit of her as her priest."

"Would you call her stable? reliable?" Neel smiled.

I wanted to say no. I wanted to describe her as neurotic or paranoid and full of unresolved conflicts— I said, for I believed it to be the truth and felt I must say it, "She is completely reliable, as far as I know. I depend on her in parish activities. She's efficient, works well with others; prominent socially, member of Junior League. Not too good in her relationship with Susan—"

"I doubt there's much of a relationship. They are objects to each other to be manipulated. Both are pretty good at it, too."

"Perhaps so. Certainly Susan's something of a pest, so other parents tell me."

"In any specific way?"

"At church school, for instance. The kids are listening to teacher. Everything's fine. Then Susan walks in. No more listening to teacher. Just chaos. And they tell me it happens without her saying a word. Her presence does it."

Neel laughed. "I felt it, myself."

He was suddenly standing. He thanked me, said he would keep in touch. I followed him through the hall of the Parish House to the street door. As he walked down the steps, he turned, asked in that casual way of his if I'd be willing to make an affidavit as to the time I had seen Dr. Channing on his terrace. "No doubt about its being Monday when you saw him?"

"None whatever," I said.

He said it would be fine if I could drop by his office within the next day or two and take care of it. I said I would. He then said, "Your statement will be important to the Chief."

I watched him get in the car, swing quickly around the corner and head downtown. I went in to heat that coffee I had forgotten to drink. Picked up his cup and as I did so, I saw the *Anabasis* lying on the table. It is curious how your mind can make of one small incident a push button that will set off the complicated delicate machinery that floods you with anxiety. That he had forgotten to take the book acquired an intense and ominous quality: We had talked along with each other almost as if this were another of his cases; now, I realized that he had withheld quite a few facts. No mention of what Mark had told him, no mention of the time of Susan's dramatic entrance into the beauty shop until I had committed myself to that five-thirty.

It fell on me: what this could do to Mark, if the Newells— Grace . . . she was in that house across the street not daring to think. . . . And they had not told me. Why didn't they come over immediately after Neel's visit? What made them reluctant —we were close friends—what was it? what will this do to them —to the lab— And now, questions that did not bother to form themselves raced through my organism.

I dialed her phone number. She did not answer. In ten minutes I tried again. No answer. I went over. The front door was unlocked. I opened it, called to her, went inside and foolishly looked in every room, then went to the glass wall of the living room which gives a clear view of the back terrace and the ravine below. I thought, She's walking in the ravine. It was October. The maples were magnificent. She's down there sitting on those rocks, thinking about it— I went to the back terrace and called her name. No answer. Perhaps she had gone into the city on an errand. The door being unlocked meant nothing. She often leaves it so.

I decided to phone Mark. I rarely called him at the Laboratories but I went inside the house and dialed the number. His secretary said he was in the animal rooms; if I could hold on for two or three minutes she'd connect me with him. From the alcove where the phone is, I could see Grace's blue sweater lying across the arm of the sofa in the living room; her sketch pad was on the table; two empty glasses—they had had a drink after Neel left, probably two or three. On a shelf above the phone were two fine photographs of her, from dance sequences. One was of the young Grace when she was in New York studying; the other was done last year by Paul Pottle and was from her dance called *Lost Memory*. Paul had a large copy of it in his book shop. I was looking at the picture of the young Grace when Mark said, "Hello, Dave."

The voice was so quiet and calm that I was left without words. I finally said, "Mark, I don't like to interrupt you, but can you tell me where Grace is? I called but there was no answer. She doesn't seem to be at home. It is not too important but—"

"She teaches at Miss Drewry's School on Thursdays. I am sure she is there."

"Of course."

Then I asked him as casually as I could how they were. Fine, he said. Voice even, cheerful. I asked him if they could come over to my study, perhaps tonight. He said he didn't think they could make it. "Tomorrow night?" He seemed to be hesitating. I said, "I hope you can. I have a personal matter I'd like to talk over with you—if you can arrange it without too much inconvenience." He said he thought they could. "Will it be all right if we drop by, after Paul's? You'll be there, too, won't you?"

I said I would. That I had forgot about going to Paul's. Afterward would be fine.

3

I can see her now, sitting on the old scuffed-up leather hassock in my study, that Friday night. She was pale and kept rubbing the fingers of her left hand. Mark was quietly chain-smoking. Their mood was not desperate: they were tired and unbelieving. It is difficult to go back to that confused week and piece things together, but this is what stays with me most persistently: their inability or refusal to believe it was actually happening to them. They knew, of course, but they were pushing it off, denying its consequences somewhere in them.

They had spent two hours, in the late afternoon, with the chief of police and Neel. Certainly it was not an easy interview for them. They had got back to the house just in time to have a cup of coffee and a sandwich before going on to Paul's book shop for the monthly meeting of our informal discussion group. The topic, that evening, was Camus and his philosophy. As we sat there, the fourteen or fifteen of us who are in the group, listening to the paper being read, I was amazed at Mark's obvious interest in it and the perceptive comments he made, afterward, on *The Stranger* and *The Plague*. I had the feeling it was not a front he was putting up: he was interested, his mind was on Camus. Grace sat near me, drinking her Scotch, turning the glass round and round as she looked down at the floor. But she, too, was easy and aware and sometime during the discussion, made two or three witty remarks about existentialism. I don't think I said anything. I was not managing my anxiety as skillfully as they were.

But when we left Paul's and came to my study, some of their ease left them. I don't know why they had not told me before but now they seemed ready to. Grace said almost immediately, "We want to tell you what's happened to us, Dave. That is, if we know." Then she sat down on the hassock and let Mark take it from there.

Mark gives you the impression that he has everything under control: voice, musculature, eyes, slow smile somehow convince you that his world-in-depth is in order and he can keep it that way without undue expenditure of effort. He shows tension only by chain-smoking, or now and then, by playing with his car keys, or groping for words when things get too personal. He showed no strain now, other than smoking, as he reminded me he had seen me at lunch on Monday, etc. "I went back to the lab and worked until about three-thirty, I'd say, then decided to take the rest of the afternoon off. I had been working late for weeks. It was a fine day— When I got home, Grace was planting some bulbs." He put out the cigarette stub.

"The black tulips I told you I had ordered, Dave."

Mark said, "I went out and helped her. We planted seventy or eighty and then I suggested we take a break and have a rum and Coke. I went to wash my hands, she called to say we were out of Cokes, did I want a Daiquiri, I said I believed I'd go over to the shopping center and pick up a carton of Cokes, anyway."

"You usually drink Daiquiris, don't you?"

"Usually, yes." No more.

Grace had stopped rubbing her fingers. Her black hair has a ragged cut, nice for her face; now she pushed the hair behind her ears. They are well formed but rather large and the gesture left her looking like a twelve-year-old who has not decided which sex she belongs to. I smiled, and she smiled like an echo and then suddenly her eyes were full of fear. I thought, She's having the worst of it, up to now.

I said, "And you did? Go for the Cokes, I mean."

"Yes. I went to Matthews, got a carton and came home. Wednesday night your friend Neel came to the house and told me Susan Newell's mother had accused me of molesting the child in that vacant store next to the beauty shop. Have you heard this?"

I said Neel had talked to me.

"Well, that's it. That's all I know."

"When do they say it happened?"

"Late Monday afternoon."

"You went to the shopping center late?"

"About five-ten. Close to then."

"You came right back, of course."

He looked at me a long time. There was one split second when I felt those eyes were about to tell me an involved and difficult story, then it was gone. The eyes said nothing. I said, "You must have. I saw you on the front terrace at five-thirty. You were reading."

"At five-thirty?"

"I think so." He looked at me, slowly smiled. "I don't think I could have made it back by then. A little later, I'd say."

I turned to Grace. She said, "I don't know, Dave. Mr. Neel asked me, too. I just don't know. I put the roast in the oven after Mark came back. He went out on the terrace with his drink. It was five-fifty when I adjusted the oven temperature. I don't know why I remember this but I do. But I don't know when he went to the shopping center or when he came back."

As I remember it now, we pushed those minutes round and round for a long time that night. I held on to the five-thirty; Mark kept saying it was probably five-forty-five or -fifty when he got back: Grace said she was sure it was five-fifty when she checked the roast. "I went out with my drink and sat on the terrace step. I knew we should finish the tulips and I said so but without much conviction—it was too pleasant just sitting there. Mark must have been on the terrace at least five minutes when I came out, for the ice had almost melted in my glass—and of course, he had opened the Cokes when he came in and fixed the drinks, that took time— oh God, is all this important? do the minutes count? how, Dave?"

Obviously, they didn't know. I told them Susan ran out of the vacant store and into the beauty shop at exactly five-thirty, saying a man had scared her.

"So people know," she whispered.

"I'm afraid a good many. Neel didn't tell you this?"

He was friendly, they said, but had told them very little. He had made rather a point of asking them questions about the time Mark went to Matthews and came back but gave no reason for doing so.

"And you said?"

"I said I didn't know." Mark speaking. "I had looked at my watch at five-ten. I was sure of that. I was not sure of anything else—except I had gone to Matthews and had come straight home, afterward."

"And he believed you?"

"He and the Chief seemed willing to. Or perhaps it was what you had said. You told him you saw me at five-thirty?" I said I did. "Anyway, I am not under arrest."

We said more: repeating for the most part what we had already said, as you do at such times. I gave them a detailed account of Miss Nella's version of the beauty shop episode. When the tall thin business came up I reminded them that Susan's father is tall and thin.

"Then you mean the child might have dreamed it up? Perhaps no one was there?" Grace asked this.

It was possible. I didn't know. None of it made much sense. You keep it on the surface: it won't work out. Try it in the depths: it still doesn't come together.

She asked me why Susan had chosen Mark as a stand-in for the father, if it was fantasy. Or did the mother do it? I couldn't answer this. I turned to Mark. It was as if he had not heard us. I asked him if he had ever had trouble with either of the Newells. He didn't seem to hear. I asked it again.

He said, "I haven't spoken twenty words to them in my life."

We stopped talking. Grace had begun to rub her fingers again. Mark was still smoking. I finally asked them if they'd like some coffee. They thought it was too late.

She said, "I think the worst of it is over, don't you?"

I told her I hoped so. There was a good bit of talk, of course, but it would probably die down soon unless Claud Newell took it into his head to swear out a warrant for Mark's arrest.

"You think he might?"

I said I didn't know what to think. He had seemed to me to be a sensible man, level-headed, not apt to do anything on impulse. But then, I certainly had not expected Renie Newell to do what she had done. I mentioned that he would come home for the weekend.

"That means he's here now." She looked at both of us, we saw she was scared and we smiled as reassuringly as we could, I said I thought we might reasonably assume that Newell would do nothing except maybe tell his Susan not to wander around in dark stores any more.

This seemed so sane and sensible that we laughed rather immoderately about it.

She said softly, "Strange . . . a man you sit across the aisle from at church, you nod to but never talk with, is suddenly in control of your life. Everything depends on him, his mood, judgment, values—" She said, "Have you anything to drink, Dave? some brandy?" I poured her a spot of brandy. Mark said he did not want anything.

She drank it slowly. Mark smoked. I couldn't think of anything cheering to say.

I had known these two people for four years. They were as close to me as anyone had ever been. I don't know why this kind of thing happens but it was Mark's presence on the vestry, at my first interview, that determined my decision to accept the invitation to come to All Saints as assistant rector. I can say it was his easy, humorous questions, cool intelligence, the sense I had at that first meeting of his integrity—but that is not saying much. After the interview, he asked me to his home to meet Grace and his eight-year-old son, Andy—and it was as if I belonged there. Grace's off-beat beauty which edges close, at times, to a gaunt homeliness, fascinated me. Her interest in the dance, painting— a deep soft way of speaking—long, relaxed silences—all this I liked. The boy and I hit it off at once: he was a little on the tense, thin side, eager, bright; we talked football, tennis, sports and were suddenly friends. As for Mark: there is nothing remarkable in his appearance or manner. In his white gown or coat at the

Laboratories you might pass him without a second glance: unlike Grace, he merges easily into a group. It is when you see his eyes that you look the second time: glowing, purposeful: you feel here is a man who knows what he is searching for—and you believe he will find it and you know it is worth finding.

I discovered other good, sensible reasons for accepting the opening at All Saints, of course, but these three people had much to do with it. I see that, now. And as we sat there, that Friday night, no longer talking, I searched for a way to help them but could not find it.

Grace finally took a letter from her bag, smiled, handed it to me. "From Andy. I thought you'd enjoy it." I laid it on the desk to read later, said the usual, He still likes New England? We forced ourselves to talk about him for a few minutes, laughed about his new ice skates which each week he reported he had not yet used; he was impatient for winter to come; wanted to learn to ski, skate. She mentioned his housemaster, Tom Eliot, whom Andy liked; we talked more about the school, his new friends, the headmaster, and all the rest of it. And then, they realized simultaneously that it was late, and got up to leave. Mark said, "I'm damned glad you saw me at five-thirty, Dave, even if it isn't true." We laughed. I said, Take it easy, both of you. They went across the street to their house. I had intended asking him if he had seen a good lawyer; he should talk to Steve Bernstein; they were friends, Steve could give him the legal angle—

Afterward, I sat in the old swivel chair which had once been in my father's law office—for some obscure reason I have held on to it—thinking about the fragments that had come to me since Thursday morning. They were jagged and did not fit together. Even now, they don't fit. We were lucky to have fallen into Neel's hands, I realized it. It was about the only thing I did feel certain of, except Mark's innocence. I knew there was no doubt about that. You can't know but you do know.

After Neel's visit, I had heard nothing more about the trouble until Miss Hortense called me, Friday morning. Her telephone calls are never less than thirty minutes long, often extend to an hour, and her range is wide. She began Friday morning with the Communists, one of her favorite fears, talked excitedly about the Un-American Activities Committee and their search for Communists in the entertainment field, said she hoped they'd soon come South and investigate these integrationists, she had a few names in her notebook that she'd gladly give them, slid off this into a paragraph on Walter Reuther and the unions, bounced back to invite me to Susan's birthday party. "You remember how much fun we had last year, don't you, Father Landrum?" I remembered. She wanted it to be especially successful this year because of this dreadful thing that had happened to Susan, had I heard? I let her talk on. Renie had told her about it, first; then others. It was she who had stopped the use of the word *rape*. "Dreadful! I scolded Renie for being so indiscreet. After all, my dear Father Landrum, she should have realized that a little girl who has been raped . . . think of her debut . . . marriage—our darling Renie lost her head for a time. But I have no doubt it was Dr. Channing who approached Susie. And I tell you why I am so sure. The checker at Matthews, the tall gangly one—I used to see her there years ago before I broke my hip and became confined to this damned wheel chair—Maidee Somebody, yes; well, this Maidee says he was in Matthews at exactly five-thirty-five that Monday afternoon and bought a carton of Cokes. She remembers it because he gave her a quarter and a nickel and the quarter rolled around the table and they both caught it and his hand was icy cold. They laughed and she saw that his face was hot as if he had been running."

"May I ask who told you this?"

"Maidee, herself. I called her after I talked to Nella Perkins at the beauty shop and heard what she had to say. I asked Maidee if a tall thin man had been in Matthews just after five-thirty. At first, she didn't think so. Then I asked her to try to remember because a tall thin man had attempted to molest little Susan Newell at five-twenty-five or five-thirty in that old store, and I felt there was a chance that someone might have seen him around the shopping center. She finally said the only tall man she could remember was Dr. Channing but she never thought of him as tall or thin because his eyes were so wonderful, you just think — No use to finish that, Father Landrum, Maidee is only a silly talky old maid! I told her to put her mind on it and she finally said he was certainly in there and had paid her for a carton of Cokes at five-thirty-five."

"Why on earth would she remember the exact time?"

"Because the poor thing has nothing else to think about. She probably keeps glancing at the clock every few minutes."

I asked no more questions, fearing whatever I said would send her off in a new direction and there would be more and more phone calls.

She was back on the party now: I told her I would be out of town that Saturday and could not come. Her silence bore down. I added that I would certainly send Susie a birthday present. But I knew that she was extremely upset with me.

Miss Hortense is eighty years old and accustomed to having her way, not only in All Saints and Windsor Hills where her family have lived since long before the Civil War but throughout the city. In her mind, Susan must be reinstated socially and the blemishes rubbed off. The people at that party would be her friends and the Newells' friends. Certainly none of the Channings' close friends would be there. "Phelia, especially, feels Susan's priest should be here." I told her, once more, that I was very sorry but could not possibly make it. And then she said, "You'll excuse me, won't you, the dogs are barking so," and that ended our talk.

I had been in Windsor Hills some time before I understood about Phelia and those barking ghosts. And perhaps I should explain them, right now. Phelia was Miss Hortense's friend and had lived with her since girlhood. From what old-timers said, I have the impression that she was small and pigeon-plump and quiet and cautious—with a habit of dropping handkerchiefs and vague *non sequiturs* all over the place. At least, I have built her up in my mind as that sort of person. She spent most of her time reading while Miss Hortense, tall and husky, handled the affairs of house and estate and attended board meetings of the bank and textile company and real estate firm in which her father had held controlling interests. Like her father, Miss Hortense was successful in business matters, and like him, a fine shot. Their fields, stretching back into the forest, were full of quail and pheasant and in her father's time friends often came down from the North for a few days' hunting. After his death she continued the parties and the breeding of bird dogs—which had been his hobby—and on any fine winter day you would likely see her in hunting pants and red plaid hat moving through the fields, and ahead of her those dogs; or you'd find her at the kennels. But Phelia did not like killing things. It seems she went, one time, with Hortense and when Hortense downed a bird on her first shot and one of the dogs brought it to her she took it out of his mouth and casually tossed it to Phelia. Phelia held the warm feathery thing for a moment, tried bravely to stuff it in the pocket of her hunting jacket, couldn't go through with it, and plopped down in the grass and cried bitterly. But that night, so Hortense says—it is a story she still likes to tell—Phelia ate not one but two of the quail, once they were broiled to a turn and served with hot biscuits and elderberry jelly. "Phelia and her stomach and Phelia and her tears are miles apart," and then Miss Hortense laughs that deep rumbling laugh of hers which makes her friends say, She is just like her father; except she holds her whisky better.

Twenty years ago, Phelia died. After her death the dogs died, one by one by one. These are the facts. But since Miss Hortense has never accepted them we find it difficult to do so. She is a powerful woman: in board meetings, in the social life of Windsor Hills which her old brown joint-swollen fingers still have a grip on, and in All Saints, yes. But it is more: and as I write this, I think her real strength lies on an obscure level where she whispers those things that something in us, not amenable to reason, wants to hear.

When I first came to Windsor Hills I thought Phelia was for some reason not well enough to see people and I fell into the habit of inquiring about her whenever I talked by phone to Miss Hortense, or called on her. Afterward—well, it was too difficult to break the habit. Again and again, I have heard myself say, "And Miss Phelia? is she all right?" And always Miss Hortense replies, "Oh yes, she's fine, Father Landrum. She felt a little tired last week but she's fine today. As I tell Phelia, her only trouble is she eats like a horse."

As for the dogs: I know Miss Hortense hears them and the barking troubles her acutely.

Now I had offended her. Ordinarily, I would have laughed it off but I needed her help, it could mean a great deal to Mark. I should have managed the party business more tactfully. She was very fond of Susie and while we all knew she had the parties because she liked birthday parties, they had become important to her, restricted as she now was to that wheel chair.

I felt impatient with myself and was worried, too, about the Maidee talk. Perhaps, tomorrow or Monday, I could drive out to her place, have a cup of tea with her, find out more about Renie and this affair, perhaps even persuade her to help hush the thing up; she was shrewd, she realized it could do Susie no good —

Ali Baba was staring at me from the striped chair. Without warning him, I picked him up to put him out and he gave me a deep scratch from my wrist up my arm. We had never been friends, had barely tolerated each other. He had belonged to the old rector, and after his death, everyone—or perhaps I should say, the Auxiliary—seemed to think he should belong to me. Not having the fortitude to protest, I had reluctantly taken him into my rooms, although I wanted a Boxer and had planned to get one. I opened the door, got rid of Ali Baba for the time being, then cleaned the scratch. It was deep and nasty. I painted it with an antiseptic and hoped that would be the end of it.

I was kept busy all morning and had little time to think of Miss Hortense or Susan. One of my parishioners was extremely ill, I spent quite some time at the hospital, there were other duties, other calls— It was the middle of the afternoon before I came back to the study. Suddenly, as I sat at my desk looking over the mail, I realized one problem had settled itself: Susie's gift. I would present Ali Baba to her. She liked cats or liked to be with them—I was not sure that she really cared for them. Anyway, it seemed a bright idea; Miss Hortense would be pleased, it would give me an excuse to call Renie and discuss the plan with her, perhaps somehow Monday afternoon would come up, perhaps the right moment would arise for me to tell her I had seen the Channings— She was disturbed, naturally; any mother would be. But if I told her I had seen him on the terrace at five-thirty, she would realize the child had been mistaken. She's fair and quite decent, she is not malevolent—

I dialed the letters T-E-, and stopped. *I must talk to you, I must talk to somebody . . . Claud . . . you don't know what I've gone through—so crude, he does not understand a nice woman he—and he laughs when I—* And that was all of that; and then she was saying in a low, frightened voice, *I went into the city yesterday on the bus—my car was at the garage—I saw some-one—a Negro from home from our plantation—he kept looking at me, I think he recognized me. I am scared—*

Two years ago. It was late, eleven or after, and sleeting out-side. A terrible night. Renie had walked into my study and I realized that she was drinking and in great misery. I asked her to sit down. She went to the leather chair, sat down; got up and came over to the striped chair directly across from me, leaned toward me—her blonde hair was shining with scattered drops of water and she was extraordinarily beautiful—and then she plunged into these words, without beginning or end. It was a long time before she said more. She cried in a low hushed endless kind of way and then suddenly was composed, and quietly tell-ing me about the Negro and her. She was fourteen, she thinks, or fifteen or sixteen, she is not sure. A summer evening: she had gone to the garden back of their house to cut some okra—

"It was almost dusk . . . I remember the lightning bugs—I had a tin pan and a knife, I like to cut okra, the flowers are beautiful and I like a garden in the dusk . . . it can be soft and mysterious, that is why I went out to cut the okra— I was cutting the pods and humming and then suddenly, between the big leaves I saw two black hands. I screamed and dropped the pan— and at that moment, I saw his face and recognized him. He was laughing good-naturedly and I wanted to laugh too, I remember that: I wanted to laugh and say, You sort of scared me. But I kept on screaming and ran in and out between the rows of okra and the running scared me even more and he ran after me, I heard him behind me, I think I did. But when I looked he wasn't there any more. I knew his name, I had seen him on the place all my life. Strange . . . I remember everything about it but not his name."

But she knew it then. And went to the house and told her father who was sitting on the front verandah. And he got up at once and she realized he might kill the boy. "He was about my age and I said, Daddy don't hurt him!" Her father had smiled in a curious and frightening way and had said, You don't want him hurt? She told him no, she didn't want him hurt; she was just scared. But he had sent for the boy and right there by the front steps had whipped him. When the boy was brought to her father, he had looked at Renie and kept looking, and Renie, unable to bear the sight of his eyes and the sounds of his screams and the lashing, ran into her room and lay across the bed with a pillow over her head. And the next day or soon after, the boy disappeared. "I always hoped he ran away. I used to wonder about it, all that summer I thought about it and I'd say, But he just ran away, he went somewhere. And yesterday—"

"You saw him?"

"I am almost sure."

"You are glad, aren't you, that he is alive?"

She looked at me and her face was gentle and her eyes confused. She said, "Yes, I'm glad, of course. But I can't get it out of my mind. The way he looked at me, yesterday, was exactly how he had looked before."

"Laughing?"

"Yes. And I felt he was thinking, You see you couldn't possibly hurt me."

"And now you are afraid he may hurt you?"

She shook her head in dissent. "I am just afraid. I don't know why." She fumbled in her bag for a cigarette. I struck a match for her. She said, "Mother came into my room, that evening, and sat on the bed while it was going on, the whipping. When it was over and everything was quiet, I remember it was so quiet we heard the tree frogs, Mother said, You should not have told your father, Renie."

—And now, two years after that night in my study, she had told it again. And this time, too, she had a name and it was Mark's.

She had said more that night. She said, "Since Daddy's death, things bother me more. This happened so long ago, it shouldn't come back now. But all day, I have thought about it and about Mother there, just with Ron. We are twins, you know."

I hadn't known.

"Oh yes. But I don't talk about him. There's nothing much to say about Ron. He just stays there, drinking most of the time, and when he is not drinking, he paints. Queer things. Not abstractions or those cubist things. It is very odd. Everything he paints looks like— I don't know. Like something not ready to be born that is being born. Rather horrible. He shows it to me and laughs when I can't think of anything to say. But then, I don't like modern art. He doesn't show it to Mother. I'm glad of that. He's very good to her. But she shouldn't be there just with him and the servants and I don't know what to do about it. All this— But Claud— He is away so much. I think that upsets me. On weekends he wants to read the papers or play golf or tinker with his boat down at the lake. I feel if we could talk about things—our life together is not so good, the sex part, I don't like to talk about it, I hardly know how to. I tried to get him to read some books on psychology and he just laughed. He says he is satisfied; if I'm not, then maybe I'd better do the reading."

"You love him, Renie? I mean, do you enjoy him in other ways?"

"I don't know. I suppose I should find it hard to live without him. If he only could—he came from poor people and is now, as you know, regional sales manager for Manon's, out of Chicago. I am not snobbish, I respect him for having made his way and for having done so well, but it may be that he was never told certain things—I can't say it—sometimes I think his trouble is that he has lost his—I read a book about that once, and it may be he is so crude because he is actually—I really don't know how to talk about this. But there is a nice way, I'm sure—"

That was as far as she could get with it.

"And you are repelled?"

"Yes. Because he is not normal in the way he—" her voice dropped low, "makes love."

"You think there is a normal way?"

"Of course. There must be. There is a normal way to do everything!"

When I didn't reply, she said, "Don't you think there is?"

"People are different, Renie. How can there be one way to eat or play or vote or work or make love?"

She left this. And now was talking about Susan: the difficulties she had with her. The child was so secretive . . . wandered around . . . she was almost sure she sometimes went into people's houses . . . knew people Renie did not know. And then, suddenly, she was telling me about a dream she had had the night before. "I've had it, now and then, for years. At college, I had it. I am always in a big house. A familiar place and yet I never know where it is or quite how big it is and part of it is always strange to me. It has room after room after room in it . . . countless rooms . . . and corridors . . . and I walk down a corridor and the doors are shut and I open every one of them and all the rooms are empty . . . and I walk down another corridor . . . and no one is in the rooms . . . I call . . . and keep opening doors . . . and no one is there . . . the rooms are empty. And yet, it seems terribly necessary for me to find someone although I don't know who it is I must find and each time I open a door the emptiness seems new—I think I am upset about this, too; I dreamed it last night and it has hung over me all day, it always hangs over me so long."

After she told me this, she was quiet. And, in a moment or two, relaxed. And she was now talking in her old humorous way. She told me a funny story about one of her friends in Junior League and as she told it her face was animated and her words enormously entertaining.

The other—the scared, confused girl who had suddenly run out of a dark, echoing past into my study that sleeting night—I had seen only the one time. That one night, we had talked. I had tried to reassure her, to let her say what she needed to say, then I took her home—or rather, I trailed her car to her apartment to be sure she made it safely.

The Renie I knew, and was thinking of when I told Neel she was stable and reliable, was the wise-cracking, skilled golf player, the social leader who, with others of her friends, did so much volunteer work for the city as a Gray Lady, and at the Blood Bank headquarters, and with the cerebral palsy school. She was the member of the Auxiliary of All Saints whom I found myself turning to most often for the hard jobs, knowing she would carry them through easily and efficiently. She has her little irritating ways, of course: One is a compulsive habit of reminding you that she is from a delta plantation and was waited on hand and foot as a child, and all the rest of that sort of thing. But behind this crinoline fantasy there is, in reality, a highly intelligent woman who keeps a beautiful apartment without help, is an excellent cook, and can equal any New Englander in energy. And she is entertaining; as adept as was her old Congressman father at telling funny stories about her friends, about the colored folks—tasteless ones, sometimes, but most are only funny—and about herself. She sees her minor faults plainly and when she is in the mood she can make you see them reflected in cracked mirrors. I have never known anyone who could use her own weaknesses so advantageously as a conversation piece—

And there were other things: When old Miss Hortense fell on the sidewalk in front of the church and broke her hip, they called me. I called the ambulance. Then I thought, Who can help? Renie, of course. I phoned her. In five minutes she was there and almost at once had us doing the right, sensible things: Miss Hortense was suddenly in a room at the hospital, a doctor and nurse were by her side and arrangements had been made for surgery. This settled, Renie went home, made a bowl of orange custard so Miss Hortense would have something homey to eat when she came out from under anesthesia. She sat by her bed those few hours afterward when it is so difficult for an elderly person, and she saw to it that only a few friends of Miss Hortense's came to see her, now and then. Miss Hortense does not like too much of that sort of foolishness. Naturally, after this, Miss Hortense felt there was no one quite like Renie. And it was the following autumn that she gave the first big birthday party for Susan to which were invited not only the right children in Windsor Hills but the members of the nine financial boards Miss Hortense sits on, and her priest, of course, and everyone else she considers of importance. And most of us went to it and wore our party caps with the kids and Miss Hortense, and gathered on the broad verandah for the Big Moment when a toy hydrogen bomb was sent up outdoors while the kids gaped and yelled and clapped at the mushrooming horror, and Miss Hortense in her wheel chair finished off her fifth glass of sherry and pushed her party cap to the side of her red wig and shouted, Send up another, somebody! You, Ben (to Ben Jordan, president of First National Bank), can't we send up something else? and Ben shook his head and kept shaking it, then muttered to me, This is the kind of thing that makes you wish you had stayed a country boy, plowing fields—and then, suddenly, five or six of the younger kids dashed into the drawing room and ran around and around in crazy circles yelling *hydrogen bomb!* and little Joel Askew stopped and stared solemnly at an oil portrait of Miss Hortense's father and spread his legs and let all the liquid in him down on Miss Hortense's antique Aubusson rug— I was near the door and called, Renie! She saw it and made a dash for him, hauled him off to the bathroom and was back in a second or two with a bath towel mopping up the excess moisture the rug rejected, and kneeling there she looked up at me and we both grinned, then shouted with laughter, and Miss Hortense screamed, What is the joke? come tell me, Father Landrum—

This Renie I had always liked and depended on. The other— I hear many things, much is suddenly told me, there are sharp terrible naked moments in people's lives when they must talk and I must listen and help where I can; but afterward, I try to cover up exposed feelings and hold on to the surface man or woman with whom I deal in our daily life.

Now this Renie, accusing Mark. . . .

My hand was still on the phone. I was reluctant to call. I was afraid a scared, twisted girl, still running through an okra field, might answer; I was afraid I could not talk to a memory that knows nothing of reason and nothing of facts. And yet, I knew I must call. And finally, I did and she spoke to me easily, cheerfully. I said, "Renie, I can't possibly make it to Susan's party. And Miss Hortense is upset with me, of course. But I shall be out of town and it is impossible. However, I have a present for Susie which you may not like at all." Then I told her of my plan to give Ali Baba to Susan. I told her that while he and Susan were friends, he and I were mortal enemies and it would actually be a great favor to me if she felt she could live with the cat in her apartment, etc. etc. I told her I wanted to get me a Boxer, etc. etc. And Renie understood, and was very nice about the whole ridiculous matter. Said Susie would come over for the cat in a day or two, that she would be excited and completely charmed with the idea. Then I waited. And she waited. And nothing more was said, nor could I find any fissure into which I could insinuate one casual question. And something told me I could not wisely approach it in a direct way.

My arm was sore. I was aware of it all Saturday afternoon. I gave it a look, after dinner, and saw the redness had crept a half-inch beyond the scratch, and was puffy and hot to the touch.

Nothing serious, probably, but I called Dr. Guthrie. He suggested that I come out to his house in half an hour.

I drove down Arlington Road toward the lake, past the Newells' apartment, and turned into Oak Lane at Paul Pottle's book and record shop. Almost immediately I was in a dense stretch of pines which gives way to broad fields as you approach Miss Hortense's old three-storied turreted gray house. It is possible that Miss Hortense could have lived contentedly in a modern house with glass walls and cantilevered roof and the rest of it— she could certainly afford to live in any house of any period she might choose. But, as she said, Phelia liked the old place, the dogs would not be happy anywhere else, and it was home; much too large to keep up these days when she was restricted to her wheel chair but since Phelia felt this way. . . .

I was approaching the gate and saw her light on. I slowed down: perhaps I should go in for a few minutes. This Susan affair is on her mind. She will be explaining to more and more people why Renie should not have used the word *rape*. Yes. But if I talk to her, she will begin to quote me, she'll have a new angle—her hand will never leave that phone dial. I did not stop. Dr. Guthrie would be waiting—

He was standing on the steps of the porch when I drove up. We greeted each other and he invited me in to speak to his wife. Mrs. Guthrie was sitting in her hostess chair, awaiting my visit.

As I walked toward her, I saw she was knitting something gray and soft. Her white hair is soft, her neck is wrinkly soft, her hands are soft and well kept. But Agnes Guthrie is not soft: she is sure. This bland certitude has the pull of an undertow and as I came toward her I felt it catch me and, as always in her presence, I began to drag my prosthetic leg, a little. This outrages me but I can't fight her complacency with my mind: I simply react in this neurotic way. Out of her presence I can be analytical: I can say, Here is a totally secure person: one who never worries about the state of the world or of outer space, or her own soul; who never feels anxiety; nor, since early childhood, has she felt awe or wonder, or anguish, or ecstasy; she is not serene nor is she compassionate, but she is completely secure: how did it happen? and what does it mean? I have tangled with it in my study, and once sketched the outline of a sermon on this theme, but in her presence I limp and search for words to say.

She laid aside her needles and greeted me. On a table were her Wedgwood cups and plates, the silver coffee service and her cook's angel food cake. Her brown eyes looked me over with tolerance. She poured coffee, cut a handsome slice of cake and offered it to me. She asked Dr. Guthrie if he cared for a slice. He refused it. She saw to the cream and sugar and then cut a sliver for herself. These matters settled, she looked up, smiled, and inquired about my mother's health.

Then, in an identical tone, she asked me if my great-grandmother was Elizabeth Raynolds of Eastern Shore. I said, Yes mam. She said she thought so: her grandmother had mentioned her in her diary and something my mother once said when visiting here, etc. Then she told me they had both—Elizabeth and her grandmother—attended the St. Cecelia Ball in Charleston in 1852; Elizabeth wore a pale green satin ball gown, her eyes were green, her hair pale red, her complexion like marble and altogether she was a sensation.

I was seeing Neel's face as I said *yes, I saw him on his terrace at five-thirty,* hearing his, *you're sure it was Monday?* and my, *quite sure.* Then my words to Renie: *do you think Susan would like to have Ali Baba?* and Mark's: *glad you said it even if it's not true. . . .*

Mrs. Guthrie was saying, "My maternal grandmother was most generous in her praise of Elizabeth."

I don't think I answered her.

Then she asked me if my mother had the recipe for ratifia. I told her I did not know. I did not tell her that I had never heard of ratifia.

She suggested that I write it down: she would like to give it to my mother because Elizabeth Raynolds' father had most generously given it to Mrs. Guthrie's grandmother. . . .

I took out my notebook and gravely wrote down this formula:

One thousand peach kernels; one gallon brandy; one quart Madeira; one quart sweet wine; one pint orange flower water; two and a half pounds of sugar. Put in a heavy jug, seal carefully and set in the sun for three months. Then drink it slowly on a pleasant afternoon.

That done with, I complimented Mrs. Guthrie on the cake, asked about Friggy, her dachshund, expressed my appreciation of her oil portrait done when she was thirty years old in the manner of Gainsborough by a painter whose name does not matter; heard insistent echoes and realized I had said the same words the last time I was here—

Dr. Guthrie was standing. We went through the amenities of departure, I followed him down the back hall, across the closed-in side porch to what he calls his makeshift office. Since his seventy-first birthday he had begun to let patients come to him at his home, at night.

The transition from Agnes' satiny womblike drawing room, where the past is continually being gestated, to Dr. Guthrie's plain small hard-surfaced sharp-cornered office left me speechless.

I took off my coat, pushed back my sleeve, showed him the arm. He asked how it happened. I said a cat had scratched me. He picked up a swab of cotton, wet it with alcohol, and cleaned the wound.

I stared at the washbowl, looked over the instruments in the cabinets, listened to the bubbling sterilizer, listened to Dr. Guthrie's breathing—a bit wheezy—looked at the white waste-can, realized he was speaking:

"Funny thing," he was saying, "the way accidents seem to come in epidemics. Much like the common cold and about as mysterious. You know Jane Houghton's camp?"

I told him I did. I had been there quite a few times with her and the Channings. "Wonderful mountain," I added.

"For ten summers, Agnes and I spent the month of August at Shaw's Inn. We enjoyed dropping in to see the campers and Jane. Now and then, an epidemic of accidents would occur. A camper would sprain her ankle on the tennis court: within a few

days there'd be five or six similar accidents—all sprained ankles
—when there had been none for several summers. Same courts,
kept up in the same efficient manner; but suddenly, one sprained
ankle would precipitate half a dozen. Then, not another for four
or five years. Or a camper might fall from a horse: there would
follow three or four more falls. Jane brought it up a time or two
when we were together. I said I felt it was due to the instability
of adolescents, power of suggestion."

"Accident proneness?"

"Yes, but more. Perhaps you recall the cases of hysterical faint-
ing during John Wesley's great revivals. He mentioned these
swoonings in his journals: made careful analyses of his sermons
in an attempt to find what he had said that could provoke this
irrational reaction. He believed he spoke with moderation, even
austerity. It astounded him that his audience did not react to
him in a rational way."

Dr. Guthrie went to the table, picked up a small bottle, looked
at it, at me, half smiled, said, "You may not know I was Methodist before I married Agnes and joined your church. My hobby
is the Wesley family; I'd like to show you my collection of
Wesleyana."

I told him I would like to see it.

He wet the swab, pushed it into the scratch. It burned like
blazes.

"Rugged treatment."

"Cauterizing the tissue." Dr. Guthrie enjoys the hardier ways of
therapy. "I'd rather not give you antibiotics unless you pick up a
temperature. And you won't. Too healthy." He selected a hy-
podermic syringe, broke an ampule, put its contents in the
syringe. Held it against the light, squinted, pushed a few
bubbles out, said, "When did you have tetanus toxoid shots?"

"Last spring."

"Better have a booster." He gave me one.

"Now—coming back to these waves of accidents: I haven't
treated a cat scratch in a year. But I've had three since Monday."

He pulled off thin strips of adhesive, pasted the bandage down snug and neat. "You're lucky. Little Susie Newell didn't get off so easy. Ugly place on her arm."

How about the third one? I didn't ask, of course.

I finally said, a bit cagily I'm afraid, that I didn't know the Newells had a cat.

He said they didn't. Susan had got the scratch prowling around in the old store next to Nella Perkins' shop.

His manner was casual, no reservation in his voice. "Interesting child. Not easy to handle and more than a match for her mother. Full of spirit. Do you know much about little girls?"

"Not much. I have a sister but—no, I can't say I know much."

He chuckled. "Susie rides the horses out at the farm and handles them like a man. Sure of herself. Reminds me of her old grandfather, Congressman Addams. He thought he could manage anybody and any situation. Susie thinks she can, too. He and I grew up together in Mississippi. We fell in love with the same girl. Arundel was beautiful and gentle and spirited and had brains. And Moon won her. He always got what he went after. I doubt that Moon ever knew about Arundel's brains—" The old man was looking far away now. "He never knew much about the people he thought he loved, nor cared to know. He chose them: he thought that was enough. No need to reach out further. I practiced twenty-two years back home before I came here when St. Vincent's was opened, twenty-five years ago, this coming February." Renie had come to St. Vincent's for Susan's delivery because her father wanted it that way. Claud Newell was working out of Kansas City at the time; Renie's mother was an invalid; Congressman Addams was in Washington. "As I say, the families have been friends for a century. Stick this in your mouth." Thermometer. "Now tell me where you got your scratch." I shifted the thermometer under my tongue, said the usual "Wa-wa-wa-wa-"

"Never mind. You can tell me later." He sat down in a straight chair and folded his hands across his ample stomach. "Smart little tyke, Susie. But as I say, quirky, and not easy to manage. She has a way of hiding scratches and bruises like another

child might hide her sins. It may be she doesn't see much difference." He looked at me, smiled, "Come to think of it, the difference is pretty subtle. She hid a boil for a week, once. When
her mother discovered it, Susie had three degrees of fever. Not a
complaint. Not a sound when I opened it." Dr. Guthrie liked
the child, it was obvious. And I felt he was getting at something.
This wasn't just an old man talking—

I took the thermometer out, handed it to him. "Her scratch
was from a cat?"

"You do have a shade of temp. I'll give you a few capsules. Yes,
I'd say a cat did it."

"That is interesting. Suppose another—child, say, had
scratched her? Would it look the same?"

Dr. Guthrie shook down the thermometer, wiped it with a
swab of wet cotton, put it away. Went to the basin and washed
his hands. Said, "No. It'd be different. A cat's claw is curved and
pointed, and narrow."

I said it impulsively, not quite knowing why, "Dr. Guthrie,
the police have been asking me questions."

"About what?" No change in his voice.

"About Susan and her parents—and Dr. Channing."

He dried his hands. Put the screw cap on the bottle of
alcohol. Wiped off the table. Closed the top of the wastecan. Set
the syringe in the sterilizer. Turned round and looked me over.
This is his way. When introduced to you, he looks you over with
neutrality and thoroughness, then shakes hands with you. Introduced to a new situation he looks it over, too. Now he looked
at me, at the wastecan, the washbowl, the floor, then through the
wall.

I got to my feet. Obviously he did not wish to discuss it. I
said, "I'm afraid I have kept you too long."

"Sit down. We haven't finished."

He talked to me a long time:

It was Tuesday night, he said, when Renie found out about the
scratch. Susan had kept her sweater on all day and through
supper. She must have done the same Monday but it was
colder, Monday, and the fact that she wore a sweater made

no impression on her mother. Tuesday evening, Renie told Susan to take it off, the room was too warm for a sweater. Susan refused. Renie again told her to take it off. Susie said no. So Renie tried to pull it off.

"Renie's a shade impetuous. Can't seem to wait for things to uncurl of their own."

She, apparently, had a time uncurling Susie. Finally, she got the sweater off and saw the scratch, streaking Susie's arm from elbow to wrist. Renie insisted on knowing what had caused it.

Susie said she didn't know.

—You're bound to know. It didn't happen in your sleep. You're bound to know.

Susie said she didn't know.

Renie threatened to spank her. Susie did not give. Renie threatened to take her allowance from her for a month. Susie curled into a tight knot in the chair. After a number of threats, Susie yielded ground enough to say she got it, maybe, while she was skating.

—Where?

—Against a pile of lumber.

—But where?

Susan said she didn't know where.

—You're bound to know where lumber is, Renie said.

Susan didn't know.

Renie pulled her out of the chair, gave her a good shaking.

—You're lying to me. You do know. Now tell me where or I'll lock you up in your room.

The threat of the locked room worked and Susie talked:

She said a cat had scratched her.

—You said lumber.

—I forgot. It was a cat scratched me.

—Where?

—Just an old yellow cat.

—But where?

—Oh . . . in a store.

—Where?

—Next to Mrs. Perkins' shop, I think.

—You think!

—Yes, I think.

—Was it in that vacant store?

—I think so.

The old doctor was obviously enjoying every detail of his account.

"By this time, Renie needed me more than Susie did," Dr. Guthrie smiled. "And this is when she called me. I rarely go out at night but after that telephone conversation I thought I'd better go see what the trouble was."

When he arrived at the apartment, Susie was in her pajamas, crouched in the big leather chair. Pale and dull-eyed and looking as if she might bite. "I kept my distance."

He couldn't keep distance from Renie. He put his bag on the floor, looked around for a straight chair, sat down and let Renie do the talking.

Renie told how and when she had found the scratch, what she had said, what Susan had said, what she had done, what Susan had done, then she told Susan to show Uncle Guth her arm.

Susan said no.

Renie tried to pull up Susan's pajama sleeve. Susan fought back.

Dr. Guthrie shook his head, laughed. "I said, Renie sit down. Then I said there was no reason to worry about the scratch: we'd have it all right in a day or so. That is when Renie mentioned the man in the store. I asked what man. She said Susan wouldn't say." She tried, again, to make Susie say. Susie pressed her lips together, looked at Uncle Guth, looked at her mama.

"I asked Renie what she thought had happened."

Renie asked Susan to leave the room while she talked to Uncle Guth. Susan pressed her lips together and scrunched up in the chair. Renie repeated the words but with heavier underscoring. Susie scrunched. Renie went to the chair and began to try to unglue Susie. Susie slid into passive resistance, rolled around under Renie's pulling and struggling but never left the chair. Finally,

Dr. Guthrie suggested that Renie let Susan stay. Then he asked Renie to tell him exactly what was on her mind.

While Susan listened attentively, Renie told him she believed the child had been raped.

Why did she think that?

What else was there to think?

Quite a few things, Dr. Guthrie told her. "First, there might not have been a man. But even were one there, he might have been a workman who had come back for his tools. Perhaps he scared her accidentally."

"I don't know why he was there but when he saw Susan he —" Renie stopped.

"Renie . . . do you think it was a nigger or a white man?"

"I—don't know."

"Let me say this and relieve your mind: There are no colored workers on that job. Nobody but carpenters and painters. They're all white and we can easily get their names."

"I didn't say it was a nigger." Susan's one contribution.

Dr. Guthrie let the silence ease them down for a few seconds. Then he asked Renie what she wanted him to do.

"Examine her."

"We'll get to the arm, after a little."

"I don't mean that. I want you to examine *her*."

He asked her why. He was trying, he told me, to catch hold of the rational end of her fear.

Renie stared at him. "Because . . . we must know, of course."

"Why?"

"If a child has been ruined— I don't think it's unreasonable for a mother to want to know it."

Then she began to cry in a low hushed way. All her life, he told me, she has blown her top over small matters but when she cries he knows she is deeply disturbed.

"I have always thought of Mrs. Newell as poised, efficient, cool in a crisis—"

"Depends on whose crisis it is. Somebody else's—yes: she's cool, quick, ready. And people think of her this way. But when it concerns her or her family: she turns into a different person.

I've known her since she was a baby. She never has one trouble: all the old ones come back when a new one appears. I tried to reason with her. Told her I'd like for her to get that word *ruined* out of her mind, and we'd go on from there."

"And Susan?"

He smiled. "Taking it all in. Eyes bright. Watching me. Watching her mother. I tried it this way with Renie: Suppose a truck had run Susie down: suppose she was lying here without legs or arms or sight or had been left paralyzed—or her face was burned, disfiguring her for life: there'd be something to worry about."

But Renie heard only the jagged translation her fears made for her. "It'd be a thousand times easier to bear than rape! You know that, Uncle Guth!"

"Now I could have kept on," Dr. Guthrie said, "but I saw she didn't want reassurance. She wanted me to confirm her fears even though she felt her life would be unendurable if they were confirmed. So I said, How about making an old man a cup of coffee? This was Moon Addams' daughter I was talking to, and I knew Moon. He had reared her to believe raping is the most hideous of crimes and an ever-present danger to every nice white girl—yet, in his own life—" He sighed. "Well, all that was a long time ago—" He was looking down at the floor. Looked up, said in a different tone, "Moon was a shrewd, capable politician who could make a mighty eloquent speech. He was successful because he learned early to keep his right hand and his left well separated from each other. He had his good qualities: was kind to anyone who was sick or hungry or needed five dollars, was a great bargainer in Congress—but Renie's own mother was subjected by him to unspeakable indignities of the spirit. She never leaves her room now; never speaks; sits in her chair and stares out of the window which faces her garden; day after day, year after year. A delicate, sheltered, protected woman, the world thinks, but she has seen all the evil there is to see, and Moon showed it to her. Once a year I go down to see her."

That old placid, calm, stodgy face had broken into agonized planes. "I tell you this. Why? I don't know. Everybody talks to me, now I talk to you. Moon never knew the meaning of tenderness, except for babies—and his dogs. It stopped there. I thought what happened to Arundel would dim out as I grew older but it is the other way round: it comes clearer each year, and I have lived seventy-two of them. As I said, Moon and I grew up together, fished, hunted, wandered around and did our young meanness together. He went to Princeton and I went to Johns Hopkins and we both loved Arundel or thought we did. We both wanted to marry her and she chose Moon. I tried to believe she chose the better man. Love is a miracle or a disaster: Arundel brought out the best in me, qualities I didn't know I possessed until she showed them to me—and she brought out the worst in Moon; and yet it was Moon she loved."

"Would you let me say, sir, that, sometimes, a delicate gentle woman seems irresistibly drawn to cruel men? I know it is easy to call such women masochists, but could it be that something in them wants to see the dark side of human nature and chooses a certain man to take them there since they are afraid to look at it, alone?"

He smiled. "It may be. But that doesn't explain anything. It only makes the lot of man more miserable. Coming back to Renie: *rape* is a powerful word and most of us don't understand its effect on people. For instance: a child says she has been raped: we doctors are then asked to make an examination so that the law may properly punish the man. But few realize or care that in this child's mind the medical examination may be as much a violation as the act of the seducer."

"Without the actual violence?"

"When a child is frightened, there is inevitably an amount of duress and restraint while the examination is being made. Yet nearly everyone is willing for her to be subjected to it. I take the position that one should be concerned only with what will heal her. I do not minimize the evil of raping or the menace of a psychotic raper. But I am not speaking of psychotic rapers. Had a psychotic been in that store Susie would have been left there dead."

He rubbed the mole on his chin reflectively, looked at me,

rubbed the mole. "Have you ever heard of a posse going out and stringing up a careless drunken driver for tearing the legs off a child or crushing its skull? No. Of course you haven't. There's something about a raping that upsets people, deeply disturbs them, but it isn't what happens to the child that concerns them most.

"But now, I'll finish my little story: I said, Renie, Susie hasn't been raped. She said, But something happened! Maybe so, I said, but Susie hasn't been raped. Then I told her I wanted her to try to imagine what this child would have ahead of her had a truck torn off her arms or legs. I said, You think exhibitionism, even seduction, even attempted rape is as bad as that? Well, I don't—and I've seen the results of all of them."

Renie stared at Dr. Guthrie as if she were about to step on a swamp rattler. Then she looked at Susan hunched up in the big chair.

"Oh my precious baby—" She rushed to Susie and tried to pull her into her arms.

"Get away!" said Susie and kicked hard.

Doc laughed. Stopped. Laughed again. It was evident that he enjoyed Susie. "My my my. All my life, I've been trying to decide which are queerer: men, women, or children. There was Mrs. Morton and her Sally: back in Mississippi. Thirty years ago. Sally was a pert-eyed bright little thing and, as you might have expected, if you knew her and her family, became pregnant in her sophomore year at college. Having a baby when you weren't married was a catastrophe in those days. No picnic today, but then—people really let their feelings go. I got Sally straightened out with a few plain facts. Told her I knew a quiet place where she could stay until the delivery; I told her if she wanted the baby and loved the wretch she'd better marry him but if she didn't love him we'd find a good family who would adopt the baby. Sally said she loved him and they both wanted the baby and wanted to get married. So I felt things might level off pretty quickly. After I persuaded Mrs. Morton that this was a sensible solution, and Sally had got her to bed, and I had thoroughly sedated her, I thought I'd go home and catch a little sleep and in the morning I'd talk some sense into Jeff Morton—when in came Jeff, all lit up and with a gun. Been out looking for Sally's boy friend. Was going out again, he said, and blast his head off. Just wanted to drop by to be sure his poor little Sally was all right. See? Before breaking her heart for sure. Things were easing down too reasonably. He had to have a bigger show, more fireworks, so he was going to turn murderer and see to it that things around town got real interesting.

"Well—I saw I was getting nowhere with Renie, so I told her I wanted her to go to the bathroom and wash her face and pretty up her hair a little, then go to the kitchen and make me that cup of coffee—and stay there while it was making."

After she left the room, he said, he didn't do a thing for several minutes. He was close to fifty when he mastered that difficult trick; but once learned, nothing had served him so well. Finally, he winked at Susan and she giggled. He took out a cigar and smoked a while. Susan watched him. Every now and then, he winked at her and she giggled back at him. They were communicating nicely. He let this continue a bit longer, then he said, "Susie, last time I saw you skating your left skate was wiggling. Ever tighten those screws?"

"Yes sir."

"Do you know about the new horse out at the farm?"

"No sir."

"Like to come out in the morning and ride it?"

"Yes sir. But I can't. It's school."

"How about in the afternoon?"

"OK."

"I'll come by and pick you up. Did you go skating this afternoon?"

"Yes sir."

"Walk to school this morning?"

"Yes sir."

"Keeping those muscles hard like I told you?"

"Yes sir."

"Mind letting me see how hard?" She came over. He told her to roll up her pajamas to the thighs. Then he examined her legs carefully. Pressed in the muscles here and there. "Sore?"

"No sir."

"Now, let's see those abdominal muscles. They hard, too?" She pulled her pajamas down below her thighs and let him poke and push her muscles and thighs.

"Muscles in fine shape. You keep them that way, hear?"

"Yes sir."

"Now—let's see you do a cartwheel."

She did four.

"You want to do a split? Don't do it if you feel sore anywhere."

"I don't feel sore," she said. She did a split, looked at him, grinned, said, "I can do a backbend while I am in a split." She did one.

She had just got to her feet when Renie walked in carrying a silver tray. There were slices of cake in her milk glass plates and coffee in her grandmother's eggshell cups. She had changed into a pale blue dressing gown and satin sandals to match.

"Never did a woman live who could make as complete shambles of a situation or smooth it up as fast," Dr. Guthrie laughed. "No wonder she drives Claud crazy."

After he drank his coffee, he sedated Renie, pulled Susie's hair and asked to see her arm. She showed it to him without protest; he cleaned it up and gave her a shot of penicillin.

"Something happens: people can't leave it as it is. They always get busy and make something else out of it. Usually something worse."

"The old psychic elaboration, as Freud called it."

"Never read him. Never felt a need to. I don't mean I am closed-minded. But when you poke around in as many houses and in as many back yards as I go in you don't need to poke around in books much. You watch enough people die, watch their families watch them die; you watch people get well when their families had counted hard on their dying; you watch women have their babies, you watch the family watch them have their babies; watch them starve their bodies or gorge them: you do it long enough . . . and you sort of catch on. You catch on to the meaning of love and the meaning of hate and the meaning of greed. You find out fear doesn't have one face:it has a hundred, and some of them smooth as gravestones; you see a man live when he ought to die according to the books; and you know he's living because he's got something he still wants to do or somebody he still wants to torment. We doctors get more credit than we deserve. Many a mortal keeps breathing just to make the folks round him miserable. It is guilt that kills. Not hate. Hate makes you last a long time; sometimes it won't loosen its grip until the whole body rusts out; while love . . . now and then love has the grace to let go, knowing by stopping its breath it makes another poor mortal breathe easy." He sighed and hushed. The drip drip from the tap in the washbowl and the bubbling of the sterilizer were all I heard. His hands were clasped across his stomach and his thumbs rubbed each other.

I finally asked him if Susie went to the farm.

"Susie?" He seemed to have forgot her. "Oh, why sure, sure. We went out and she rode the new horse for an hour. Cantered, posted, did a slow trot, a hard gallop and when she returned to the stables she stood up in the saddle and singlefooted around the lot. I'm taking her to the horse show next spring. She's riding Sky Foot."

"So you knew she was all right?"

"Of course she's all right! She hadn't been touched. Had she been—" he looked at the washbowl, then at me, "She's young; she's been protected. Nature makes a child shy; there'd have been a recoil, a faint tremor, at least, had she recently been through such an experience."

"Do you think, sir, that someone was in that store?"

He looked straight at me. "I doubt it."

We did not talk for a full minute, then he said, "That's what I know." He eased out of his chair. A sharp twinge of pain crossed his face. He went to the desk and wrote a prescription, handed it to me. He led me to the side entrance, explaining that Agnes had retired. Then he said, as if it were of no importance, "You say the police have been asking you questions?"

"Neel of the Juvenile Bureau came to my study, Thursday morning. It seems that Susan ran in Nella Perkins' shop after she left the store, so quite a few people have heard about the incident."

"Do you know who reported it to the police?"

"Susan's mother."

"Do you know when?"

"Wednesday evening."

Dr. Guthrie pressed his pudgy forefinger into his cheek. Felt the maxillary muscles, pushed them around a bit. Finally, he asked with no curiosity in his voice, "How did Dr. Channing get in the picture?"

"I don't know, sir."

More probing of the maxillary muscles. Then, "By the way, where did *your* scratch come from?"

"Ali Baba, the rectory cat."

He stood at the door, unmoving, and looked straight at the middle of my face. He can stare at you longer than anyone I have ever known, except a six-months-old baby.

He finally said, "Let me know if you have any more trouble with the arm."

When Saturday passed and no arrest had been made, and Sunday and Monday, I decided the worst of it was over.

Claud Newell had come in from Chicago on Friday night. I had seen him at church Sunday morning, had shaken hands with him afterward. He was affable and calm and gave no indication that he was disturbed about anything. On the contrary, he had seemed more interested than usual. I noticed as I was midway my sermon that he was listening attentively. I glanced at Renie and she smiled. She's decided not to tell him, I thought. A little of it, yes; probably told him Susie had been wandering around and had gotten scratched by a cat. She made that accusation on impulse, regrets it now—Neel and the Chief must have talked some sense into her—she probably liked the old Chief, she likes people with the common touch—her politician father had it to an extraordinary degree—I had seen him on TV years ago, voice warm, colloquial, as he spoke of the sacred system of segregation . . . maybe Dr. Guthrie had talked to her—

This scudded cloudily through my mind as I stood in the pulpit speaking. And then I thought, *they are going to drop it.* I was startled by the sudden confidence and hope that amplified my voice. My congregation was a bit shaken, too, I think, for there was a quiet rustle in pews as masks slid off and real faces peered out at me for a moment, then as suddenly the masks went on again and I continued my sermon on the urgent need for a new moral commitment to be made by all of us.

Mark gave me a quick look, glanced at the Newells, then at Grace, she seemed far away and I don't think she noticed anything.

On Tuesday morning, as I was having my coffee, Dewey Snyder called. He said he had liked the sermon, Sunday: it was carefully organized and to the point and was greatly needed at this time. Then his voice changed, became warm and confidential. He said "Dave—" he calls me this now and then when he is about to put a little pressure on, "I want to tell you that everything is set up for the TV program. Did you, by chance, see the write-up in the morning paper?"

I said I had not read the paper, as yet. He apologized for calling me at such an early hour, said he had done so because he wanted to call my attention to the fact that Dr. Channing's name was not included in the notice.

"By mistake?"

"No."

"But he *is* the program! How could his name—" I didn't complete it. I knew.

He waited. He presents you with a *fait accompli* then makes you take the initiative from that point on. I walked straight into his trap. I just wasn't up to matching him trick for trick. So I said what he expected me to say, "Because of the talk?"

"Yes," he said, "I felt you would understand."

I told him I didn't understand. There had been no arrest, the talk would die down. I knew there was quite a bit of it in Windsor Hills and around the shopping center but surely not in the rest of the city. There had been no mention of it in the papers— He said he had heard nothing but talk of this scandal at the City Club, Katie had heard it at the Yacht Club, one of his friends had heard it at the golf club, it was everywhere; his secretary brought him in a new story each day; she had just told him about the checker at the supermarket seeing Dr. Channing there at five-thirty-five that Monday afternoon, five minutes after the Newell child had run into the beauty shop. . . .

"It makes him absolutely useless to us. It would be impossible for him to speak on television. Even if we were willing the station probably would not be. It would be highly offensive to people—"

I said, "Mark Channing is no more guilty of what he has been accused of than I am, or you. A silly, confused little girl happened to think of his name—"

We went into quite a hassle. I must have used the word *innocence* a dozen times; he matched it with *controversial*. He spoke once more of a man's losing his usefulness when accused of this sort of thing. "Once you are smeared, that is it."

"But we are doing the smearing."

He did not reply to that. I felt my temper rising at this point and paused for a moment, forcing my voice down to a more relaxed level, trying to push back that rush of feeling which makes you blow your top. I tried it this way, "Do you know the actual facts?"

"Does anyone?"

I ignored that. I asked him to let me tell him what I did know about it. He said he'd like for me to. And he listened without interruption as I carefully enumerated the discrepancies in Susan's story. I, naturally, stressed the point that at the moment Susan ran out of the store into the beauty shop I had seen Mark sitting on his terrace, reading—

"I realize," he said, "that you are close friends and this is hard on you."

Well, that was his way of calling me a liar, I suppose, and I had to take it. After all, I wasn't too sure I was not one. The only thing I was certain of, at this time, was that Mark had not been in that store and I could not accept what was happening to him without making strong protest. I said quite a bit about the madness of suspicion, its uncontrollable energy when released, said I felt it was our duty to protect a man against reckless and irresponsible accusation; any man; but especially someone we knew and believed in. "Isn't it a curiously hypocritical form of Puritanism for us to insist that everyone who appears before the people on TV, or in any other way, must be without sin? what does this actually mean? are they, Dewey, without sin? those who do appear? and the people listening: are they without sin?"

I didn't get anywhere with this, so I dropped it. I tried it from another angle, "The Cancer Committee is raising funds for research: are we, who make up this committee, willing to humiliate and possibly destroy one of the best men in research in the country in order to raise funds for the very research he is doing? does this make much sense?"

He said quietly, reasonably, "No one wants to humiliate Dr. Channing. And certainly in no one's mind is there any thought of destroying him. It is a very unfortunate thing, but it is plain common sense, Dave: you can't have a man who is involved in a sex perversion scandal on this kind of program. Our purpose is not to start a controversy but to raise money. It is your friendship that is keeping you from seeing this. You are always reasonable— I understand why this is hard but even so, surely you see that we have to bow to the inevitable and find someone else. That is all we can do. There is no alternative."

I didn't argue with him more. I knew there were arguments, but I couldn't get hold of them quickly and persuasively enough. I said only this, "It scares me to think I live in a world where eight-year-old children make our decisions for us. It is Susan who is deciding who is to speak on cancer research, who will appear on TV, and who is to do research, perhaps, in our city. This is fantastic. Unbelievable." I am afraid I put all the feeling into my words that I had been repressing. I had been troubled by the fact that Mark was showing so little fear, so little perturbation. I had said, He's not admitting what is ahead of him, he's blocking it off. Well, I had blocked it off, too. Certainly, I had not anticipated this from Snyder.

There was more talk, of course. The details do not matter. He wanted to know if Mark usually wrote out his speeches. I said I thought he did, although he never read them. Then that would make things simpler for he would, of course, be willing for someone else to read the paper. I knew Mark would. His integrity, his profound interest in research—he would not hesitate. Then Snyder said the committee would like for me to read the paper. I told him it would be quite impossible. He accepted this decision without protest. Would I find someone? I finally said I would try. Would I tell Dr. Channing about the change in plans? I saw Mark's eyes: it would humiliate him less, coming from me than from the others, yes; but it was difficult to agree to it. I said I'd like to think about it; would phone him, later. But I knew as I postponed my decision what my answer would be. What else was there to do?

Names ran through my head. I eliminated the members of the staff. They were too loyal to Mark, this would be deeply embarrassing to them. There were two or three intelligent, young businessmen, friends of Mark's, who had the personality to put it over. But after a little thought I reluctantly scratched their names: too many tie-ups, complex business relationships, they might turn me down and for Mark's sake I did not want to be refused.

During the day, as I kept busy with my parish responsibilities, I was thinking of all of it: the little, the big, the sudden twist of events— Who could read this paper? Miss Hortense's party —I must go see her and drink a cup of tea and make her laugh about Ali Baba. Duveen . . . running into that half-dark place, running out again with her story about Yellow Cat sliding back on the lumber pile . . . who was brave enough to read this brilliant scientist's paper? questions questions—

Susan . . . where had she picked up Mark's name? If he had been in the store she would have recognized him, surely. She had seen him too many times at church and is alert and quick. I had thought this again and again and again and again. But all day I kept thinking it, trying to find something to catch hold of that made real sense in terms of these people who were not names in a newspaper but people I thought I knew well. I seemed to remember hearing Renie speak of the Channings once and with rather a bit of feeling. But I was not sure of that memory; it was vague, shadowy— Neel had said something undoubtedly happened in that store. Yes: Susan wandered into the place, picked up the cat, was rough with it and it scratched her. The emptiness and half-darkness and the pain were enough to scare her and she imagined or made up the rest of it: the tall thin man— What I had said to Grace and Mark about her father being tall and thin had come to me on the spur of the moment, a kind of facile improvisation. But Mark did actually look like him. Both are tall men and thin, both have sandy hair— There was no real thinking behind this. Just a vague stirring as if I were about to think. Susie's a lonely child. You never know what lonely kids are doing inside their heads. Her eyes had always interested me. Like dark wooden beads, most of the time; but they can turn a shining cat-yellow and as suddenly they can look tired and lost as if they have wandered away and forgot the name of the street they live on. I had seen her like that, many times, as she sat in the fourth pew below me. She looks fragile and at the same time unbreakable, like leather. That pale shining hair— Yes, she got scared when the old yellow cat scratched her, she suddenly realized she was alone in that big place, thought of her father, probably wished he was there to protect her, then her feelings took a sudden dive—

I could not keep on improvising without facts. Back again on the paper: who could read it? I thought of young Dr. Sydney Ainsworth. He and Katie Snyder with whom he was in love were friends of the Channings; he was a brilliant pediatrician and popular, interested in cancer, of course; he and Mark had often talked about the forms of malignancy which invade children's bodies most frequently. His attitude would be right; he would be outraged about this happening to Mark, at the same time he was deeply interested in the Cancer Committee's work—and they had done a fine job in our city— This might be the answer. I'd talk to him.

5

I let six days go by after talking with Snyder before I gave Mark's speech to Sydney Ainsworth.

That afternoon, I felt feverish. I swallowed a couple of aspirin and decided to take it easy for an hour or so. Went upstairs and lay down.

To get comfortable I had removed the leg and put it on the floor by the bed. This is my habit. I have had poor luck with a prosthetic limb. Mine is modern enough, well fitted, etc., but lying down with it on is no good. Perhaps because the amputation was above the knee and AK's have a way of causing all sorts of complications.

Now let me be explicit, even to an embarrassing degree: My duties as rector involve many people; someone is likely to drop in at any time. That day, I kept my shirt and trousers and shoe on, even though I was lying down. If someone came to the study I knew I could quickly slip on a coat, pick up my crutches and go downstairs.

So: the leg lay there on the rug: wearing its well-shined black shoe which matches the well-shined shoe on my other foot, the real one. Unwittingly, I had set the stage for what happened, later.

I picked up a book of essays on Christianity and existentialism, read a few pages on Berdyaev—couldn't take it. Turned to Paul Tillich's piece on Picasso's "Guernica." Vaguely disagreed with him as I read but could find no sound reason for my reluctance to go along with him. Found myself drifting . . . *what is behind this thing—what's got into Snyder—if it had been Esteridge, yes; fat, jolly, powerful, always joking but hard, ruthless—Dewey—no, I couldn't see it.* Concentrated on the Tillich piece, again; he's difficult, yes, but worth it—and sometimes enormously exciting as in *The Shaking of the Foundations.* But this time, he didn't hold me. I turned the pages of the book, back and forth, back and forth. Held on to an essay on Kierkegaard for ten or twelve pages. Couldn't make it. Picked up a book by Karl Barth and doggedly read a chapter, made myself mark sentences, here and there, made myself reread a difficult paragraph, here and there.

It was no good, my trying. All I could think of was what I had done to Mark. I had slogged it out with my conscience half the night after I talked with Dewey Snyder. Then, what did I do? Like a slinky manservant I carried out his errand, and like an efficient one, I did it successfully. Now, everything was arranged: there had been no talk, no publicity about it, no embarrassment for the committee; I had finally persuaded young Dr. Sydney Ainsworth to get in there and pitch for us.

I had postponed telling Mark about Snyder's decision as long as I could. Finally, I called him at the lab about eleven o'clock Friday, and asked if I could drop by. Felt this was the best way. He would not want me to discuss it before Grace nor could I possibly do so.

His secretary took me into his small office, off the larger one where she and the others worked. A cubbyhole of a place; crowded with two wall files, his desk, shelves of technical books, a table with a file of tissue slides on it, other things. As I sat waiting, miserable and full of dread, I looked at Grace's photograph on his desk. Above it, on the wall, was a water color she had done of Andy when he was five. Mark liked it very much. I think Andy actually looked more like Grace, but somehow, in this portrait, he looked like Mark—bone structure like his—maybe my eyes had not seen that—eyes like his, too, and that mouth. As I looked at it now, I realized he did resemble Mark. New England is a far-off place. But Andy seemed to like it. I must write the boy; hadn't managed but one letter to him—

A technologist passed the open door, a tray of slides in her hands; another, with a wire tray of staining jars; someone came in, smiled, picked up some charts from his desk, put some freshly sharpened pencils in a glass where already there were several, went back into the main office.

In the tissue room, I heard voices. At first, thought I recognized Mark's. Decided against it. In a cubicle of its own, directly in front of me, was the electron microscope. I remembered the night he showed it to me: his enthusiasm as he explained what this had meant to the study of viruses. We had had a steak supper, at their house, and somehow the virus theory came up and we began to talk: I said I knew practically nothing about all this: he said, Let's go to the lab, I'd like to show you a few things. And we had gone, the two of us, and he had talked to me about the Warburg apparatus, and the spectronometer, the electron microscope, and all the rest of it—had shown me through the tissue rooms, the animal rooms. And that is when I had seen Dr. Otto Warburg's photograph on his office wall. He had talked to me about this great scientist. Now I looked at the photograph, hanging there above the bookshelves. The man's eyes. Thought of Mark's. I suddenly felt I couldn't go through this, could have no part in it. *Get up and leave! Tell Snyder to do his dirty work himself!*

Down the corridor, I heard Mark speak. Pleasant, interested voice; calm, sure. A stranger would never have guessed that voice belonged to a man whose life was tumbling down on his head.

He came in, pulling on his white gown. He had been in the animal rooms. An assistant followed him. They were laughing. The assistant held a flask of blood. Said something—but I know little of the jargon; could pick out a few words, yes—as you do in a foreign city when sitting at a sidewalk café listening to talk around you, without really knowing what is said. He mentioned the Warburg apparatus, said something a moment or so

later, about nitrogen molecules, commented on a batch of slides
that were questionable and went into a quick complex sentence
out of which I got only a ragged phrase or two. One fantastic
word stuck with me: desoxyribonucleic. Their everyday talk:
of great meaning to them and of such small clarity to me. It is as
if we are all working in glass-walled but soundproof rooms: we
dimly see each other's minds and the products of those minds
but we don't really hear or comprehend. I think this now. Then: I
was feeling only dread, and shame.

They came in. The three of us exchanged the usual amenities.
They checked a paper quickly, the assistant went out. Mark
looked keen, alert, completely committed; his eyes had the
steady glow that is always in them when he is at the lab. I've
seen it many times. He sat down. Looked at me sharply. The
ardor left his face. He was, suddenly, a tired man. Perhaps my
face had already told him for he showed no surprise, no feeling, as I explained the committee's decision not to have him on
the cancer-drive program. He smiled quickly when he got the
point of my stammering words, said, "It was to be expected,
Dave. Don't sweat so hard." We tried to laugh.

Then he said in that even, monotonous tone his voice slips into
when he is under stress, "It could have been predicted by either
of us. They want their drive to go over. To make it do so, they
need the best possible man on that program. I am no longer that
man."

He went to his files, pulled a folder out, removed the speech,
handed it to me. "You might scan it," he said, "then we'll go over
together the spots we should change if someone else is to give
it. Have they decided who will take my place?"

I told him no. Told him I had in mind Dr. Sydney Ainsworth.
If he thought well of it, I would ask him.

"Then we won't have to change much. Leave it. Sydney can
change it to suit himself. He's all right."

I should have been relieved but I felt worse. If he would get
mad and fight back, tell me and everybody else that we were
fools and cowards, it would help him. Help me, too. Instead, he
took out a cigarette, smoked it, stared out the window. Finally

he said, without looking at me, "We can't fight this one. It is not on the fighting level of things."

We smoked in silence for a minute or more. I said, "I can't understand Snyder. Ever have a run-in with him?"

"No. We don't always agree about vestry matters; in the nature of things we wouldn't, I'm younger, we are different." He turned, looked at me. "But you don't have to hunt for a motive: I've been accused of making immoral approaches to a little girl. What more do you need?"

"Nothing has been proved. How can a man—"

"They don't have to prove it, Dave. They don't live in a lab."

"Look—you've been accused by a silly half-delinquent little girl and her hysterical mother. I told Snyder the child was in that place at five-thirty and you were on your terrace reading at five-thirty. I saw you there. But when I said it he did not even listen, he went on saying what he had planned to say."

"Did you see me there, Dave?"

"Of course I did."

"Wasn't it about five-forty-five when I went out on the terrace; or five-fifty?"

"Mark, I saw you there at five-thirty and I'm sticking to it."

He smiled, he suddenly laughed.

Then his eyes tensed up again. "The only important thing is that I've been accused. That is what they can't forgive: I'm the malignant virus in the neighborhood's organism." He laughed. "Maybe I'd better prove the theory before I use it as an analogy."

Finally, he said evenly, quietly, "If you find anything in the paper you and Sydney want to change, tell him to give me a ring."

I left in a moment or two.

This was on Friday.

Saturday morning, Dewey Snyder phoned and thanked me for what I had done. It was his coziness that did me in. And a tone I had not heard in his voice before: moral superiority. All he said was, How about going out to the farm with him? wonderful weather; he wanted me to see his chrysanthemums. "And I want to tell you the rest of that story about the pervert at my college. You know, the homo I mentioned the other day. My, my," laughing shrilly now, "his escapades will amaze you."

He had a right to feel morally superior to me for he had done what he deemed good and I had done what I knew was wrong, but the coziness was more than I could stomach. Heard my voice grow cold as I told him I could not go; heard him say confidently, Perhaps you can make it next week.

After I hung up I sat at the desk a long time. Thinking? No. Brain stupefied. Just feeling.

There are times when anger and shame and guilt fuse in a man's mind—or in his glands—and become something new and different: if there is a word for it, I don't know it. But I felt it as it tore at my sense of decency and honor and love for Mark. So deftly, Dewey Snyder had set Mark off in a dark dirty little corner with the so-called pervert he had known at college. And I had let him do it.

And worse, I had the nasty feeling I had been tipped: in his mind it had been done: I'd hear the details of it six months, or a year, later. Time has a comfortable way of letting us forget which chick came out of which egg. Snyder would wait, oh sure. Then, at the proper time, he'd suggest to the finance committee that my salary be increased, or he'd give something fine and elegant to the new rectory; and word would get around to the bishop that I was an up-and-coming young man. . . . Yes, I knew how things were done. Would I accept the tip? would I rub all this out and accept it?

It is a nightmare to watch one's clerical robes metamorphose into a valet's coat. Suddenly, I saw just that happening to me. I tried once more to justify what I had done: you have to work with people; you have to give in a little; compromise a little— I said everything I had said to myself that night after my talk with Snyder. I said, The cancer drive is important, you can't jeopardize it; the money is needed. For what? For research. Sure: and to get money for research you are now helping to destroy the most brilliant researcher in your region. And you are doing this to your friend. But what else can you do? I'd like to hear what some of the perfectionists think you can do—

I was hearing again Snyder's voice: like the wet edge of something that should be dry. And I turned on him all the shame and disesteem and fury I had begun to feel for myself. Tension eased: I had found a way to siphon off feelings, a scapegoat to turn them on. . . . It worked for a while. A few minutes. Then it came back: the nightmare feeling—and with it a sore throat.

As I am writing now, I see it this way: had I held firm on the TV issue—small as it was—had I refused to go along with Snyder at the beginning, the rest of it—no, some of it—might not have happened. I could not have stopped Claud Newell from swearing out that warrant, of course; but I might have blocked off the events that trampled us during the weeks that followed. But on that Friday morning when I talked with Mark, I had convinced myself that his speech would be canceled anyway, no matter how firmly I stood up for him; therefore my telling him, instead of someone else doing it, might save him pain and embarrassment. That is why I agreed to take it on. I would not let myself see what I see today: I made it easier for him, yes; but I made it easier, also, for the committee: a priest cleared them of their guilt by his collaboration in their sin, and by doing it opened the door a few inches wider to disaster.

I stared at the two books I had tried to read but all I saw was Mark's face: in his office at the lab, immobilized, as I said the words. I remember his hand—the thumbnail was blackened—rubbing the edge of a tray of slides. The hand left the edge of the tray and moved to a glass full of pencils, lifted one out, laid it on the desk, rolled it slowly back and forth as I talked. The rest of him was still. I tried not to think of that flat, toneless scene. I had said it badly as if it meant nothing to me; he had replied as if it meant nothing to him. And we had sat there: tied and gagged by feelings that had overpowered us.

Throughout those two weeks he had said so little. Doggedly kept at the lab working all day and half the night—as if he knew he must do what he had to do quick. Or did he block it off? Did he blind himself to what was coming? I have never been sure. Had he been able to talk much to Grace? I doubted it. And I was shaken by a sudden glimpse of his loneliness.

My love for him is deep. It goes into places in my nature that are unexplored terrain: no other relationship has left a footprint there. I cannot explain it: but must we? are we compelled to explain a relationship that does not fit the stereotypes? does any real relationship fit a pattern? whose pattern? what pair of giant scissors snipped the one, two, three, four, or five, or six patterns out? who is the pattern-maker?

And then, I thought of Grace. How different was my feeling for her: a delicate tie; shadowy. I had been reluctant to spell it out for fear it would blow away, exposing itself for what it might be: a dream, not a real thing at all. Let me say it crudely: she had done something big for me and I loved her for it. That is not quite true, perhaps; I would have loved her had she done nothing. I cannot easily find words. For how I felt then is not how I feel now. But let me try:

Something stopped breathing in me after the leg came off, it had to do, in large part, with my girl—her name was Jean—and our broken engagement. She—how can I talk about it?—Jean's world begins, and ends perhaps, in her muscles competing with other muscles. That may explain it. We used to have great tennis games together; sometimes, we'd swim a mile or so in heavy surf, bodies moving side by side in slow driving rhythm through the water and she'd look at me and blow the water out of her mouth and laugh and I'd laugh and we felt: not fused, not one, but two, moving in perfect synchrony.

No. *I* felt that. I don't know, now, what my girl felt.

Well, anyway—when we had done battling that surf, I'd pull her into shallow water and take her in my arms—two cold wet bodies close together—and I'd hear our hearts pounding and I'd begin to warm up and would find her mouth and then, quickly— well . . . she'd pull away laughing, and say, Race me up the beach. Then we'd lie on the dunes, smoking; not talking much; or if we talked, it was about sports, about her chance in the golf tournament, or mine for all-American; then we'd go home and have a big steak or maybe cook it there over a charcoal brazier; and lie on the sands afterward, looking at the sky and listening to the slow shush shush of tide going out. And, after a while, she'd sing. Folk songs. It was the kind of music she liked. I remember I tried a little Stravinsky on her once, and some Bartók, and she said it didn't make sense; then I tried Bach and she said it made her dizzy if she tried to follow the polyphony and sleepy if she didn't; and then I tried Prokofieff and that meant nothing to her either. Well, anyway, she knew hundreds of folk songs and I liked hearing her sing them against the pull and drag of the sea. But when I'd draw her close and feel for the soft warm part of her, she'd stiffen a little and laugh and kiss me quick, and sit up. But being a big naive hulk of a guy I loved her and believed she loved me.

Once, we swam out to the sand bar and lay there until the tide covered it. This was a game of ours: we'd lie on the finger of sand until the tide was strong and deep then we'd swim in through the breakers to the beach. But this time, there was a stiff undertow and we had to swim a slow curve. As we were doing it, I saw a dark fin rise above the shine of a swell and disappear, then rise again: and I knew it was following us. So I swam up close to her and told her a shark was easing toward us. Her eyes looked startled for a split second then took on a bright, competitive gleam and she said, OK, let's race him. I said, No, you get ahead and I'll cover—go ahead now fifteen feet and I'll follow. Her face hardened: We do it side by side, *side by side, Dave!* Well, she's quite a gal, amazing nerve and all that, and I was proud of it— and yet I wasn't proud. We made it, of course; the shark was cautious and preferred the quieter waters far out, and maybe he had already had dinner. But we didn't talk that night; and I hoped she wouldn't sing, and she didn't; we lay there and listened to the sea and I listened to a desolate feeling that washed over me, ebbed, came back. . . . But I still loved her.

We never talked much, except about sports: talk wasn't to Jean something interesting in itself, like tennis, as it is to me. You felt she talked as she dressed: words were manufactured objects you took out of a drawer or off a coat hanger. When you needed them, you used them. Not material you made something new and exciting out of, something you might not use every day, or any day. But one night she said something that was not manufactured: it came out of the deep part of her. She said she liked the gulls: as she lay on the sand she never tired watching them fly above her, the sharp cutting curve of their wings, the slow drift, the deadly swoop . . . and then she said she was jealous of them, a little, because she couldn't fly like that. And she meant it. More than she knew.

Well . . . she wouldn't marry me before I went to the war. She had a heavy schedule of tournaments ahead and—"It is better this way, Dave."

And then, when I came back without a leg and could no longer play with her. . . . This sort of thing, of course, has happened to a lot of men, no use to make it big. And, in a sense, it was my fault; not hers: I pushed her too hard. I felt— I guess I was scared and I pushed too hard. She was affectionate, more so than she had ever been before; but once, while I was at the rehabilitation institute, she took me out for a ride; and somehow her hand touched the empty trouser leg—I was still on crutches, it was before I had learned to use the prosthesis—and she shivered, I saw it ripple through her body—and then she began talking about politics, of all things; for she knows nothing about politics.

I knew we had to face it. So—like a fool, I arranged for her to see me exercising. I know, now, that I made it pretty rough on her.

But I had to: she must see me as I am *now*, I kept saying to myself: the stump, everything. And she came and watched me at the bars, in my trunks, and she took it with her chin up and cheerfully talked to the other vets who gathered around her, for she is a wonderful-looking girl, all right. They thought she was terrific. Then afterward, two weeks afterward, she broke down and cried and said it quick: that she could never sleep with a one-legged man; she loved me, but she couldn't. "I am so damned normal," she said, "and I've always liked normal people, you know that, Dave; something about the abnormal scares me, you know that, Dave." And she cried like a little girl and I patted her and told her, Never mind, never mind, honey. And afterward, I said to myself, If you can't, you can't.

But later, oh I don't know: everything turned rocky and dry inside; and I was like that when I came to All Saints. Then it happened: Grace started the dead place breathing again. That is all I know to say. And I thought for a long time she did it without realizing what she had done. Now—well, I'm not so sure. But anyway, she did it and so simply: by asking hard things of me. Or was it only the verbs she used? *Hurry, hurry,* she'd say; *climb up here, Dave,* she'd say; *let's go down the rocks, let's cross the creek here;* and *will you run over, Dave?*

One day, she asked why didn't I use her bars in the basement for my exercise? I was shy. Felt the sweat break out when she said it. But a week later, I went. Got into my trunks and went to work at the bars. I thought, if she comes down here and sees me I can't take it. But I soon forgot as I began to give myself a workout. I was soft. Tried to stand on my hands and couldn't make it at first. It bothered me. Came back next day. Worked nearly an hour. Came back.

Then one morning she came—in her leotard. She slipped in, said hi, lay down on the floor, began doing her stretches. She did not even glance at the bar. I exercised, she exercised. She left before I finished; said bye—and was gone.

She came again. Again. And never once glanced my way. I can see her now: black cropped hair, with those slivers of it on her forehead, small lithe body in black leotard, sitting on the floor, legs stretched out wide, grasping her feet with her hands . . . going through those grotesque movements the modern dancers use. Now and then she'd say, *Ouch I'm stiff.* Then she'd stand and do a dozen swift long steps across the floor—and a few magnificent slow wide circles, and a back bend or two, and I'd stop and watch her. I began to see what the distorted stretches were for: for the mind more than the body: to break old rigidities so the new feeling could come through, the new thinking. I'd go back to my bar work, stand on my hands, hardening muscles that had gone soft on me; tensing, stretching. But I kept watching her, and thinking: about strange new dimensions, new designs, new feelings that body and imagination together can create. Don't believe I'd ever thought about it before. The body had always been something to compete with. One day she caught me at it: She laughed and said, Dave, mind helping me here? I hobbled over. She said, Here, hold me, here in the small of the back, that's it; now: hold; and I held, knowing if I slipped I might break her back but I sweated it out and held her as she did those back bends, and then a twist, and came up. Another time she said, Put on your leg, will you, and help me here? I fastened it on as casually as if I were putting on my coat, and came over and supported her as she did a bend that put her head on the floor; she said, Turn, and I turned; she said again, Turn, and I turned; and then she said, Now I'm going to swing, hold me—and I held her; and there we were, dancer and cripple, doing a kind of adagio together.

And that is the way I learned to feel like a man again.

Then she taught me to paint: what she actually did was teach me to see my world in a hundred new ways. And I loved her for it.

Yes, I loved her. Like a clumsy puppy, rolling over himself, I'm afraid. Anyway, one day we'd been down on the rocks below the house in the ravine. We'd had a fine time scrambling over mean tricky spots and I was high as a kite—to see that I could once more use my muscles with fair skill. We came in and had a glass of sherry. She put on Brahms' *Double Concerto*. We were in the living room, at ease, completely relaxed. I looked at that black shaggy hair, and those deep gray yellow-spangled eyes and then suddenly I pulled her up and into my arms and kissed her and said, Thank you, dear. And she so coolly, so quietly eased out of my arms and said, "Do you mean thank you or something else?" and then she grinned—her face soft and gentle but lit up with a sense of the absurd, and behind that, a knowledge of danger. I said, "I mean both."

"It can't be both, Dave. You know I love Mark."

Yes, I knew.

"He loves you, too."

"I know."

"And I love you, very much."

"I know." I felt like a miserable hound dog.

She went over and poured us more sherry.

"You see, people miss so much by thinking there is only one way to love; there are dozens of ways, Dave. We must find a way that fits you and me and Mark—and Andy." She smiled in that quick, almost sad way of hers and came over and kissed me on the nose and then put her hand on my shoulder. We never mentioned it again—not until that terrible time, later. We, together, put up the old barbed wire, twisting it this way and that, while we drank another glass of sherry and listened to the concerto.

But Mark: it was the stillness at the center of his nature that I responded to. There was equilibrium there: I felt it as one of body, brain, feeling, imagination. He never tried too hard: never strained for what he was after. Maybe, he did not want it too much. So he relaxed—and got it. Anybody in the sports world understands this: it is not only the Japanese who in their mystic art of archery understand that old secret of Zen; or the Hindus with yoga; every tennis player who is good knows something about it; every pole jumper. Maybe only superficially, but we know. We call it the follow-through; but it is more: it begins at the beginning of the stroke or the jump; but it is more: it begins down at the center of the personality, before the beginning of the stroke or drive or jump, in a profound concentration: in stillness. This, which I have taken for granted since childhood in physical skills, Mark does with his mind; and I respond to it; he seems to begin deepdown and never look too hard at the goal. Maybe this disinterestedness of his gives me a curious sense of security for I try too hard, except in sports. I struggle too hard to comprehend the incomprehensible, to find what I call "integrity," to realize what I call "beauty." With him, somehow, things fall away, don't press too close.

Perhaps I am evading those deeper pulls that tie one man to

another. Perhaps. Now, as I write it down, I can sum it up only by saying I miss our talks most.

They were a game we played: these talks about mysticism and poetry, India, and symbol and myth and art. Oh, we talked politics too, of course; but it was ideas that we got excited about. Mark liked to say poetry and mysticism are blood kin: born out of the mythic mind of man, out of the womb of the archaic word; on the other hand, he'd say, theology is logic's motherless child. Yes, I know: his figure is easily torn to shreds; and indeed, even when brilliantly right, nothing he said was ever new—except when speaking of his work in the lab. Cassirer had said it years ago, or Suzanne Langer had said it, or Tillich had said it, Jaspers had said it, or Plato or Kierkegaard or— New only to us because *we* were saying it, because *our* glands had warmed up and *our* minds were tingling with quick minute connections we had not, until then, made between, sometimes, quite distant ideas.

For hours, we'd engage in this philosophical skin-diving. I admit our oxygen supply was limited and we rarely stayed down long, but we'd plunge deep as we could into those fabulous regions of the mythic mind, the imagination, and swim around among its dangerous beauty and wavering grotesqueries. And then we'd surface and look at that lonely achievement of man's of which he is so justly proud: his reason. Compared to the undersea creations we had been swimming among, the million-year-old mountains and valleys scooped out and piled up in the deep pregnant wetness of man's undermind, reason looked pretty much like a young tight-lipped island. But Mark would say, Yes, but each man makes it: each grows his own painfully, slowly, out of *his* accretions of facts, his—and other men's— proved experience. Just the same, I'd answer, it is a small bleak place to spend a life; sure, fine for breathing, fine for taking off into outer space but. . . .

Important talk? No. Our talk, that is all. But it gave us awareness of a vast Unknown within ourselves and outside us which our words and minds could never envelop. And it left us humbled by the frailty and the greatness, the superb miracle of the human reason: this small island threatened by swirling waters, riptides, storms, undertow, somehow surviving, somehow making itself a little larger each thousand years or so by its minute accretions of knowledge. . . .

And I lay there, that Monday afternoon, saddened and shamed. For it is good for men, in twos and threes, to plunge into the ancient questions and bring up their own small answers. It is good, even if they never bring up an answer: the hush is left the richer for it.

Now what? Now, when Mark and I talked, we seemed to talk only about Susan. Our world was constricted to a small size-eight: iron dimensions that would not give. How had this incredible thing happened? by what legerdemain had one small girl lifted us clean out of our world—not a giant-size world, perhaps, but at least it held some poetry in it, a bit of art and science, a little music, a few ideas, a respect for reason and knowledge, a modicum of dignity and mercy—and a humble sense of not-knowing and yet wanting to know, of not-loving and wanting to love, of never quite feeling the edge of it, yet yearning to relate one's whole self to the Great Enigma. . . . How had one small child lifted us out of this, our world, into her playhouse and locked us up? She did not do it alone, of course. I knew that, even then. The monster helped her, the machine-monster powered by deep fears and dark yearning to hurt something, to squeeze knowledge into a smaller thing than its own ignorance, to mash the life out of compassion: this thing had scooped us up in its great shovel and given us to her: new toys to play with—

So: we talked about Susan. And Renie, of course. And what Nella said happened in the beauty shop and what Miss Hortense said, and what Duveen told Johnny and what all the others were saying—and that hour: that hour and its ticking minutes. Mark would tell me, as if under compulsion to say it, exactly how he had spent every one of those minutes: He had come home early; he had helped Grace prepare the flower beds and plant the tulip bulbs until five-ten; he had then come in to rest a bit; he had washed his hands and said he'd go get the Cokes; he had gone to

Matthews, got them, brought them home and put them on the kitchen table, opened two, mixed the drinks, given one to Grace and taken one out on the terrace.

"I know," I'd say—I said it a dozen times—"I saw you there reading, at five-thirty." That *five-thirty* was a raft in the swirling waters and we clung to it. Or, rather, we tried to. Now and then, I felt my grip loosening for something inside me would whisper, "But you don't *know* it was five-thirty." And I'd push the doubt away quick and clamber back on that slithering bouncing fact: *five-thirty*.

"I'm damned glad you did. But it wasn't quite five-thirty, Dave. Must have been nearer five-forty-five." He said it two or three times; then he seemed to forget—and when I'd say, "I saw you there at five-thirty," he would nod as if now he had accepted my memory of Monday afternoon instead of his own. Until Friday morning in the lab. Then, he said, It must have been five-forty-five or five-fifty, Dave; it couldn't have been earlier. And yet, all the time he was withholding the big fact; the one fact that made all the small facts totally irrelevant. Why? To this day, I don't know. I've brooded about it for two years. I just don't know.

I laid the book on the table. Found myself staring at the leg on the rug. At its black shoe. As if I'd never seen it before.

Curious: how it belongs to you sometimes as much as the rest of your body; then it doesn't. When this happens, it turns into your mortal enemy—exactly as an old memory can do, or an experience you have lived through, and never understood. Suddenly, one day, it separates itself from you and begins to live a life of its own: then it is likely to fight you or maybe turn you into its slave.

I mentioned it once to Sydney Ainsworth: the ambiguous, intense feelings I sometimes have toward this inanimate object. Yes, he said easily, as if such talk held no bizarre overtones for him, he'd seen it in his young patients. One little fellow hated his leg brace, called it a Communist; said he was going to turn it over to the FBI. Another wanted to give his prosthetic arm a bath whenever he took one. We had laughed; then we talked seriously for half an hour, perhaps, about the image men have of their own body, their rejection of it, their distortion, sudden reconciliation. I liked the man. And we became friends. We saw each other at Paul Pottle's book shop, usually. Rarely anywhere else. He was not a member of All Saints but since his engagement to Katie Snyder had attended fairly often.

I like Katie, but her smooth exterior baffled me. Her face is usually expressionless. It is her shield, this mask of indifference, and not many people have made a dent in it. Why she liked me I didn't know. It surprised and pleased me, and puzzled me, too, but it was fairly obvious that she did. Perhaps, she took it for granted that one likes one's rector. I discard that possibility even as I make it. Katie doesn't take it for granted that you like anyone. Her mother died when she was twelve; Katie had been devoted to her. Mrs. Snyder had been active in All Saints, perhaps there was a half-unconscious identification. I wasn't sure.

It is difficult to understand anyone's personality but Katie's seemed to me too devious and secret to guess at. There are a few obvious facts, however, which add up to hardly more than a stereotype and yet they say something about her, as she was at this time. She was just out of an Eastern college and girded with pessimism. Her exterior—except for her extraordinary beauty—was pretty much like the others her age: That is, she wore her hair in a "pony" when everyone did, and now wears it in a soft loose chignon; wears expensive tapered slacks when she gives a party and shorts or blue jeans when she goes out in her Jaguar with the roll-back top. With her blue jeans she wears expensive, imported sweaters. Katie laughed at the idea of coming home for the debutante ball but came and wore a knockout of a dress—one of Ceil Chapman's, she told me.

She adored Auden when she was a freshman; adored Dylan Thomas in her senior year. She had read Sartre and Camus, of course; and she had plowed through *Fear and Trembling* and a little of Heidegger and Berdyaev. During college vacations, she read Kafka and Rilke and Dostoevsky—not so much for their intrinsic quality as writers as because they had been dragged into the existentialist camp and "belonged."

I suppose there is no one of us who is not a refugee from either the past or the future or what we feel may be inside ourselves. These were merely the escape technics Katie had chosen. Existentialism gave her a place to run to. What she longed for, I think, was security from hope. If she felt hopeful she'd have to assume her share of responsibility for the mess the human race had got itself into. I understood her feelings—I did not agree with her but I understood, and liked her for at least protesting the complacency she felt smothered by.

"It is no use to try to change me," she had said, "I don't like people who think the human race is progressing. Because it isn't; it can't! I don't like prejudiced people, either. And certainly I don't want to hurt anybody. But why, why, try to do anything, Dave? The world is evil, man's nature is evil, science has failed us, who would dare say, today, that there is such a thing as objectivity! All that matters is what we feel, what we experience, and the inescapable fact of death; our obligation is to accept ourselves, for what we are: which is nothing. You're a darling," she had dropped in to tell me goodbye on her way back to college, "but you're such an optimist! You actually believe in the goodness of people. You do, Dave—why not admit it? You believe man can become something better—and that's as old-fashioned as the nineteenth century."

"I know," I said. "It is as archaic as the human race, sweetie." We both laughed and then talked of other things.

This kind of thinking, this attitude was true of her two, three years ago. Today? I wrote this about her in the present tense, changed it to the past tense, put some of it back in the present tense because I'm not sure. As I think of Katie now, I have only a deep sense of humility. She measured up so gallantly those last weeks when everything tumbled on us and when I made so many mistakes.

Sydney is older and more shellacked with what looks like cynicism than is his Katie. Actually, she is not cynical at all. Her hurt goes deep. I had shied away from Sydney when he opened his office here. He was a fine pediatrician, I knew, but somehow I could not, at first, see anything but his professional skill. And then, one day, we met at the bedside of a child who could not get well; and there, in the presence of death, I saw a different man. While I read a prayer with the parents in the other room, Sydney was holding that little girl in his hands and whispering a fairy story to her. The mother went in, after I left, and found them so; and he stayed with the child, whispering his stories, until she slipped away. His derisive laughter at the idealists never irritated me, after that; only disturbed me: he was so nearly right, and I knew it.

I called him early Monday morning, at his apartment. I had put it off as long as I could. He came by the study on his way to lunch to pick up Mark's paper.

"I don't like it," he said. "How do you feel?"

"Pretty bad."

"You won't argue with me, then?"

"No." I handed him the paper.

He glanced at it. "It's probably a hell of a good speech."

"Yes, I know."

"Stealing his brains and banning him. Because he's not fit to be seen on television. Why are we letting ourselves in for this?"

I didn't answer.

"You and me! Why, Dave?"

"To get money."

"The old merry-go-round: to get a little money for more research we destroy—well, there you are!"

No answer from me. I had said it a hundred times to myself.

"Who made this decision?"

"Dewey Snyder."

"I might have known. When?"

"Last week."

"Went right after him, didn't he. You wonder what he has against him."

"Nothing personal, I'd say."

"How about the others on the committee? Didn't they protest? Hasn't Mark any friends there?"

"Sure he has. But they agreed with Snyder that they couldn't jeopardize the campaign by having Mark on the program. Not now."

"Sure. The sponsors are pure, the audience is pure, nobody's guilty of anything but Mark, and he's guilty only because an eight-year-old says so." He looked at me and smiled. "And if I wait about a minute you will tell me they're decent people who don't intend to do harm."

"They are. They work hard on this committee, they are deeply concerned about cancer. But they are blind and unaware of—" I stopped.

"Of the human beings who have cancer. Sure. They think any man is expendable. No matter who he is. Somebody else can be found who is just as good, just as smart. On with the drive for money!"

"You're talking like these idealists you laugh at."

"Maybe I am. Maybe it had to happen to a man I admire and respect before I could see it straight. The thing that scares you is that it hasn't occurred to one of them that this man, this man named Mark Channing, may be the one, the very one, who might stumble on the answer to cancer. And yet they are doing their full share to destroy him. Why are they willing to run such a risk?"

"I don't know, Syd."

He was standing now, looking at me. "Yesterday, at church," he spoke slowly and more sincerely than I had ever heard him speak, "you almost won me. I actually began to believe, as I listened to that sermon of yours, that there might be enough people in the world with the guts and the sense to pull us through. And because you made me feel this way, I wanted to help with the pulling. Yeah . . . I had quite a shine in my eyes. Me! You did this to me, yesterday. Now look where we are!"

"Sydney—you haven't heard of Mark's arrest?"

He shook his head.

"It was on page five in this morning's paper. We tried to keep it out. The editor did his best. But it was news, you know. So it is there."

"I was in surgery all morning. Haven't read the paper. I suppose it has been on radio."

"I suppose so. I didn't listen."

"That makes the committee feel completely justified now."

I let that go by.

"Well, I'd better be sliding along. Keep half a dozen more kids alive. Don't ask me what for—that fifty-thousand-dollar house on the lake I've got to have to compete with Katie's father, I guess."

"In your mind or hers?"

"Mine. All mine." He grinned, closed the door after him. Opened it, came back in. Eyes grave. "What else has happened to Mark?"

"Three or four anonymous letters. Grace has been getting telephone calls telling her to leave him, telling her no decent woman would live with a dirty pervert, that living with him makes her a pervert, too—that sort of thing."

"That must be fun. Last week, a patient from the Flats brought her baby to the clinic. While I was working with the baby she asked me if I had heard tell of that labbitory, over in the north part of town. Said there was a man working there named Channing, and she'd heard he raped a little girl in an empty store. I told her it was a mistake. The little girl had not been raped, had not even been hurt and Dr. Channing had noth-

ing whatever to do with it. She said folks in her neighborhood
had told her about some mighty peculiar things going on in that
labbitory. I didn't go into it with her. The baby was pretty sick, I
had to take care of it."

I didn't answer.

"Thought maybe somebody had better know this kind of talk
is going on."

"Much obliged, Sydney."

He closed the door softly behind him.

I had preached the sermon Sydney mentioned before I knew or
any of my parishioners knew that Claud Newell had sworn out
the warrant against Mark. I preached on trust in one's fellow-
men. At least, that was my intention. Am afraid I wandered pretty much everywhere before I was done, for I felt I
was preaching at myself—at least, no one in that congregation
could have felt more guilty.

I began by saying: Trust is a hormone our spiritual metabolism
requires: without it, resistance breaks down and malignancies
begin to grow. I said, Animals, as far as we know, neither trust
nor suspect each other; but the human being does both and has
to do both: it is the delicate balance that matters. I said, The
human being got out of the cave because he gambled on the
goodness and decency of his fellow-men; he lost, yes; as a matter
of history he lost rather frequently but he won a shade more
often, every thousand years or every ten thousand years, than he
lost. Now: the balance has tilted again; today, man is gambling
on the evil in other men and if he keeps doing it, he will end up
in the cave again—or nowhere.

I said, I could not talk easily about God. No man could. For
words are created by men: they are no more than open cages
men have made to catch and hold their small dreams and dis-
coveries; and man has not yet dreamed or discovered much
about the meaning of God. But each generation, each person,
keeps whispering his own definition—or else refuses to whisper
it. Each sets up his private altar in his own privately endowed

temple and worships the Word he feels most deeply about: whether that feeling is love or hate or fear or awe or greed.

I said, God means to me the unknown, the eternal mystery beyond the certainty; all that is yet to be learned about our universe and ourselves, and all that is beyond the human capacity to learn; God means to me both the Ultimate Form and the Forming Power beyond the chaos and the order; God means to me, man's unknown capacity for tenderness and compassion and love, and sacrifice, and forgiveness; God means our hunger for illumination of past and future, and our hunger to understand good and evil and the eternal tensions between them.

I said, I believe it is not possible to set limits on human goodness but limits on evil are easy to set. When a man decides to set a limit on the good in his own or others' nature, when he resolves that the human race can go so far and no farther on the road to mercy and beauty and understanding and truth, when he settles for less than ultimate concerns: then it is that evil's outpost is reached. Thoughtful people, today, are deeply concerned about evil: but are they not thinking of evil as a corncob used in a moment of dark violence? or as a concentration camp? or a lynching? or other forms of body desecration? Fascinating modern ghost stories are being written about the totally evil man, the sleepwalker without awareness. And, as we read, goose flesh comes up on the mind; but the authors of the ghost stories fail, even so, to shine a light on the evil in man because they have forgot, or don't know how, to shine the light on the good in him. I reminded my congregation, that morning, of the ancient wisdom of the Medusa myth: men could not look directly upon Medusa's evil countenance without turning to stone. Nor can they, today, look evil in the face without growing numb and hopeless and apathetic, for looking, yet they cannot see. Evil can be clearly seen and measured only when mirrored in the bright vision of what is good. When that vision of man is lost—when we forget that Jesus Christ not only died for our sins but lived as the luminous Example of human goodness so that we might have hope, might find courage—we are doomed.

Renie sat in the fourth row, below me, listening—her eyes soft and shining, her hair glowing like a nimbus. Listening to every word I said. I felt warmed by her empathy. There is a place in me, in most preachers, I am afraid, that is like a greedy child: hand it a tea cake of attention and it brightens up. I felt, My words are helping; she is not incapable of understanding; hearing this, surely she is seeing the enormity of what she has done—

I cut the abstractions short. Began to talk about the trust a child gives an adult. Eloquently, I built up a child's frailty, its lack of strength, its vulnerability, its dependence upon the adult who holds so much power to destroy or create its future—and yet the child trusts. Why? Because the parents deserve his trust? Of course not. He does it because he must: because there is a stern survival-necessity centered in this word. Then I told a short story, illustrating this theme. And Renie followed me, smiled at the right place, looked gentle where she should have—

Susan was sitting next to her. Biting her nails. She looked tired and pale as if this Thing roaming our neighborhood had come too close and she had seen too much truth in her own lies. Claud was gray-pale and as tired-looking as Susan. On the sixth row across the aisle, were Mark and Grace, listening courteously. I was puzzled by a curious blankness on their faces. Nothing showed. I had not yet heard of the warrant Claud Newell had sworn out for Mark's arrest on Saturday afternoon. Nor of what happened later that evening. But Renie knew. At least she knew Claud's part in it. As I think about it, today, I am afraid that is why she looked so relaxed: she had accomplished the secret mission a mysterious boss inside her had sent her on.

But in priestly naiveté, that fine November Sunday, I preached my sermon on the human need to trust and be trusted. And I was sure others besides Renie were listening for there was a warmth on faces, an attentiveness: surely some of it sank in. Oh yes, I smile at myself as I write it down now. Not in bitterness—that is an irrelevant word—but with a jagged hurting knowledge of complexities I tried not to see then, or perhaps I could not see. That Sunday morning, I felt—and with decent humility—that the sermon had done my congregation a little good.

I followed the choir down the aisle, slipped off stole and surplice in the tower room, returned to the door to speak to my parishioners. As they shook hands with me—quite a few went out the side door—some told me they were moved by my words. Mrs. Riley (she had a brown scarf wound around her neck which made her look as if she had a sore throat, and her dress was pinned over as if she were wearing a sweater under it but it is always like that) said it was most inspiring—but Mrs. Riley, bless her, inspires easily. Dewey Snyder (he had a dwarf white chrysanthemum in his lapel) said, It is a fine November day, isn't it?—and of course I knew what he thought. Sydney Ainsworth murmured, Keep it up, and winked; and before I could smile, Mrs. Graham (she is president of the altar guild) shook hands and asked me to tell her what I really felt the meaning of trust is, *really is:* as if I had withheld the secret and would now pour it only into her ears. She keeps shaking hands as she talks and I began to repeat what I had said in the pulpit (as we pumped each other's hand in moist fellowship) then I thought, You can't shake hands and talk about trust, like this; so I asked if perhaps I might call on her soon and we'd talk more; she set a date. Then Mr. Foster, head of the English department at the college, shook hands. He does not pump, he fractures or tries to: as if he is reminding you that explicating Eliot and correcting themes on *Moby Dick* do not keep him from being a bone-crusher equal to any ex-football player like me. As he crushed, he said, Don't you think the Grand Inquisitor had a real point when, etc. and I said Yes, etc. and he said, But—, and I said, Quite probably; and then he said he liked what I said about treason, he'd like for the seniors to hear it, would I come, etc. and while I couldn't remember saying anything about treason, I said I would.

Then Grace and Mark came by and Grace whispered, *They've done it.* I was so appalled that I forgot to shake hands with either of them. They went out, two blank faces, into that fine November day and I stood there hearing her stricken words as I listened to the organ telling Bach's immortal arguments, binding and resolving, pulling up to a more complex order and binding and resolving . . . *they've done it . . . they've done it . . .* and

Charlie played on, as he always did each Sunday, on and on, and I stood there, alone now, in that hushed sanctuary, listening to Bach and Grace's broken words, listening and lost in the ambient blue-gold-violet silence beyond the sounds. *It is a fine beautiful old church, All Saints:* those nine words formed in my mind and I do not know exactly what I meant when I said them to myself, that day.

Later, about one o'clock, Jane called me. She had not attended either of the morning services. Now she called to say she and Grace and Mark were driving up to the mountain. Would I like to go with them? I went, of course. On the drive up, we did not mention the arrest. We talked only of the beauty of the autumn trees, the light on the mountains, we talked about politics, Grace mentioned a letter she had had from Andy—

"He still likes school?"

"More every day. This letter was asking me to send him his arrowhead collection. Every letter asks me to send something. He told of a trip out to the school's hut, a mile or two from the campus. Don't let me forget it, Mark; the collection."

Still no mention of the arrest.

Mark told me he was enormously pleased with the new assistant who had come down to him from Sloan-Kettering. Still no mention of the trouble.

But once we were on the mountain, and in Jane's library, Mark stretched out in front of a small fire and quietly told me. Jane and Grace were in the kitchen, doing something about supper. It seems Neel and the Chief were out of town when Newell swore out the warrant; the officer left in charge didn't feel as friendly as they had; a cop came to the lab where Mark was working late and took him to the lockup. "For four hours I couldn't get in touch with anybody. They wouldn't let me phone Grace. Finally, they let me. Just changed their minds and let me. She called Jane, they got Steve and worked out the matter of the bond. One thousand dollars. Jane got the money for us, bless her."

His tone was curiously casual. Mine was, too. I think now we didn't actually believe it had happened. Anyway, we pushed off our feelings. I asked why had Newell done nothing for ten or twelve days, then suddenly sworn out the warrant? Mark knew that answer. Newell was charging him with having followed Susan and having made immoral advances to her on the street.

"She claims I followed her last Tuesday. I have no alibi. I was at the lab at that hour but I don't know anyone who can say so."

"Your secretary?"

"Her mother was ill. She had gone home shortly after lunch."

"What are you going to do, Mark?"

"Not anything this afternoon." He smiled. "We are going to forget it, and talk the way we used to. Do you remember there once was a time when we had interesting things to say?"

We laughed. We didn't say anything interesting but we did manage to talk about casual things. The four of us walked over to their cabin, a quarter of a mile away, to get the arrowhead collection. Mark picked up a book he said he needed at the lab. Grace took home two or three records she wanted. She mentioned the play at the Red Bank theater, said rehearsals were beginning this next week. I spotted a leak. Mark went out and looked at the roof. We managed to keep everything empty and trite. But we were watching each other. I caught Mark looking at me hard. Once I saw Jane looking at Grace as if studying her carefully. As a matter of fact, I think we were all relieved when we started back to Windsor Hills about nine o'clock.

.

My head was aching. *Why don't you put on your glasses when you read? And stop thinking! Read!*

I turned to get them from the bedside table; saw them on the bureau across the room from the bed, hated to hop over for them; lay there. Sunday morning seemed close: in the room with me: fusing with and changing the present moment called Monday afternoon—and last Tuesday, and Friday and Saturday and Sunday evenings . . . all of it changing hue and shape, becoming different, becoming independent of me—and monstrous.

I turned. Was staring now at the small blue bowl on the bureau: a dark blob against the light but reflected in the mirror it acquired a lucent paleness that glowed and trembled, like magic. When I was a kid it was magic. Not its color nor its shape but its contents bestowed mystery on it: My mother kept her earrings there. And my sister and I would slip in and play with them; we'd tip in as if it were forbidden play . . . stand in front of the mirror . . . try them on: pair after pair, enlarging our image of ourselves, and at the same time distorting this image in strange secret ways. I remember, one day, I felt sudden deep shame—as if this were girl's play. And I said in a loud bold voice, *I'm a pirate,* because pirates can wear earrings if they want to: and this restored my maleness, a little; but I was uncomfortable all day, as if a fence were there and I had crawled under it into the wrong side of things.

My mother is vague in her talk. I am surprised when she remembers things that happened in our childhood. But she remembered the bowl, for when she visited me last year she brought it and placed it on the bureau. I left it where she put it; what else could you do! It meant something to her, to give it to me. I felt this. Since the leg came off, the little lady has been giving me things and feeding me: making cherry pies, huckleberry pies, and cake and cramming them down me—as if, somehow, if only she feeds me enough, perhaps, perhaps the leg will grow back. I know . . . such a thought would never dare creep into her tidy mind; but I think below the tidiness, down in that uncharted part of her where she lives more freely, she rather believes it. My little mother and I never visit in each other's front minds for we don't speak each other's everyday language; yet it is curious how much I think I know about what goes on in the unlighted part of her.

As I looked at the bowl, wavering in the mirror, I wondered when I had written her. Wondered if it was time for another visit; if she ever saw my girl; if she attended the game at the University last Saturday. She was there, I knew, unless she was sick. She never misses a game. She wraps herself up in a heavy old coat, takes along a hot water bottle, and settles down for the happiest hours of her life. Her name is Mary Lou; she never played rowdy games—that is her phrase—when she was a child, not even tennis, her mother would not let her; but she had me playing by the time I was three; and my sister Meg, too; she coached us like a pro; and as soon as I walked, she had me in the water, on the court, the ball diamond, the football field. As far back as I can remember I belonged to three or four teams; and the little lady was always coaching me on the sidelines. Mary Lou is tiny; my father was small, too, and despised sports, always sat with a book, usually in his law office; hated walking a hundred yards. I don't know how I turned into such a hulking six feet two, and a hundred and eighty-five pounds; or how I became the "lazy guy who always got there"! As I have mentioned, the fellows used to call me "Preacher"; perhaps because they knew I was an acolyte when in high school; or maybe because once, down in the shower room, I told somebody I was going into the Church; it seemed incongruous, somehow; I was "Preacher," after that. They were good guys and we were great friends; they rarely trampled my vague dreams.

I closed my eyes. Wished the old brain would stop remembering. When I opened them, I was once more staring into the mirror. The blue bowl was still there . . . doing things to me, like an incantation. But beyond it, in the mirror, I saw the white knob of my bedroom door: slowly turning.

7

As I watched the mirror, the door began to open. Slowly. Susan's face crept in, then her body. She slid around the door without making a sound and went straight to the bathroom. I had not moved and apparently she had not seen me. In a moment or so she came out, darted to the closet, opened the door, burrowed through my suits and topcoats to the shelves back at the far end. I lost her for about a minute, then she slid out, darted over to the corner where my crutches were. From the way she grasped them I knew she was quite used to them. She skillfully lifted herself, handling them as stilts.

"Susan."

Crutches fell to the floor. Her composure was superb. She turned and looked at me.

"Did you come for something?"

"Yes, I came for Ali Baba. He's gone somewhere. I think he's here."

I decided to play it as casually as she was doing. "Why not look on the terrace?"

She opened the French windows as if she had done it a hundred times. Eased out on the terrace. Eased in. She walked slowly toward the bed. "Are you sick?"

As she came near I saw the dilated eyes, the stiff facial muscles. She was scared—a deepdown fear that might have driven a grownup into a heavy trembling or into flight—but her body was tight and rigid and completely under control.

"No. I'm reading."

"Is it a story?"

"No. It is a book written by some famous theologians."

She listened gravely. Her cat-yellow eyes were on my face. They shifted now to the leg lying on the rug. She swallowed hard. She said without taking her eyes off the leg, "Is it a nice book?"

"Yes, it is."

"Do you read bad books too? like my mother?"

"What is a bad book?"

"Oh, just bad. You know what bad is."

She inched over for a view of the leg on the other side. "My daddy hates bad books. He hates them and he yells at her when she reads them and she says what you yelling at me for—"

Susan's eyes shifted again and found the black shoe on the foot of the limb—

"—and she gets real mad and says you're afraid to read psy-psychology that's what's wrong with you—"

Susan's eyes moved from the floor to the bed. They were searching for the shoe's mate—

"—and Daddy says what's wrong with me and she says you read page 148 and you'll see what's wrong with you—"

Susan had found it now on me—

"—and then my mama yelled at him and he said go get some fresh air Susan and do it right now I don't want you hearing such talk and my mama said you just won't face the facts of life that's what—"

"Susan," I said, "I have some good story books downstairs. Do you like *Hans Brinker?*"

Her eyes began at the toe of the black shoe on my foot, crept up my ankle, up my leg to the knee, up to my hip and then skittered across and slowly, carefully, crept down the deflated trouser leg and then back to the floor to the black shoe on the foot of the limb lying there and crept back to the bed to the deflated trouser leg—

"I like it OK," she said—

—and back to the leg on the floor and up to the straps and buckle at the top of it . . . and then she pointed at the leg on the floor . . . and at the deflated trouser leg . . . and swallowed hard and kept pointing.

There was an urgent question in that pointing finger. So I said it quickly and plainly: my leg was cut off in an accident and I wear that thing on the floor because it helps me walk.

"It is called a prosthetic limb. Or you can call it an artificial one if you want to. And it straps on and makes it easy for me to walk."

"How did it come off?" she whispered.

I had just told her but I said it again. "In the war. The plane I was in crashed. My parachute didn't open quick enough, the leg was crushed and the surgeon had to amputate it."

"Amp—"

"Yes. He operated so it would heal."

"He cut it off?"

"Yes."

"Had you been bad and he cut it off because you did something real bad?"

I explained again.

"Where is it now?"

She had me there. It was my turn to point. I pointed at the crutches. I said, "You bring them here and I'll teach you a funny trick."

She chose not to hear. She said, drawing in a deep breath, "Now—I'll tell *you* a story. I can tell stories, too."

Most of the time, when I look at Susan, I see a thin small face that has ferreted its way through impenetrable grown-up moods until it has become sharp and polished. Or, sometimes, I see a hard dry seed of a face that has never sprouted. But now, it was as if it had only one skin and suddenly it lit up inside like a stage and the bell was ringing and the play was about to begin:

She said, "Once upon a time a pros-prosthetic limb went out for a walk. And while it was walking along real politely, hopping and skipping now and then but not too much, it met a real leg that had been amputated by a surgeon. The prosthetic limb stopped and took off its glasses and said, Well well! I did not expect to find you here taking a walk. I thought you had been buried in a box in the ground and couldn't get out. And here you are! And the real leg said, Here I am—so what! This is a free country and I can go for a walk if I want to. If you want to, ha, said the prosthetic limb, if you want to. But you can't want to because you're dead, that's what!"

Then she laughed. I thought she was coming to pieces, she laughed so hard. And I was afraid, suddenly, I might come to pieces, too. For I was not seeing Susan, I was looking at a Thing I had not seen in eleven years: I was in England, forty miles outside London. Early dawn. The night had been quiet and empty with only a wind blowing through it. All night long it blew, an easy relaxed wind, but somehow it set the doors in my childhood banging . . . and I had not slept. No planes had come over for three nights. Better sleep while you can but I couldn't sleep. Now it was dawn: a July dawn, a black-green wet cool blurry hour and I went out for a walk. There was a blurry house over in a meadow and I heard a sheep's bell somewhere, a thin tinkling somewhere along the fog drift, then it came: the plane, abrupt, bearing down. This time, somehow, I did not fall to the ground. I stood there, I didn't care or maybe I had gone too far into the past to scramble back to the present, so I stood there and let it happen as a cow might have done. I simply did not react: object in the sky, siren in the village, scream, roar. Back in the meadow was that house, not far. I didn't know it had been hit, am not sure it was a direct hit. It was there, solid; something a man had built, a place people slept in and ate in and made love in and quarreled in and walked out of and back to—and then it came to pieces: walls and roof and beds and chairs and people rose up and flattened down. I don't know how long I stood in the road. My head whanged and my bones ached and I felt I was bleeding somewhere but I wasn't, later I found I wasn't. I must have walked over to the rubble and stuff and the smoke there was smoke but no fire it must have been a lamp and maybe the falling plaster put it out before it burned much. I suppose I thought maybe I could help somebody. But there was nobody to help. I found fragments—that was all. I kept pushing broken things around, turning them over, looking . . . and there was half a room left one half gone the other there, and on a piece of a chair was a doll, a whole doll, and as I came up to it, its face disintegrated before my eyes into bits of dust—as if it had held together only until somebody could share its final shame. It is one of my most bothersome memories for I am not sure the doll was on the broken piece of chair, I'm just not sure. But now, suddenly, I saw it again—and I knew I had better shift the present scene to get rid of that distant event. I had to and I did.

"I'll tell you another one," she was saying.

Oh no you won't. "No. We're going to have a piece of chocolate cake. We'll have it down in my study. You run along now and I'll bring it."

"But—" Her face suddenly caught on and became a greedy kid's face. "OK. I like chocolate. Where is it?"

"It's in the kitchen but you run on and I'll bring it downstairs to the study and we'll have a tea party."

She did not budge. She stood there waiting for the big scene to bang out its first note. I felt trapped. I sat up and slid over to the edge of the bed. Her eyes were on the leg on the floor. She wanted to see it hop off the floor and join its mate or maybe its mate would hop off the bed and join it or— Then, as I was trying to figure this one out, another horrible thought occurred to me. Suppose her mother were to come looking for Susan and found her upstairs, like this, with me. Then suppose Susan were to tell Renie that I had tried to—or suppose Renie were to decide herself that—or suppose Neel came in—or suppose my mother came into the nursery and found me— Did I actually think that? about the nursery? No. I felt it—the way you feel a big wave wash over you.

I was in a heavy sweat. But once more I tried to play it the casual way.

"You go downstairs to the study and wait. I'll bring the cake. You can have a Coke and I'll have coffee."

"I'll have coffee, too."

"OK. But you run on now and look for Ali Baba. He's probably in the big chair this minute. I'll be down soon."

"The story is real nice," the temptress said sweetly. "It is about a pink and a blue and a purple parasol that went walking one day just like three mushrooms—"

She almost caught me: I was about to say it, *But mushrooms don't walk.* Instead I said, "I'm sure it is. Now get out, Susan!" I yelled the words at her and she ran quickly as if I had threatened to shoot her down. I was startled by her loss of poise, the quick terror on her face. I sat there after she was gone, unable to move. Disoriented by a child's face. By my having torn— Where had I seen terror in a child's face before? In a war, yes; in bombed cities . . . but where in time of peace—in a mirror—what mirror—what peace— I wished I knew whether I had actually seen the doll disintegrate or was it something I made up in post-surgery delirium, and what was Susan actually up to—was she looking for the cat—was she looking everywhere for something she could never find?

When I entered the study with the cake she was waiting in the big chair. No Ali Baba. She had set up the card table. She had taken the blue and white mats out of the drawer and moved the bowl of flowers from my desk to the table. She had found everything: the blue and white cups and saucers and plates (the Royal Copenhagen ones Grace and Mark gave me) and silver. *Found* may not be the appropriate word, for it was obvious that Susan knew better than I where everything was in my rooms. She had turned the switch and the kettle was beginning to simmer. She sat in the chair, quietly waiting, with a dignity only a child could have wrapped herself in at this moment.

We dispatched the chocolate cake and coffee. While we were doing so, I showed her Saint-Exupéry's *Little Prince.* Suggested she take it home with her.

She casually turned the pages. Then she said, "I know another story. It's about—"

"Susan, excuse me, but isn't it time for you to go? Your mother will worry."

"No she won't."

Face tightened into a knot.

"I'm afraid she will."

"No she won't."

"How do you know?"

"Maybe she's drinking." She giggled. "She drinks when my daddy's gone. He wouldn't like it if he knew—"

"Making up things again?"

"No I'm not. And I don't want to go home."

I could not discuss Renie's frail defenses with Susan. I said, "You said you had a story to tell me. About the parasols?"

She drew a deep breath and her face lit up. "I'm not going to tell it. I have another. It's about a little girl named Boody who went somewhere."

I waited.

"Ask me where."

"OK. Where?"

"Well—she went into a dark store. To get some candy, maybe." She giggled.

"Can you get candy in a dark store?"

"Oh sure. Why not? She played with a cat, too."

"What color was the cat?"

She was silent. *Better let her tell it.*

She stared at me coldly. Then drew in her breath and went on, "She went in for some candy but she found a cat. And she went way back where it is real dark and she got scared and screamed."

She stopped.

"Because it was dark?" I whispered.

"She just did."

"Because a yellow cat scratched her?"

No answer. *Pay your line out more slowly.*

"It was dark and it was a bad scratch Boody got."

"How you think she got it?"

Susan smiled mischievously. "She won't tell me."

"Was it a bad scratch?"

"Of course. I told you. A bad scratch."

"Who is Boody?"

"Just Boody. We play together."

"What else happened?"

"Nothing."

Thought I'd sting her professional pride. "Not much of a story, is it?"

"It is, too. It's a terrible story."

"Tell it then, if it's so terrible."

No answer.

Our talents for staring competed. I lost. "What else happened?" I said.

"Nothing."

"Were you with her?"

"No."

"Well, where did your scratch come from?"

No answer.

"Did Yellow Cat scratch you too?"

No answer.

"Something must have scratched you. Probably an old moth-eaten tiger with a bad cold in his head and a pink shawl around his neck. Enough to make him scratch, I'd say."

Her eyes gleamed. She drew in her breath and said firmly, "Your Ali Baba scratched me."

"Well, he scratched me too, so we're even."

She giggled and began to bite her nails.

"Did Boody see anything in the store?"

"Yes."

"What?"

"A tall bad man."

"Why was he bad?"

Silence.

"Did he hurt Boody?"

She tightened her lips against her teeth.

"I don't believe you have a story. You only make like it."

"I do, too."

"Did he hurt Boody?"

"No."

"Did he do anything to her?"

Once more the dry seed of a face and boring eyes.

"Did he?"

Not a word.

"Oh well, a flop of a story, if you're asking me. Thought you could tell a good one."

"His name was Dr. Chenin."

Flatly I said, "It was not."

"It was, too."

Snarling like a mean kid I said, "You wouldn't know because you were not there."

"I was, too."

"Ha! no you weren't. It was Boody who was there."

"I got lots of presents because a bad man hurt me."

"You were not hurt."

"You gave me Ali Baba."

"Yes, I know, because it was your birthday. But you were not hurt."

"How do you know?"

"I see it in your eyes. You're making it up."

"I got a lot of presents."

"Not hurt."

"Was, too."

"Boody was hurt."

She looked at me, bit her lip, pulled her legs up under her in the chair. Scrunched there like a curled up question mark.

I glanced at my watch. In a bored voice I announced that I must make several telephone calls.

"I was just playing-like Boody."

"It was you in the store?"

"Yes."

"How do you know the man was Dr. Channing?"

"My mama says so."

"Was she in the store?"

"No. She wouldn't go in that old store for anything."

"Why?"

"She's scary."

"What of?"

"She says they'll do something to her."

"Who?"

"Oh, men. You know. Men are real bad. And you mustn't listen to a one of them."

"Why?"

"She says they want to rape us."

"What does rape mean?"

Giggling now. She pulled up one shoulder and coyly looked over it at me.

"Tell me. What does it mean? If you use a word you ought to know what it means."

"It means he gets near you."

"I'm near you."

"Wel—l. . . ." She drew in a breath, let it out; giggled hard.

"Susan, tell me: were you hurt the least bit by anybody in that store? Remember I know when you are making it up and when you are telling the truth."

"What is the truth?"

A desperate try: "It is what actually happens. Not what you want to happen. Not what you're afraid will happen. We make up stories when we want things to happen or are afraid they may happen. And sometimes we do it for fun—or to scare people or make them do our way or to hurt them. And sometimes we do it because it's a pretty story and we tell it just as we fly a kite or send balloons floating."

"I do it because it's pretty. And for fun."

"I know. But this time, let's hold on to what actually happened. The real truth. See?"

"OK."

"Were you hurt the least bit by a man in that store?"

"No sir." Her voice was suddenly ladylike and dignified.

"Not a bit?"

"No sir."

"He didn't touch you?"

"No sir."

"Not even your dress?"

"No sir." She giggled and there were no more *sirs*.

"Did he say anything to you?"

She shook her head.

"Then what on earth did he do?"

She giggled and hid her face against the chair.

"Don't be silly."

"I can't tell."

"Yes you can."

"No I can't. It's a bad word and my mama told me never to say it."

"Where did you hear it?"

"She said it."

"Where did she hear it if it's so bad?"

"She found it in a book."

"What kind of book?"

"Oh one of those books my daddy gets mad about."

"You mean a psychology book?"

"Guess so."

"Susan, tell me: is it a short word or a long word?" I know I sound like an ass but I did not dare say the two words in my mind for fear Susie would tell her mama I had—well, there's no use in completing that sentence.

"It's a real long word."

"Real real long?"

"Uh-huh."

"Four syllables or five syllables?"

"Oh that's real bad!"

"What's real bad?" I felt I was standing on my head.

"That word you used."

"*Syllable?*"

"Uh-huh." She stared at me disapprovingly.

Well, there was no percentage in this. I quit. I stared back and lit a cigarette.

"You want me to tell the truth?" she asked gently, after we had spent several moments probing the exterior of each other's heads.

"If you can."

"I told the bad word to the chief of police. My mama said for me to. She said say it once and never say it again. People who say bad words are vulgar, my mama says. That means not nice. She says we come from a real nice family and ladies don't—"

"Susan,"—I wanted to get off this for a moment—"why did you say it was Dr. Channing?"

"It looked like my daddy, at first."

"In the store?"

"Yes. But I guess I forgot. He was in Chicago."

"Who said it was Dr. Channing?"

"My mama."

"How did she know?"

"Well—she asked me what he looked like and I said it was a tall man like my daddy and she said it must be Mark Channing."

"She said that?"

"Uh-huh. And she said she reckoned we'd better be sure." She giggled and giggled.

"Why are you giggling?"

"We hid in the rose bushes," the words floated through hysterical laughter.

"Where?"

"In front of their house. And he got out of his car and—and he had a sack of groceries and a newspaper and my mama asked me if he was the man. And I said maybe. And she said now look good. And I looked good and said I reckon so. And she's been real nice and hasn't fussed at me any more."

"Did she used to fuss at you?"

I should not have said it. She did not reply. A new relationship with her mother had begun; Susie had pleased her—maybe for the first time in her life—and Susie was going to make the most of it.

I tried a new approach. "What you said, Susan, is hurting Dr. Channing."

"No."

"Yes it is. He is having lots of trouble. He's losing his friends. Some people won't even speak to him."

"Why?"

"Because they think he is a wicked man and that he hurt you in that store. He is a good man, Susan, as good as your daddy."

"My daddy's bad, too. He has ladies in his hotel room in Chicago. My mama says so." She began to laugh wildly. "My mama phoned him one night and a lady answered and said he had stepped out and my mama was real mad and I heard her tell my daddy when he came home—"

I switched again. "Susan, tell me: why do you say it was Dr. Channing?"

"My mama told me to."

"But Dr. Channing was not in the store. Nobody was. You imagined it."

"He was, too, and he scared me."

"Susan: listen to this carefully, will you? When you were in that store, Dr. Channing was sitting over there, across the street from here on his terrace, reading. *I saw him there.* He couldn't have been in the store. You were making up a story, I think. See? You were playing-like and maybe you told it to the cat; maybe you were playing-like a scary kind of story and maybe you began to imagine it was really happening and it was dark and you *thought* you saw a man but you only imagined it, see?"

"I—"

"You were not hurt."

Her face emptied out. The old look crept back, the look that used to bother me as I stood at the lectern reading: as if she had no home address. I wished it hadn't happened. I suddenly realized she had been looking happy since the store episode, happy and sure. Scared, maybe; but no longer lonely; for she had a collaborator now, somewhere in a dark corner of Renie's mind, Susie had found a new playmate.

"But my mama said—" Susie did not try to complete the sentence.

I thought, *You're brainwashing this child.* I began to realize with a kind of chill in my blood that every grownup she had come in contact with had been doing the same thing to her.

And yet, even though I thought this, I deliberately cut her another slice of chocolate cake. She said, Thank you, and began to eat it. While she did so, I wrote a note on my typewriter. The note said: *"There wasn't anybody in the store but me. The cat scratched me. That is all. Yours truly—"*

"Read this, please."

She read it.

"Is it true?"

She stared at me as if she wasn't sure I was here in the study, either.

"I reckon."

"Will you sign it, please?"

She was plainly puzzled.

"You know, way you would sign a letter you wrote."

"I didn't write it."

She didn't, of course. "Then will you write one yourself—just like it?"

She looked pretty blank but nodded assent. I brought her a pencil and a clean sheet of paper. She slowly began printing out the letters. She had finished and had printed S-u- when the phone rang.

I turned to answer it. It was Charlie. He was in difficulty. The motor in the organ had overheated. He had called the electrician but the assistant he sent seemed unsure of where the trouble was. Would I drop by the church and look at it with them? I told him I'd be there in ten minutes. I turned back to Susan. She had finished and was sitting relaxed and quiet in the brown and white chair, watching me.

"Now, we must be going." Am afraid my voice was full of cream. "It is dark. I shall take you home."

I deliberately left the note where it was, as if the whole matter were forgotten. I locked the door of my study. I dropped her at her apartment house, watched her enter the hall and get into the automatic elevator, then I drove around to the church. I must have stayed there close to an hour with Charlie and the electrician.

When I left, it was after eight and I was starved. Went halfway to Hart's Restaurant, where I usually have dinner, before I remembered that I should call Neel or the Chief and ask for an appointment. Her letter was enough, surely, to clear Mark. Maybe with this we could persuade Claud Newell to drop the case. I returned to my study—it wasn't the kind of call I wanted to make at Hart's—and dialed the police station. They were at their homes, the desk sergeant told me. I dialed Neel and made an appointment for Wednesday morning. Thought I'd better slip the note into a safe place. Nothing safer than my wallet. I picked up the note, saw Susan had added a postscript. She must have done it while I talked to Charlie. There it was: *P.S. I was joaking. He did hurt me too, that bad man. Susan.*

I put it in my wallet, and went on to the café, wolfed down three hamburgers, a bowl of salad, a piece of lemon pie and two cups of poor coffee. Haven't been that hungry since training days at school. Guess I was devouring Susan, too, along with the hamburgers. I was outdone enough.

The food changed my feelings. I cheered up. Maybe it is a good thing, that postscript. Revealing. Obviously the kid is having fun with us, making fools out of the whole community, showing us how primitive and childlike we are, nobody caring a hoot about the real facts. I'll enjoy watching the Chief's face when he reads this one, I thought.

Went home. Put two hours of records on the hi-fi. I couldn't take anything as reasonable and genial as Mozart or as orderly and of the balanced complexity of Bach. No, I needed Bartók, and a little Hindemith and a little Milhaud and then for a night-cap I put on a record of Lully's—but somewhere along that twisting tortuous path of dissonance, long before Lully, I went to sleep.

When I waked up, the hi-fi was silent. My heart was racing as if I had played two or three hard sets of tennis. There is no point in telling my dream. It was like most dreams: a senseless business, if you don't have a key to it and I didn't have one, but the last scene of it was a conversation between Susan and Prosthetic Limb and Real Leg, all of whom were tiptoeing on the edge of the Grand Canyon and daring each other to jump it for a piece of chocolate cake. And Dewey Snyder was standing there in a judge's black gown with the cake and had solemnly cut two slices. That was all. No, not quite—because just before the man in the black gown turned into Dewey Snyder, he looked like my little mother Mary Lou, and then for a dazzling second he looked like me.

8

Breakfast with Neel. Apartment uncluttered, spacious. White rugs
on floor. Saarinen chair. A bench from Norway. An excellent
reproduction of a Kandinsky abstraction. A water color done by
a friend in New Mexico. Greenish bronze artifact found by Neel
while in Guatemala—a stunning piece, used in death rites, I
think he said. Two masks from Orissa. Shelves of books on
prison administration, penology, psychology, child guidance, family guidance, recreation. Books on delinquent this, delinquent
that; on drug addiction; ballistics; jujitsu; architecture, city
planning: Neutra, Lewis Mumford, Frank Lloyd Wright, Mies
van der Rohe, others. Penal codes of the State. A recent report
by the Mayor's Committee on Housing. A report on crime in our
city made by the Chief of Police—Neel probably wrote it. Lives
of famous prison wardens. Practically everything of Dostoevsky's.
Three or four Kafkas. Two shelves of Bertrand Russell, Hegel,
Whitehead, Unamuno, Nietzsche, Kant, Goethe. Above his hi-fi
was an excellent collection of modern and classical music, and a
number of jazz records—progressive, Dixie, etc. He had recently
said he could get nowhere with the members of one teen-age
gang until he began to talk jazz with them—"that's the only way
they can dig me." A few hillbilly records: "they're my kind, you
know." On a shelf where the magazines and paper books were
stacked was something called *How to Commit Murder and Leave
Full Evidence Behind*. Must be a gag: I picked it up, found it

in typescript, inside hard covers. Began to read: fascinating, crazy stuff. . . .

Neel was in his copper-lined kitchen (not literally, just seems so at first glance) and called to me to turn on the eight o'clock news, if I wanted to. I preferred to collect the full evidence but I turned on the TV for him and went back to my book.

He was coming in and out, now, setting up a small table for breakfast. Laid mats: each a famous murder trial sketched out in the manner of a treasure hunt map—I saw this later, at breakfast. At the moment, I was pretty absorbed in the Full Evidence thesis. He saw me reading it, grinned, finished arranging the silver and plates, and the rest of it.

"I'm shaking the omelet around," he shouted from the kitchen. "Be with you in half a minute."

He came in, proudly bearing a perfect omelet in an enameled iron pan. He brought in sausage and waffles on a handsome platter—from Finland, I'd guess. I admired it aloud; admired the table. A little shy now, so he had to cover: said, "Not bad for a boy who ate with his hands until he was twelve years old, is it? Three tin spoons and five of us—the pup and I managed with our paws." We laughed. With sudden gravity, "I have the feeling it is bad taste to push my background into the lap of a guest. Perhaps I need to remind myself, now and then, to keep the record straight, but I shouldn't—" He was deftly serving my plate. "I had a rough dream last night—it took me back home. I haven't quite returned, to this." He smiled, quietly became the courteous host he wanted to be, and was.

After our first cup of coffee, "About Susan: shall we pitch into her now? the Chief wants to see us at nine-thirty."

I gave him an account of her visit to my bedroom. Repeated one of her stories in detail so he'd get the drift of her imagination. Then I gave him her note. He read it, laid it on the table. Picked it up, read it again.

"What else did she say?"

I mentioned her reaction to those four-syllable words.

Neel laughed. "She used two of them on the Chief and lost

him. He said nobody could convince him an eight-year-old would know those words: the kid was too glib to suit him. I suggested her mother probably told her to use the words as a decent way of saying what had to be said. It didn't ring true, he said."

"I agree with you about the words. But I think the Chief is right that the story was made up. The act Susan was describing in those four-syllable words occurred inside her own head, nowhere else. We're dealing with a bright, imaginative child who has a gift for telling stories. She's a lonely child—"

"They all are," Neel said.

"I know. But Susan's brand of loneliness is pretty inclusive. This Boody she told me about: the imaginary playmate: she's old for that sort of thing, isn't she?"

He nodded.

"All right. This suggests, don't you think, that while she seems to play well with the neighborhood children, actually she doesn't make much contact."

"Could be."

"This contactless association is what I'm trying to get at. For instance, she and her mother just don't speak the same language. It may be the mother's fault; or the child's, I don't know. Whatever caused it, everything with Susan is now a top-drawer secret. Then suddenly she bursts forth with these wild stories."

"She's talking in code, don't you think? She can't say what she feels in plain words so she says it in a kind of explosive fable."

"Something like that. But you're the psychologist."

We studied each other for a moment. I was not at all sure he was going along with me. He asked me what I knew about her father. Not too much, I said. At home only on weekends. Was usually at the pier tinkering with his boat. I had never seen Susan with him except at church.

He said slowly, "Her mother hates her. I saw it the first time I talked with them. There's something powerful in Susan which Mrs. Newell can't control. She resents it and fears it, yet is trying to exploit it for her own purpose."

"I'm not sure about that. In fact, I am not sure about my

analysis of the Newell family. I don't know enough to say what I've just said."

Neel looked up, smiled. "Nor do I." He read the note again, turned it this way, that. Seemed restless.

My admission of ignorance did not deter me, however, from further theorizing: "But Susan feels closer to her mother since this occurred," I said. "She's never had her approval. She's got it now."

"Because she said she was approached by a man?"

"Because she fell in with her mother's suggestion that she had been approached by a certain man."

He smiled. "You may be right."

"I may not. But this is what I think: She's got something now she's been craving a long time and she's going to hold on to it. If it means swearing Dr. Channing was in the store, she'll swear it."

Neel said slowly, "I'm playing my hunches, I admit—but I have a feeling a man was there."

"Why do you think so?"

"I see it written in invisible ink, you might say, on that note."

I suppose my disappointment was splashed all over me, for he smiled and said, "But I don't think it was Dr. Channing." He looked at me too long for my comfort. "It couldn't have been because you stated you saw him on his terrace at five-thirty."

It began again: When, exactly, did I see him? He said, himself, it wasn't five-thirty. "Yes, I saw him at five-thirty," I said firmly. "I'm not too good about time—but this clicked. I happened to break a bottle of hair tonic; cleaned up the mess, and when I finished I went to the window and saw Mark on his terrace, reading."

"Sure," he said softly. "It's down in the written statement we took from you. That's why we didn't arrest him in the first place."

"Look, Neel: Susan added the postscript not because it was the truth she was determined to tell but simply to tease. It's a weapon she's found her mother vulnerable to—and most grown folks. You should have heard her tell those stories. When she finished one she had another ready. Her fantasies are flooding

her and she has the gift of organizing them into stories, then
tells them to upset people. She added that postscript simply to
give a surprise twist. She's discovered it works, sometimes. She
was scared all right when she ran out of that store but—" I
hesitated. Had the feeling he was more interested in my motivation than in Susan's.

"Why?"

"I don't know, of course. But this is what I think: Here's a
half-dark place: nobody in it but her and the cat; fantasies pouring into her mind—forbidden fantasies, let's say, about her father; then the cat scratches her and she feels as if—well, almost
as if God has punished her for her bad thoughts. Then: what
does she do? She runs out of the store and into the beauty shop
and tells them a man has frightened her. She also tells Nella
Perkins and the others that she does not know the man. But:
when her mother pointed out Mark Channing, she said he was
the one. The actual facts are: this little brat has seen Mark Channing for years at church; the Newells sit in the fourth pew on
the right, the Channings sit in the sixth pew across the aisle. She
has big eyes and big ears and she doesn't miss a trick. When she
isn't sticking out her tongue and walling her eyes at me she's
wriggling and squirming and staring at everybody in the congregation. She would have recognized Dr. Channing instantly, had
he been in that store."

"I said I was merely playing my hunch," Neel spoke quietly.

I realized my voice was too urgent. I eased it down. "Mark
Channing is my close friend, as you know. I realize I have a
predisposition to the theory that Susan made it all up. But I also
think there are solid facts to buttress my theory. Will you go
along with the kid's loneliness?"

"Yes."

"And the poor relationship with her parents?"

"It's worse than poor."

"All right. Her loneliness for a father—the tall, thin man she
imagined—father image—will you go along with that?"

"Yes. To a degree."

"OK. The sex part of it: an eight-year-old girl starved for

healthy affection might settle in her fantasy life for something crude and perverse, don't you think?"

"Quite likely."

"And these crude, perverse daydreams might very well concern her father since she's had no real relationship with him?"

"Possibly. Yes, I'd say it is quite possible that such Oedipal symptoms might show up."

Relief is a mild word for my reaction. I have my doubts concerning the Oedipus complex theory, certainly the stripped-down, literal form in which it is often stated, but now I was clinging to it as if to a life raft.

He poured a third cup of coffee for me. Rubbed his thin nose. "Even so, I somehow feel—" he stopped. "But go ahead."

"I think—this is not a fact but an opinion—that to take this case to court can do nobody any good. Susan, least of all."

"I agree."

"I know—this is a fact—that Dr. Guthrie could give testimony that would completely exonerate Dr. Channing. But whether he would, I'm not sure."

"May I ask where you obtained this information?"

"From Dr. Guthrie. He examined Susan on Tuesday evening after that Monday afternoon—at the urgent request of her mother who thought Susan had been raped. He found her untouched. He told me that a little girl who has gone through such an experience, whether of rape, attempted rape, or exhibitionism, would instinctively shrink from close contact with any man, at least for a few days. Susie showed no fear; she was completely poised.

"Now my third point: Mrs. Newell seems to have a phobia about rape. She has told me, in confidence, things I cannot go into. I can say only that when she was in her early teens, she had a most unpleasant—you might say, traumatic experience. All this has—"

He interrupted me. "She's a bitch from way back. I know her kind, Dave. I should: I have a sister just like her. It has been difficult for me to be objective about this case because I knew what she was, the first five minutes I talked with her. I have been afraid I'd cause a miscarriage of justice because of my personal memories, and my prejudice against this kind of woman. So I've leaned backward: to be fair to her and her child."

To my astonishment, his quiet manner had disappeared. His voice was low-pitched—he's a mountaineer and like most of them he does not let his feelings show too much—but his eyes were bitter, agonized.

I was as shaken by his change of mood as if I had stumbled on a human skull while walking on somebody's front lawn. My first reaction was to defend Renie. I knew I couldn't. I realized the center of things had shifted abruptly from her and Susan.

"They could be twins. Not just morally or psychologically: they even look alike. Take those British tweeds and Dior gowns off of Mrs. Newell, add ten pounds, put her in a cheap chain-store dress, let her hair get dirty, let her stop brushing her teeth and you have my sister, Hattie Belle. They have the same way with a man—inviting him—then stripping him clean of whatever it is he values most. They always find it. Money: they take it; his work: they destroy it; his secret image of himself: they dirty it up.

"I don't know what Mrs. Newell was like when she was a girl. But I know about Hattie Belle. Since she was ten years old, she's been layin out of nights"—he had slipped as naturally into the old vernacular as if he had pulled on a pair of overalls—"with any man she can cheat. She's married now and has four children but she still cheats: cheats him, cheats the kids. At least two of them are not his. I am not sure any of them are. If I could get up the nerve, I'd have the Welfare Board take them away from her. But it is more than I could go through."

He sighed. "I don't know what makes a woman a bitch. I've read hundreds of books on psychology, delinquency, crime, broken homes, all the rest of it. I've never found out. The theories won't stick to Hattie Belle. She slides right out of them. They won't fit Mrs. Newell, either. You can say it is something they feel about their body. It is, but it's a lot more than that. They use it like a lethal weapon, sure; and without scruple. They take care, too, because it's their bank account and insurance policy.

But there's something else: they're addicted to men. And they hate them the same way an alcoholic hates his whisky; loathes it and yet must have it. I say this and yet I know it is not right, either. Not quite. When Hattie Belle was no more than two or three she was already at it, standing by the side of the road holding her dress up and no pants on. That kind of thing. Laughing, daring them to look, saying, *Give me a penny.* But—now this is the point: anybody who didn't give her a penny, paid for it; and anybody who did, paid, too. She'd run tell pappy on all of them." He went over to the mantel, picked up one of the Orissa masks, turned it this way; that way; set it back in its place.

"Children do these things. You know it better than I do, Neel. They have one point of view, we have a different one."

"You think I'm hard on her. I am, and it's wrong, and I know it. I don't know why . . . maybe it's because you want a little something that's decent to remember about the two or three you used to love. You hate the sheer poverty of your memories. I planned to send her to college, after I got mine; thought she'd like to be *somebody.* She laughed; said she knew all in the world she needed to know." He smiled. "Of course she does. And plenty you and I don't know.

"Anyway, she kept it up. Ma would whip her: tell me to run git a switch—there was a wild cherry near the creek, and I'd run and pull off a switch. Felt I was on the side of God when I helped Ma whip her but I'd end up blubbering with the kid." He stopped.

The Kandinsky abstraction, Saarinen chair, the books, the handsome platter from Finland, the copper jugs and pots . . . fading out—

He was saying ". . . taught her to read when she was four."

I said, "How old were you, Neel?"

"About eight. You mean when I taught her?"

His eyes were in such pain. I nodded.

"Bright—was reading fine by the time she was five. But once she learned, what then? I mean, around her. How did books tie up with what was around her and inside her? Landrum, can you conceive of the environment I grew up in? No. You came

from one of those white-column shacks with blinds on them—"
he grinned.

"More Williamsburg." I laughed a little. "But small, Neel. We
were not rich people."

"Maybe not. But your father was a famous trial lawyer. You
had books, knowledge in your background—manners—ideals—
traditions—well, never mind. I know you can understand, that's
why I'm telling you. We lived way back in a cove near one of
the Balds—unpainted cabin—no furniture except one double
bed, a wood-burning stove, two straight chairs and a packing box
we used for a table. Hattie Belle and I slept on the floor. They'd
take us and put us in the bed to go to sleep, when it was freezing cold, then pick us up, wrap us in a quilt, and lay us on the
floor." He stopped. "Never thought it before but that was a gentle
thing, wasn't it? Maybe they did have a little feeling." Stopped
again. Shook his head. ". . . I just don't know—it'd be easier
not to think so.

"But sometimes we didn't stay asleep, and we'd lie there on
that freezing-cold hard floor and listen to what was going on in
that bed. We thought, or made like we thought, they were fighting. Hattie Belle would say when she was about four or five, *They
fit all night, did you hear um?* And she'd giggle and I'd feel hot
and shamed and would laugh big and whoop it up and then stop
and push her hard and tell her to shut up or I'd slap her down.
I think she slept harder than I did; a lot of times she'd be asleep
while I lay there thinking about it . . . with no words to help
me. Then I got the habit of not thinking. I learned to deliberately put my mind on something else: I'd put my mind on squirrel shooting, force myself to see those squirrels flitting around in
the trees, feel myself out in the woods easing up on them, close
enough sometimes to see the heart beating in one."

He stopped, looked around the spacious room. I don't think he
saw a thing in it. He was back in those mountains. "There was a
big poplar, no nuts on it, mind you, but they loved that tree."
Looked at me. "We don't know much of anything, do we? Why
did those squirrels like a poplar when there were hickories and
oaks around with plenty nuts and acorns for them?

"Sometimes, lying on that floor, I'd make myself think about a big rock I knew on the side of old Bald. It had a place under it big enough for two or three mountain cats. There were always tracks there. . . . One night, when I couldn't take what I heard going on in that bed, I slipped out and went to the rock and slept under it, sort of hoping a mountain cat would come along and stay with me. I was never scared of wild things—it was what lived in houses that got me.

"Next day, Pap wore me out. Said a rattler could have bit me walking through those woods barefoot. He didn't catch on that the house was full of things that scared me worse than rattlers and copperheads. I just let him beat. Knew better than to try to explain.

"Sometimes, on a winter's day, I'd sit on an old stump out in the field—where you could see the mountains stretching out, watch the black-blue whiteness of them, the shadows sliding down them, let my eyes move from the far ones to the close ones, peak to peak, along the rough tree-edge—wondering what was on the other side, wishing I knew."

He stopped. Said, "This is unpardonable. I intended only to compare her with Hattie Belle. That dream, last night, must have blasted me wide open. Strange . . . how we think we know people when we've never heard their dreams. Like seeing half a man walking around—"

"I wish you'd tell it, if you feel up to it."

He smiled. "I feel up to it—in fact, I'm holding back with the greatest difficulty. But I won't inflict it on you.

"Back to the other: I got to stealing. Must have been about twelve. Went with a gang of boys who lived round about. Most of them were fifteen and sixteen but they took me along because I was glib with my tongue and they found out I could pick locks." He laughed. "It's my one talent. I can pick any lock ever made. No use to brag—better say, almost any. We'd go around, nights, opening the houses owned by the summer people. We called them furriners.

"Breaking into those places gave me my first view of a room with rugs and furniture in it, and pictures on the wall.

"First, I'd pick a lock and open the door, and then I'd invite the rest of them in as if I owned the place. That was my big moment: I actually felt, because I could get in, I owned the place. That was all I wanted: just to open it, and own it for a minute or so. I guess I stole a little, too; when the others did. I must have.

"Remember in one house there was a chest of drawers and on it a silver tea caddy (I didn't know the name of it, then) and a bowl and a small carved box. I looked at it and something happened inside me—a wonderful, strange feeling crept through me. Maybe it was joy. I don't know. I stood there, looking at all of it together—I knew whatever gave me the feeling had to do with its being *just as it was*. I didn't know the word *arrangement* or *pattern,* or *design* but I knew I wanted it to stay *just as it was*. And then one of the big guys came up and said, You take that tin thing and I'll take the rest. But I didn't want it, and I didn't want any of it touched. I said, No you aint and I aint, either! So he knocked me down and began stomping me and the others had to pull him off. They remembered it was me who could pick the locks."

But after a while, to open houses and steal wasn't enough so they started breaking things. "We'd pick up cups and hurl them against a wall; plates were tricky, they'd bounce back on you sometimes, but cups were reliable. We'd take our knives and gash the surface of the tables and chests. We'd break a mirror— and seeing our shattered selves in that shattered glass. . . ." He looked up. Smiled. "Sort of made modern art out of us. Everything we destroyed made us want to destroy more. As I look back now—it was as if a door had swung open and let in air and the small smouldering fire down in us had turned into a roaring holocaust. I don't know . . . I think this now. Anyway, we behaved like monsters. Some of them would stand on the beds and do their dirty business, right there. Our feelings rose like flames; then somebody would say, *I gotta lay a woman*—only they said it in worse language than that—and they'd laugh and look at me for I was a runty kid of twelve—then one of the big ones would come at me and try to make me do things with him. I'd fight him off . . . it scared me, it made me sick, and yet something in me wanted to do it.

"We were bucking poverty and ignorance—and monotony. We didn't know the words but we were crazy with the disease."

I didn't speak but I moved my hand—in slight disagreement. He said, "I know. That's looking at it the small way. There're plenty of decent people in the world who are as poor as I was and as ignorant and who live a monotonous life. But when they're decent they have something I didn't have—and those other kids didn't have. If we could find out what, we might get rid of this delinquency we're so concerned with. Until we do, we won't." He looked at me earnestly. "You agree to that?"

"Yes, I think I do."

"Well—anyway, coming back: we grew too sure and got caught and that is how I met the Chief. But I've told you about the years I lived with him and his wife when he was sheriff of our county. I didn't find out until I was studying sociology at the University that they had kept me because of my poor environment. I thought they had me there because they liked me."

"They did."

He smiled. "Sure, I know. I'm not mixed up about that.

"But I'm as off the main drag as the old lady in your church who begins everything by telling when she was a blue baby. I wanted to tell you about Hattie Belle because Mrs. Newell is exactly like her—and Hattie Belle pulled me right back home. She always tricks, you see?" He tried to be light about it. "And Mrs. Newell tricks, too. She was determined to ruin Dr. Channing. And her child presented her with the opportunity she needed."

My face apparently showed the doubt I felt, for he said, "You find it hard to believe, don't you?"

"It doesn't fit what I know of her."

"A literate, charming woman who dresses like a quiet million dollars can be just as bitchy as a dirty ignorant—"

I couldn't let him finish this cruel sentence. I said, "Neel—I see it. I know you think Mrs. Newell has a compulsive need to ruin men and that in doing so, she finds satisfaction. But I can't for the life of me see why it had to be Mark Channing."

"Because he's repelled her advances at some time or other. It wouldn't take more than that."

"But we don't know this. We're guessing wild."

He glanced at his watch. "Lord! it's nine o'clock. You think the main point is that Susan said the man in the store looked like her father? She said she thought at first it was her father. Right?"

"Right."

"Then she said she forgot—he was in Chicago. You think this proves that she was making up a daydream of a tabooed kind."

"I think it is likely."

"You think a trial will do nothing good for Susan but will ruin her social reputation in this city."

"I think they'll regret it when she grows up, yes."

"And this argument will count with her father."

"Unless he's lost his senses. And I don't think he has."

"And you're sure we are not circumventing justice as far as Dr. Channing is concerned: first, because you think the child made it plain she was fantasying the man; second, because you saw Channing at five-thirty on his terrace. And, to sum it up: Since he couldn't have done it, and we have no evidence concerning anyone else: why not drop the case? Hmm?" There was an odd light in his eyes.

"Yes. And use our efforts, instead, to persuade Claud Newell to do something constructive for the child."

"Such as?"

"Consulting with the Family Guidance Bureau or a psychiatrist. Help the child make some real relationships."

He smiled, looked at his watch. Made no move to go.

I said, "Do you have reservations? Can anything good for the Newells or Channings or this community or the cause of justice come out of such a trial?"

"Not a damned thing. Like to wash up?" He showed me the bathroom.

When I came back, he said, "There's quite a bit of talk going on. Heard much?"

"No. Mrs. Channing has had anonymous phone calls urging

her to leave her husband. Quite a few of them. Also some anonymous letters. Two on pink paper. Rough stuff."

"Through the mail?"

"Slipped under her door."

"Why didn't they tell us?"

"They thought there was nothing you could do about it. Is there?"

He shook his head. "Not much. We must go. Sorry to end our visit so abruptly. I've enjoyed having you here. And I am embarrassed about dumping my decayed fetid past on you."

"Neel . . . will you let me say something?"

"Sure."

"I've watched you work with the delinquent kids of this city for three years. You've done a superb job. I wish you could see Hattie Belle as if she were one of them."

"I wish to God I could. It is my major weakness; what you might call my cardinal sin: and I am superstitious enough to believe it will throw me, one of these days."

We were in the elevator now. He said, "Objectivity is a difficult thing to achieve—desirable as it is."

"Nobody can achieve it and I don't think it would be desirable to do so even if we could."

"Wait! Let's leave that one for next time."

We laughed. I said, Fine breakfast; didn't know you were up to such waffles. He said he hated to admit they came out of a package. And after that, we were silent.

Neither of us said much on the way downtown. As he parked the car, he asked me to make the rounds with him some night soon. I said I'd like to. I asked him about the Vested Interests, a new gang he had run into in the Negro slums; asked him about the Guided Missiles, the white gang in our section of Windsor Hills.

He said, as we went in the building, "Any threats in those letters? or phone calls?"

"None that I know of."

"Try to find out, will you? And keep me informed."

I promised I would.

He stopped at the door of the Chief's office. Lowered his voice, said, "I don't believe in God, but lately I've been wishing I did. Not for my sake. I feel no need of religion; I feel only a terrible need for a world where there is kindness and understanding—well, never mind my philosophy. I just wish you could help more with these young hoodlums of ours. They need something I haven't got."

"I haven't got it, either, Neel."

"But you're still searching—and they are. I quit—long ago. We'd better be moving, the Chief gets nervous—"

We went in. He was waiting for us. I had been warned he had slipped this interview into a crowded schedule. I let Neel do the talking. Somewhere along the way he said, "She's just like Hattie Belle, Chief; so you know what we're up against."

I saw the Chief understood what Neel was talking about. He had picked up a pencil and was drawing wavy lines. Not saying anything. Face sagging a little—he has a moon-face, bright red; two brown splotches on one cheek, sparse gray-yellow hair, head set on a bull neck that falls in strings of skin and muscle in front. Drawing wavy lines . . . not saying a word. Drawing a wavy line, putting dots under it, drawing another, putting dots—

He looked at me. Shrewd, knowing eyes. "What you think, Reverend Landrum?"

"I think the Newell family's in trouble and it didn't begin in that store. I'm not too sure there is a beginning to a family's trouble—"

"I know it aint," he said.

"Mrs. Newell is well liked in Windsor Hills. I have found her extremely thoughtful of the sick people and old people in the parish—and they love her. I depend on her in our activities and she never lets me down. But you can't reason with her about a few things. As for her husband:"

"Wouldn't be in his shoes for a million dollars."

"I know. But it's his fault, too. He's run out on them, in a way. Driving too hard at his job—"

"A man's got to do something."

I decided to let him figure it out at his own speed. He kept drawing those lines. Neel was smoking. I was thinking how to get the child's point of view over when Neel said, "Chief, you ought to hear those stories Susan told Mr. Landrum. How about telling the one about the prosthesis?"

Neel was smiling a little, not much, as I told it. The Chief listened solemnly. When I finished, he said, "You ought've taken a crutch to her. She's a menace!" He looked angry. Began doodling again. I saw he was shaking with laughter. I was so taken aback that I did not laugh with him. As quickly as he could, he said, "I want you to excuse me, Reverend. I know it's no laughing matter to you." Gnawing his lip, looking shamed, as a small boy might.

I told him I thought it as funny as he did, etc. "We're dealing with an imaginative child, Chief. In my opinion, she made up nine-tenths of what she says happened in the store. She was certainly there; she picked up that cat, all right, and he scratched her; but the rest of it, no."

He was doodling rapidly now. Wavy line, dots. It changed: he was drawing a cat. "You don't think anyone was there, besides the cat?"

"No. I think she was walking around in the place making up a story. She did something to the cat, perhaps; I don't know about that, of course. Anyway he scratched her and jumped out of her arms, she realized how dark the place was, things turned round in her head, and suddenly she felt a character in her own story, so to speak, had hurt her."

The Chief's eyes gave nothing away. "How about you, Neel?"

"She makes up stories, Chief; no doubt about that. But I am inclined to think she can't tell things straight because she doesn't feel or see them straight. Always they are distorted. As I see it: She was in that half-dark place dreaming things, feeling death wishes"—the Chief looked at me sharply—"toward her mother, maybe; wishing she had a father to whom she meant a great deal. The cat felt her tension, scratched her, and all of it together scared the daylights out of her."

The Chief looked at me conspiratorially. "He's a Freudian, you know—whatever that is."

We laughed. I felt tremendously relieved as Neel moved in to hedge his position. He said, "Chief: there's something else you should know." He quickly told him about my talk with Dr. Guthrie. "That's important evidence. A little girl who has been the object of rape, exhibitionism, anything of the sort, is going to be anxious and nervous afterward. Wouldn't you think?"

The Chief nodded.

"But, according to the doctor she was at ease. Completely at ease."

"When did the doctor tell you this, Mr. Landrum?"

"Saturday night, after the trouble on Monday."

Still drawing cats. "Claud Newell did not swear out the warrant until after the child claimed Dr. Channing had followed her from school. You know this?"

I knew what Mark and Grace had told me. "I've heard a little about it. What time did she say she was followed?"

"Around four-thirty."

Neel said, "It seems nobody was with Dr. Channing after three o'clock, that day. His secretary went home shortly after lunch because her mother was ill. Dr. Channing says he was in his office studying a batch of slides and had closed the door in order not to be disturbed. He says he left his office at six-thirty and no one happened to be in the automatic elevator when he went down."

The Chief said, "Can you think of a motive the child might have had for saying this, if he didn't follow her?"

I could think of a dozen. Susan might have thought it was time to throw more fat on the home fires to keep them burning brightly. I said this. I had an idea—but I didn't say it—that she was also flexing her new power. A few words: and the entire community falls flat on its face. She'd try it again, probably— and soon.

The Chief wanted to know how we figured Dr. Channing had been pulled into it, in the first place.

I went at this cautiously. "The two men are curiously alike in appearance," I said. "Both have brown hair, graying at the temples; both have thin faces, blue eyes, an easy slow walk. Both are tall and thin. Both drop the left shoulder."

"You're not saying her father was in there?"

"Certainly not. But my theory is that this lonely little brat wished he was there. When she talked to me about it she said she thought, at first, the man was her father—but he was in Chicago, she added. She didn't say she remembered he was in Chicago. She said it in a different way: as if, later, she *realized* he was in Chicago. She has an imaginary playmate; why not an imaginary father?"

"I'm as lost as if I was back of Clingman's Dome," said the Chief. "You're telling me this Susan imagined her father was in that dark store making immoral advances to her? I won't buy that one."

"Chief—you remember the things you ran into up home when you were sheriff?"

"Yeah, but this aint up home. Those poor ignorant folks were shut off, lonely—"

"You ran into incest cases, didn't you? pretty often, didn't you, Chief?" said Neel softly.

"Not pretty often. Let's don't make it worse than it was. Now and then."

"All right. But you see, don't you, how a little girl might imagine that sort of thing and become frightened at her own thoughts? then, when the cat scratched her, how she might feel as if *somebody* had scratched her? She knew better, one piece of her brain knew better; but it triggered off a lot of fear and other things too; more fantasies, maybe."

The Chief was drawing cats: big cats, little cats, pussy cats, day-born kittens; picked up a fresh piece of paper and began on more cats— Stopped. Reached in his drawer, felt around for his tobacco, cut off a piece, tucked it in his mouth, said, "And how did the story end?"

We laughed and eased down a bit. I told him what Susan had said about hiding in the rose bushes in the parkway in front of the Channings' house.

"That woman told me her child recognized him in the store. The reason they hid in the rose bushes, she said, was because she thought the child might be wrong. She stressed it that she didn't want to accuse an innocent man. She said Susie recognized him instantly."

"Exactly the way Hattie Belle would have done it, Chief."

"All right, boys, what we going to do? Hold a private trial and settle it our way?"

Neel carefully made his points: Newell should be told what a trial would do to the child's future in Windsor Hills, even if they won; he should also be told he didn't have much of a case and if he lost—"

"You know better than that, Kel. He'll win if it goes to court. No jury is going in for all that imagination business. They imagine too much, themselves; it'll seem like solid fact. Dr. Channing having had those colored doctors at his place won't help him with a jury either."

"Where did you hear that, Chief?"

"Picked it up, Reverend, here and there."

We waited. He finally said, "I take it, we're to persuade him to withdraw the charges, mainly for the sake of his child."

"That's right," Neel said softly.

The Chief was moving around in his chair and belching softly. It was a hint for us to leave. We stood. "Bring Newell in, Kel—and I'll see what I can do. But it's my opinion we've got a stubborn man on our hands. When you having your little talk, Reverend?"

"After you, sir—if you'll let me time it that way."

He shifted his tobacco from one cheek to the other. "OK, boys. You know what's in the books—I just know what's in folks' nature. We'll see how it works out. Drop in again, Reverend. I've got a story I think you might like. It sort of matches Susie's."

"I'd like to hear it, sir."

I felt pretty good about the interview. But Neel seemed on the somber side. We didn't say much as he drove back to his place where I had left my car. As I turned toward the Parish House, I saw him heading for the downtown district.

9

Around nine, Katie and Sydney dropped in to see me. I knew when I saw her face with its carefully cultured indifference that she was disturbed about something. I looked at Sydney. He was going to let her say it, whatever it was.

She began by kidding me, "Why don't you speak to a girl friend when she screams hi at you?"

"Where was the girl friend?"

"On Highway 401-A. The rector of All Saints was making a nice leisurely seventy-five. I know because you passed me and I trailed you. What was your hurry?"

"I guess I was thinking about my sermon. I've had trouble this week finding time to work on it."

She dropped this and announced that Charlie had finally got going on the third act of his opera. He had played the first scene, still unfinished, for her that afternoon. She had also read it. "This is Charlie's music. Nobody else's. There's something in it he has never found before—a new simplicity— But I still think the title may be wrong. *The Coward* . . ." she said it tentatively and looked at me so long that I smiled and said, Don't!

"That is exactly what I mean. The audience may say *don't*, too. I am not sure people can get emotional distance from it—"

"I think Katie may be worrying too much. Who minds a man's cowardice if he is of another nationality?" Sydney speaking. But it was obvious that they had not come to discuss the third act of Charlie's opera with me.

Finally, "Dave . . ." and then she began to say it:

Her father had called an unofficial meeting of the vestry. Four of them, the important ones—she said—had come in after dinner. "It is none of my business what my father does about his church affairs. I know I am meddling but he should have asked you. Since he didn't, I think you should know."

I suggested that her father as senior warden might feel he had the right, or privilege say, to call an informal meeting of the vestry. "After all, he has been senior warden for nine years."

"Without asking you?"

"Yes, since it was informal."

"Church canon states that the rector is to be present at all vestry meetings."

"You've been reading up?"

"Yes."

"Your father probably felt he was not stepping across his legal rights."

"Daddy never steps across his legal rights. But as a matter of simple courtesy he should have asked you."

"Not necessarily."

"Dave . . . it was about Mark." She didn't explain further. I looked at Sydney, got nothing from his face.

"What about him?"

"The trial coming up, newspaper publicity, the talk, TV. What this scandal will do to All Saints. In my father's opinion, any considerate man would have resigned from the vestry the day he was arrested."

It must be extremely embarrassing, her father had said, for the Laboratories. He was surprised that Dr. Channing had not been asked to leave. It certainly had hurt the Cancer Committee's drive for money, there was no doubt about that. But he was thinking now of All Saints: he felt the time had come when the vestry must face up to its obligations and request Dr. Channing's resignation.

I interrupted her, just here, and asked who were there.

Ben Jordan of First National Bank, she said; Lee Esteridge,

chairman of the board of Allied Industries; Dr. Guthrie; and Simon Reid of Reid, Levin, Weinstein and Winthrop.

There followed a discussion, Katie said, of procedures, church canon, etc. Simon Reid reminded them that the vestry had no right to ask for a vestryman's resignation; it might possibly be requested, it certainly could not be demanded; a demand could be made only by the parish and only if the rector and parish found just cause.

In his opinion, Ben Jordan said, this would be a sensitive matter. Extremely so—since Dr. Channing's guilt had not been established. Coming before the trial—

Lee Esteridge of Allied Industries did not wait for Jordan to finish. He said he was amazed: there was no earthly doubt of the man's guilt! He had not heard it questioned before. The Newells were responsible not to say prominent people. Mrs. Newell was highly thought of. How under God's heaven had Ben arrived at this asinine conclusion! The damnedest thing—

"His face and bald head turned purple. I remembered his blood pressure and went over and asked him if he would like some water. He whispered that he never drank it, just pour him a double one, sugar, of that Tennessee whisky; that was all he needed. I gave it to him and he sipped it slowly but the purple didn't leave his face so I asked him if he should take one of his tranquilizers and he winked and pulled out the vial and I opened it for him and he took two with his whisky. He said he had to double his dosage when he was around Ben.

"All this time, Daddy was concentrating on Ben."

He asked him quietly, smoothly, if he would like to see a vestryman of All Saints in the headlines. It would inevitably be a sensational and sordid affair.

Ben said of course he wouldn't like it. It was going to be a most unpleasant experience for everyone. Nevertheless, in his opinion, they must keep in mind that Dr. Channing could be, and probably was, as innocent as any man here. This kind of thing had happened before. He remembered reading something in the *Saturday Evening Post*, once, or the *Readers' Digest*, or somewhere. In his opinion, the vestry should move cautiously. Certainly it was embarrassing, extremely so, for All Saints. But who was to blame for that? Dr. Channing? the Newells? or the irresponsible talk sweeping the city?

In his opinion—in committee, Ben tends to overwork that phrase—Mark Channing should have been given more support at the beginning of the trouble. If the thoughtful people of Windsor Hills had spoken up—but that was water under the bridge, etc. The point he wanted to make now was this: Dr. Channing was a distinguished scientist; he had made a notable contribution to the city and to All Saints as a man of intelligence and even wisdom, you might say; to take him off the vestry now . . .

"He really stood up to Daddy. I have never seen anyone do it before. I am afraid—"she shrugged.

"Of what?"

"I am afraid Ben slipped into momentary amnesia and forgot the facts of life."

"That your father is—"

"Yes, dear: chairman of First National. Ben is only president."

"What did Dr. Guthrie have to say?"

"Nothing. Perhaps a comment about the weather. I am not sure. He just listened carefully and drank his coffee."

"Who spoke after that?"

"Nobody." She was rubbing her left hand, exactly as Grace does. "Daddy recapitulated the scandal, the empty store, what the child said, what Mrs. Newell said. Then he reminded them that the Newell child had also accused Mark of following her, after school—and that was when the police force finally came to its senses and arrested him. The way he said it: *following her after school*—" She left that. "Every one of them knows Mark well. They know he was at the lab, is always there every afternoon, studying his slides and mice. But when Daddy said it: There was a terrible moment—I told Syd about it, it was most strange—when I could not see Mark at all. What I saw was a faceless man, a kind of giant abstraction of evil stealthily creeping up behind every little girl in the world. I don't know what those men saw. With me—I suppose it was a kind of throw-back to age six. Because Mother, even as sensible as she was about things, would warn me when I was little to be careful and never speak to a strange man, never let myself be left alone with one, with even the men I knew, in lonely places—"

She looked at us both. "It must do something to little females to be warned from the time they can walk, against men. Of course I see why Mother did it. But—this is what I am getting at: Grace and Andy and Mark have always seemed to me—not a perfect family but my kind; how any sane person could fail to feel Mark's integrity—and yet, when Daddy said this, it flashed across my mind, *He may have a dual personality: there may be two Marks or three or four*—you read just enough not to know anything! I thought this: *We think he is somebody who is rational, brilliant, completely decent, our friend, but he may be Somebody Else.*"

"We are all Somebody Else. I am. You are. Sydney is. Mark is, too. It is only when a man is severely ill that he can lose complete contact with his self-awareness, his memory, values, conscience; but you know this, Katie. I am no psychiatrist and I have only the muggiest notion of the dynamics of how the wall is built or grows inside a man, cutting him off from the rest of himself. It must begin early and I have the feeling it isn't so much that he never finds his own identity as it is that he never makes a fundamental identification with the one or two human beings he can believe in. I am guessing, I don't know."

Sydney said, "Drugs can split a man more easily; put part of him to sleep, while the other part goes on a binge. I've meant to discuss this with you in terms of theology. How can you—"

"We'll do it, one of these days. But I'll tell you now that I don't have the answers. But Katie is—"

I turned to her. I said. "The point is, Katie, you know Mark. Hold on to that."

"Yes. But Daddy hypnotized me. His voice was so calm and reasonable and he said it with such moderation and sympathy: as if this were something he had reluctantly brought up only for the sake of God and the church and all the nice little helpless girls in the world. What I am trying to get at is this: He was completely sincere. He believed his own words. He actually felt it was a most painful duty for all of them but they owed it to All Saints, et cetera. He was completely unaware of his real motive. Does this mean *he* is severely ill?"

Sydney said, "Your father is sane, Katie, whatever else!"

She looked at us both. "I don't see the line. If it is here, I don't see it: between a sick man and an evil one; or a good man and one who splits his acts off from his real motives."

I thought we'd better leave that, just now. I said, "What is your father's real motive? do you know?"

She looked at me, at Sydney, swallowed hard. Too dry, too terse. Her eyes were bright and cold. Katie learned long ago another way of weeping: her tears rarely show: they slide down into an underground channel. A lake of unshed tears must be inside that girl. This telling had been difficult. I looked at her: her long, smooth, slender browned hands lay in her lap, limp, nerveless.

I said, "Thank you for telling me. It was good of you, Katie—but you mustn't worry too much about this."

"Don't offer me a piece of candy, Dave!"

I deserved it, of course. I should have done better than that. The three of us said nothing for a full minute. Sydney was watchful of her. Now and then, he looked at me. I felt he had encouraged her to come. I knew she now wished she hadn't. I saw her face tightening up. She had transgressed her code: which is, of course, to stay out of things and do nothing.

She said, "I came because—" She couldn't finish it.

"Because you are concerned. I understand." I tried to pick up the mood a bit. And yet, all the time I felt I was talking like a professional clergyman. "Remember when you used to tell me you'd never be guilty of concern about the world's troubles?"

"It is not the world's troubles—it is Grace and my Andy. Does he know?"

I didn't think so but I didn't know. "Probably not. They think it will level off soon, they'll tell him something—afterward."

"After what?" she lit a cigarette. Pulled her legs up under her, turned in that slow easy way of hers and looked at me. She is almost tall, almost Sydney's height. Her hair is ash blonde and smoothly drawn back. Her skin is not dark, not light: amberish. She has a way of pushing her chin out when she's thinking. Odd habit but not unattractive.

"I saw Grace at the Red Bank theater last night. She is rehearsing the Anouilh play. She was completely absorbed in it. It was fantastic, her concentration. One of the dancers said to me, She's wonderful, absolutely—but how can she stand up to it, like this! And I said, She has to.

"But it worried me. She seemed too absorbed, as if— Why do they think it will level off?"

I didn't try to say.

"Why, Dave? Surely they—at least, they know he is under arrest and facing a trial. It will ruin them!"

"Let me try it this way: Mark believes—no matter what he may think—something in him believes this is basically a reasonable world. He doesn't believe a community like Windsor Hills will take a child's word instead of that of a responsible adult. He probably has never said this to Grace or himself. You don't. But he is counting on it: on the fact that he is innocent and most people are rational and decent."

"Is he? Or are they refusing to look at what is ahead? He couldn't possibly believe what you say. All he has to do is listen to TV or read the newspapers. If there is an unreasonable choice open to people, they take it; a lie they can believe instead of the truth, they believe it."

I decided I wouldn't argue it. We had been through it before. Anyway, I agreed with her more than I wanted to admit.

Sydney said, "Tell him the rest, honey."

"Daddy has a dossier on them." My face must have protested the word. "Yes, really. He read from it to the others."

"In your presence?"

"I count about as much as the piano. He expects it to tinkle now and then but he knows it doesn't think or see." Pulling shoulders up a notch.

"Walter served another round of drinks and my father told him he would not need him any more. Then he read from it."

Sydney gave her a cigarette, looked at me, raised his eyebrows as if to say, Wait until you hear this one!

"The dossier says many things that are true: for instance, that Mark went to Cornell for his medical degree and did his graduate work there in biochemistry. It mentioned his Ph.D. degree. Cited two labs he had trained in. Told of his service in the Air Force in World War II and his two years as prisoner in a Japanese camp— I didn't know about that." She looked at me for confirmation.

I nodded. "Sounds accurate, so far."

"Where was he?"

In a camp near Shanghai, I told her.

"That is what the dossier stated. This was the first time Daddy editorialized. He looked up and said, Of course Dr. Channing may have lost his loyalty there. As if it were an acknowledged fact that he had lost it! But Daddy knows it was a Japanese camp, not Communist. He deliberately tried to confuse them—"

She grinned. "Of course that's not too difficult. What they tied it up with was the Korean war, the Communist brainwashing of American prisoners; all of that. But Daddy—"

Sydney said, "Tell him, Katie, about the other things."

"Yes." She looked at him a long time, turned to me, "He's sweet, isn't he." Grinned like a bad kid, but almost at once slipped on her tight expressionless mask.

"He has found out things about Grace. She studied ballet in New York one year, and then modern dance with Martha Graham and Hanya Holm. Three years in all, the dossier says. We know that is true. But in her dance group, at one time or another, there were some Negroes. Daddy mentioned two men. He has pictures and passed them around." She almost smiled. "The silence creaked. One would look and pass the picture on to the next one, and he would look— You'd have thought they were little boys peeking at their first French post cards.

"But this is the point: Daddy did it deliberately. He knew what it would do to their fears or guilt or memories or whatever it is this sort of thing works on." She swallowed hard. "He *did that!* My father. If he had been a sleazy demagogue running for

election and had done this to his opponent, you could—"
Stopped.

"You don't know where he found the pictures, do you?" I kept my voice as easy and casual as possible.

"No. I have pictures of Grace, of course. Dancing alone—a few with her groups up in New York—some of our group here at Red Bank and with the kids at camp. I was there after Grace was counselor but Jane gave them to me. He may have seen them and it may have given him the idea, but I have none of her with the Negro dancers. What I think, Dave: he hired an investigator, detective, whoever does this sort of thing for pay. Does that sound probable?"

"Yes."

"Could this spy have slipped into their home and found the pictures?"

"It is possible."

Sydney said, "Do you mind, Katie, if I mention the point—I believe you said it was the one he stressed—that Grace's roommate in New York was a Communist."

"When was this?"

Katie said it was in 1941 or '42, she was not sure. She asked, "Is that true?"

"I don't know. She has never mentioned it to me."

"He skimmed the dossier; slowed down only to make his points. One thing he stressed was the fact that Grace went, several times, with her roommate to a meeting of a front organization. Oh yes, he told them that she was, right now, a member of the American Civil Liberties Union. This is when I goofed."

"How?"

"I laughed. I said, You'll have to find something else, Daddy, I'm afraid. The ACLU is strongly opposed to communism. What it tries to do is protect all people's civil liberties."

Same thing, Esteridge muttered.

Then her father said something light and casual about his little girl having picked up a few naive ideas while she was at Vassar. "It takes time, you know, to outgrow them."

"They gave him a big hand. I mean they laughed."

"Then you—"

"Played dead again. I had tinkled, they were annoyed. Except Ben: he winked at me. Slyly—but he winked."

"They were rude, of course."

"They are evil. But you are thinking that, in spite of it, they do many good things, aren't you?"

"Katie . . . they are trying to hold on to a world that no longer exists. They are blind and terrified because they feel it slipping away from them. They are gripping thin air but they keep trying desperately to hold on to it—hoping the air will turn into something familiar and solid. I just don't think we get anywhere by condemning them."

"They are evil. I know you think it is your duty to try to believe in the human race. You think if you trust it, it will finally come through. I don't. I think the human race is ratty. I understand perfectly that they had to choose: diminish me or diminish Daddy. The choice was easy to make. But all that isn't important."

She fumbled around for her cigarettes, remembered she was smoking one, picked it up. It had gone out. We both tried to light it for her.

"But he is right. I am naive. I keep thinking it is only illiterate people who talk the way he did—and politicians, like McCarthy was and his cronies still are and the breed we grow down here. I know it but I can't believe it. He went to Chapel Hill; to Oxford for three years; stays at the Waldorf in New York; is a patron of the Philharmonic; goes to London, Paris, Frankfurt two or three times a year—how on earth—"

We were smiling. She stared at us, then laughed. "You see! I *am* silly. But you know what I mean: the idea of a witch hunter in Brooks Brothers clothes blocks me." She stopped. Began again, "I can't see it, Dave; so I'm afraid what I've said may be untrue. I have told it as I see it but is it that I am not seeing it right? I've never tried to understand my father: the idea has seemed too terrifying. All I can put together about this is: Mark is searching for the cause of cancer; Mother died of cancer; my father is chairman of the Cancer Committee. If this is true, how can he be against Mark?"

"I don't think he is."

"You mean *personally.*"

"I mean in every way. Mark is a scientist. Your father is not opposed to science, he respects it. Mark is not political-minded; not enough, he always says. Nor does he go around smashing other people's economic idols. On those levels he is certainly no obvious threat to your father or your father's world."

"Then why this fantastic business of the dossier? Why is he witch hunting?"

I had no answer to that.

Sydney stood up. "We must go, honey." She said, "I'd leave tomorrow and camp out on the nice old Left Bank the rest of my life and forget everything, but Sydney won't go with me. And whither he stays, I stay. Is he worth it, Dave?"

We laughed. They told me good night and left.

10

I was still there—standing, thinking or beginning to think about what she had told me; knowing it was a shade distorted, too full of the feeling she had hidden so many years—when the door opened. She came in. She said softly, "I am going to Sydney's apartment for the night."

I waited.

"Shocked you?"

"Not beyond the point of recovery. You may have shocked a little tyke who rents the nursery from you." We liked each other. I felt I could say it.

"Don't analyze me!"

"I have no talent for it. Just a good guesser."

That neutral face. But this time the eyes were soft. I said, "Katie . . . are you going because you love Sydney or to punish your father?"

"Both. I'm frugal. Always looking for bargains."

"When are you going to marry him? You want to, don't you?"

"Very much, Dave. And I'd like to measure up to that marriage." Her voice was honest and gentle.

"I know you would. And he would, too. Why put it off?"

"Money."

"You don't think he is doing well enough? or he doesn't?"

"I think he is doing marvelously. It is the money Mother left me. Dad's too—although he is not leaving me much. He is setting up a foundation—a kind of shrine to Capitalism—to keep the government from spending the inheritance taxes on foreign aid and all the other socialistic things he hates. Syd has worked very hard. His people had enough—that is, his father was a small-town Ford dealer and did all right—but Syd had to borrow, finally, to get through those ten years of medical training."

"I thought he told me he had repaid it."

"He has."

"Then why not—"

"He says if he marries a rich girl there is nothing, really, he can give her. To me, that is materialism in a big way." I waited.

"I try to tell him what he means to me. The fact that we can actually talk and understand what the other is saying, at least two-thirds of the time—"

"That's a high rating."

"I know." She smiled.

She was still standing. She picked up a round glass paperweight, held it, rubbed it.

"I suppose it sounds like the first act of the same old play: I say money means nothing to me, he says that is because I've always had it; oxygen means nothing, either, until you're cut off from it. All the old lines. Then I try to tell him about Mother: how she felt about money, that it was hers only to be used for others in the world. He doesn't believe she was like that. He says, Why did she leave you half a million if she felt it belonged to the world? I don't know why. At the last, when she knew she was dying, she weakened: I suppose she was afraid something might happen—a depression might come—anyway, she left me a third of what she had. And now Syd feels he has to match it. Could you help him see?"

That was the most she had ever said to me. I told her Syd and I would have a talk.

Then she said, as if feeling her way, "Dave . . . my father is fond of you." She was looking at my Marin reproductions. She said, "I wish you had the originals. You like Marin very much, don't you?"

"Yes. But I can't afford real Marins. Anyway, I like these, I've hung around them a long time."

She smiled. "Would you let me give you two?"

"No."

"One?"

"No."

"As a special favor to me, would you? I happen to know where there are—" I was shaking my head. She didn't complete the sentence. I couldn't see quite how this had come up. Now I realize she was trying to block her father's little tipping scheme —but I couldn't see, then, and I felt annoyed with her.

I said, "You must not buy Syd any paintings, either. Let him buy them for you."

"You both value *things* too much."

"I value my relationships. Things can twist them into peculiar shapes, sometimes."

She looked at me. I couldn't read those thoughts. She said, "You give me a bleak view of myself. And I suppose you are right. When I care for people I go out and buy them a present— I don't seem to know anything else to do." Then she said, "Forget it. I came back to tell you this: Daddy is very fond of you." I didn't like the sound of it. "I think because he is, you—"

"Might influence him? If you're suggesting that, I think you are wrong."

"I'm not. He wants to influence you. When he likes anyone he must dominate him."

There wasn't much to say to that.

"What he is after is to destroy your friendship with Mark. He wants him out of your life."

Nothing to say to that, either.

"Because he thinks Mark dominates you."

"Wait a minute! I'm not aware that anyone dominates me."

"Daddy thinks all clergymen are weak; all can be dominated: by the bishop, the senior warden, the parishioners, their own ambition or greed, or a friend who has brains—"

There was a snake-coldness in the girl's face. I was infuriated. Whether with her or her father or both or only with myself, I am not sure, even today.

"He has contempt, only contempt, for those he can dominate and hatred for those he fails on. You can't win."

No answer from me. I felt she might be warning me in this nasty oblique way; or was she only trying to hurt something, anything—

"I've carried on a cold war with him since I was eight years old."

This gave me a chance to pull away from her father and me. "Why eight? Something interesting happen when you were eight?"

She smiled. "I begin at eight because that is as far back as I can remember."

"Nothing? Clean sheet of paper?"

"Blank. Not clean. It was probably such a mess my memory locked it up. But from eight, it seems to be fairly respectable. Full of Mother and Alice, my governess. Alice B. Toklas." She smiled. "One of Mother's sad little jokes. At least, she made it once or twice and I've held on to it."

Syd was in the car, waiting, but things were on her mind. I

offered her a chair. She didn't seem to hear me but she sat down. She said, "Don't worry about Syd. He likes nothing better than to sit in the dark in a car by himself. He really likes to."

She was looking at my father's old desk. Not quite as if she saw it; looking through it. "My governess was named Alice Brown. Mother added the other for fun. Mother met Gertrude Stein in Paris, years ago. She had admired her writing and her theories and she was enormously impressed when she met her. But it was Miss Toklas whom she really liked. Mother thought my governess was a wise and sensitive as well as learned woman and since she happened to look amazingly like Miss Toklas, Mother called her that. A time or two. Not much of a joke. I am not sure Mother had a real sense of humor. Mother . . . was always searching—not so much for the *avant-garde* as for the handful of people in our time who might, just might, be changing the human race by a poem, a novel, a painting, an idea, a belief, or simply by being a more complex and aware and loving, brave person than the rest of us. The germinal ones, she called them. Mother thought the human race could change, was always changing. Of course I don't. Of all of them, the one she wanted most to meet was Gandhi. She called him Gandhiji, just as his followers did."

Her tongue was rattling. The closed-up, masked Katie was talking as if she could not stop. Her mother had planned to go to India. She had written Gandhiji many times and now and then he wrote her a brief note, or his secretary did. And finally, it was arranged for her to have a talk with him. He was assassinated two weeks before she was to fly over. She postponed her trip. A month later, they found she had leukemia. "They didn't tell me. I knew she was dying but they pretended I didn't know and I pretended and the big mysterious moment came nearer and nearer and it had no name and all the time her eyes were saying, Don't look . . . pretend with me it is not here, let's pretend a day or two longer."

My irritation was gone. "How old were you, Katie?"

"Twelve. An old twelve, they say." She smiled. And once more the blankness slid over her face.

I waited. She said, "Dave . . . *something is happening,* and we can't see or hear it. I felt the same way when Mother was dying. I dreamed of her last night and the night before and the night before: We were somewhere and at the same time nowhere nobody no background no scenery or climate nothing but us, but I definitely felt we were somewhere we had been before and she was talking to me as she had done those weeks—she always talked to me but even more those last weeks—about love and pity and compassion, and opening up so that you can understand—she used that phrase. She'd say, If you are tight and small you can never understand, you have to let yourself open up and that means seeing and feeling things you've never seen or felt before in others and yourself, things you don't like but only in this way can you become a person and a free one: you'll understand what hate is only when you feel your own hate destroying you, and you'll never know love until *you* love so passionately you are willing to risk everything—"

That closed-up, tight face telling me her mother's words—

She was saying, "And now in my dream, Mother was talking, like that. But when I waked up I could not remember a word she said. But I felt it was very important for me to remember. But not a word came back. It was as if she were still near me and trying to make me hear. I know that cannot be. I know she is not near me. I know what death is—"

"Do you, Katie?"

"Annihilation. When it comes, that is the end." She looked at me, expecting me, I think, to argue with her. I had better sense, this time. I was beginning to understand that Katie climbs toward the truth by jumping from one lie to another. Says it, says what she does not believe so that she will finally have the courage to say, Maybe I don't really know, after all.

She was saying, "But I felt she was near, in that dream. And I've thought today and yesterday almost constantly about what she said to me, those last months she lived. I suppose she was trying to say enough to last me a lifetime. I understood so little of it, then. She read me the poets she loved, Valéry and Rilke and St. John Perse—and Jeffers. Of course he is not fashionable, now." She stopped. "That would have hurt her. She read and she talked about the philosophers she loved and she talked about the contemporary music she loved, Stravinsky, and the young moderns she wanted me to be sure to listen to—and she told me about places in the world she loved, and sunsets she had seen, and moonlight, and she even wrote out her favorite recipes—and all the time I was thinking of what was happening to us, what was coming closer and closer, I didn't care in the least about anything she was saying, I was watching the other—

"But I shouldn't talk about it. And yet, I feel compelled to."

"I'm glad you do."

"Dave," she had left that, "in the dream, I felt she was warning me: to be careful, to watch out—not for me, it was someone else I must watch out for. Someone whose face I could not see. Strange . . . and then, when I waked up I was thinking of Charlie. I lay there wondering why. I didn't know why. I was just thinking about him—I could see those wonderful hands of his, could hear him playing, and then I was remembering his breakdown a few years ago, and his terrible terrible agony and fear of people, his inability to trust himself to do anything but play his music, and write it. He wouldn't drive a car for so long; he wouldn't go out to see people, and his stammering which is not bad at all, only when he loses his confidence, was so awful. And then, I suddenly remembered she had said to me once, *Charlie is my good and beloved friend. I want him to be yours, too. He has a fine talent. Whether he will develop it, I don't know; his life has been hard; you may hear things when you grow up but if you do, I want you to know they are not true.* And then she told me I must do all I could to see to it that he never stopped composing. That I must help him if he ever needed it."

She turned to me. "Dave . . . what did she think I might hear? I haven't ever heard anything. Have you?"

I shook my head.

"He couldn't possibly be involved in—all this, could he?"

"Not possibly. Not remotely involved."

"Strange . . . how I felt it had something to do with him, what I dreamed. Of course, I don't believe in that sort of thing.

But it pulls you. Then I remembered something about my father. She had told me, once, that she thought I was like him in many ways—and I hadn't liked her saying it a bit. She smiled and said it again: *You are like him in many ways and because you are, the two of you may not get along too well, when you grow up. He can be difficult. But you can be, too. I want you to remember there is something very good and generous in your father. You find it. That is your job.*

She was looking down at the floor, those slender brown hands limp and passive. She looked up, "I have never found it, Dave. If she had lived she would have kept him from doing this to Mark. I can't."

"Because you don't love him?"

"I don't know." Stopped. Stared at the desk. "She wrote me letters, one for every birthday until I was twenty-one. She wanted them to help but they— I dreaded those birthdays! knowing the letter would be there: knowing I had to read it: knowing it would turn my birthday back into the day of her death. She wanted so much to live those years with me but all it did was—"

Constance. She'd managed it, though, somehow; for she was here with us, in my study, and she was pushing and nudging her daughter—whether in the right direction, I didn't know. The firm hands that reach out from the grave blindly pulling and pushing. . . .

I said, "You came because you think I can do something to help, didn't you?"

"Yes. My father has called a meeting, informally I'm sure, of the full vestry for late Sunday afternoon. At our house. I hope you will be there."

"Barge in?"

"I don't care how; just come. You can't swing Daddy—and don't try—but you can persuade the others not to listen to him. Will you?"

I told her I would be there. I'd try to have a talk with her father before the meeting, if I could; perhaps Saturday morning

—he had asked me out to the farm, perhaps we could have a little talk while there.

She said, "I must run along. There is a patient at the hospital Syd wants to look in on. I don't see why being a vestryman is important to Mark. It may not be. But it will hurt him to be pushed out this way."

"It will hurt the church more."

"I care only for what it will do to him and Grace. Night, dear." She slipped out the door.

Splintery. That is the word that came to my mind. The pieces of Katie. . . . Maybe her love for Sydney would finish the fusing, someday. A year or two ago, I had tried to talk to her as her priest: I got nowhere. She pushed it off angrily, would have none of it; saying her mind rejected the basic assumptions of the Church: she could not believe that Jesus Christ was actually God's Son, she could not think of the Cross as I spoke to her of it, or the Atonement, she could not believe in God, she did not see sacrifice as essential to the human person, she did not believe there is cosmic purpose in our being on this earth, it was sheer accident. And yet, the Sunday after storming out at me, she partook of Communion with the deepest gravity, as she had always done. Believing and not believing, accepting and rejecting; unable to find what could speak to her modern mind and just as unable to give up the ancient symbols that whisper persistently to the measureless, yearning unhistoric part of all of us.

I tried to stop thinking about her. It was more urgent now to think about her father and that dossier. Why did he care so much about Mark that he was willing to spend money and time to destroy him? Was she right? Fantastic! *Daddy is very fond of you.* The next thing, she'd be naming it, so that I'd make no mistake as to what kind of feeling the "fondness" consisted of. I laughed. Katie's sophistication can get you down, sometimes. She is, too often, that "old twelve" she smiles at.

But I couldn't laugh off the microbes Snyder had let loose by reading that incredible dossier. All I could do, right now, was hope those responsible vestrymen would be responsible enough to keep their mouths shut. Once Newell withdraws those charges —once that is done, things will clear up and the talk will stop. I didn't actually believe that. As usual, I was fighting my fears with an overdose of optimism.

Neel. Now and then, throughout the day, I had thought about him. Strange . . . you start on one thing, then you're on another. Hattie Belle: he couldn't get her off his mind or out of his heart. Trying to force her out with hate—as if you could. But he doesn't hate her, no; he is just ashamed that something in him still clings to something in her.

When I left him this morning, I had felt our plan would work, Claud Newell would almost certainly be amenable to our arguments. I had thought, I'll call Mark during the day and tell him what we are up to. But I didn't. I couldn't forget Neel's face long enough. Perhaps he had said too much about Hattie Belle—this sort of thing leaves you washed out, afterward. I wasn't sure. I had the feeling Neel believed the situation had slipped beyond our grasp. I decided not to call Mark. Maybe tomorrow.

This dossier. . . .

I went upstairs and to bed. Katie's dreams—back with me again. She had kept thinking about Charlie. So she had never heard anything. Good. Not even about his attempted suicide. That was good, too. She didn't need to know.

What I knew came from Charlie and when you're talking to a man who has tried to kill himself twenty minutes before, you're not likely to get it too straight. I had stayed with him all night, for he was pretty confused for a while, memories sloshing over him as if he were drowning in them. But gradually he quieted down. Left his early memories and came closer, I think, to the big thing that bothered him most. I may be wrong here: there may have been a dozen big things I don't know which the psychiatrist may know and certainly if he does, can evaluate more expertly than I. But what Charlie finally told me was this:

There had been an accident: a cliff somewhere not too far

from High Falls: a child had fallen and been killed. Charlie was sixteen, seventeen, maybe. The oldest in the group. In a sense, he was in charge. The boys were staying with their families at one of the summer hotels and he had taken six of them on a hike and while exploring a great mountain of a cliff one of them had gone too near the edge. Charlie blamed himself for this, for everything. Said he should have been more explicit in his warnings, should have set up some rules for them. Anyway, the youngster fell and by miraculous chance caught on a narrow ledge twenty feet below, rolled half over and stopped himself when part of his body was on the edge of it by grasping a small azalea bush growing in a crevice of the ledge. Below that azalea lay a sheer two-hundred-foot drop. Charlie called to him to hold on, he was coming, just hold on to that bush. Then he sent the rest of them back to the village and farmhouses for help. He shouted to the boy to pull himself back a little. The boy said he couldn't. Charlie saw the crumpled leg, broken, he decided, so he told him to hang on, he was coming. Then he looked at that narrow ledge twenty feet down; looked at the awful drop below it; looked at those slick moss-covered rounded boulders; finally saw between two of them not a path but a thin split, wide enough for his body if he handled himself sidewise, that seemed to extend down to the ledge. He couldn't see down, the split had a sharp twist in it, he assumed it went to the ledge. He slid in, easing his body this way, that, through the fissure, bracing himself against first one boulder then the other, feeling for something solid to get a toe hold on, shifting, easing, bracing. Then abruptly, the split widened and there was nothing under his feet. Directly below him, about eight feet below, was the ledge. He couldn't hang on to the boulders, bracing his body against one then the other as he had been doing, for they were too wide apart; he couldn't choose one and cling to it for there was no toe hold or handhold on either of those rounded slick rocks. He couldn't slide down the rock, there'd be no way to brake himself, he wouldn't be able to control the speed of the slide. He had no choice but to drop to that ledge below, or go back. He looked down, he saw the boy, yes; he said he'd always see him, but he saw that two-hundred-foot precipice too, and he panicked. All he had to do was let go and drop eight feet to that ledge, relax, and drop easy and be sure he used his ankles to pull his weight around, just a little. You might as well tell somebody all he has to do to handle a jet plane is this and this and this. If you've disciplined your body all your life, bone against muscle and tendon against bone, made it do your way in water and air and on slippery terrain, if you've taught it about weight and checks and counterchecks, all right. But Charlie hadn't. His hands could do miracles with a keyboard, but he just didn't have that kind of body. He kept saying to me, *The ledge was only about two feet wide but that was no excuse. I couldn't do it and I knew it. I just couldn't do it.* And then, for a while, I couldn't follow his words because of his sobs and his stammering. Well, anyway: there he was. And all the time, the kid's body was hanging half over the ledge just below him, out of balance, too much of him hanging in space, and he was hurt and couldn't pull himself back, too much weight was on that hand clutching the azalea, and finally the kid called softly, almost like a sigh, *I'm gone . . .* and the body slowly rolled over the edge and disappeared while Charlie watched it.

When help came, he told the truth about what had happened. A local boy said before he had finished, Get out of my way! and Charlie pulled up again just as he had pulled down. Then the local boy slid edgewise between those boulders, as if on glass, got quickly to the spot where the split widened, looked down and then dropped as easy as a cat to the ledge; lay down on his belly and grasping that azalea hung over, far out, trying to spot the body two hundred feet below. He couldn't see it. When he came back nobody said anything: all of them just looked at Charlie. They had been born in those mountains, their eyes and muscles and inner ear were as used to the sheer drops, the precipitous slick moss-covered sharp jutting cliffs as city kids are used to traffic-jammed streets. They didn't say a word, they just looked it. When Charlie got back to the hotel nobody said a word of criticism, he told me, they just looked it. In the village, people would say when they saw him, Yeah, he's the one, and then they looked it. This is what he thought they said: *He's the one.*

There were many Windsor Hills people on vacation up there and the dead boy was known to all of them.

All this, Charlie told me in choked stammering words that night four years ago when he tried finally to use the 38 and stop those looks. "And then, when I loaded it, I couldn't even pull the trigger. I am afraid to live and afraid to die." I emptied the gun and slipped it in my pocket. The accident had happened years ago. Gradually, slowly, not all at once, Charlie's whole life had got caught in that thin crevasse between slick rounded boulders and everything finally, except his music, came to the place where he had to let go and drop—and Charlie couldn't do it.

He was much better, now. But it had shaped him—not only his feelings and mind and acts but his body: he walked cautiously, he almost minced, and I've seen men raise their eyebrows and smile a sliding sort of smile as he passed and I knew what they were thinking. Oh sure.

It was about three years ago, I think, when I suggested the boy choir to him. I thought a good choir would be fine for All Saints, and Charlie—and the whole city. Of course he was afraid of it. He said, "Y-y-y-y-you'd t-t-trust me . . . with them?"

"Anywhere, under any condition. Grace and Mark want you to try Andy out if you decide to do it." He looked at me a full ten minutes. Then he smiled that gentle sad smile which he turns on people and dogs and the ideas he likes. He didn't say a word. A year passed before he finally felt up to it. All had gone well. A few months later, at Neel's suggestion, we had added ten youngsters from the Flats who had unusual voices and nothing else much. About the time he took on the choir he started his opera, *The Coward*.

I wished Constance had stayed out of it. What Katie had told me and all I remembered left me restless and wakeful.

I picked up Heidegger's *Existence and Being* knowing it would either get my mind off of this or put me to sleep in about five minutes. The latter, probably, for I must say Heidegger can write the most involved opaque sentences I have ever plowed through.

Sometime in the night, I found myself awake. Thinking not about Mark and Grace or Charlie or Dewey Snyder or Susan Newell or any of the rest of it, but about my sister Meg:

I was fourteen and she was sixteen. We were on the tennis court. Mother, as usual, was coaching us. We had gone out to play, just to play and have fun; but Mother came out, too, and turned it into a hard hour of coaching: Watch that drive, Dave, your balance is not good; Meg, lift it from the shoulder, no, lower down, lift now with your hip muscles—sure you can, Margaret, watch Dave—Dave, show her your footwork—show her how you smash it—lob it, Dave, easy now, relax and follow through easy easy—Margaret, show him your wrist work, show him— Margaret, put it on the line six inches from the alley—and Margaret's sudden *I don't want to, Ma! we're just playing, we want to play a little*—

And then Dad drove up, got out of the car, walked past the tennis court, with his brief case, glanced at me, at Meg, quizzically; we both saw the look; and then Mother followed him inside. And suddenly the court was a battleground: we began driving those balls at each other, at each other's body; I aimed for her breasts and she aimed for my genitals and we both aimed to hurt, kill, maybe—if we could; and the fury rose in us, and a terrible resentment, and we made each other the object of it, there was nothing but hate in her eyes and nothing but hate in my mind, and my muscles and footwork were perfect and so were hers, so was our skill in dodging, until, suddenly, she lobbed a deceptively soft one and almost got me, and I aimed two at the backline and she relaxed, then suddenly I drove one straight at her left breast, she ducked, it hit her shoulder and hurt, I saw the agony and I was glad glad! And then Mother was there again calling out to me, Stop it, Dave! And I stopped, breathing hard, thinking she would scold us both, thinking she might say a great deal. But all she said was, Your footwork is abominable. And Meg laughed and I laughed and we kept on laughing, almost yelling, and suddenly we were friends and it was Mother who was the enemy—

Meg . . . what a sister to have! always competing with you and winning more than her share. She is still a superb tennis player. Cool, quick, sure; placing those balls within half an inch of where she intends them to go. Thinking of life as if it were a tennis court—all so simple to Meg; politics so simple to Meg; she always knows why she's a Democrat and is curt and impatient when I say, sometimes, I wonder why I am; liberal, yes; but when she tells you why she is, you almost decide to try to understand the conservative point of view better; just as sure of her theology, impatient with my doubts, my fumbling, my questioning. "If you're not sure, get out of the Church, Dave. You'd be good at half a dozen other things." Then she begins to tell me what I'd be good at—as if she were a vocational guidance counselor. And suddenly, we are at each other's throats again and she finally ends it by saying, *Oh, these men, these men; the women are the realists of the world, they are the ones who know the grubby facts.* So it goes: I am as opposed to segregation as Meg is and I think I have better and deeper reasons than hers for being opposed to it, but when she gets started on segregation and integration,I find myself answering her as if I were a cautious, vague Moderate. She can twist you and turn you until you are defending all you are opposed to, and although I think I know her well, I don't know why she can do this to me. She married a few years ago and has three children. Her husband is a man about Dad's size, and Dad was small; a quiet fellow, who makes a lot of money but doesn't say much; doesn't, as far as I know, think much except about financial affairs and sports. But when Meg gets going, when she says, *Now isn't that just like a man!* Ed chuckles, looks at her, looks at me, and chuckles. It makes you wonder about them—you feel Meg has met her match in Ed but you wonder how, and you begin to think about things that are no business of yours to be thinking about if you are somebody's brother.

I turned over, trying to get some sleep. Yeah . . . sure . . . Meg would know exactly what to do about all this. . . . She'd have the answer . . . she'd place it . . . right on the line . . . but where? what line?

11

On Friday evening I thought again, Why not tell them about my talk with Neel and the Chief. It is not settled but—go ahead and tell them.

I had seen Grace at the shopping center late in the afternoon, coming out of Walgreen's. I was in my car. I called out to her but she was too preoccupied to hear. She looked wan and unrelated —as if she had been torn out of a book and picked up by a wind— It bothered me. I wished I had not thought it. As I drove on past Town and Country Clothes, past Nella's Beauty Shop, past Toni's old store, I could not shake off the sense of her isolation. Somehow, I had not realized it: she puts up such a good front when she is with you. *Front* is the wrong word. Grace hides herself, yes; but not behind a façade. She hides herself behind you. It is difficult to define what I mean. I am not sure I can. She seems to possess to an extraordinary degree sensitive antennae which instantly pick up whatever message your personality is sending out and she responds by adjusting with fabulous ease to your mood, your rhythm, your interests. There is nothing passive or neutral about her: you feel her, all right. But you don't go to her—if you did you might not reach your destination. She comes to you. And the closer she comes to you the farther away the real Grace seems to be. She slips through words because the part of her that *is,* she keeps aloof; the part of her that *becomes you* is all you are aware of; so you fall into the habit of taking for granted that what you see in Grace—which is usually a most charitable reflection of yourself (or of Mark for they were together so much of the time)—is all there is of her.

The realization came to me as a genuine shock that she might be having a difficult time of it on her own personal terms; that she might possibly be experiencing something which Mark knew nothing about and had not given a thought to.

As I drove away from the shopping center and down Arlington, toward the lake—I was taking a Graham Greene suspense novel to a retired school teacher who is kept in by an invalid brother—I tried to pick up a few pieces of the real Grace, attempting to see her as if the rest of us did not exist. An impossible try, of course; but I did catch on to the fact that here, there, she was not looking at this trouble in the same way Mark was or using the same defenses.

I delivered the novel, then went to Charlie's apartment for dinner. While he was doing the steaks he talked about the third act of *The Coward*. He had made headway, he said; it was becoming a real thing after two years of too much talk about it. "It's Katie," he said. "She's made it seem possible. I don't know how. She is hard to please; and she won't let me talk to her. She says, Let me hear it." He laughed. "So—I write something for her to hear."

Two fine steaks were on the table. He was carefully placing braised mushrooms on the plates. "Do you think she'll marry Sydney?"

I told him I thought so. We settled down to the steaks. After dinner, he played the beginning of the third act for me. Stopped. Said, "That's it. I can't move it on from here." It seemed the music was not the problem. It was the book. "I can't see the resolution of the coward's fears. I'm blocked on it." He talked about his feeling that he had slipped away from the essential truth of the opera.

"Psychologically?"

"In every way. Musically, too. I don't know how to separate one kind of truth from another."

But he looked confident and his voice sounded confident. I

had never seen him in a better mood. And so I left early; partly, because this time Charlie didn't need my encouragement; partly, because I had a sermon to finish.

Once back in my study, I found myself thinking of Grace. Why not tell them? It may not work out but the Chief and Neel think it will; if it does, if Newell withdraws the charges, things are bound to ease for them; whatever the outcome, it is a spot of good news and they can sure use a little.

I turned to dial their number. As I did so, the phone rang. Mark. Could he and Grace come over? I said yes, of course.

He came alone. Grace, he said, would be along presently. She was finishing up a few things— His voice trailed off. He was looking at me as if formulating a difficult sentence but seemed unable to find the first word. Just stood there.

"Sit down."

He walked across the study, looked at the Marin print on the west wall. "Always liked it," he said, as if he had been away a long time.

"Coffee?"

"No, believe not."

He turned away from the Marin, walked over to the fish photograph, looked at it a long time. Said, "Be fine to spend a week on the Gulf—right in the middle of it."

"Do you good." Waiting. "Like to go along with you." Waiting.

He turned toward me, took out his cigarettes, shook one up. "Dave—"

I saw he couldn't make it. I said, "Has something happened?"

"It's about Andy." He pulled out the cigarette, forgot to light it. I had the feeling, again, there was something else he had tried to say first, that he felt he must say.

He said, "Some fool has written him a letter."

"About all this?"

He nodded. I waited.

He was caught again in thick gluey wordlessness. I tried to throw him a sentence to catch hold of. "We should have expected something of the kind, don't you think?"

"I guess so."

"Anonymous?"

He nodded.

No more.

"It shook him of course. Have you talked with him?"

"Yes. We both did."

"How did he seem?"

"I'm not sure."

I saw it had hit him hard. I'd leave him alone for a few minutes. Struck a match for his cigarette; then went out in the hall,
opened the door, looked across the street, saw their living-room
light on, thought, She's having a rough time, too. I knew she was
sitting there thinking what to do next. Or perhaps she had
stopped thinking. I saw again that isolated face in front of
Walgreen's. A face like that stops thinking. What I wanted to do
was go over and talk to her; I felt she needed someone to talk to
more than he did, maybe. But of course I couldn't, so I went
back into the study, turned on the electric unit, thinking, We'll
have some coffee when she comes. Diddled around with cups and
saucers, fixed a tray, turned off the stove, came back to my chair.
He looked better.

He said more easily now, "Seems Andy wouldn't tell what
was in it." Smiled briefly.

Said, "Eliot somehow found out it was anonymous."

As he finally told it, it added up to this:

The headmaster had called them around nine o'clock. He was
relaxed, easy, shielding but said Andy seemed unduly depressed;
he believed he was disturbed about a letter he received in the
mail that morning. Andy's housemaster, Eliot, had talked with
him a long time, had found out the letter was not signed but
Andy seemed unwilling to disclose its contents. Eliot was now at
the headmaster's. They had been discussing the matter. Mark
asked if they knew where the letter was from. The headmaster
said, Yes, Andy had told Eliot it was postmarked in his home
town. The school nurse had seen Andy, he was not sick, she
thought, but seemed tense and shaken. She suggested he stay in
the infirmary but he did not want to, so Eliot had suggested that
he stay with him. Andy was in Eliot's rooms now. The headmaster

thought it was not too serious but the boy was disturbed more, perhaps, than he should be; if they could reassure him etc. . . . telephone him—or better still, perhaps one of them could come up?

They knew, of course, that he would not have suggested a trip to New England unless he felt the boy was in real difficulty. Mark phoned Andy at once, before Eliot had returned to the house. Could get nothing much but yes and no out of him.

"Kin to you."

Mark half smiled. "Afraid so." He had tried to explain about anonymous letters: he said quite a few people receive them these days; you can't take them seriously, they're written by crazy people or cowards and are usually insulting and full of lies.

"But no matter who writes it," Mark said to me, "you take it seriously when you are thirteen—if someone says what I think was said."

"You couldn't come straight to the point and ask him."

"How could I?"

"I was stating a fact. It would have pushed him too hard. You can't win against a thing like that."

"I kept trying. Told him one of us would fly up in the morning; that we had received a few letters, too, probably like his; full of dirty words and accusations."

Andy said, "Why, Daddy?"

And Mark had to say he didn't know. He said he probably had an enemy. Then he felt compelled to add that whoever the enemy was, of course he was not actually dangerous—just the silly crackpot variety. Then Andy asked why do we have an enemy and Mark had trouble with that one but said there were quite a few people who misunderstood research. Some people didn't approve of the use of animals in lab experiments; felt it was wrong to deliberately inject cancerous tissue into mice and rabbits. They don't seem to understand, he told Andy, the importance for human beings of studying the growth of the disease. Did he perhaps remember the letters in the press last summer when the shipment of monkeys arrived? Andy said he did. "You remember how angry and critical some of those letters were?" Andy said yes sir. "Perhaps it is one of these people doing this."

Andy did not say anything. Mark asked him if he was still on the line, he said he was, and Mark said, "You're not worrying too much, are you, son?"

"I guess not," said Andy.

Then Grace, listening in on the extension, told him she was coming up on the morning plane. She was terribly sorry about the silly letter but it would be wonderful to see him so soon. Then she said it, too: "Lots of people, darling, get anonymous letters. They just do. Remember whatever is in yours is a lie. Only a sick, mixed-up person would write one. You understand that, don't you dear?"

And Andy said, "Yes mam."

As I try to write this down, try to recover their words or the gist of them, I keep thinking about the fragmented quality of human awareness: You take your blindness for granted most of the time then suddenly it stuns you: how little you see as you plunge ahead from minute to minute, day to day, year to year— vision cut down to the arc of a flickering flashlight, never sure how your words and acts are affecting someone else because you never really see that someone as he is. I know we should find even the most serene life unendurable were we to possess to any real degree those extrasensory perceptions that bridge space which our grandmothers believed in and scientists are now studying and claiming a few people possess. And yet— Well, here they were: and there, a thousand miles away, was Andy: the three of them trying to cross the blankness, unable to perceive what was happening to the others. Had Mark and Grace been able to see that newspaper clipping pasted on a piece of paper which Andy pulled out of a pink envelope—but of course they couldn't see. And he could not tell them because it stated baldly the fact of his father's arrest on November 5th, on the charge of making immoral advances to a small girl, and his release on bond. Andy could not have repeated those words. And, perhaps, had they known, they could not have done much better than they did.

Anyway—Grace plunged on through the dark, saying, "Try not to worry, dear. It is just a silly letter written by somebody who is sick and upset. Whatever is in it is a lie. I'll explain it when I see you. And Daddy will write you."

Andy's whispered words, "Don't come, Mummie," overlapped hers as she was saying he and Eliot perhaps could drive in to Boston to meet her, they would let Eliot know when the plane was due—perhaps there might be a show they could go to—

"Yes Mummie," and sobbed and hung up. They both had heard the whisper and the muffled sob.

Well, there wasn't much to say. This disease of anonymity sweeping across our times—this symptom of sharp angry rejection of personal responsibility is too vast, too complex and hideous in its implications for easy words, even had we been thinking about it in generalized terms. But of course we were not thinking in those terms at all; we were staring at a handful of obscene specifics and neither of us knew what to do about them.

After a long silence I said, "I suppose you have felt it was better to keep the entire thing from him?"

"Not better. The only thing we knew to do. We've worried but we didn't see how we could do anything else. I kept believing it would blow over; that we'd get it settled somehow; I guess I was wrong but I believed it. I never lied to the boy in my life, until tonight. He knew I was lying. The whole affair is incredible. I can't be sure it is happening."

I knew he meant it. He had never quite believed it. Not quite. A sliver of his mind knew; knew he had been accused and arrested but the rest of him had not quite acknowledged it. There was in Mark, as I had said that night to Katie and Syd, a deep rejection of the irrational in human affairs. The laboratory was the world he felt secure in, where facts are collected, scrutinized, tested and retested in relation to other facts, where reason and order and method prevail, where hypotheses are put into strait jackets and not allowed out in the street until they are labeled "true." That many people live in a world where they don't bother to check anything and where they ride their hypotheses as if they were hot rods—this world, Mark could not fully admit the existence of.

He said, "We'd planned to tell him at Christmas, when we met him at his grandmother's in Baltimore. We had decided it wouldn't do to let him come home."

He sat there rubbing the side of his face, staring at the floor. I wondered what was keeping Grace. Then I had the feeling again: he intended to tell me something else, first, and had been unable to. I was about to say, Grace upset much? when he looked up, said quietly, "Someone has to hate you a lot to send a boy a letter like that."

"Do you know anyone who does?"

"No."

"They hate something, of course; not necessarily you."

He sighed. Did not answer.

I thought, They think you've broken a taboo: that you've dared do what they have only dared imagine. It makes you radioactive. Every time they hear your name the Geiger counters start ticking. Naturally, they want to hurt you in the worst possible way.

I tried it this way:

"Somebody thinks you raped a little girl and he wants you punished, right now. If you're not, his controls may break down, too. He can't wait for you to be tried by the courts, so he becomes judge and jury both, tries you himself and punishes you by raping the mind of your little son. And he feels he's helping the whole community by doing it—and in a crazy upside-down way, it makes sense: he's kept himself from committing one sin by committing a worse one."

He was staring at the floor. I was not sure he heard a word I said.

"I know I've made it sound pretty simple. But the man who wrote that letter doesn't necessarily have to feel a personal grudge against you. You are a symbol of all he dreads in himself."

He was still staring at the floor.

"When you become a symbol to people you're in for bad trouble."

He almost smiled. "I see it theoretically. I just can't get a grip on it."

We sat smoking. Looking at each other, now and then. Not talking.

He said, "We've always got along fine. The boy and me. You know how we've been."

Yes, I knew. They'd fished and hunted together, camped in the Smokies, just the two of them, for a week at a time. He met Andy last summer at the close of his camp and they took a four-day canoe trip down the French Broad. They'd go up to their cabin near Jane's, on Saturdays, and mess around having a swell time: Mark helping Andy find quartz, all kinds of rocks; or the two of them squirrel shooting, or taking pictures, or talking about excavations they'd go on some day in Mexico and Egypt. Everybody knew how they were.

"I had to lie to him, but I've got to set it straight. I think this is between him and me. Grace doesn't. She says she is the one to go. She's packing her bags now."

So that is why she is delayed.

"She insists she is the one to do it. It isn't like her."

"No . . . but I think she's right."

"Why?"

I didn't find it easy to remind him there were questions Andy needed to have answered that he'd feel he could ask her when he couldn't ask his father.

"All his life, we've taught him when he has something to clear up to go straight to the one concerned and do it. If I let Grace do this—this thing I should do— I know I'm no good talking about personal things but we wouldn't have to say much. We have our own way. Good God, Dave, this is almost more than—" He swallowed the rest of it.

I knew it was hard on him. But I felt she had to do it. A man can't defend himself to his young son. I was thinking how mercifully she'd do it, for them both. There were things she needed to tell the boy about little girls, the way they are warned against men, how it gets on their minds, etc., their feelings about their bodies; the kind of woman Renie is, her obsessive fear, or whatever it is, of raping. Mark could never say this, even if he tried. And I didn't think he'd try.

"She'll say it in such simple words, Mark. You know how she is."

"I know she can talk to him better—"

"The big thing is he'll feel how absolutely sure she is of you."

"I don't think she is."

"How can you say that!"

"Not since—" Grace was tapping on the door, was coming in. As she walked in, I got a swift preview of what she will look like when she is seventy years old. Then it was gone. She looked merely tired and pale but not as unrelated as she had that afternoon. She was tied up again with these two.

"Dave?" She smiled, she was under control.

I'd try to keep it easy, casual.

"Sit down, dear. We're getting our ducks in a row." I asked Mark if he had called the local airport.

"Yes. No good connection from here. We can save time by picking up Eastern Air Lines. Their first plane is at seven in the morning. I made a reservation."

"Good. Let's figure a bit. How about letting me take Grace to the airport?" It was a hundred-mile drive. We should leave close to three-thirty, I thought.

We made plans. And as we made them, I watched her face and she watched his. And I saw how much she loved him, it was so plain. His sudden doubt of her worried me. It was to be expected, perhaps: you are accused of a crime that is completely outside the field of your conscious temptations; you cannot conceive of yourself committing it; but other people can. Quite easily, apparently. Strangers, of course, who don't know you. You begin to receive anonymous phone calls and letters. Then you slowly begin to realize that people who know you suspect you, too. Then incredible things happen: you find you are unfit to appear on a TV program; your professional prestige is stripped from you by one small humiliating incident after another; finally you feel that only a handful of people in all the world still believe in you and then you are struck again, this time where it is unendurable, because it concerns the son you love, and you turn and begin to fight back by doubting the ones closest to you, those who have stood firmly with you; you tear them away from you as if you cannot bear their belief in you, as if you must now stand alone and abandoned in your agony. It is not only true, I think, that in our agony we feel alone, something in us wants to feel alone. As I watched his face I could believe this might be happening to him: that letter to Andy had gone deep.

He said, about here, that he wanted to take her to the airport —and she wanted him to, I could see that.

I said it seemed to me it might be a good idea for him to go to the lab, as usual. Just in case he was being watched. I mentioned the janitor. Said I had a feeling he wrote that letter. Mark didn't think so and didn't like my saying it, I felt. Mark trusts the people in his lab; it is not easy for him to believe anyone who works there even on the periphery, even a janitor, would do an irrational thing like this. Anyway, he couldn't see what difference it would make now; then he said again that S. K. couldn't have done it because he couldn't have got Andy's address. I said maybe Mark's secretary gave it to him. Mark said she wouldn't. I said she might think he wanted to send his boss's son a Thanksgiving card, it would be natural for her to give it to anyone who called up if the request were made in a reasonable way. We pushed our suspicions and certainties back and forth, jabbing them into each other. We got pretty tense over it. I began to feel, Maybe he thinks you just want to take her—you do, don't you? sure I do; but not that way; sure I want to see if she is all right but—

I asked him about his bond: would he be permitted to leave town? He thought so; I said I didn't know; why not call Steve? But nobody did, somehow. Everybody was too tired to think straight; we jangled each other quite a bit; but we finally agreed it must not leak out about the letter. It might be better, therefore, for me to take Grace and for Mark to go to the lab at his usual time. We'd leave at three-thirty; this would give us a good enough margin; I'd get back about eleven, in plenty of time for the funeral of one of my parishioners at twelve.

Then Mark asked me if I happened to have any money. He smiled in his old way. "—because we have between us exactly seventeen dollars and sixty-five cents."

I had about nine dollars. That wouldn't help much. Then I remembered the church money I had not deposited. I unlocked a desk drawer, took out my security box, gave him the money, one hundred and fourteen dollars, and Mark wrote a check to cover it. I noticed the check was drawn on his savings account. They were running thin, obviously: payments on the house, the boy in school— It was like a ghost story—one they were being compelled to live out against their will, their strings pulled by invisible hands, as if they were puppets. This raced through my mind in a split second. I turned back, said, "But this won't do it. Not a round trip." Grace could cash a check at the school, he reminded me. "It is OK, Dave, and thanks a lot."

They were standing now. I told them I'd phone the airport, when my alarm went off, to hold Grace's space, we were on our way, etc. Mark said he'd do it; I said, good. I thought they were ready to go. Grace was looking at him and he was looking at her. They were talking a swift silent agonized language. It seemed interminable, that dialogue. Finally, Mark pressed his cigarette against the ash tray, dropped it in, picked it up, looked at it, said,

"Dave—guess I'd better tell you: I was in the store that afternoon."

12

I felt my mind spin out to a point . . . *but you didn't harm the child did you?*

What I actually said was, "Think we'd better have some coffee." I clicked the switch.

They stared at me as I walked over to the hi-fi, put on the first record I touched. It happened to be the *Brandenburg Fifth.* I'll never forget the awful shock of that joyous confident blast of piano and violin as the thing begins. Grace did not seem to hear a sound. Felt for the hassock as if she were blind, sank down on it. Mark took out a cigarette, did not light it. Stood there. We were three flat faces. There was nothing warm between us, we had recoiled from each other. I remember how that word *store* kept pounding me—

Finally, I had sense enough to turn off the record.

Then I said it: "All right. You were in the store. But you didn't harm the child."

Mark swallowed hard, lit his cigarette. Just stared at me. Finally shook his head.

"Then spread it out, won't you? Why you went? Let's get it down where we can look at it." As I turned, I saw Grace's dead-white face. "Or can it wait?"

"Let him tell you, Dave."

Mark began:

"I went in—" Stopped. Walked around the room. He looked crowded—a lot of things were pushing—

"Mind if I take it from the beginning? I was on my way for the Cokes; had no thought except to get them quick as I could and come back. I cut through the park and pulled up in front of that old store. Saw they were remodeling the place—and went in."

"Wait. You walked? you didn't go in your car?"

"No. Thought the walk would do me good. Takes only four or five minutes. My intention was to buy the Cokes and get home as quick as I could. I'm sure of this. I had no other thought but this. But I detoured and went in that store. I don't know why."

He stopped. Looked at her, at me. "I've thought a hundred times: a machine set to buy those Cokes would have taken the shortest route to Matthews, bought them, turned round, gone home, deposited them on Grace's kitchen table. Why didn't I? I don't know. Guess automation's brain and mine just— I was set to get the Cokes all right, but I must have been thinking about other things, too. Don't mean consciously, I mean—"

It got me. "You don't have to tell us why you went in the store. Anybody might have stepped in and looked around."

"I want you to know—if I know, myself. Not sure I do. Must have been—"

"Dave, have you some Scotch?" She was shaking.

I poured a drink for her. "Why don't you go home and rest a little?" She whispered no.

"I'm sorry, Mark." She smiled at him. His face and body had stiffened as if—well, I had the absolutely crazy notion he expected his plane to crack up any moment. I realized what he was doing now was a near unbearable ordeal.

I asked him if he'd have a drink.

He seemed not to hear. "I'm not talking about the unconscious part of the memory," he was saying. "I'm talking about the easy-to-get-at part. Think I went in that place, think I went because it smelled like Dad's construction work used to." He picked up his cigarette. Gone out. Dropped it.

"But I wasn't thinking about Dad. And I didn't smell a thing before I opened that door. Unless the paint, maybe. Not sure

. . . let's leave it. What made me stop, turn the latch and go in —let's leave it."

You could see he had retraced his steps a thousand times during these weeks.

"Say my muscles pulled me in. Dad was a building contractor. Down in Georgia. Lowndes County was where I was born. Don't know if I've ever told you about Dad."

He stopped as if expecting an answer. "No. Don't think you ever did," I said.

"We were living there when my mother died. There were ponds and lakes everywhere, surrounded by big oaks hanging in moss; there were cypress in the water, thousands of them, with big swollen knees. Some of the oaks were dead—and some of the cypress were dead; they were like old gray skeletons with long beards of moss. Water was reddish brown. I remembered all that while I was in the store. Don't know why. Dad used to take me around with him on jobs, after she died. I'd watch them mix concrete . . . stand there half a day, watching . . . liked the clatter and that thick stuff pouring out of those jaws. I'd make up stories about it: it was a giant who chewed up rocks and people; chewed up things that happened—and then they had not happened. Must have been about seven when I thought that one up; remember I felt good, afterward, like I'd been in swimming. Used to ride the big shovel, too, when Dad had a road job. Sounds pretty dangerous for a kid—guess I wanted to and now think I did; don't know. Can't seem to remember much. He died when I was nine. Then I went to Ohio to live with my grandparents. Dad's people."

Mark stopped. Looked hard at Grace. Her mouth had opened, a little; her eyes were looking through him at something else: maybe Andy, maybe the store, maybe she saw a little boy she'd never heard of before, maybe he saw a little boy he'd never quite seen before; I don't know. I took the glass out of her fingers. She asked for another drink. I gave it to her.

He was talking again:

"I went in. Wait—the door was closed. I went in and shut it after me. I'm sure I shut it. I'm sure the place was empty. It was half-dark and not a sound. I looked around. They had torn out the floor to repair the foundation; termites probably. I saw they had been planing boards. There were pine curls all over the ground. I picked up two or three. Smelled good. Stood there pulling one out, letting it snap back into a curl. Suddenly—I heard him saying, *You want to be a silly girl? why are you doing that!* Grace—" he turned to her as if I were not present, "can you believe me? It was like a dream—strong and awful like a dream—I must have been about five, maybe: I was in a building he was constructing, the carpenters were planing pine boards and I picked up some curls of wood, a bunch of them, and stuck them under my cap. I thought it made me look like a clown. I was capering around trying to think of something comical to do when he turned on me and said, *Take those damned things out of your cap.* His eyes were cold and looked as if they could forget and leave me behind. I was scared all right. Funny how scared a kid can get. I remember the carpenters laughing. It seemed to me everything stopped dead. There was a moment when nothing in the world was happening. And then they laughed. Terrible sound. I don't know . . . maybe I thought that later, after I was grown. Well, it came back. All this. Hadn't thought about it in years. Somehow it bothered me. Think I may have stood a minute or so—sort of—

"Then I saw a row of paint cans—on a board laid on two nail kegs. Wall paint, Textron or something. Went over and read the colors: *sea gray, foam green,* things like that . . . one of them was labeled *shell blue.* Remember thinking: ought to be *shell pink,* shouldn't it? Thought of a sailboat I used to own—well, hardly that; a boat with a sail, I should say; couldn't remember what became of it. Used to sail down the creek in Ohio—another boy and me—we'd make like we were going to the Gulf of Mexico and on to Tahiti. Had a second-hand outboard motor. We'd take a can or so of baked beans and a bottle of catsup and blankets and camp out overnight. Remember the tree frogs. Other things. A cow—there was a cow walking around as we lay there on the grass one night—remember she—oh well; and Bill died laughing and it didn't seem funny to me—tried to laugh but it didn't seem funny—just seemed a lot of it—remember looking at the sky and wondering why he laughed—remember the Big Dipper was bright that night, remember I thought, I'm going to fly an airplane someday, going to fly all around the world and to the moon maybe. And I lay there dipping the wings, nose-diving, climbing, banking, doing everything I'd seen in movies, while all outer space watched me—I sort of thought it was watching."

He stopped. Caught in it, again. Grace's eyes were full of tears; she had not moved; just looked at him.

He went on, "Could remember everything but what became of my boat; whether I sold it or what. Kept working on it, as if it were a problem I must solve. Strange, how you can forget a thing, seems like I would—"

He walked across the room, turned, walked back.

"Then I pried the lid off that paint can. Sure enough, stuff was blue. Looked like it might taste good. Put the lid on. Remember pressing it down hard—air's not good for paint. Then I sat down on a stack of lumber. Was smoking. Remember telling myself, *be careful with that cigarette.*

"Just sat there. In that half-dark place. Can't see why Grace or anybody would believe it."

I saw he had to tell every detail. He had been sealed up so long: it was all or nothing, now.

He looked at her, at me. "I'd been in the lab pretty much, lately. Good many evenings. It was so near done, this phase, I didn't want anything to go wrong. Must admit you had worried me about S. K.—when was it? last summer? when you first mentioned him?"

I had forgot that. I think I merely said, There's something about your janitor that bothers me; he seems afraid he'll catch cancer. What the man had said to me was, "Better wash your hands when you leave this place, Mr. Landrum."

Mark smiled. "Oh, not much but—one day I saw him tilting the museum jars that contain the breast tumors. Rocking them back and forth. Queer look in his face. May have imagined it but— Anyway, I spoke to him pretty sharp. Told him never to touch them; he said he was just looking; told him to keep his hands off. He muttered, walked out. Saw him another time looking at the mice. We had planted tissue in five, that day. Covered the implantations with Algire chambers—you put a fold between plastic plates. I think you've seen them out there. I caught S. K. opening the door of a cage, a few inches. I told him not to handle the mice. He seemed to resent it. Oh, I don't think there's any harm in him. Only thing that bothers me, it seems to hold a peculiar fascination for him. But I've made a point of coming in now and then at night when he's cleaning, just to be sure.

"But that Monday—I came home early. I wanted to think about something else. I remember that. I was suddenly tired of the lab, I wanted to forget it. That's why I helped Grace plant the bulbs. I wanted to see something else growing besides cells, I guess. Maybe that's why I went in the store: to smell lumber, paint, see building going on." He was caught again, for a few seconds.

"Anyway, I sat there, looking around.

"Then I remembered Dad's last job: a six-story office building. Not much of a skyscraper but it had the first automatic elevator I'd ever seen. He let me ride it soon as it was installed. Let me punch the button: up, 2, 3, 4, 5, 6; down. . . . Can see those numbers and Dad half smiling; never saw him smile a whole smile in my life." He stopped, looked away. Came back.

"Well, that's about it, I guess. I dropped the cigarette. Checked to be sure it was dead. Started out the back door—that's where I was: near it. Saw a latrine in the corner rigged up for the workmen, stepped in to use it. No door. A flap of canvas. Djdn't bother to drop it. Place half-dark. Nobody but me. Then—as I turned around, I saw the kid: standing right there in front of me. She had a yellow cat in her arms—I swear she did. She didn't move. She was looking straight at me. She said, 'You bad bad bad man don't you hurt me don't you dare!' I turned away quick—couldn't work the zipper—kept trying—it wouldn't— all in my mind was to get out of the damned place. Then things happened so fast I don't know what came first: she screamed—

terrible scream—cat jumped out of her arms and landed on the lumber, and then instead of running away the kid ran up to me and began to beat on me like crazy. Her hands beat like sticks. I dodged and went out that door as if a thousand witches were after me. Ran down the alley. Saw I was near Matthews, braked up, caught my breath, went in the back door, got the Cokes, paid a cashier, cut across the street and hurried back to the house. You know the rest: I opened two Cokes, added the rum, gave a glass to Grace and took one out on the terrace."

I poured him a drink. He gulped it. I poured three cups of coffee; put one by each of them, took mine over to the window to give him time to level off.

I tried not to think. Something in my mind seesawed and whanged but I wouldn't listen. I stood at that window and stared at the rhododendron below the ledge. Watched a car come up, park thirty feet beyond—under the big sycamore. Taillight on. Nobody got out.

When I came back from the window he and Grace were looking down at the floor. Grace rubbing her fingers.

13

Here I begin to blur. I find it almost impossible to recall our words from here on. I mean the way they built up. The tensions press today as if it happened yesterday; but the sudden mood we slipped into, my state of mind I should say, seems in retrospect so melodramatic that I can scarcely believe my own memory. For instance, that book: why it loomed as large as it did, why I felt I had to say all I said.

This is how I remember it:

"Did you smoke one cigarette or two while you were there?" I asked.

"One."

"You thought about quite a few things on one cigarette."

His voice was calm and courteous. "Yes. Seems like I did." Not a sign of defensiveness. He said, "Believe it was like this: you remember events simultaneously, a lot of them, sometimes. They just operate on different levels."

"It happens like that, Dave." Her voice was pleading. She reminded me how you wake up, look at the clock, go back to sleep, have a long involved dream, wake up and find only a minute has passed. "Remembering is like that. It comes all at once."

"Sure it does. I'm trying to see how the others may shape it up. Mark, you were in the place ten or twelve minutes?"

"Probably. Not sure. May not have been that long."

"Mind telling me why you didn't mention it, afterward? You didn't, did you?"

He did not answer at once. Grace shook her head.

He was sitting in the striped chair. He felt around for his cigarettes, found the package, kept his fingers on it, did not take one out. Stared at the package. Then he turned to me. "When it happened I was bowled over. No man wants a little girl— But I didn't think beyond that. Didn't dream anything would come of it. Didn't recognize the kid as belonging to anybody I knew. It was one of those things that just don't happen. When it finally does, you try to forget it.

"Thought I'd tell Grace. Sometime. Had no idea— I hadn't done a thing, so didn't worry. Or if I did, I didn't know it. By the time I walked home I could laugh, not much I admit, but— well, I must have looked an all-fired ass loping down that alley. I was embarrassed. But I wasn't too upset. Would have told Grace, right then, if I had been."

But later—when you were accused, why didn't you tell her? The question pounded my brain but I could not ask it.

"I said to myself," Mark still explaining, "*forget it forget it,* went out on the terrace, drank the rum and Coke and read my book."

"What were you reading?"

"*The Possessed.*"

"Dostoevsky's *Possessed?*"

"Sure."

This is when it started. I had been as certain of him as of anyone in the world. But the name of that book did it. I cannot explain it. Except to say it unloosed something. Perhaps not it alone; perhaps it was the book linked on to the knowledge that he had held the other back, until now. I knew his reading it was pure coincidence. I was sure of it. They both read a great deal. He was more likely to be reading philosophy, Whitehead or Unamuno or Berdyaev, but why not Dostoevsky? if he wanted to, why not? Just the same, my whole organism took a leap and landed on a more irrational level—not only my mind but my glands, too, for my heart was hammering and my head felt tight. And as I remember things now, I feel my senses were distorted: I saw things too black too white too large too small too out of shape, somehow.

I looked at Grace. Her eyes had turned into black holes. She has so much empathy—I feel she caught it from me, the doubt, suspicion—but not as formulated as those words suggest—perhaps lack of confidence is a better way to say it. I was no longer sure of him; I felt she was no longer sure: and now I feel—not then, but now—that a new gestalt was forming: we had looked at the Mark We Know, now we were looking at the Mark We Do Not Know.

I felt she wanted to speak; decided not to.

"Is something the matter, Dave?" Mark's voice was the only sane sound in my head.

"No. Not a thing. I just thought—"

"What is it, Dave?" Her voice was urgent.

"Nothing of importance." Relieved that my voice sounded

easy. "I was merely wishing you had read—something else."

Neither said anything.

Then I said, "Does anybody know you were reading it?"

"They don't, do they? You didn't mention it, did you, Mark?" Grace's voice was low and frightened.

Mark has one of the fastest mental take-offs I know. But always when things get personal he goes into that slow motion. He looked at her, at me. He seemed to have lost every word in his language. But he finally made it. He said, "No. I—didn't. As far as I know."

Then he said, "I'm not sure what you're getting at, Dave."

"As I say, it's not important. I was just wondering why you happened to be reading that book. Instead of something else."

He looked at me hard. Looked at her. "This is why: because Grace was saying, while we planted the bulbs, that she had just reread Virginia Woolf's translation of *Stavrogin's Confession* and she thought it—oh I don't know; what's the use—" He sighed, rubbed his face.

Grace took it up. "I was talking about its strange tranquillity. Mrs. Woolf's translation. Its theme is—but her words create a curious calm. I said it was like a deep undersea calm with the storm raging on the surface, then I switched and said I believed it was the other way around: a calm surface with a terrible undertow and suction underneath it. Then I said, it seemed more than Dostoevsky when she had done with it. I mean it isn't a translation: it is a metamorphosis. And I went on to say, I wish she had done a translation of *Crime and Punishment*. You know, the way we talk about things."

"You were reading the *Confession?*" My tone must have been inquisitorial.

"No. But what's wrong with reading it, for God's sake!"

"Don't you *see?*"

"No I don't." He walked over to the window.

Why didn't he? It had stabbed me like a chest pain. This Thing: I could see it dim, way off: Stavrogin and the little girl he seduced and raped: her terror her grief her shame her guilt, her slow slow and then, so quick death. And its shadow:

Mark and another little girl. . . . It blazed up in my mind like a picture on fire. Then died down to slow smoldering words: they were talking about Stavrogin and his confession . . . no, it was Woolf's prose they were discussing not—yes, but just the same, they both knew the Stavrogin story . . . suppose Mark . . . suppose the power of that story, the steep downward-spiraling stairs Dostoevsky makes you lean over . . . suppose thinking about it had released a locked-up impulse, had pushed him down to another level of feeling, into a savage, dark place, way down where the conscience cannot exert its controls, or your sense of reality—suppose—yes, but a book can't—maybe it can —but this book evokes pity terror stirs your conscience your moral sense not your sadism not desire not—but maybe it was already stirred, the desire, the need— What am I letting myself—the child was not hurt, you know that!

"Dave." Voice a whisper. I felt she might have called me several times. "Nobody knows he read it. I'll burn it."

Mark turned on her. I'd never seen him like that. "What's come over you two? would you do that?"

"I'd burn the house down if it would help you and Andy." She tried to hide her crying. "I'm scared."

He looked at her gravely; then smiled and said, "I'm scared too, honey—but not because I read a book and think somebody's going to find out about it. You two don't actually think the police would search our house to see what books we read in order to decide whether I tried to seduce a little girl?"

Grace said, "Somebody might. Whoever sent that letter to Andy might. Whoever phones me."

She was deeply disturbed and showed it. All along she had been poised and steady. Now—

I felt it was my fault. I tried to put the brakes on. I said, "Grace, if S. K. wrote that letter—and I think he did—he wouldn't know Dostoevsky from Mickey Spillane."

"Yes he would. The *evsky* would do it; he'd say we were Communists and then somebody who did know would—"

Mark was watching us both. He said, "Let's take it easy."

He reminded us that nobody could have been more reasonable than Neel; that the Chief was all right, too. He told us Steve Bernstein had informed him that the judge was widely known for his fairness and happened to be, also, a subtle sophisticated man who knew his way around in human nature. "The people who count are sensible—let's hold on to that. There's nothing new in the situation to cause us to panic."

Except you were there; and the child didn't make it up; and you read that book; and somebody, a dozen, maybe a hundred people who don't count, and some who do, are stirring things into a mess—how about those letters and calls to Grace, and now to Andy—

It bothered me, this sudden evasion. Mark knew as well as I did that the man or woman who wrote that letter to Andy was out to hurt and hurt bad.

Grace was walking around the room. I felt she had stopped listening to us. She seemed to be hearing something else. She said, "Mark—do you think Andy's all right? I'm afraid he's not all right. . . ."

"He's sound asleep, honey. And Eliot's with him. Nothing could possibly happen to him tonight."

She stared at the closed door. I had an irrational feeling, for a moment, that she had walked through it and had gone away.

I said, knowing as I said it that it was not perhaps a wise thing to say, "I'd like to know who sent that letter to Andy. If we knew we might see who is whipping the froth up."

"Some crackpot. You said so, yourself, a while ago. There're always crackpots everywhere who do these things."

Grace was pale, distraught, and seemed under enormous tension. I should have let them go home. But I forgot her, he forgot her too, and we talked across her. I suppose we were too worried to know what else to do but talk.

I said, "It's not just the crackpots stirring things up. A lot of people can't think straight about a thing like this, who can think straight about everything else. Sensible, astute businessmen whose judgment is good on most matters will fall flat over this."

I was thinking of Dewey Snyder, of the vestrymen, and some of those on the Cancer Drive Committee. "It is because—" Well, I wasn't sure I knew. So I stopped here.

"Why?"

"I'm not sure. We've talked about it before. When it gets close, it is not easy to see— It is different from breaking the law. Or breaking a moral law. It's deeper; goes way down. Beyond words, probably. Take killing, for instance: killing is not taboo. People think it is wrong, sometimes; but not always. They think there are plenty of extenuating circumstances for killing even children: in war, in H-bomb tests— But this kind of thing is wrong all the time, in people's minds."

"You're talking as if I raped the child or had been accused of raping her."

"In a lot of people's minds you did rape her. That's the point I'm trying to make. That's why the book worries me. Suppose it does come out in the testimony that you were reading it: think what a jury could do with it."

I could see those twelve men hunched up reading it; minds already inflamed with half-repressed fantasies; most, maybe all, reading it for the first time. They'd identify him with Stavrogin, they'd strip all the differences off and merge the two as the Guilty One—unless, unless by some miracle, they identified him with themselves. Then, of course, they'd believe him innocent. Neel thought they might do this because quite a few men are being framed by little girls on charges such as this; all men are vulnerable, just here; there was a chance that they'd identify with him. It would depend, of course, on how much they felt they had in common with him. Would they feel they had much in common with a scientist? with a man who had entertained Negro scientists in his home? whose wife is an artist and modern dancer and has had her picture made with a Negro? I didn't know.

I said, "Make up your mind. It can't be that book. How about the New York *Times?* You take it; you were reading the theater page."

He laughed. I did, too. But I meant it.

He was studying me now. "You thought that, didn't you? about the Confession? that if I read it, I might then have—hurt the child?"

"I thought it. I don't believe it." Was that true? "But if the others thought it they would believe it."

"But *your* thinking it . . . I be damned."

Well, it got me. Partly because I was shaken by his having been in the store and the fact that he had not told us; shaken, too, that I had felt suspicion. I didn't like having felt it; of course I didn't. It put me right down with Snyder. Just the same, it seemed to me he was riding too smooth on his innocence— ignoring too much that just couldn't be ignored.

I see it now. It was necessary for him to tunnel in and go ahead without looking anywhere except in front of him. That is how he endured those two years in a Jap prison; how he carried out those missions over the Hump through sleet ice snow with Jap fighters tailing him. How he had kept on with his work at the lab, these weeks, behaving as if he weren't worried, as if everything were going to be all right. He knew he was innocent. He believed people are basically reasonable and just, therefore he would be cleared. Once cleared, his life would smooth out and the work at the lab would go on and his normal life with Grace and Andy would begin again. He was compelled to keep acting on this assumption—even though he was now living, and knew it, on a level of human affairs where men rarely behave reasonably and rarely are just.

But I couldn't see it, that night; and I resented the seeming moral arrogance in his calm attitude—as if I were the one who had done wrong—

I didn't answer him. I suppose he felt my reaction. He looked up, sighed, said, "I'm sorry, Dave. We came here for help because we need it bad; and if anybody in the world will help us, I know you will. I seem muddle-headed, somehow. I have the greatest respect for you—including your imagination." He smiled in his old easy way. "You know that. Your hunches are usually good, and I know it. We both feel indebted to you. Hope you know that, too."

I told him to forget it. Told him maybe I worried about S. K. and Miss Hortense—I had not mentioned her but I had thought about her—because I saw too many people like them, every day. (I was worried more about Dewey Snyder, but decided not to mention him.)

But in spite of our quieter words, I did not feel good. I felt, What else is he holding back? I wasn't sure. And I wanted to get things straight. It was late but I said, "Mind going back a bit? Did you tell the police or the magistrate you were in the store?"

"No."

"Did they ask you?"

"Yes. I said I was not in the store; I was at Matthews."

Now Grace was listening to us. "What else could he have said, Dave?"

"I don't know. It's a funny thing: you count on the truth being accepted as the truth. We live that way. Then a time comes, you just can't tell it."

"Because they'll take the part of it that fits what is in their minds and discard the rest. I seem to have jumped over on your side of the argument. They'd believe I was in the store if I said I was; sure; but they'd never believe I sat down on a pile of lumber and thought about things that happened thirty years ago."

"But why perjury? You don't have to give evidence against yourself."

"Two minutes ago, you wanted me to lie and tell them I'd been reading the New York *Times*. Now you—" He stopped, rubbed his face. "I know I don't have to give evidence against myself. But suppose I had refused to answer that question—what would they have thought?"

We didn't bother to say it.

"What I think I did was withhold an emotionally charged fact that is irrelevant to the information they need. That's not double talk. I don't like perjury any more than you do. But what they needed to know was this: (a) was the child hurt? (b) did I hurt her? The answer is no. I didn't hurt her nor was she hurt. But if I told them I was in that store—*that one fact* would push all the other facts out where they couldn't be dealt with, no matter how relevant they might be. There're facts and facts. You know that, Dave. Inside a man, outside him. Some you can measure; some you can't. We forget the dangerous facts are those that don't speak a modern language: those that can talk only to the primitive part of us. You believe this—even more than I do."

Of course. That was why I was worried about the book. That was why I worried about him, for until this moment he had seemed to be denying this primitive, irrational part of us.

Then she said it: "Dave, you wouldn't tell the truth, would you, if they called you as witness?"

We laughed, Mark and I. We had to. It was an incredible mess and painfully real and close—for Andy was on the periphery of our thoughts every moment we talked.

But I must admit I had been wishing Mark had not told me.

I said, hoping it was true, "I would not be required to divulge what is, in effect, a confession he has made to his priest."

She was as direct as a child: "But would you still say you saw him on the terrace at five-thirty?"

I evaded her—and my conscience. Said, "Was that why you didn't tell us, Mark?"

Once more, he studied his cigarette. Said, "When Neel walked in our house that Wednesday night and asked his questions, I didn't have time to think. And I wanted Grace—" he looked at her for a long time, "to feel sure of me."

She turned to him quickly. Her face, all of her, said everything a man needed to hear.

"That first time, it was reflex—my saying I hadn't been in the store. And after you said you saw me on the terrace at five-thirty— But when we talked to Andy, I knew I had to tell you both. I couldn't handle it any longer by myself."

It was late. But we sat there—each of us withdrawn and silent. As I think about it now, there was a curious emptiness in that room—as if we had left it, one by one.

Finally, Mark looked up, said, "It's strange how she knew my name. I'd never been around her."

I told them I was about to phone when they asked to come over. Then I told them about Renie and Susan hiding behind the rose bushes, watching him as he got out of his car, as he walked into the house. Told them the Chief and Neel had decided to try to persuade the Newells to drop the charges, for the sake of the child. Neel had never believed in the validity of the case.

"When I told them about Susan's visit to my rooms—I can't go into it now; perhaps some other time—Neel agreed with me, and the Chief, too, with a few reservations, that Susan had fantasied the whole thing with her mother's collaboration. I was sure of it. Am afraid I did a first-class selling job on her talent for lying—plus the fact that you could not possibly have been in the store because I saw you on your terrace at five-thirty." I looked at Grace. She almost smiled. "They said they would talk to Claud Newell this weekend. I promised them I would, also. We were sure we could persuade him to withdraw his charges. I had hoped it would be good news for you."

"Dave!" Grace whispered this. Not a muscle moved in Mark's face.

She said, "I must go. Stay as long as you need to, Mark. I'll be all right. Night, Dave dear."

Mark stood up. "Thanks, Dave. I— Thank you very much. I'll run along." He put his hand on my shoulder, his eyes tried to say something but I was not sure what. We agreed, once more, on three-thirty. They left.

I walked over to the desk. Was unable to think what I wanted there. Saw Grace's glass and cup. That put a thought in my head: wash them. I picked up the things and washed them. Turned off the light, started upstairs. I had not locked the window. Decided it might be a good idea since I'd be away the next day. The light from the hall was sufficient to see by. Went over to the window. As I locked it, someone turned away from the shrubbery, got in the car parked at the sycamore tree and drove off. It happened before my eyes could adjust to the dark. I thought it was a man; don't know; have never found out. And, I must admit, I have never given it much thought since.

14

At three o'clock the alarm went off. I turned on the light, fumbled around for the phone to call the airport, remembered Mark was to do it. Went in the kitchen, put on the water for coffee. Got under the shower to wake up. Then did the bacon while the coffee dripped. Drank coffee and ate strips of bacon as I dressed. Saw a light on in their kitchen and decided there was time to pack my vestments. Knew I should take them along in case of a delay: I could then come into town on the west side, save thirty minutes on the cross-town route to the funeral home where the services for Mrs. Bailey were to be held.

I pulled out the vestment case. Went to the closet, found a surplice, did not find my cassock. Pushed through pants, coats, topcoats, jackets: no cassock. Looked again. Thought of Susan— I knew she had not taken it but I thought of her. Susan and that clothes closet were now tied in a hard knot. (I do not know why I pull these inconsequential details to the surface of my mind; perhaps because I tend to hang on to trivia when the big things begin to speed around the curves.) Anyway, I gave up, plugged in the razor—and at the first *burr* remembered the cassock was at the cleaners. There was one of the same weight in the robing room. I'd go over and get it, and pick up a stole.

Shaving now. Thinking of small affairs. But Susan stayed in

my mind. Last night, she had not mattered much. It was Andy, Mark, Grace. Now, she began to assume importance. It was beginning to come to me that she might be in more trouble than Andy. She had had so few breaks. Andy had had all the breaks, until now; and Grace would straighten him out; I did not minimize his hurt or the shock—I knew nothing, of course, about the newspaper clipping—but I felt his relationship with his parents was basically good and because it was they would work it out. And I had realized—belatedly, I'm afraid—that I was Susan's priest, too; and the child needed a friend.

Last night, she was no more than a name to me. We mentioned her again and again but I don't think we felt her as a person. She was an obstacle we tried to shove out of our way. At this bare hour between night and dawn, she came clear: her small sharp face pushing as if nothing ever opened up easily for her; eyes changing color as mood changed; her absurd pretense of sophistication, hysterical giggle, quicksilver imagination —it appealed to me, suddenly.

Well, she had sure prowled the neighborhood: must have been in my rooms a dozen times; in other people's too. Opening doors, opening drawers, looking at herself in other people's mirrors—I could see her preening . . . staring . . . preening— behind her a different room, a different world, each time. Inside her mind—what? Something vague like cloud pictures? A little one-act play, maybe? I don't know. The kind of kid who might steal, too. Not because she wants it but because she needs something whose name is not in her vocabulary; so she settles for the synonyms: running off with a box, a ring, watch, pin, thimble, a hat, a picture, a dollar, maybe. . . . But I had not missed a thing from my rooms.

It is possible she had been in that store before, talking to the carpenters. Many times, perhaps. Which one of them would admit it now! She was, apparently, on familiar terms with that old yellow cat. All the alley cats, maybe, liked to go along with her on those little journeys. Who wouldn't? Then, one day, one Monday afternoon, her search collided with Mark's: both, looking in that old place for something needed: Susie, wanting what she had never had; Mark? I don't know—was it what he had lost long ago? How little I know about this man who is my closest friend! One edge of his life, one edge of mine have touched. That is all.

And yet, we thought we knew Susan—at least enough to name her. To everybody, she was The Pest. There had been moments, as she sat in the fourth pew making faces at me while I tried to preach, when I had thought up stronger names than that for her. The child seems to bring out the worst in every grown person she meets. You keep trying to figure out why. Maybe she knows something we used to know and pretend we've forgot and she reminds us, by a kind of dead odor clinging to her, that we still belong to "the brotherhood." I don't know. But I do know: had a sensitive intelligent dog sought his owner, say; had he kept looking for him or for something that belonged to him, coming in with a shoe or sock or old sweater, we'd be moved by his devotion and need and we'd pat him and say *nice doggie,* and the rest of it. But when Susie does it, she's the Menace to everybody, including me.

I was shaving under my eyes now. Saw how black they were. They had always been black, of course; but I had concentrated on Susie's pale yellow eyes until I was a bit startled to see my own staring back at me. Mark . . . I could see his eyes, too—when I let myself. They were tense last night; pupils dilated. I knew things were crowding him harder than he would admit. And Grace—something snapped in her when I said that book's name. Why did I do such a thing? My brain was twanging like a piece of elastic; when that happens, you don't know what sounds will come out of your mouth.

Odd . . . how you try to think of a situation as one: when it is always two, three, four, five and so on. Totally different events had happened to those two in that store. Had begun there . . . now— Yet we try to make them one. We hunger for form: but we have so little sense of form. Last night, Mark kept saying she was not hurt. The kid just wasn't hurt, he said. Simpler that way for him, I guess, not to think about it. And yet, had the incident been intentional, it could scarcely have—

I saw her as she was, in my study: scrunched up in my arm-chair, making up her stories about toadstools and parasols, Boody and Renie and a Chicago hotel room-phone ringing and Mark's following her. The little liar . . . and yet she was the only one of us who had told the truth about the store. In spite of my brainwashing, she'd stuck to it. I'd lied about the five-thirty terrace business—unintentionally, the first time; after-ward, I guess I did it deliberately; and I'd lie more if I talked to Claud Newell and I had to talk to him; and if there is a trial I shall— Well, I don't know. Mark had lied to everybody and would keep it up. The only disagreement we had was which thing to lie about. The whole mess was unreal, incredible. It made me sick. I felt we were caught in the nets of somebody's Big Lie struggling to cut our way out with dull little lies, and we'd never do it. Why couldn't we think straight?

Putting on my dog collar now, and *rabat*. A clergyman's puzzled solemn face stared back at me from the mirror. I turned away.

As a matter of fact, nobody had thought straight. Neel cer-tainly had not. What a fine case he and I concocted about Susie: except it just wasn't true. We were sincere in thinking it was. But it wasn't. Makes you feel pretty silly. Worse: it scares you to watch yourself make escalators of theories and push every lost human being you know on one, hoping they will soon be out of your sight. Well, I was the one riding the escalator—not Susie. Susie was the sanest one in the lot. She knew she needed something: she tried in her child-way to find it, and she hadn't hurt anybody. She had not intended hurt—but of course she had hurt—

It was Renie. Renie . . . Neel had done a demolition job on my image of Renie: Red-blonde hair pulled back in a shining smooth chignon, her stunning classic face, slim neat figure, warm laugh, helpfulness to people, her engaging sense of humor about small things—I had not forgot that night in my study but it was back in the shadows—all this I had tried to hold to, feeling you can't let everything good you've known about a person slide down the drain. Well, it had slid, all right. As I thought her name now, Renie's face turned slowly into Hattie Belle's cheap lush cosmetic-smeared calculating face. Hattie Belle . . . *take those Dior clothes off Mrs. Newell, get her out of her British tweeds, add ten pounds to her, put her in a cheap dress from a chain store and you've got Hattie Belle*—his voice snipping like a tailor's shears; his eyes agonized. He loved that bitchy sister of his—it was so plain—and he believed he despised her. I stood there in my room, tangled in the maze of Neel's feelings. I pulled away. You can't begin on Hattie Belle. . . .

Yes, Renie held Susie's hand while she lit the fuse. Gave her the match, all right. But where did the fuse come from? who tied it to this network of buried explosives that were detonating in heart after heart, mind after mind? I felt, It is going to rock us all before it is done with. Immediately, I told myself to take it easy. Things like this have happened before, hundreds of times: if they can make a case that sticks with the jury the man is sent to prison and that is that; if they can't, they free him—

But this man is Mark. . . . What a difference a name makes to you. A dread began to press me. *Free him—for what?*

I saw it was three-twenty. Slipped on a tweed coat. Hurried out. Drove around the corner to the church. Went in to pick up the cassock. Turned the lights on only in the small robing room and at the side entrance. Suddenly, it was as if the whole church were lighted up: altar, Cross, candles, reredos, pulpit, lectern, choir stalls, nave, baptistery—windows glowing, music streaming, the ancient liturgy. . . . All of it opened up in my mind so swiftly and completely, as I turned to lift the robe off its hanger, that I was transfixed. For a minute or more I stood there in that dim cold anteroom, caught in a radiance that slowly illumined my heart and mind and memory: All of it, all the Church had meant to me, all I called my religion was there: its heart-twisting words whispering, the great and terrible Moments of the Last Supper, the Passion, the Cross, the Atonement; the Holy Trinity. . . . All this: all that the Church had meant to me when I was a small boy hungry for something bigger than a man to believe in, straining toward something more lasting than my small present, yearning to come closer to a goodness that I dimly apprehended but had no word for; all it had meant in my teens; in college, when the feeling was somehow transformed into concern for my fellow-man, and then had changed again into solace and a source of comfort, as I watched men die in the war—for I believed my own words when I told the dying that God was not indifferent to a man's death; even as I lay embittered and hopeless on the hospital bed after the leg was torn off, I had still clung to something, hardly more than a sliver of Place, still and wordless and swept clean, but it had caught my heart firmly and had held me; all this suffused me and surrounded me and I felt as if I were about to be lifted to another order of feeling and perceiving and living, that a wisdom was about to be revealed to me— And then, the illumination dimmed and faded; and I was left alone in that cold small room standing there with my hand on a limp black robe. And everything was as it had been.

I felt emptied out. Cut off from the Presence of God. And I wanted to cry as a child cries when his small view of things is blown out by sudden windy events. I switched on the chancel lights, went in. I must have thought, It will return—the illumination will return if I see the real altar, real Cross, the real— I walked up closer to the altar. I wanted to kneel and pray, to bend my body, yes, and my mind, in genuflection to what is beyond my comprehension, beyond this obscene hour we were caught in and the small ineffectual way we were responding to it. I cannot kneel now, although I desperately needed to. But I stood there and prayed: clumsily, agonizingly: for compassion, forgiveness, courage. (How reluctant is one's vocabulary! In my anguish it released only those three words.) And then, I went into the small room again, took the cassock from its hanger and hurried out into the night, feeling I had prayed the wrong prayer, feeling I should have asked God for much more and much less. And yet, how could I? I did not know what that more was, nor the less. I had lost it just as it was about to be revealed to me. And I, too, was lost; I no longer understood the meaning that the Church has for this time we live in; I no longer understood my relationship with God.

I stare at these words as I write them down now for they have a pitiful and arrogant look. How can a man understand his relationship with God? when he does not even understand his relationship with his own mother or father; or the woman he chooses to live his life with; or her children he works for; or his friend; or his relationship to the earth he walks on, or that vast unlighted unknown part of his own self which stretches back into his childhood and on and on into the limitless past of the human childhood. Understand? It is like saying, I do not understand a form that is round, or the smell of violets, or the smell of dung, I do not understand the sounds that streamed out of Beethoven's head, or the love of a child.

When I was a young acolyte, I had felt a Hand holding me steady, giving me direction: I had believed in something that seemed enormously significant to me. And I had loved something beyond my own self. Had I then said my belief aloud it would certainly have sounded naive in its minute concreteness and wondrously vague in its generalities. But somehow, it had form, and it held me; it gave me not purpose but a sense of purpose, not a destination but a sense of direction. But every year one's belief changes—or is it one's love? I don't know. But I do know this: when the heart expands, when the imagination opens, when the memory becomes more aware, when the mind grows or one's personal relationships acquire depth and complexity, this changes one's relationship to God. "God" is a symbol for God, as Paul Tillich has said many times. Yes. A symbol of a symbol of a symbol, I think it must be: But that is not enough: It is a symbol of a truth that must be created anew—for it cannot be discovered— by each of us and as continuously as our bodies and minds and spirit are re-created. What I had not done was keep on creating and being re-created, and now—

Now: At this moment we needed, I needed and Grace and Mark and Andy, and Susan—and her mother, too—needed something we did not possess. And Those Others, the anonymous ones who seemed to be causing most of this fantastic trouble: what had my Church and I as its priest done to transmute their fevered sick imaginations and impulses into mystical yearning and creative act?

Unformed words piled up in my mind and pressed hard. As I try now to translate that pressure into words, it seems to me I feared that perhaps the liturgical beauty of the Church, its tradition, its poetry, its awesome rituals of penitence and need had seduced me. The Church can be prison more easily than door. Perhaps it was prison to me. This feeling, for it was no more than feeling, was almost unendurable. I got in the car, deeply troubled, and estranged.

As I turned the ignition key and started the motor I thought, *Something has gone wrong with us all.* I had little idea of what I meant. But I resolved to take a day or two off as soon as I could manage it (when this trouble was over, I meant), borrow Jane's cabin up on the mountain and try to think it out; try to find what had gone wrong with me, at least. A day or two? Sure. Keep it small and sensible. Always, something urges me to keep it small and sensible as I reach out for the big realization, the Great Form. Something always urges me to think it out clearly when I know I can do no more than open myself up so that wisdom or vision or simple goodness and love may enter me at its appointed time. Religion is a creative act, a discovery, as is an artist's painting or a composer's symphony, and yet—well, a hard nub in me stubbornly refuses this knowledge; and I keep trying the down-to-earth approach and I end with my mouth in the mud.

As I went across Arlington and into the Channing driveway, I saw them waiting in the cold dark of the terrace. I slowed, brought the car to a stop. They turned to each other. Mark took her in his arms. I believed their minds were as close as their bodies. I felt it, and I was relieved. Last night I had not been sure. There had been a few minutes when—but I could have imagined that. Now, things had leveled off, I could see it. And I was glad, for I cared more for these two than for anyone else on

earth and I had begun to realize, during these weeks, how en-
twined my life was with theirs.

And yet—as I walked toward them I felt completely outside
their lives.

Strange . . . how it happens: cold, dark, silent moment:
two people in deep embrace: and the Watcher stands there, a
million miles from human warmth, drifting farther and farther
away in his loneliness. I know: the milk of that loneliness has
nourished all the poetry and art and music and magic and
mysticism, and science, too, maybe, this old human world has
created for itself; but it can be a sour thing in one's own mouth.
I was almost overpowered by my feeling of isolation: I envied
these two their brutal dilemma, was jealous of their tearing
anxiety about the boy: at least it was theirs; it was real;
they were suffering but they were living out the deep human
things—

Mark picked up her bags. They met me halfway down the
walk. We went to the car. Mark got her settled while I put the
luggage in the car trunk.

"I'll call you, dear—and take care," she said. And he kissed her
again and turned to me, "OK, Dave?" I said, "Everything's fine."
And my voice sounded as if everything was and would always
be. It is like that, my voice: confident, sure, hopeful; I have
nothing to do with it; it's the shape of the larynx or something,
the way my palate wobbles, maybe. (They used to tell me at the
Seminary that sooner or later it was bound to make me a bishop.
Fine joke; sure.) I hated the sound of it, now, as it reached my
ears.

He stood there as I backed down the drive. Was standing
there when I slowed to make a left turn as I cut into Briarcliff.

I gave her a cigarette. Did the things you do to make a woman
comfortable, seeing about coat, handbag, and so on. And then
I drove up the highway past dark streets dark houses on on until
we were out of the city and in the country. The sense of being
completely cut off from all that counts in a personal sense—how
shall I say it? all that concerns body, intimate ties, had settled

down on me. I couldn't shake it off. I could not talk. It was cruel timing: this: cutting across that sudden crashing sense of loss I had felt in the robing room. Perhaps both feelings were one. I don't know. But it bore down. I was ashamed but I could not pull free of it.

Ten miles—perhaps it was—later, she said, "Dave?"

I drove a half-mile before I could say, "Yes?"

"You mean so much to me. To both of us." Not the words but the voice said what counted. She was answering my mood; she always seems to feel you. Always she's like that.

Yes, he means something as a friend, as their priest, sure; but not— *What else do you want?* But I didn't ask it, I stifled it before I quite heard it inside my head.

I took her hand. I intended only to let her know that my mood was nothing for her to worry about. It is a thin strong hand, used to working with clay, stone, paint; used to washing dishes and cooking and the rest of it for Grace does her own work and those other things, too. (She is not too neat about it, I must say; she's likely to shove a stack of canvases under the couch, a pile of messy drawing paper, plus a piece of wet clay; and the dishes may stay in the sink for two days; but she's a good cook; and anybody would like to be invited to her house.) Her hand softened and warmed as I held it. I realized I had no right to hold this hand; released it, patted it, offered her another cigarette. She said no.

I felt she was smiling: at me, with me, maybe. She had put me firmly in my place, long ago, after she had done so much to help me get my bearings. Gently. She had been gentle all right, but she had been honest and direct, too; and I knew she was right; and she knew it. Mark probably knew about it, too. I guess she told him. But he had never given the slightest indication he knew; nor shown jealousy—*how could he be jealous of a one-legged man!* I almost jammed the car in front of us. I felt her stiffen but she said nothing. *Snap out of it,* I told myself, *you'll kill both of you.*

We were passing through a small town. Stopped at a crossing while a freight train crept by. A street light was overhead: I could see her face now, the sharp curving line from ear to chin; her black straight hair; she had not put on her small hat; probably would forget to until Boston reminded her. She seemed so valiant, somehow, sitting there quietly, her worries pushed back from my view. I was swept by feeling. I buried it quick; word and feeling.

I turned and looked at the watchman, swinging his red lantern. Heard myself say to him, "Cold morning." He said, "Shore is."

I said to her in a low voice, "Seems old to be doing this kind of thing."

She looked at him, said it would be interesting to try a lithograph of his face. There's something cruel in it, and harsh, she said. "They're such different feelings." He'd been beat and he'd beat back. And she liked that. But the cruelty was deeper: she felt it was reserved for those he loved, maybe; and yet he's warm and sentimental. "You feel his eyes would fill up quickly if you mentioned the two or three right things. I am not sure I'm a painter. I care too much for the psychology of a face. You feel his face could slide off in pieces. They're just barely overlapped now."

The traffic bars were open. I was driving across tracks as she said this.

"Guess we're all in pieces and overlapped," I said.

I thought, as I drove down the one business street of the town, that a bank is a lonely thing at four-fifteen in the morning. One light on. No tellers. Vaults closed. No customers. Just dead money: pieces of metal; stacks of paper; still and meaningless until a human eye looks, a hand reaches, then they take on life, they become more alive than people, sometimes. Next to the bank, a grocery store. New modern front. One light on. Dark, except near the wide show-window which was full of rusty country hams. Next door, a hardware store. New modern front. One light on. They'd left two plows outside. Forgot them, I guess. A cat was lying on one of them. Looked like Ali Baba. I thought, Suppose all this were buried; and a thousand years from now somebody excavated it and began to study the artifacts to see what kind of culture this town once had; what its people had valued and deemed beautiful, what ugly hard truths they had had the fortitude to hold on to, what they had created with their hands, what kind of God they had worshipped—

She was answering me. I had almost forgot what I had said. "Yes," she was saying, "but some faces show it; others don't." Face . . . oh yes, the watchman at the crossing.

As I remember his face today, I see nothing but an old dark cap with the earflaps pulled down, yellow bushy eyebrows, a mole near his mouth, and the jaws working as he chewed tobacco. I wonder if she still remembers him.

I thought, She has herself completely under control. She'll be all right with the boy. Easy, calm. She is worried all right but she'll never show it. They're both lucky to have her.

"Dave—" It must have been twenty minutes later, "when you were Andy's age, how did you feel about things?

"The real things," she added softly.

I didn't know what to say.

"Your father—did you feel close to him?"

"No."

"Do you know why?"

"No. I never did, somehow."

"You respected him?"

"I think so. In the home—I'm not sure. It was different when I went to his office."

"Do you mind telling me how it was different?"

I didn't quite know. These things are not easy to say. I think I liked the walls lined with his lawbooks, most of them a dull yellow and brown— I remember I liked that; Dad sitting at his desk studying important-looking papers; the clerks taking books down and looking up precedents as they prepared briefs, everybody talking legal jargon. It was impressive. When he'd lean back in his old swivel chair, swing around, put the tips of his fingers together and quote something from Justice Holmes, as he was fond of doing, or Justice Brandeis, or cite Somebody versus Somebody it was impressive. But at home, he wasn't impressive.

"I don't quite know," I said.

Strange . . . it is gone, then it returns: Meg and I would be eating our breakfast in the small breakfast room. Dishes were white with yellow bands, I remember that. Mother reading the sports page. My father reading the financial page of New York *Times*. Mother would tell Meg and me every sports event, as if she were our age, and I'd say *Gee . . . golly*. My father would say nothing. And Meg's big gray eyes would look at me and look at Mother and look at Dad and then she'd eat her oatmeal very fast and Mother would say, "Not so fast, Margaret!" It swings back as if you had pressed a button: enlarged a bit, or diminished a bit, sometimes with words, sometimes without words, sometimes lighted differently—but always *there*, those feelings —pulling loose or tightening.

I drove on a mile or two. I said, "Mother took us to hear him argue a famous murder case. I was twelve. She told us it was an important day in our lives. It was." There were many people but the ones I watched were the reporters from the city newspapers, and the photographers, outside the court room; inside, the judge, the men in the jury box, witnesses taking the oath on the Bible, the attorneys. I didn't pay much attention to the man being tried—it was Dad's role I watched. When he stepped out and began to cross-examine the witnesses I felt a tremendous excitement. He had a quick, fiery, wittily aggressive approach. Like a good net player in a tennis game.

"Did he win?"

"Yes."

"Suppose he hadn't."

I didn't reply to that. "I remember Mother saying to us, Your father is the most brilliant lawyer in the state. Then she'd add, He has a magnificent vocabulary. But somehow she left us feeling there was something else he didn't have. Something important. It bothered me."

Grace said, "Was there antagonism?"

"Not that I remember. We just didn't seem to have anything to say to each other." I thought about it, a bit more. "He and Meg hit it off fine. I'm pretty sure he didn't like my playing football, going in for sports, the way I did. He wanted me to read more."

"But you do read."

"Yes. But not then. Not while he was alive." That is true. I stubbornly refused, while he was alive, to do the things he wanted his son to do. Especially the reading. Now—were he to return and see my study lined with books and his old swivel chair, what would he think?

I said, "I know I missed something big. That is why Mark's relationship with Andy seems—well, pretty wonderful."

She said slowly, "I'm not so sure. Things hurt more when you care too much."

I didn't agree but I said nothing.

I was thinking about the boy: He was about eight when I came to Windsor Hills. Not a husky, but skilled in the use of his body. He spent a good bit of time working on dance routines with his mother, in the basement. Mark didn't like that. I remember he said, "Let's get the boy out in the open." He wasn't upset; just seemed to feel uncomfortable about Andy dancing. So I taught Andy to box. Gave him a bow and some arrows for Christmas. We rigged up three bales of hay behind the target so we wouldn't nip our neighbors, and I practiced archery with him. I took him to the pool that summer; taught him to swim. By the time he was ten, he was the best diver in his age-group in Windsor Hills. An absolutely fearless youngster. At camp he did everything well. But that was his body. Mind? subtle, quick. Feelings? too sensitive maybe; maybe too much imagination, too much empathy, but a fine sense of humor. Honest and generous. That letter had hurt him, all right; and would keep hurting; but it didn't seem to me to have disastrous possibilities.

I said, "I suppose you have looked through the electron microscope at the lab? at Mark's nuclei and viruses?"

"Yes."

"An incredible experience, isn't it?"

"Yes, of course."

"It would be a nightmare if we had the power to see our human relationships as clearly. Even as it is, we may be too sensitive, too aware. With our half-knowledge, we see the human child as frail but he is also tough and durable. Andy can take a lot of hard knocks." That kind of reassurance doesn't help much and I knew it but it was all I could come up with at the moment.

She did not reply.

We were winding now through a village of small houses where mine workers live. Lights were on in some of the houses; some were still dark.

I remembered how I used to lie awake on the train when I was a kid and watch the lights come on in houses. I'd lean my face against the cold window pane and wait for that first light to pop out of the blackness. The fields would be dark blobs sliding by, higher blobs of hills sliding back of them, then one by one the lights would come on. They held me: I'd always wake up for this dark hour when it is day for so many people you never know.

You look at it when you're a little tyke and think one thing: think another when you are older. When I was small it'd be how things smelled: in yard, barn, house: how they sounded: I'd wonder if milkers listened to the ping-pang of milk squirting into empty pails or were they too cold and sleepy; wondered if the cows were sleepy, too. When a worker left with his lunch pail, I'd make up a lunch for him to take along: peanut butter sandwich, cake, the things a ten-year-old likes.

When I was fifteen or sixteen, I thought about Them, the Two of them: as they ate breakfast before dawn; did she cook it? or did he go to work and leave her in bed? Wondered how she felt as she lay half-asleep against him; was she soft and warm? smell good? did he kiss her? did they laugh? did he touch her the way I would so she'd remember all day while I worked? or did he just get up and leave, and go to the mine or the factory?

And then, when I was much older, I'd wake up pushed by the old sense of wonder but my brain would now feel compelled to ask dull questions about farm prices, wages, unions, housing— And He and She, and the cow, the ping-pang of warm milk in pails, the crunch crunch of live creatures feeding, the man with the lunch-box taking a kid's lunch along with him, turned into "economic conditions, social conditions, farm conditions," which I, a clergyman, must try to understand. But I'd never understand the real things . . . no woman would give me—she couldn't, I guess, forget the leg—if she could forget I know I. . . .

I sighed; covered it with a low laugh.

Grace said, "Something funny?" I said, "No; guess not."

15

We had left the town and were in the hills. Two freight trucks were in front of us and close to each other. I was timing the moment to pass when she said, "Dave . . . you don't think he —did anything? do you?"

I was passing, a car was nosing around the curve, I cut in quick behind the front truck, the rear one gave way, the approaching car went by. I said, "No." Passed the other truck, got in the clear, speeded up. "And you don't, either."

No answer.

"You can't, possibly." I was surprised that she had put it in words. Shaken. How could she?

We must have gone five miles. Ten, maybe. "Even if—" Voice almost a whisper. "I'd understand that he was sick—something had given way—it can happen to any—"

I cut her sentence off. I was startled by the anger in my

voice. "He's no more sick than I am. Or you. Not as sick as I am, probably."

Silence.

"We've got to believe in him. Not just understand—believe in him. A man's got to have—" Wagon rose up out of the fog. I put on brakes, eased over on the shoulder to use up speed, crept along behind it. There was something in the back of it, covered with a piece of canvas. Moving now and then. Animal? Wasn't sure. It bothered me. Box? I was dangerously close to that wagon, couldn't pull away from it, car lights back of me. Two animals, maybe? Piece of machinery—why would machinery be moving. . . . If I had been alone I might have concentrated on that covered-up slow-squirming lump; my mind sticks fast, sometimes, on the irrelevant. But I wasn't alone—and everything in the car was racing and everything outside was moving slow as death.

I felt her physical nearness as I had never felt it before. I began to think it in words. Blocked the words off. Said, "You love him?"

"You know I do."

Yes, I knew; that one thing I was sure of. And it didn't make me feel better— "Love isn't enough." I left it there for half a mile. "Not nearly enough." Then I said, "Loyalty isn't enough, either. It'd break him to think you cared and were standing by but had lost your faith in him."

Whom are you preaching at? her? yourself?

"Look: everything was all right until last night. Nobody could have done better; you were sure of him, he knew you were and it steadied him. You knew Susie's story was made up. Somebody made it up—if she didn't. You told me you understood how little girls or their mothers, or both, imagine these things and then project them— You told me you had heard of a similar case. In Maryland, I think you said."

"But—"

"But last night, everything fell on you: that letter to Andy; then Mark telling you he was in the store when he had said for weeks he wasn't; then, like a crazy idiot I dragged in the Dostoevsky business. I want you to forget that book. It has nothing to do with Mark. Nothing!"

"We were talking about it, Dave. It could have—"

"How?" She didn't answer. "How?"

She said, "I knew a girl at school; she was at a house party —somehow they got to talking about ways of committing suicide. The next day she killed herself. It has happened many times."

"Have you ever engaged in a discussion of suicide?"

"Yes."

"You didn't kill yourself, next day."

"But the talk oppressed me. I kept thinking about it."

I tried again. This time, I was glad to hear my voice coming through more relaxed and sympathetic. "You and Mark were talking about Virginia Woolf's problems as a translator, were you not? How she handled her material, the imagery, speech rhythms and so on?"

"Yes."

"You were not, actually, talking about the subject matter, were you? the seduction?"

"No. But he knew the story. It could have released something—"

"What?"

"I don't know—maybe an impulse—"

"Not possible. I'm sorry to keep interrupting you but it couldn't possibly—not in Mark. He wouldn't have had such an impulse, to be released."

"But you thought it, didn't you? last night?"

I had eased too close to the wagon. Tried to get some distance between us.

"You did think it, Dave?"

"I thought about it—or it flashed through my mind. I don't believe it."

"Why didn't he tell me he was there? All these weeks. . . . I can't understand it."

Yes. This is what is bothering her. But there was no sense tangling with it. To find out we'd have to follow every footprint Mark had made since he was born, maybe. I said, "He didn't want to worry you. The fact that he was in that store put him in a shaky position with the law and the community. He knew this. He knew it was hard enough on you as it was. Look: Let's don't ask the whys we can't answer. We're not talking about a theoretical man, we're talking about Mark. We both know he finds it almost impossible to talk about things that go deep with him. Let's leave it at that. The important thing is Mark's values—morals—controls: Are they skin-deep?"

She sighed softly. It got me. I thought, I'm asking too much when she's—

She said, "No."

I pushed on. "Suppose one of his assistants in the lab were found dead—say, in the tissue room—and Mark was the only person you knew who had been there; *but he had been there:* would you think he had killed him?"

"Of course not."

"Are you sure?"

"Yes."

"But you can suspect him of seducing a child? or trying to?"

She was silent.

Silence can be easy; it can also become unendurable. I felt compelled to break it. I said, "Does he love you?"

"Yes."

"Would you know?"

"Yes. I'd know." Her voice shook me. It was so confident.

"All right. Then why would he want—why would he even think about a silly little girl? What in him would need this experience? What is the hunger he must satisfy?"

She said, "Haven't you thought about it? don't all men? sometimes? half-think? half-want? wonder? Not on top of the mind but deepdown. I've thought horrible things, savage things. I've wondered how it would feel to do them, too. You haven't? are you so pure—or just simple?"

I laughed. She laughed, too. It eased us for a moment. "Sure I have. But you haven't done them—and he hasn't either." My voice had assumed a priestly quality. Are you putting on your cassock to protect you—

She didn't answer, at once. Then she said in a lighter tone—
it surprised me: "You remember Millie?"

"The girl who shared your apartment in New York?"

"Yes. Millie used to think— She'd be walking along the street
and see herself, suddenly, plunge a knife in a passer-by. She'd
see the knife, in her mind. See it sink in. But she could never see
her own hand or the face of the person. Now and then, she'd
look out the window and think, Suppose I dropped a flower-
pot on that old woman's head, down there."

"But she didn't."

"No."

Why on earth had she said this!

She was still on Millie. She said Millie would tell her:

—If I can't shake it off, I'll have to go to a psychiatrist. And
that costs money. And he'd tell me to break off with Joe and to
adjust to Daddy's values or make me remember the nasty things
I used to think and do as a kid, all of which I remember anyway.

—How do you know he would, Millie?

—Oh, you hear things. You just know. I'll stick to Millie's
method.

Millie's method was this: when she thought about that
knife she'd try to carry the feeling, tension, over into her acting:
sharpening movements, voice. It seemed to work. Her acting
improved and the knife disappeared. She called it her variant on
Stanislavski. It's a triple deal, she'd say: her method. She got
rid of the thought, improved her acting, and kept Joe.

"Who's Joe?"

"I was never quite sure. She met him at a Communist cock-
tail party."

"How is she now?"

"Fine. Six children. She's good with them, too."

"Never plunged that knife?"

"Not yet."

I drove along for a minute or so. "Joe's children?"

"No. She married a junior executive in her father's mills.
Her father retires next year and her husband will then become president of the mills."

A hundred yards on, I laughed. She laughed.

The wagon. Too much fog to pass. We were moving at less than ten miles an hour. The drag made me tense; and her words were exacerbating. Why Millie? Why on earth must we talk about Millie? We had laughed about her, all right; but we had not relaxed, and what was the point of it? I thought, I'll switch to politics if I can. Thought, No; you'd better not slip away from it.

I said, "Of course it shook you. What he told us, last night." No reply. "But being shaken up and losing your confidence in him are two different things. If we can't feel the absolute truth of what he said, how he felt as he sat on that pile of lumber . . . his loneliness as a child . . . the sailboat . . . the cement mixer —if we can't see the truth of it there's something wrong with us, not with him. I never believed you'd—"

I left it there. There was no sound. I was afraid she was crying. I could not be sure. Since we got in the car, all the way, I had been tense, irritable. Actually fighting her. And I knew it. I was amazed at myself. Why was I behaving like this? She'd been through weeks of it. Had geared her organism to accept what had happened as an insane accident; now—it was transformed by his admission, last night, into something quite different. He *had been there.* The child had beat on him. The two had experienced, together, an intimate and ancient terror. Then— Well, they were different afterward. Both of them. And somehow he had felt incapable of telling Grace about it. Now—Andy. She'd had no sleep, no solitude. She'd been fed some pretty raw facts during the last twelve hours. And here I was, demanding the correct answer from her. What did I think she was? an IBM brain?

Her voice was quiet and under complete control when she finally spoke. "Dave, you love him and respect him, as he does you. And you feel it is wrong for you and me to talk about him. You think we should just stand by him without admitting what is in our minds."

Of course I felt that way. Felt it intensely.

"But that is a conventional attitude. It is not necessarily right for him or Andy—or me."

I did not try to answer that, either.

"I don't know what you think belief in a person is. But whatever it is, it is not certainty that he won't make mistakes. Or sin."

As she talked, my feelings rather than my reason argued with her. Sin, yes; but what sin? a man is not capable of all sins!

"Or become sick and do— There may be pressures on Mark I know nothing about. Something may have caused a psychic upheaval in him—you know he wouldn't show it, it could be happening and he would go along as quietly as ever. Calm, composed—you know him this well, Dave! He's worked much too hard, lately; I've realized that."

"He loves his work." I meant it. But think of spending your life concentrating on a speck so small that you can see it only through an electron microscope! Those viruses. Looking at them —analyzing what he sees, measuring, comparing, measuring, watching minute changes, minute transformations— Maybe she's right. Maybe the rest of him can't put up with it, maybe something revolted—

She was answering me, "I know he loves it. It is his life. But those memories last night—they forced him to think about them, they compelled him to hurt again as he had as a child. Suppose— I think you can be too scientific. I don't know how to say it because I'm muddled about it but suppose it, the other part of him, the memories, feelings pushed him too hard and he did something irrational—something completely uncharacteristic of him— I don't think this has happened but *I don't know!* What I know is, I love him—regardless of what may or may not have happened inside him. Because I do, I want to consider every possibility— not to judge him but to know what to do next!"

Is there something else? are things not right between them— has he stopped— I wouldn't finish it.

Then, "Could you forget you are Mark's loyal friend and be my priest for a little while? Let me say what is so hard to say?" I felt irony in that voice, as if she had read my thoughts; and under it, desperation. I knew she was trying to smile, too, although she was dead serious. "I need to say it, Dave."

I apologized and told her I wanted her to say anything that would help her.

And then I passed that wagon.

She seemed to have forgot we were talking. I said, "You want to tell me something?"

"Yes." She stopped. Began again. "You remember I told you, once, what happened to me when I was not much older than Andy?"

I remembered but I didn't say anything.

"I keep thinking if only I could—" She didn't say more.

I drove on for another mile or two.

She said, "Dave—I can't tell Andy that Mark was in the store."

"Why should you?"

"Mark says I must."

"Why?"

"I'm not sure. I told him I didn't think it was necessary, it would be better not to. This seemed to upset him. He rarely gets angry but he seemed very upset. He asked me why I felt Andy shouldn't know. I tried to remind him that it might be hard on the boy—children feel things deeply because they've had so little experience and can't find a name for what they are feeling. Then he looked at me in a queer way, a bitter, sharp way, and said he wasn't sure of me. Not sure at all, he said."

"Meaning?"

"I don't quite know."

"Was he drinking?"

"The one drink in your study. I don't think he drank anything when he came home. He said he felt something change in me when he told me he was in the store. He said it two or three times, *You changed when I told you.* I told him I was surprised, of course; I was so sure he hadn't been near the place. But I made it worse. He said, All right: I lied to you and Dave, and I lied to the boy over the phone. Then he said he was not going to lie again or let us lie. He kept saying over and over, The boy has to hear the truth; we cannot lie to him again. He said Andy would believe him because he had always told him the truth."

"And you think?"

"Ever since Andy was born we've tried to be as honest as we could with him. Both of us. Ever since he was a baby. But there comes a time— How can you reveal everything about your life to a child? why should you? why subject him to such an ordeal? why does Mark want this?"

"I don't know." I know a combination of shocks can work like a powerful drug on a man causing him to have unpredictable reactions—but I could scarcely believe this. And this doubt she was feeling—this was hard to believe, too. Had she thought it up during our ride? did she feel this during the night? If she goes to Andy feeling this way, the boy will feel it, too.

I finally said, "Suppose you do what he wants: tell Andy everything that happened. Can you explain it as a kind of guilt-by-association incident? Here is his father: in the store looking around, as anyone might do. Then in comes this Susan. But he doesn't hear her. He is sitting on a pile of lumber remembering things and thinking; and the kid doesn't see him. Then he goes to the latrine—and she sees him and the rest of it happens. Then everybody accuses him of something he didn't do—just because he is tall and the crazy kid said the man in the store was tall. Would he believe you?"

"Every word I'd say—if that were all. But he has the letter: he knows other people know. And he knows we kept it from him. He's thinking about it in those terms, and in other terms too. His imagination is involved. We don't know what he is seeing in his mind—what pictures are there— He must have thought things —all children do—about us, about me, maybe; about Mark, tabooed things— An anonymous letter—it is curious, Dave, but it is as if it were coming out of you, your own self. The ones they pushed under my door frightened me."

"Of course they did. They were obscene and insulting."

"It was more than that. You feel, something in you feels, that they came from an unknown place; and this brings up associations: hell, caves, labyrinths, mysterious powers, oracles, demons— I lay awake last night thinking what it would do to Andy—

Your grown-up mind sees it simply as a misspelled, stupid, nasty anonymous letter—but something on a wordless, primitive level in you reacts. I—I don't know how far it has pulled him." For the first time, she was crying. She fought hard to regain her control.

After a moment, she said, "If this had happened to you, even if I told him you were in the store, I should have no difficulty convincing him of your innocence. It would be almost as if I were reading a suspense story to him and by a strange twist of circumstance he knew the accused. He'd say, But of course Father Dave didn't do it—he just happened to walk in that store and look around. But when it is your own father, it is different. He can't help but think—"

"What everybody else is thinking—only more so."

"Yes. The details Mark told us will make it worse."

"Omit the details."

"I see no reason to mention the store. That letter has done enough."

I thought, She's working on it too hard. Pulling it this way, that; probing too much. He'll feel her feelings. If she is sure of Mark and calm, he'll react the same way. On the other hand—

She said, "When you're young, you think things you can't possibly say. You're defenseless. You've nothing to measure your thoughts or feelings by. No frame to put around them. I keep thinking what happened to me, Dave."

"What do you want to do?"

"I want to tell him only what Mark told you and me, in the beginning. I want to say we were planting the tulips on the terrace. The tall black ones I wrote him about. That we had worked a long time; it was a warmish day and his father said, Let's give ourselves a break and have a rum and Coke. So we went inside and I discovered there were no Cokes. So: Mark went to Matthews and got a carton, came back, and we had our drinks. In the meantime, this child—this Susan Newell—went in the vacant store and something scared her. She said a tall thin man did something bad to her; then she saw Mark on the street, afterward, and said he was the man."

"He is going to ask why."

"I'll tell him she thought it because he is tall and thin. And other people happened to see him at Matthews—"

I said, "Does Andy know where that vacant store is? How near it is to Matthews?"

"I'd think so."

In a moment she said, "Yes. He asked me—I remember now—it was a year or two ago: he asked me why the store was closed. I told him Toni had gone away and no one seemed to know who owned the store; there was an uncertainty about Toni's death, too; no one had proof that he had died and no one knew who his heirs were. I remember now: Andy persisted in his questions. Had I ever been inside? I told him no. Had anyone been inside? I told him I didn't know. He wanted to know what was in there. Was it empty? or were things still in there? I explained that the store was closed when we came to Windsor Hills and I had never heard anyone discuss it. He ran to the window and tried to look in. The glass was covered with that white soapy stuff. He came running back—I was parked in front of Town and Country—and he told me he had seen a yellow cat asleep in the window. He was extremely excited, wanted to know how a cat could be in a store that had been shut up for years. He wanted to go to the alley to see if a window had been left open or if the back door had a small hole in it through which the cat could come and go."

I said, "If I were you, I'd tell him nothing or I'd tell him everything. Why tell him about the Cokes? Just tell him the whole thing was made up. That Mark was with you all afternoon. Don't mention the fact that he went to the shopping center. Say you planted bulbs, the two of you; then you sat on the front terrace and read. Tell him Susan went in the store, all right, and was scratched by the old yellow cat he had seen long ago and it scared her; then she ran into the beauty shop and told them a man was in the store prowling around; then everybody began to talk and make up things. She said the man was tall and thin and Mark happens to be tall and thin; so does her father; and that is that. Tell him Susan is a liar. And her mother is a worse one. Tell him I saw Mark on the terrace at five-thirty at the exact moment Susan was inside the store."

She began to laugh. It was hysterical laughter, close to tears. I tried to stop her, then I began to laugh too. Finally she said, "We may all be absolutely wacky."

Then she said, "Mark is never unreasonable. There must be a reason for his wanting Andy to know. I feel it is important for me to find it."

"It is possible he is tired. When you are your judgment is likely to be poor."

She was still working at it:

"Andy is more than a son to Mark," she finally said. "He's everything Mark missed as a child: home, mother, father . . . he's all of it. Mark talked all night about it. He thinks he will be telling Andy the truth when he tells him the literal facts. Mark said to us—didn't he? last night? that facts do not necessarily add up to the truth. There are facts and facts—and they don't all speak a modern language—am I wrong?—didn't he say it? If not last night, he has said it another time. Some facts by-pass the reason and go to the primitive part of us. I'm sure he has said it to me."

"He said it last night."

"Then why is he insisting that I load Andy with facts that are bound to add up to a big lie— And one the child can't take?"

"I don't know."

She said slowly, "I suppose no one ever had an emptier child-hood— That lonely little fellow he told us about last night, play-ing clown, with the pine curls stuck under his cap—and his father's suspicious, blazing anger. He had never told me this, un-til last night."

"Yes, but I think we can overstress these things."

"I know, Dave. I know there is not just one reason, or just two or three or four. But his father didn't trust him long ago when he needed trust. Now his son must give him that trust: must prove himself the all-understanding person his father failed to be."

"Does this seem like Mark to you?"

"Not in the least. But none of it seems like him. That little memory was there, though; and he thought about it in the store;

and he thought about it again, last night, because he told it to us."

"And you think all the commotion has brought the memory wide awake, the hurt or need, and now it wants to be fed, or something?"

"In a way; in a devious way, yes."

Neel and I had trapped ourselves with theories about Susan. And we were dead wrong when we had been sure we were right. This might or might not be right. You know the theory: you try to fit your unique experience, or somebody else's, to it: you pinch it off here, pull it around there—but it tricks you because there is usually one detail that is different and one detail, or two or three, can wreck any theory.

I said, "It is possible. Mark's under terrific pressure. He may want something of himself or Andy or their relationship that he hasn't needed before. I don't know. He has always seemed to me about the most sensible, rational person I ever knew. I just don't know."

"I don't know, either. Because he's always seemed that way to me, too. But last night, after we left you, he seemed different. He couldn't stop talking. He walked up and down the living room, talking, talking. He told me about those years in prison—he'd never talked about it before. The loneliness. He described everything in precise detail as if it were necessary for me to see it, too. The nights . . . the days . . . the nights . . . how he wanted me; then he stopped wanting me; he decided he couldn't have me ever again so he stopped wanting me; he just wanted a woman, any woman . . . then he wanted anybody, any live human being. It was then, he said, the terror began: when the loneliness hardened into concrete wants. He tried to explain how loneliness is first a feeling of isolation, of being cut off from all you need and feed on, all your mind, body, heart need—then suddenly it becomes an object, a thing threatening you, and you must not let it touch you, you must fight it off with other objects. . . ."

He described how he fought it; how he piled up all he knew to keep the loneliness from touching him. He said he didn't have many personal memories to pile up; he tried to go back to his childhood but he couldn't remember much; then he tried to go back to his years in Ohio but he couldn't remember them; so he piled up facts, all the facts he knew about biology and chemistry. He'd put his mind on the bloodstream, and think about it day and night: It became as big as the Mississippi River as he filled it with the facts he had learned about it. He'd say, Tonight I shall think about plasma; another night he'd think about blood cells or blood patterns; another time it would be enzymes; or he'd think about sugar levels, let them rise and fall in this great Bloodstream that flowed across his mind. Then he'd think about tissue: healthy tissue, malignant tissue; then the endocrine system, the hormones; he'd try to break them into molecules, and then he'd try to break the molecules. Sometimes he'd begin with the cells: he'd say, There are two hundred billion cells in a baby's body and he'd go on from there, differentiating them; or he would begin with one cell: he'd break that cell down into its constituent parts until he'd get to the nucleus, then he'd try to break the nucleus into its acids. . . . He tried to remember poetry but he couldn't remember much and this bothered him. But he could remember facts. One night, he bounded the states of the Union, telling himself that Arkansas was bounded by Mississippi and Tennessee on the east, Texas and Louisiana on the south, Missouri on the north, and Oklahoma on the west, then he bounded Missouri and from Missouri he moved on to Ohio, and on until he had bounded every state in the Union. Then he named the Presidents of the United States. He tried to do the Secretaries of State but broke down around Cleveland or McKinley. One night he began to make colors in his mind: He remembered watching Grace paint, so he took the idea of gray and mixed the colors in his mind until, a week later, he had sixty-four shades of gray. He felt much better, afterward. Then he remembered a little play he had been in. In the third grade in Quitman, Georgia, or Madison, Florida; he spent almost all of one night trying to decide which state he was in when he was in the little play. With that settled, he remembered the crude paper flowers they had made; the teacher had brought rolls of colored tissue paper to school, it swished when she unrolled it and the sunlight caught the colors and the paper unrolled down an aisle, and he felt something turn over in his stomach. He thinks it was his first esthetic experience. He said the colors did something tremendous to him. So in that dark prison, he tried to make those bright-colored paper flowers again, in his mind; then he began to think of flowers in botanical terms and constructed petals and stamen and sepals and pistils and all the rest of it. And, about then, he remembered Goethe's symbolic plant. He had always considered *The Metamorphosis of Plants* a kind of scientific-literary curiosity. But shut away from the world, he found he liked to think about it. It turned into poetry, the poetry of morphology. Then he remembered Heimholtz's arguments against that book. He tried to follow the argument through but he'd lose it and return to his facts. There seemed to be plenty of facts in his mind. So he piled them, like bricks, around him. Then the nightmare began: the bricks liquefied, the facts melted like syrup candy and ran off the edge of the world and he was left with nothing between him and the loneliness.

She said, "Once he spent a week, maybe a month—he said he had no idea of time—remembering every place in New York we had been together: what time of day or night we went there, how long we stayed, what we did, how we got there, whether we went by cab or subway or walked, what we ate, then he'd try to remember what clothes I had on. And sometimes he could remember but always, after a time, I seemed to have on nothing. He said he distinctly remembered, as he lay there in that prison, an afternoon at the Museum of Modern Art: We were looking at an exhibit of French Impressionists: he remembered we were looking at a Renoir, and I walked over to two Seurats, and he noticed as I stood there, that I had on a blue tweed skirt and a black jacket. And then the clothes were not there. I was naked. And then, I was not there. My personality faded first: I was just a body: then I turned into a Picasso-like cubist construction broken into quite interesting planes and tensions, he said; then that faded, too. And there was nothing. This was when he began to want something: anything, if only it were living and breathing. And finally he knew he was close to losing his reason, he felt it sliding away. And there followed a black empty time when he was fighting fighting. . . . Then, finally, he began to clear. The first thing he remembered was that he had a little son named Andrew whom he had never seen. It began, he said, as a kind of depersonalized idea; a clean abstraction. Then, he slowly realized he did actually have a son whom he had never seen—a flesh and blood son who breathed and cried and laughed and might even now be saying two or three words. He held on to this—as a person drowning might do. And slowly he believed it. And then he began to plan for him. He could see him growing from day to day. His imagination was living again; every day, he created this son anew and watched his creation grow and change, grow and change. And this held him; this staved off the Enemy. It was not me; it was Andy whom he had never seen who saved him.

"I understand," she said. "I almost understand. And I am glad he felt he could say it."

Voice low—and trembling now and then; but otherwise she was holding herself steady. "It was just so much, coming at one time. Something in his mind opened in your study: once opened, it wouldn't shut. Everything poured out. His friendship for you: did you know he cared so much?"

I didn't know.

"His research—you realize what that means to him?"

"I think so."

"Did you know his mother died of cancer when he was a year old?"

"No."

"I didn't, either. Until last night. I knew she died when he was a baby. That is all he had told me. I keep thinking about it."

After another silence she said, "Once, he fell out of a tree and landed on his head." She tried to laugh. "He told me about that, too; everything, the big the little; he told me everything. So much. It is like a flood. It drowns me, sort of. His research, the feeling he has about it—is it because of the way his mother died? he never knew her—but is he now determined to know the enemy who killed her? is that part of it? for him?"

"Not necessarily." I wished she hadn't said it. Why try to find the primal cause of everything! A man's choice of work—surely there must be a hundred reasons why it chooses him or he chooses it.

"Mark's mind likes to work with facts. It is full of curiosity and at home with abstractions. You know that. He is by temperament and the quality of his mind, a natural researcher. Let's leave it at that."

"Yes, I know. It's just that I felt I understood him so well a few weeks ago. Now he's turned into a stranger."

"You haven't had time to fit it together. But it does fit; there's nothing, is there, that tears up what you had thought about him? It makes him bigger—you are aware of a little more of him but this gives him depth. The old iceberg analogy: only a small part of us thrusts up above the waters. This is true of all of us. You know this as well as I do."

"Dave . . . why did it happen? I have sworn I wouldn't ask it. I know how silly it is to ask it. I know it's primitive— But why— why—" She stopped. Said quietly, "Don't try. Don't try."

She began again. "Just before we were married, I told him what happened to me at camp, in New England. With a woman. I was nearly fifteen." It had swung around again. Why on earth—

I wanted the fog to lift, daylight to come. I looked at the speedometer, wondered if I could push it up a bit; then, perhaps, she'd realize we'd better not talk more, just now. We were in a dip of the road and the fog was thick and wet; vision blanked out thirty feet ahead. I slowed down, said, "Would you like a cigarette?" She said yes. I pushed in the lighter.

We smoked a while. Neither of us said a word for a long time. We had eased into open space where there was no fog. She said, "When I told him, we were falling in love and I was thinking only of what it might do to him and his love for me. Now I'm afraid it may have something to do with my whole life. I feel—"

She was groping, she couldn't find it.

"In what way?"

"I don't know. I feel it has caught up with me."

"You think you're being—punished?"

"Not in a crude way. But I have the feeling it may be one thing, among others, that could have—" Unfinished.

I thought, She's fallen into a stream and is being swept away by a swift cruel undercurrent. It is not characteristic of her—this guilt. She's modern in her point of view, informed, has always been relaxed. I was remembering how easy and natural she had been with Andy when things came up—masturbation—all the things—

I said, "Something happened to you, once, when you were fifteen years old—and now you think Mark has brooded over it?"

"That isn't what I mean. Will you let me try to tell you?"

"I want you to."

She said softly, "It is dawn. I hadn't noticed." She turned away and looked at the countryside. A meadow was shining with heavy frost, weeds and dead goldenrod and sumac were stiff and white with it, and fog was rising now from the pavement, spilling over the shoulders of the road. She did not turn back until we had left the meadow behind us. Then she gave me a quick imploring look and began to talk— I think she intended to begin with the woman. But instead, she began with Mark: telling me of their first weeks together, long ago, in New York:

16

They were in her walk-up apartment.

But first: They had met three weeks before. One cold rainy night in 1942. In front of the Royale Theater. He was a colonel in the Air Force. Had done a stint in England; was home instructing at one of our bases. She was studying modern dance with Martha Graham or Hanya Holm, with both maybe; was studying sculpture with Zorach. On that rainy night, they were two strangers standing near the curb. She glanced at him, thought he looked interesting. She said she must have looked like a drowned rat. Everybody wanted cabs, of course. He stepped out, signaled, she ran out and signaled too, the cab driver ignored her, said to him, Yes sir! He opened the door, she called, You meanie; Mark turned, saw her, laughed, said, Come along, I'll take you home.

It couldn't have been a more stereotyped beginning, in wartime. But it was their beginning.

"I let him pick me up because I could see he was nice and I was soaking wet." They went to her apartment, she asked him in and they talked all night. Her roommate, Millie, came in, went to bed; but they talked on and on. He told her about his research in biochemistry. "I thought it fascinating," she said. "Me: who flunked in chemistry; only thing I ever failed in." She told him about modern dance, what it meant to her, and he listened as if he cared; she told him about abstract expressionism, and he asked her to show him some paintings in the galleries. Tomorrow, he said. He built a fire in the small grate; she cooked bacon and eggs in the small kitchen; they drank wine, they drank coffee, they talked until dawn. She said, Tell me about flying. He said, Let's walk across Brooklyn Bridge. They did. They ate more bacon and eggs somewhere on Fulton Street, and then went up on the roof of the old Hotel Margaret to look across the harbor at the Manhattan skyline. He came back at noon for her and took her to luncheon at the Plaza because she and her mother had always stayed there on their trips to New York. That afternoon, he took her to Sloan-Kettering, the great research institute where he had worked. "That's the way he began to make love to me: showing me mice and malignant tissue and tubes and slides, explaining technics, and introducing me to his fellow-researchers. I told them my father was a surgeon; one of the doctors had heard of him while studying at Hopkins. That made me feel good. I felt I belonged."

They went somewhere for dinner. Then to the Blue Angel.

Then on to a place in the Village and danced for hours. Next time he was off duty, they took a Seventh Avenue subway to Fulton Street, Manhattan side, and walked over to the fish market. Awful smells, fine sky, gulls greedy, clamorous. They went upstairs to Sweets for lunch. There was a big fat cat under their table. The old waiter shushed it toward the kitchen as he firmly told them to order the small scallops. They obeyed and were glad—but they would have liked anything, that day. They wandered around old narrow streets down at the foot of the island, walked through the churchyard at Trinity; cut across to the Hudson River side and went to Washington Market. Wandered up and down the stalls. "We'd stand for minutes looking at geese and ducks and pheasants. We'd examine a thick sirloin steak, cherry red with creamy islands of fat; then gravely estimate how many people could be served from a certain rib roast."

Detail, detail, detail. I had never heard her remembering aloud before. It had meaning for her, their afternoon in the Market, and it was necessary to pull every stall and its contents back in order to recapture the experience she was seeking— She had finished with the cheeses and was now at the vegetable stalls: "We looked a long time at eggplant and purple cabbage and I knew he loved me and I said I'd never seen anything so beautiful." Then she told him she loved the name *escarolle* but hated the thing it stood for; they talked about names; he liked water cress best of all—its taste and its name. This seemed important to her, for she did, too. They went to the fish stalls: looked at clumps of oysters in the shell, and mussels and turtles and piles of gray raw shrimp and bowls of pink cooked ones. She said she liked sea turtle; and he said he liked the small terrapin or whatever they are you get on the Amazon; he told her how they mince the terrapin meat down there and season it with all kinds of peppers until it is blazing hot and then stir in farinha and bake the mixture in small shells. She asked when he had been on the Amazon; he said he hadn't, he had read about it in the *National Geographic,* or somewhere. This made her laugh hysterically.

As I listened, her voice was young again, expectant—

Her memory had arrived at a flower stall: he bought her a bunch of winter violets and stuck them in her coat. He said, It's time to buy supper. So they bought mushrooms and caviar, and cheeses whose names they liked, and a pheasant and some snails and freshly ground Honduras coffee, and French bread. Then he bought a dozen big double-yolked eggs. He spotted them among pyramids of eggs, picked one up, turned it on his palm. He said, "I want a dozen." The hearty red-cheeked woman behind the stall said, "They're double." He smiled, he said, "Yes, I know." He asked her where she lived; she told him on a farm on Staten Island; he told her about his grandfather's farm in Ohio. And Grace listened and watched his face, his hands. ". . . how gently he picked up that egg—as if he had just slipped it out from under the hen."

He hailed a cab. They took the things home. He unwrapped them, he folded the big paper bags, he said where do you keep the bags? She said she had never kept one. He said they might be useful. So she found a place to keep them. He handled everything easily, carefully. "As if he were in his lab." He said he'd do the snails if she would do the pheasant. While it roasted in the wine, he made a fire in the grate and poured drinks. She set the table. They listened to a Poulenc record. He had never heard Poulenc; but he remembered that she had mentioned Poulenc when she was talking about her mother playing the piano; so he asked to hear Poulenc. "He's always been like that; always wants to hear, to see." After the snails and pheasant and the rest of it, they washed dishes. Then he said, for the first time, I love you; she said yes, she knew; and she loved him, too. He handed her a fresh dishcloth. When the dishes were done he said, Let's clean up the place. He poured two glasses of brandy and got the mop and broom. "Millie and I weren't very good housekeepers." A homesick boy without a home met a girl who thought she'd had too much home and now they were playing house together down in the Village. "It was an odd way to make love but it was fun." When he had things as neat as he wanted them, they drank more brandy and listened to Gershwin because he knew all about Gershwin's music. Then, toward midnight, Millie came. Millie had a small part in a Broadway play; usually she cleaned up before she left the theater but that night she hadn't. She looked tired behind the make-up, and worried, but she stayed with them; she would go in the bedroom, then come out; she'd go to the kitchen, pick up a piece of bread and a bit of pheasant, and come out and sit on the stool and nibble. She seemed to be feeling what they felt. She said, "Let me stay." They laughed and she stayed, hunched up on the stool, chin in her hands, watching them.

"I remember how sorry I was for her," Grace said. The three talked for another hour. Then he kissed Grace good night, and Millie laughed at them; then she asked him, like a little girl, to kiss her too. And he did. He ping-ponged a few words with her; kissed Grace again, and left. They both listened to him go down the stairs. Millie said, "You get him if you can." She walked around the room; she sat down, took off her flats, rubbed her feet; walked around the room some more; took a print off its hook— it was Picasso's *Two Sisters;* she said, They're too sad, they have no bones, they're melting; she turned it to the wall. She always turned a picture to the wall when she was upset. Sometimes, all the pictures were turned to the wall. "The only fuss we ever had was when she turned my one Klee water color toward the wall. I wouldn't put up with that."

Millie said, "He's better than my Joe."

"What do you mean?"

"He's real. You don't find somebody who's real—not once in ten years. Maybe not ever. You hold on to him."

"You love Joe."

"I know; but he's not real. I love phonies because I'm not real, either."

Grace told her she looked worried. She said she was. She said, "Joe's sold out. The CP's bought him. All of him he knows about or they know about. I'm through. He's no better than Daddy. The other side of the coin. They both sell out too easy. Dad fights the commies and the commies fight big businessmen like Dad.

But they're all—oh I don't know. I sell out too—but I don't know what buys me."

"They don't either, maybe."

The two girls went to bed. Grace tried to worry about Millie; she couldn't; she was too much in love with Mark.

Now—three weeks later—Mark and Grace were once more in her flat. They had been to a show, had stopped by Sardi's. They had ordered some food. He said, "Something's on your mind. Want to tell me?"

The drinks had come. She drank hers quickly. "I was thinking about things."

He did not ask what, but gave her his close attention, the way he does if he thinks you want to say something you are having difficulty with.

They finished their drinks. She said, "I'm sort of scared. You don't know me."

"I'll know you better after we are married. Tomorrow?"

She asked him how much longer before he'd be sent across. He said he wasn't sure. She said, A month? He said, Maybe; maybe two months.

She told him she meant what she said—he might not feel the same way when he knew her better.

"That goes for you, too. But I'm not worried."

The food was being served. They ate it. They didn't talk much. She was thinking, You don't have to tell him now. Next week you can do it.

He said as they drank their coffee, "What is it?"

She said, "Nothing much. Let's go home."

And they had gone to Fourth Street.

He was building a fire now—and she had gone over to the cupboard for a bottle of wine and glasses. He said, "I meant what I said. I want to marry you as soon as possible."

She said, "You haven't met Mother and Dad."

He laughed. "You mean they need to meet me."

"Both. They'll like you."

"It'll be rugged but—yes, I know they need to meet me. Let's go tomorrow. The fire won't burn." He found some paper, he struck a match, it flared up.

She brought the bottle over to the low table near the fire. Brought the glasses. He said, "You are trembling."

And then she told him—about Her. Blurted it out. She said to me, "I don't have any idea what I said. I just felt he had to know."

And he stood with the blown-out match in his hand and listened as she told him. His eyes meeting hers every moment. At the hard spot, when she found it almost impossible to say the next words, he took her hand and held it as she talked. He let her say all she wanted to say. Then he said, "Sit down." She was so weak she fell on the stool. Then he looked at her a long time; he was almost smiling. Then he said softly, "It is the saddest little story I ever heard."

That made her cry. He stood beside her, touched her hair, touched her neck. He poured two glasses of wine, lifted up her face, wiped it against his sleeve, said, "I want you to drink this." He put a glass in her hand. He lifted his glass and said, "To the girl I love." And slowly drank his wine.

"While I cried like a baby, Dave."

He went to the bathroom, brought back a box of Kleenex. Almost anybody else would have given her his handkerchief but Mark always did the sensible thing. Then he made her drink the wine. Then he worked on the fire, a little. Then he stood looking at her; suddenly he grinned, said, "Guess I'd better tell you what I've done, too. Come over and sit real close. It's going to be rough but if you can, I can. Once, when I was about seventeen I went berserk and—"

She put her hand over his mouth. He kissed it. They laughed. They drank another glass of wine. He pulled her close, kissed her—

"Then I asked him to make love to me, right then. I didn't know how to ask it, I fumbled with my words, I was terribly shy, but I told him what I wanted."

Mark looked at her so long it scared her. He eased her down on the stool. He walked over to the fireplace. He looked at the fire which had not burned much. He turned around, said quietly, evenly, "When I make love to you it is not going to be a lab experiment. Let's get that straight. That's what you want? not me—but to be sure of yourself?"

She was too stunned to answer.

"To prove something to yourself. That you're—what?"

She couldn't answer.

"That you're normal? is that it? I know a little about a normal cell—don't know a thing about a normal person."

She said she didn't know what a normal person was, either. But she wanted to be normal for him because—

"Because why?"

Because she'd hate to—ruin everything.

"Because?"

"I love you."

He looked at her a long time, then smiled and said, "Sounds interesting—but it isn't in my line. When I make love to you, it'll be because we can't help ourselves."

"I feel that way—right now."

And as I drove along listening I was feeling *I have never been young, like that. Why? Why?*

Mark didn't seem to hear. He finished his cigarette. She watched him. She tried hard to get inside his mind. She felt he was already inside hers and she was frightened at what he was seeing there. He spoke casually about meeting her at Penn Station next morning. How about in front of Information? Yes. About nine-twenty? Yes. He kissed her good night; did it lightly. It hurt. She heard him go down the stairs, heard him stop. He stayed on that step a long time. Then he ran up the stairs. She opened the door. He came in, took her in his arms, kissed her, made her kiss him, said, "You do love me?" She whispered yes. "You're sure?" She said she was sure. "Sure enough to spend the rest of your life with me?" "Yes." "Then hold it. Don't think about anything else until tomorrow." And he was gone.

At nine-twenty he met her at Information. He told her she looked wonderful; he liked her in that shade of blue. She tried to say something easy to him. Couldn't think of a word. Just smiled, and swallowed hard.

They went down to the train. They didn't speak as they walked down the stairs. She saw a brown and white wrapper from a candy bar on the cement floor. She saw two fat legs, two wobbly high heels in front of her. She saw a hand with black hairs on it pulling a crying dragging child in a red coat. She looked up and into the eyes of an engineer in his cab as they passed another train. She said his eyes had the same intent look that Mark's often have; but they were a different color, she couldn't remember what color but they were different; she'd never forget that engineer, she said.

They walked through two cars before they found seats. He took her coat, he put a small canvas bag at his feet. He said, I have a present or two for you. I got your father a bottle of Drambuie, hope he likes it. She said he did. He had a Prokofieff record for her mother, hoped she liked Prokofieff. Grace said she did. Did she have this one? Grace thought she didn't. Neither said more. But she felt good being quiet. "There're so many kinds of quiet," she said to me, "and we were moving through this one in the same rhythm."

They left the tunnel, passed the Jersey marshes, left Newark, left Elizabeth, had passed that big Squibbs sign, wherever it is. Finally she asked to see her present. He took the small case out of his pocket: she knew: he had shown it to her before but she had asked him to keep it a few days. Her ring. He slipped it on her finger. He said, I've got something else. This time he seemed unsure. He took out a small white prayer book wrapped in tissue paper. He said it was the only thing of his mother's he owned. Inside was her name: *Nancy Livingstone. With love from Mother and Father—on her wedding day.*

He said, "She was sick a long time before she died. She marked it up quite a bit." He opened it, showed her the pencil marks, said softly, "That's all she left in this world, just a few marks on a prayer book." She wanted to whisper, *She left you.* Couldn't say it. He asked her if she'd keep it while he was gone.

"I read it to pieces," she said to me now, "the years he was in prison."

Then he showed her two faded pictures of the young Nancy

and his father. Then snapshots of his grandparents who had reared him on that Ohio farm. Then he said, That's it, I guess.

"That's the man I married, Dave. I wanted you to know."

But I already knew.

She told how it was when they arrived at her home in Roland Park. She had telephoned her mother before she left New York. They took a cab at Pennsylvania Station, went up Charles Street, up the Parkway. Mrs. Ryder was waiting. Quietly cordial; quietly observant. She led them into the music room. She asked them if they would have some sherry. Grace offered to get it; her mother said, No; you're company, today. She left them and went to the pantry. He walked over to the Stieff piano, he picked up a Mozart piano concerto lying there, turned the pages. He whispered, She doesn't look a bit like you; she's a little like—Billie Burke.

She whispered that she'd never thought of it but she was, kind of.

Then her mother came in with the silver tray and a bottle of Dry Sack. Mark poured the sherry. Somehow, in a moment or two, he had her settled in her comfortable chair and was talking easily to her. "I knew they liked each other."

She heard her father's car in the driveway, ran out to meet him. He kissed her, said Sugar, etc. And she said what a girl always says when her father says, It is pretty quick, you know, etc., had she thought it through, etc. He came in, shook hands with Mark. Grace poured him a drink of Scotch, knowing he was up to no foolishness like sherry. Suddenly, the room seemed extraordinarily bright. A muscle in her father's cheek had moved quickly and relaxed, and she knew—"he is so obvious"—that Mark was not off to a bad start. She said she had never seen so much sun in one room. She went over and stuck her finger in the cage and touched the canary. She looked at the miniature cacti and African violets in the window; she moved the cacti and rearranged the African violets . . . and then she moved them back as they had been. And all the time she was listening as Mark talked music with her mother and medicine with her father. She saw Mark look wistfully at the Scotch; she winked at him. And he, at once, concentrated gravely on his conversation with her mother about Stravinsky.

"Dad was sly as a pickpocket: the way he eased Mark's credentials out of him: Cornell, medical degree; Cornell, Ph.D. in biochemistry: names of teachers; names of one or two scientists with whom he had worked at Sloan-Kettering; name of his commanding officer at the base. She knew her father would fade into his study after lunch and call these people. She hoped Mark wouldn't guess it. But nothing mattered now. She was high on sherry and love: home seemed a nice place to be, at least for a day; Mark fitted in; she knew her parents felt it.

After lunch, Mark said he believed he'd go out in the garden and walk around. She stayed and told her parents about him. Everything she could remember. It wasn't much, of course. Then her father went in his study, as she knew he would do. And she and her mother asked Mark if he'd like to drive around Johns Hopkins University and he said he would. When they came back, her father asked Mark to go to the hospital with him, he had a few calls to make. "It was like an old dance everybody in the world knows the steps of."

They took the ten-fifteen back to New York that evening. Went to Fourth Street. Millie had left a note pinned on an orange in the middle of the coffee table. It said she was spending the night with Joe. "Joe's overpersuaded me. Pray for my soul." When Grace read it, her heart began to beat fast. She handed it to Mark. He laughed. "Good old Millie." She said she'd make some coffee if he would build a fire. As she went back and forth, she told him how the Committee had been putting pressure on Joe not to marry Millie. She's bourgeois and stupid, they told him. Joe's in to his neck, Grace told Mark. She wished Millie would drop him. Millie joined the CP because she hates her family's hypocrisy: they're big church people but it is money money things things; they're anti-Semitic, anti-Negro, anti-labor, anti-TVA, anti-modern art. Everything they fear or don't understand they call "communistic"—so Millie joined the Communist party, of course. "They practically pushed her in. But she's only playing around."

"The CP doesn't play dolls," Mark said.

"She knows. But to her anything's better than her parents' values—the ones they say they have. But nobody's going to boss Millie. Not Joe—not the CP—not even Millie, I'm afraid."

They forgot Millie. Mark came over, kissed her, said quietly, "I would like to stay tonight."

She said, "Sure it's not a lab experiment?"

He said, "Sure."

They had an early breakfast, next morning. He went back to the base. Three days later they were married—attended by her father and mother and a fellow-officer. "We had five weeks together before he was sent to India. I knew I was pregnant when he left. Somehow I felt this would bring him back."

She was talking to herself, not to me. Searching for the unique something that made it only her experience, and Mark's. She laughed. Her voice was full of tears as she said, "I tell it, and it could be anybody's love affair. I thought we went through something special and rigorous and came out of it stronger, more alive. But now it sounds only very young."

After a little, she said, "I meant to tell you something else, that has to do with that old relationship of mine. I feel—I don't know quite what I feel." She did not say more.

"I remember you told me of the woman's death. Do you know why it happened?"

"I can only guess. I know a little, yes. It happened seven years after I had known her at camp."

"How old was she?"

"I'm not sure. I was fifteen when I knew her and she must have been twenty-two or -three. I'm not sure. She must have been twenty-nine or thirty, at the time of her death. She lived with a girl her own age, three years. The other girl married and made a go of it. On the surface, at least. She—the one I cared for —took up flying. She was a fine pilot, daring, cool, relaxed, expert. The men at the field liked her enormously. She was fun, a good sport, keyed people up; made you feel that something special was about to happen when she walked in a room. And men felt her as much, I think, as women did."

"You saw her after camp?"

"Once, by accident." Yes, I remembered. She had told me, one April afternoon in her living room. She stopped. Seemed to be searching for something. She said, "She was different. It was as if she had just arrived from a country where customs are a bit shocking, perhaps, and exotic but interesting. More than that. She made everybody feel they had missed something important by not having lived her life although she never talked about it. She was not afraid of anything in the external world. But inside— I think, now, there was a place she had never dared go near."

They felt this, too, I thought, and were attracted by it.

"Then—one of the pilots at the air base fell in love with her and apparently she was in love with him—or hoped she was. They were married. Two days later, she took a plane up and headed out to sea. She radioed, *no fuel*. They asked her to give her bearings, asked her again and again. Then they heard, Tell Bill . . . it is OK . . . tell Bill he has been wonderful, tell him . . . tell him I tried— Her words slid together and that was all."

"And even now . . . it is with you."

"Not the way she died, Dave. It shocked me, yes; at the time. I've told you how it hurt then; I was so young; and it hurts now, in a way. But I feel . . . it was her death. She had been making it all her life—shaping it to fit her exactly when it came."

Last year, yes, we had talked about it. It had come up quite casually, and she had told me a great deal but we had not talked much about the woman's death. Had life grown, suddenly, too large for her? or too small? Strange, how the way you die can change, make over the life you have lived as if there is a hidden design which only your death can make visible.

She was saying, "What hurt was not her death but what I let a few words do to my image of her—and of me." Groping for an inner connection she could not find. "And now it is happening again—not to me but to my son."

"But this is—" I wouldn't say it.

"Different. I know. Because Mark has done no wrong." She had firmly pushed her doubt away. "But it comes rushing back at you and you can't understand it or yourself or—this world—"

She was trembling and looked much too pale. I suggested that she not talk any more but try to rest.

She closed her eyes. Opened them. Said, "I thought it was settled, that I had made my final peace with it. I suppose you never do, quite."

No. You shove it on that carousel tootling its sad-gay music and finally it comes round again and you recognize it and say, So there you are! —And sometimes it has shrunk into a small thing and you smile as if at a broken toy; and then again it has grown big and misshapen and evil and the sight of it leaves you trembling and sweating and you watch it as it moves along its orbit and disappears and you know it will come again—in someone you love if not in you.

She said, without opening her eyes, "That night long ago, Mark said a wonderful thing: *You can't prove anything that is important to you; you risk it if you love a person.* I believe that. But Andy is too young—he doesn't know you must risk—and he couldn't, even if he knew." Tears rolled from beneath her eyes. "It is so wrong! If he must doubt, it should be me, not Mark."

We were nearing the city. A big paper mill, a school, a long stretch of field and rough eroded hills slid by.

I looked at her. Breathing softly now. Pale. Limp. Why had this come back to tangle with her at the moment she needed all the objectivity she could hold on to? I wasn't sure. Why was Mark suddenly demanding so much of Andy? I didn't know; I still do not know. It happens: the blow falls; and parts of you explode: memories heave, the underside comes up, you look, you cannot believe what you see for the old experience has turned over an inch or two and there are no words that fit the new vision. Her breathing was regular now. I hoped she was sleeping. You need to hold on to what is happening *now*—and what do you do? you swing back into inner space, you are lost suddenly in the pulling twisting ambiguous experiences of ten years ago, fifteen, twenty—

I turned away and looked at those fields with the frost on them, and the trees. Most of the leaves were gone except on the red

oaks and white oaks. A persimmon had lost its leaves but a few
of its small purplish-yellow globes of fruit were still hanging on
bare branches. The kudzu covering red clay banks was limp
and dead. I held on to leaves, briars, brown kudzu, a split rail
fence; I made myself remember a cold frosty Saturday morning
when I was a kid and had gone hunting and stopped and rested
my gun against a fence and shook a persimmon tree and ate the
soft squudgy sweet fruit that fell. A little of it. You never want
many persimmons. Not a thing unusual had happened that Saturday, long ago. I just remembered it. And then I looked at her, at
the shaggy black hair, the curve of cheek, the closed eyelids . . .
so young—as if there were a few years she could not leave—and
so terribly old . . . and now I was praying God to give her the
strength she had to have . . . and to forgive us our pitiful ways.

We were drawing near the airport. I said, "Grace . . . maybe
you'd like to use your lipstick? We're getting in now." She opened
her eyes, smiled, dug into her handbag, brushed her hair, carefully rubbed the lipstick on.

17

We were near the airport. A Piper Cub swoofed low overhead,
circled toward the control tower to the left; two DC-6's eased over
the northern horizon; a helicopter was churning along parallel to
the highway. I turned out of the clover leaf, was almost immediately in front of the terminal and hunting a parking place.
Here, everything seemed curiously rational. I thought that word.

I meant *in order:* marked, lined off; signal lights where they should be; runways where they should be; warning signs: *watch for low-flying craft, exit, enter, no entrance,* where they should be. This seemed real. The rest of it—last night, last week, that interminable time in the car—was a disorderly dream: pressing down like a low ceiling as important dreams do, but a dream. I knew I would try to sort it out, later: the store, the Woman, Mark, Millie, the Ryders, all of it: what she had said, what I had said, what Mark had said, had felt— In that car we had strained to respond to an unknown situation and unknown possibilities within ourselves. Where had we got with it? knowing this much, did we know anything? Something had changed: what? something had entered that had snapped the equilibrium of—of what? of their relationship with each other? with me? Words say too much; and never enough—

I picked up her bags, we went inside to the counter. The clerk smiled, said, We were expecting you, Mrs. Channing.

Most men smile at Grace; most find something to say to her. Her offbeat attractiveness sinks in. A porter weighed her baggage. She went to the women's room. I was astonished at how fresh she looked when she came out: black hair shining, gray eyes full of depth, lips cleanly outlined, a smell of "Tapestry"— (I had asked her, years ago, what scent she used when she wore suits or skirt and sweater; apparently I should not have said it, for she had laughed and said your sister is right, you do ask funny questions; then she told me it was "Tapestry.") She had put on the single strand of pearls she often wears. She smiled, she said she was afraid she had left her hat in the car, would I mind— I went out for it. When I came back, she had misplaced a glove. Seemed enormously distracted, fumbled in her handbag, looked in the women's room, came back quietly saying, *I can't find it*— but her words had anguish in them. I saw it lying on the counter, retrieved it. She smiled, said, "I am behaving like Mother."

We had a spot of time on our hands and walked up to the glassed-in terrace. Planes circling, awaiting their signals to come in. One was about to depart: we watched it take off. We didn't talk—except the trivia you say at such times. Gray day, cold, no wind, no rain, no heavy clouds; visibility good in spite of strings of fog a foot or so above the ground. Plane coming in from the south. I said it was probably hers but there was no hurry, it would refuel here. Gas truck moved in below us. Fire truck moved in. Ground crew moved in. The plane landed rather far out and taxied in. We saw it was hers. We watched the passengers come down the ramp. We laughed at a worried little man in a checked coat who raced into the building raced out to the plane raced back again and then stopped—frozen; feet turned in, pigeonwise; he felt in his pocket, pulled out a paper, looked at it, put it in his pocket; removed it, looked at it, put it in his pocket; never stirred, after that. We watched the fuel truck drive up, hook on. We watched the crew at their routine work. I said, It is about time.

We started down the stairs. Heard the loud-speaker calling my name: *David Landrum, David Landrum, telephone . . . booth number four . . . Reverend Landrum . . . telephone . . . booth number four—*

She looked startled, touched my arm. I said, "Mark's calling to see if we made it all right."

I went on ahead. She was following me. I closed the booth door to shut out noise. Saw her standing on the other side: watching, waiting to speak to him—

Mark said, "Dave—" his voice prepared me for the next words, "it's about Andy."

"Yes." I took care about my face, knowing those eyes were searching it. What he was telling me was this: Andy had gone out for a walk, while Tom Eliot was at the headmaster's home. He'd left a note saying he would be back in a little while but hadn't come back. Snow was falling when he left; it had grown heavier, had turned now into a blizzard. They put out search parties, early, had called Mark at four o'clock. No trace of the boy. Were to call again at six. No call. He tried: lines down in New Hampshire. He was taking next plane. (Voice monotone now.) Tell Grace to go to Ritz Carlton; tell her if plane can't make Boston to phone you where she is, in case she can't get me. Don't tell her I am coming. Tell her heavy snow. Tell her school will get in touch with her as soon as they can; to wait at hotel; tell her they'll bring Andy in to see her just as soon as possible.

"Would you like her to wait and go up with you?"

"No. Only one seat available. It is better for her to go on. You won't tell her about the boy."

I said no. "I've got it, Mark. I'll do my best. I'll keep in touch with you."

I hung up. Opened the booth door. Smiled. Tried not to see her eyes. Said, "He was calling to be sure you'd made it."

"He didn't talk to me." Voice soft, hurt.

"He knew the plane was due and thought you might already have got on." I sounded foolish, and knew it. But it was all I could think to say. "This is what he wanted to tell you: A blizzard is sweeping across upper New England. If your plane makes it to Boston you are to go to the Ritz and take a room; if it doesn't, if it is grounded somewhere, New York, New Haven, anywhere, you're to phone him; if you fail to get him at once, transfer your call to me. If trains are running and your plane is held up in New York, go by train to Boston and wait at the hotel until the school gets in touch with you; telephone lines may be down so don't worry if you don't hear right away. Don't try to go to the school—you might get stranded. Just wait at the hotel."

She said, Yes, she would do what he said. Her face had tensed up; eyes dark now. I knew she was looking hard at me. I took out my address book, pretended to jot something down. I said, "I'll telephone the Ritz for a room reservation."

Then I looked at her and said, "If he had called you and you were on the plane he could not have got you. He knew I could relay the message. He's all right. I told him you were, too, your plane was in, you were about to board it. You'll be delayed seeing Andy, of course. But not for long, I hope."

They were calling her plane the second time. She searched my face, searched my eyes, did not say a word.

I pushed her gently toward the gate. I said, Goodbye dear. I gripped her shoulders and kissed her on the forehead. I said, Tell Andy hi. She tried to smile. I said, Try to sleep a little, after you've had breakfast. I said, You're strong, Grace—stronger than you know. I said, Try to pray a little, won't you? I said, Think through what you want to say to the boy but don't worry; your love will do it; your love will do everything for the three of you. God bless you, dear. . . .

The words stumbled through my lips.

I watched her go across the strip to the ramp. She looked as slight as a young girl, bare head, back straight as she ran lightly up the steps. I saw the plane's hostess speak to her, they smiled at each other; she turned, I waved, she waved, and disappeared inside the plane.

Engines revved up; plane taxied down the strip, paused, taxied again, paused; engines opened wide, plane lifted, made altitude quickly, turned a slow quarter-turn, headed northeast—was gone. I stood a long time looking at the empty sky.

I went to the counter in the restaurant and ordered coffee and something to eat. Ate it. Paid for it. Called the Ritz; bad connection but they heard me and made a reservation for her. Checked Mark's space on the plane; checked the departure time; everything all right there. Went to the men's room. To the car. Was halfway home before I realized it was not snowing everywhere on earth. Looked up—sometime, don't know when—saw the sun coming out, only a little but enough to pull off the ground-fog and open up a pale winter day. Saw people; they seemed busy, they looked cheerful, most of them; a few worried; a few cold; nobody looked as if his world had gone to pieces. Saw the frost had disappeared from weeds, grasses. I must have passed Mark's car—perhaps in a town where northbound and southbound cars are routed on different streets.

Don't remember much else about that trip home. Know I arrived in time to get into vestments for the burial service for Mrs. Bailey. Know my mind was completely on her family and their grief and on the prayers I read for their consolation and strength in that small bleak chapel at the funeral home. There they sat: old Mr. Bailey and his sister and four cousins and thirty or forty friends. And a gray casket and flowers. . . . And yet— in another glass-walled room in that limitless inner space we call our mind, were Grace and Mark and a school in New England and a boy and a letter and snow falling—and beyond it but somehow a part of it was a little boy named Mark and a father he feared and could not do without and a store and Susan and Renie, a young Grace and Millie and the Woman and a prison in the Pacific, all of it weaving and unweaving, winding, unwinding, twisting, and yet moving implacably toward a point as if this Thing, this disaster just ahead of us, had been fixed at that point in time and during our lifetime we had been moving steadily toward each other, converging on it— No. This is a lie. It could have been avoided easily, easily! If only—if only— What? I didn't know.

—And yet, as I thought this, I was deeply aware of the family gathered here in this chapel to express their respect and faith and awe, to bear witness before God to an honorable meeting of life with death. To old Mr. Bailey and his sister, Miss Annie, and their handful of friends, this moment was not a dread brush with death but a solemn glimpse, through the cleavage death makes, of God and his wondrous ways. They did not see a hole dug in the ground into which she would be laid: they were seeing a future which God had prepared and they saw it as something much better than the earth had given them, much better for the one lying there who had, at last, been released by God's mercy from her pain. And I felt their feelings, their unwavering trust and confidence and hope reaching out to the words I read and entering them, making them larger, more true: *I am the resurrection and the life, saith the Lord: he that believeth in me, though he were dead, yet shall he live: and whosoever liveth and believeth in me, shall never die.* . . . Never had those old words seemed so strong, so powerful, so filled with the pathos and the sheer wonder of the human experience as they did at that moment; never had they been so illumined for me. This was not a monologue I was reading from the Prayer Book but a dialogue taking place between a handful of people and their God in whom they believed unwaveringly. They were what we call "simple people": They could not have talked about "man's destiny" or the human condition; they had only a vague notion of the universe, even of this earth; they would have thought it not only wrong but completely irrelevant to ask the big questions—as irrelevant as many scientists think but for quite different reasons. But they were as ready to start out on the endless journey into the unknown we call "death" as are the intrepid scientists and airmen who are, even now, ready to be rocketed into Outer Space—and they were waving goodbye, with tears and with confidence, to the member of their family who had started on her way, just ahead of them. For them, death was not a crashing end to life but a pushing back of the human frontier, a few steps farther into the expanding universe.

Only when I left them—when I returned to my rooms, only then, was I grounded again to this earth and its agonizing tearing realities. Once grounded, I was swept by fear, anxiety, torn by angry incredulity. The world I lived in was not the world of old Mr. Bailey and Miss Annie. Their faith which half an hour before had stirred me deeply seemed now to have nothing to do with us—it was as if I had read a scene in an old-fashioned book and had responded, warmly, to its quaint simplicity. This, this monstrous thing happening to Andy, to Grace and Mark and all of us: I made no effort to understand how it fitted in with the other. No. I was feeling, *It can't happen; it doesn't have to happen and yet it is happening.* This is what tortured me: *none of it had to happen*—and yet it was happening as irresistibly as a Greek tragedy unfolds sequence after sequence.

I went up to my bedroom and lay down. Needed sleep. But I couldn't sleep. Lay there staring at the blue bowl on my bureau, staring at Niebuhr's book on my bedside table, looking at my watch, worrying: Suppose she had tried to call while I was at the funeral home or the cemetery or out on the highway. She should be at the Ritz now—if she got through. I called Eastern Air Lines: asked if Flight 14 had reached Boston on schedule. They had heard nothing to the contrary.

I stayed near my desk most of the afternoon, waiting for Grace's call. Went, finally, to Matthews for a few groceries. As I pulled out a wire cart, I thought, I'll make it quick. Picked up orange juice at the frozen juice counter; a stick of butter at the dairy counter, a pound of grapes from the fruit counter, a package of Saltines, a can of sardines, two or three other things, a loaf of bread— I remember these irrelevant details because of Maidee: they stick to her. As I took the stuff out of the wire cart and laid it on the slow-moving surface of the counter to be checked out, I saw the checker was Maidee. Tall, bony Maidee—flesh never grows on her; whatever is in her blood makes only skin and big-jointed bones; and her voice is bony and loose-jointed, too, no tension in her. I could hear her say to Miss Hortense and the others in her slow vague yet terrifyingly explicit way: *Yes, he was here. At exactly five-thirty-five. I remember because the quarter slipped out of his hand and rolled. . . .* I wanted to shout: *Now see what you did! The boy is lost in a blizzard because you said the quarter. . . .* But of course I did not say it.

She looked up—eyes pinpointed to the dimension of dimes, nickels, bills: *was it a one? a five? a ten?*— She said, Hello Mr. Landrum. I said, Hello Miss Maidee, how're things? She said, Fine, you OK? Fine, I said. I handed her the money, she handed me the change, I concentrated on her hand stuffing my purchases in a paper sack, I gave the wire cart a shove, it slid back into the nest of carts. As I turned away, someone pulled it out of its nest and began the trek around milk counter, frozen foods, dairy, meat, poultry . . . planning Sunday dinner, planning TV supper, planning—

At three-thirty, I called the airport, asked if both planes had got through to Boston. They said yes. No planes south of Boston had been grounded until three o'clock. All air traffic was suspended at present at Boston airport. At four o'clock, I asked Long Distance if calls were getting through to New England. She didn't know; would I like to put a call through? I said yes, to Boston. Gave her the Ritz's phone number, the Channings' names. Heard her buzzing Boston . . . heard cracking . . . whistling . . . wheezing . . . then across the noise a Boston voice was talking to her. She told me the Channings' room did not answer. I asked to be connected with the desk: Were they registered? Yes. You're sure? Mrs. Channing arrived this morning;

Dr. Channing in the early afternoon. I thanked him, left a message that I had called.

Stared down at my desk. Saw a note slipped under the ash try. "Call me, please, at your convenience. Katie." I wasn't up to it. She must have dropped by while I was at the shopping center. Whatever it was—and I thought I knew—I couldn't deal with it now.

It reminded me, however, that I had things to do. A sermon to preach, for one thing. It was written. But I needed to read it a number of times to get the sequences and its end in my head. Otherwise I'd circle like a helicopter in search of a landing spot.

I pulled it out of the drawer, read it, forced my mind on it, sketched out a tight outline, read the outline three times. Fairly good sermon—but what did it have to do with us, today? Nothing: no matter—it is all the sermon you've got—get it organized.

Remembered the appointment I was to make with Claud Newell. Why go through with it now? Useless. Useless. What would Mark care if— The talk with Neel and the Chief seemed to have happened a long time ago. Too long ago to matter now. I felt this—and yet I knew it was important to go through with it, to have those charges withdrawn; more important than ever —no matter what was about to happen, those charges must be withdrawn. But last night— I had not come to terms with last night. I had not come to terms with what Grace— Don't try. You can't. Deal with what is in front of you, right now.

So I called the Newells and Renie answered. We talked about this and that; we laughed; she asked me if I had got in touch with Miss Hortense; I said no, why? and she said Miss Hortense wanted to talk to me; she was very upset, she had had a dream about some Communists— I told Renie I'd call Miss Hortense later. Then I asked her if I could speak to her husband. He was at the golf club, she said.

"Playing on a day like this?"

Her voice showed surprise. She laughed at me, she said, "It's a fine day for golf, Dave. Why—"

Would she mind asking him to give me a ring when he returned? She hesitated, said she would be glad to. Her voice changed in that split second of hesitation. Cool, suspicious— I thanked her and hung up.

Jane. I must talk with Jane. It was pushing me: Last night . . . Mark . . . the store . . . why didn't he tell us? why did he withhold it? Grace . . . all that she had felt compelled to say— that plane taking her where she could not go, I was standing there again watching it, looking at that empty sky—I knew now what was ahead. I could not endure the knowledge alone. There was nothing Jane could do for them. Not now. But I felt she could work a miracle for me. It is my role to listen to people. Now Jane must listen to me. I could not see beyond this hour but Jane might see.

This feeling I have about her is something my words cannot deal with; there're no solid facts to support it. I suppose I was the small boy who cries out for the arms of the Great Mother. I am not ashamed to confess it. But to say this no more describes my complex need than a comic strip describes a man's profoundest experiences. I felt: I felt she would receive this which I must tell her as she receives everything good and evil: as if it had happened ten thousand years ago; not as bad news or good news but as a sentence not until now deciphered in an old worn human document that somehow, somewhere has been dug up; she'd look at it, smooth it out, peruse it with care and compassion and interest. She would not deny. Jane denies nothing. She would say Yes, yes, yes. With sorrow. But she would say it. How she had traveled that long arduous way to the still point of pain, I don't know. But as I am writing this now, it seems to me that she has somehow crashed the barrier and has gone beyond the mind-breaking stabbing agony the rest of us feel. All the words seem wrong. But she is there. Or more nearly there than anyone I have ever known. Her eyes confirm you: they are like an old sailor's eyes fixed on an invisible horizon. She reminds you of the Singer in that brief hypnotizing fable of Rilke's: The men in the boat, rowing rowing across a sea to an unknown destination, going Somewhere, toward a place ten hundred, ten million miles distant, ten million years distant maybe—no one knows; but they keep on rowing with the expertness, the know-how they are masters of, for there is nothing they don't know about oars and a rowboat and its relationship to the water a few inches from their hands and the wind blowing across their bodies. But what they don't know is where they are going. And this not-knowing desolates them, exhausts them, they are drained by weariness and non-meaning and terror; and then, then: one of them, the Singer, begins to sing and his singing brings that unknown point in the future nearer, nearer . . . it is as if it is now coming toward them instead of their going toward it; and the rowers feel better, somehow, more sure, somehow; and the oars quicken and the boat moves on a few inches further into the unknown—

Jane does this: Somehow, as your words fall against her silence a resonance is set up, a new sound makes its mark on your mind, and your feelings change. She has an astonishing sense of the faraway place, of invisible order surrounding the near chaos, of a never-to-be-reached harmony that one finds only within one's awareness that it exists. And at the same time, she has almost a shocking way of dealing with everyday concerns: shrewd and down-to-earth as a peasant in her awareness of the small things people cling to. *A doll means more to a child than the whole human race*— She often says this, and like the politicians, she never forgets it; and like them she knows people remain children. She works on several civic committees; the Juvenile Delinquency Committee, League of Women Voters, Physical Rehabilitation Committee, the Library Board; she is a director of the Civic Symphony Society; and she volunteers for the grubby assignments. This is only one layer of Jane—the top layer, what she chooses to show the world; but there must be Janes within Janes, there must be a frightened human in her, somewhere, and an angry one and somewhere a lonely mixed-up one just like the rest of us, there has to be. . . .

She was at home now, I knew—where she is every Saturday afternoon, sitting in her big chair with feet propped up, a box of chocolates on the small table near her—always that box of chocolates—and reading Karl Kraus. She had told me, I think it was the afternoon we were up at her mountain place, that she was reading his *Last Days of Man*—eight hundred pages of it, in the German; doing it on Saturday afternoons. Last winter, she read *Finnegans Wake* for the second time. The winter before, I think it was Dante; perhaps Lao-Tse or Mo Ti; perhaps Kierkegaard— It was she who had persuaded me to read Kirkegaard in the right way: beginning with *Concluding Unscientific Postscript* and working back through his last books.

I dialed her number. I spoke to her. She said, "Dave? Good. Where have you been? I tried to get you all morning." I told her I had been out of reach of a phone. She asked me where Mark and Grace were. I told her they had gone out of town for the weekend. "Good," she said. "I hope they went up to their cabin." I said I was not sure where they were. Could I drop in to see her? Knew I was interrupting her but I needed to talk with her. She asked me to come at six o'clock and stay for supper.

I went over to the window. Saturday afternoon traffic was heavy on Arlington Road. People coming back from the football game. Saw Susie skating on the sidewalk across the street; in that Black Watch plaid skirt and cap to match, and that long pale hair streaming, she looked like a Charles Addams drawing. She was skimming across my line of vision. . . . Four weeks ago I could laugh and did; now she had become uncanny, if she touched you you would feel it the rest of your life— She stopped. Crossed over, paused on the sidewalk in front of my study, looked up, saw me at the window, waved, skated on down the street—

A few minutes later, Claud Newell called. Voice not friendly. He resented my interference with his life. I didn't blame him. But I was not up to pastoral overtures: instead, I said pretty tersely, I'm afraid, that I wanted to talk with him as soon as possible. Silence at his end of the line. It is about Susan, I said. Silence. Finally he asked what time I wanted him to come over. I said, At your convenience. He suggested nine o'clock.

When I arrived at Jane's, she was reading and there were the chocolates beside her. She offered me one and I took it. I sat down in a rocker—she has three—in that quiet, Victorian room (Victorian, except for her books and records and hi-fi). It was once her mother's, and her mother's things are still there. I waited as she laid aside her book and went to the kitchen for a few minutes.

When she returned, I told her as quickly as I could about Andy and the anonymous letter—the phone call from the headmaster —Grace's departure—the snow and Andy's going out for a walk. I pushed it on her pretty fast, I'm afraid, for as I told it her face paled out and the color did not come back for a long time. But she did not show it in her quiet words as she asked careful questions about the letter, the snow, Grace and Mark. She then asked me if Andy had ever mentioned a hut in his letters to me. I didn't think so. She went to her desk, found a short letter from him telling her about the school, Eliot, his housemaster, then he said they had walked out to a cabin the school had about a mile off the campus. *It is like ours, Jane, up on your mountain. We had a good time.*

"He may have gone there."

It didn't sound quite reasonable. "At night?"

She was looking down at her hands which were clasped together in her lap. She said, "His father always walks when he is solving a problem. Andy may not know it consciously but he knows it. He is not in the least afraid of the dark. It was snowing —he may have wanted to stay out in it. On impulse, he may have gone to the cabin simply because it reminded him of theirs. I think it is possible, Dave."

After this, she looked down at the rug a long time, then she said, "You've had no sleep, have you? and no food?" Not much of either, I admitted. "Then, let's push this away and have supper. Can you?" She smiled. I said it was hard to. Said I kept trying to put it together, that I couldn't quite see this.

She said, "Let's wait. There is a chance that it is all right. Phones are out, we can't hear but they may have found him by now. I think he went to the hut. If he did and saw he should not try to go back to the school, he is safe. He would build a fire and keep warm."

"Would Mark think of this possibility?"

She thought he would.

I wasn't sure he would; he had been so disturbed, everything piling— "Suppose he doesn't. I feel it is too late—everything is—"

"I know you do. But we can't create the disaster in our minds before it happens; let's wait until we hear."

Such simple words, not particularly wise but somehow comforting. It was her and all I knew of her past life, her love, her compassion, her acceptance that comforted me.

As we ate her superb food—she is a fine cook—I asked her once more how did it all start—was it Renie Newell? if so, why? why? who wrote the letter? why? why?

And once again she said, "Until we know more, let's wait; keep in touch if we can, but wait." This sort of thing, said by most people, can infuriate you; but said by Jane it seemed right. And with an effort I began to talk about other things. The Kraus book, a little—she sketched it out for me, this prophetic German who, before Hitler, had seen the Germans rushing to their doom —she talked to me about a problem Neel had discussed with her, that morning. He had stumbled on a marijuana club of Windsor Hill teen-agers. We went pretty fully into this because some of them were in my church. I asked her if she had heard of Gus Hestor. No, she hadn't heard of him. We discussed him, his silent almost invisible trouble-making as if he were not human but a disease spreading through the city. This in no way tied up with the club of young dope users, but what created the climate for one might be creating the climate for the other. And all the time, I wanted to say, Tell me about Grace: she taught dance in your camp; you were with her that day when she read the account of the woman's suicide. *Tell me about Grace.* . . . But somehow, I couldn't. It was almost like asking, Tell me about you, Jane: what men, what women have you loved? how many have you hurt? and what has hurt you so much that you are compelled to find a place to abide where you cannot be hurt again? are you sure you are safe there? She knew so much . . . but would it ever be told? Do women ever tell? They were bred to secrecy for ten thousand years—will they ever tell? They know so much—but will they tell? I felt behind this, this that was happen-

but it doesn't show—and a decisiveness that can speed like a rocket when needed. His war record proved this. Claud Newell's energy is predominantly physical and emotional. And it shows. I felt it as he stood there. An energy not as controlled as Mark's, I'd guess, but in the groove. Imagination? I couldn't feel it; it might be there, I didn't know. Can he think beyond his own small problems? I didn't know. But he has words, I was sure; an arsenal of them; and probably uses them best when fighting his own battles. While Mark—that is when he loses all his words.

I felt Newell was capable of ruthless strategy. This is a man, I thought, who sees all people as his opponents. He never wastes hate on them for they are not enemies but obstructions; if he has to move them, he moves them—and that is that. I felt he could laugh at himself; a bitter sound it would have, too. The lines in his face made this obvious. I had never heard Mark laugh in that way. Not because he lacks a sense of humor—he has a rare and subtle sense of the absurdity of the human condition, the blundering triumphs and failures of mankind—but this is philosophical humor and is set off from himself. The bitter, personal skin-close laughter of Newell's spurts out of broken parts of the personality rubbing in bruising, hurting awareness of their unfriendly proximity. Mark is too—solid? too organized? I am searching, now, for my word. Too intent, perhaps; too absorbed in a purpose larger than himself, beyond his personal existence—he just doesn't have time to be aware of what is going on inside him. Claud's personality is looser, the pieces jangle, clash. Every part of him is hungry and the hungers jostle each other: mind hungering not to discover the unknown, as does Mark's, but to dominate the known, to use it for his own purpose . . . body hungering for food and drink but here he knows when he's had enough. His hunger for women is different. I felt it had never been satisfied: he always wants more in his sexual life than he gets because he wants it only on the sexual level, and women feel this and swarm around him—I was pretty sure—lured by a primitive, undeveloped desire they know in advance they can't satisfy, and he knows it, too, and despises them for attempting what they are sure to fail at. And yet, he can laugh, I felt, at himself and them—

This glib summing up of a complex, restless human being was crashing through my mind as we shook hands, as I offered him a chair, a cup of coffee. He refused the coffee. Sat down in the striped chair and took out his cigarettes. His hand was trembling.

I wasn't prepared for it. I should have been. But I had failed to connect up with him in feeling, I had forgot that he could bleed, like me. He had been, until this moment, an object: a high-powered, dangerous object that might very well fly to pieces in my face but one I was trying to manipulate and if I couldn't do that, block. My mind was completely on the situation. I had been analyzing Susie and Renie for weeks—and him, too, I suspect, as I saw him through their eyes. Now I was taking him to pieces: not to understand him or them but as parts of the trap Mark was caught in. My purpose was to extricate Mark from that trap. And of course Newell knew it. The Chief and Neel had already put him through, this morning. He had tried to work off the effects of that interview on the golf course. Now here I was: his priest, concerned not about him and his child but about Mark Channing: using Susan as decoy—or, more accurately, perhaps, as the subject of blackmail. For we had virtually kidnaped her future by our warning—my words had not been uttered but he knew they were about to be. The price of this future was Mark's release from arrest: This is the crude translation his feelings were making of our intentions. And he wasn't too wrong, either.

He flipped the ash off his cigarette. Again I saw the trembling. Strange . . . how one small betrayal of a man's dread can change things. Suddenly, I was responding to him as a man, I felt involved with him, began to see through his eyes.

I thought, I'll offer him a brandy: over a brandy, perhaps we can quietly discuss the whole matter, his point of view, Susan, all of it, simply as two civilized human beings. Perhaps, we can work out something for Susan that will help the child, I wanted him to see that I had a genuine interest in her—or was beginning to. This morning I had seen her, had begun to see the brat as a lonely Susan, a sensitive, interesting little girl who wandered away from home, yes; from what we call the "real world"; spending too much of her time creating her play-like world—and when she did return to the real one, she prowled around too much, ransacking the place! Yes. But only in search of what she needed for the creation of her play-like world. Of course, this isn't so good. She's in trouble and gets everybody else in trouble. Just the same, with all her fantasy and her tales, she has stayed closer to the truth than the rest of us.

I left that.

Thought again: If we could talk quietly over a glass of— But Newell was not the type: he goes to a bar and takes his straight and plenty of it—or pours a stiff drink or two or three in his bathroom. And tonight, he had had his full quota. I saw this, the moment he entered my study.

All I could do was hand him a light for his cigarette.

Then I began: I tried to communicate to him my sympathy for Susan. I had, in all sincerity, begun to have a glimmer of understanding and I tried to get my new feeling across to him. I mentioned having seen her ride Dr. Guthrie's Sky Foot; commented on her skill and courage in handling the horse. I said she dropped in to see me, now and then. He looked startled. I said, Perhaps he didn't know I had given her my cat, Ali Baba—I detoured here, telling him I didn't like cats, he said he didn't, I said I was getting me a Boxer, he said he'd get an English bull —I got back on the track and told him the cat had a way of coming back to the Parish House and Susan would run over for him. A muscle in his face eased. I told him about her interesting stories. His face tensed up. I said I felt she had rather a special kind of imagination—

"Are you trying to break it to me that she is a liar? Because if you are, I'd prefer that you give it to me straight. Makes me restless," he half smiled, "to play cards with a man when I see a couple of aces slipping down his sleeve. I think you know a lot you are not going to tell me, Mr. Landrum, and the little you are willing to tell will drive me off my head."

I couldn't for a moment think of anything to say.

He plunged on. "Let's get to the point. I can take it better that way—if I can take it at all. I don't like this diplomacy stuff."

What "the point" was, I wouldn't admit, right then. I had convinced myself, by now, that I wanted him to see and wanted to see, myself, the whole picture—at least, that part of it in which his little girl was the central fact. I had hoped—until last night—that we could find out what she was searching for in that store, what her story of the man meant when decoded in terms of her fantasies, her needs, relationships, or lack of them. Now—after what Mark had told Grace and me—the imaginary man I had elaborately worked my theory around had metamorphosed into a real man whom I was hiding, like an escaped convict, in a corner of my mind. I couldn't handle the new facts. I had planned this talk with Newell before last night. Now, I felt I had to go ahead with it, but there wasn't anything to talk about if I told him the truth. If he knew that Mark had been in that store no power on earth could make him drop the case.

It was going to be rough on the truth, all right. But wasn't it better for Susan, as well as for Mark, if I kept the new facts out of the discussion? After all, Mark had not harmed the child. I went into a hassle with my conscience and came out on top, as I often do. You can't tell the literal truth. No. But you are sticking to the essence. Susan needs help; she's in trouble; she didn't lie about the store but she did lie about Mark following her; and she prowls too much and a trial will ruin her in this town—so you're basically right—

Whether I was or wasn't, I knew I was going along *as if* Mark had not been in the store and *as if* Susie had made it up. I swooped up a handful of points about the forthcoming trial, newspaper, radio, TV publicity, the gossip, and the effect of all this on Susan's friends—and her social future in Windsor Hills. I prepared to say them as persuasively as I could. I would ignore the Channings completely. I'd try to take Newell along with me, step by step, as I carefully led up to the courtroom scenes, the kind of discussion that would take place, the questions, and what the consequences would inevitably be for Susan as the center of this scandal. . . .

But I didn't move fast enough. I was slowed down by pretending this was going to be a reasonable quiet talk between two men who wanted only the best for a child both of them were concerned about, when actually my real purpose was— In short, Newell was more honest and he outsmarted me. He had put me on the defensive and he was going to keep me there. In his mind, we were not priest and parishioner—we were opponents. He was using the strategy he was adept at when out to get a big-time client from a competitor—the same that I used long ago as halfback when, heading for that line, I'd ram it down their throats—

Something else slowed me: *It is right for you to believe in Mark, sure; but how about Newell? how about his need to believe in Renie? in Susan? when are loyalty and faith right for one man and not for another if all the facts are not available to either? And Susan: she told the truth, at least about the store, and here you are trying to persuade her father she is the liar he secretly fears she is—how do you justify it?*

Whether I struggled with this for a split second or a long minute, I don't know. When I came to, Claud Newell was standing. He was saying, "You've been careful to stay off the subject of my wife, Mr. Landrum. But that is where this talk is going to begin. Not with Susan. Susan has nothing to do with it. Oh sure— she was in the store, I suppose. I even wonder about that. Maybe she wasn't. How do I know? How do I know Channing was there? As a matter of fact, I don't. What I do know is: Renie did this deliberately to shame me. Me! She didn't give a thought to what it would do to Susan, she was after me! Something happened and she found out about it—the woman meant nothing to me—nothing! But Renie—"

He was walking around the study. Looking at the photograph of the big fish—I remember how his eyes slid off the Marin print and stopped at the photograph. He was touching things: coffee pot, cup, book, ash tray—

Everything decent and honest in me wanted to say, *Look, Newell: Susan was there. And Channing was there, too. What scared Susan was seeing Channing at the latrine—you can un-*

derstand that. But what is more natural than for a man to—he had no idea she was in that place—

I couldn't say it. I couldn't count on his possessing that much reason and common sense—

He picked up a record, read its label, put it down on the hi-fi console. His voice was almost too low to be heard: "When I swore out that warrant for Channing's arrest, I didn't care whether he was innocent or guilty. Renie—I had dropped by home. We'd been having a rough time of it for a month or two but I had worried about that store in spite of not believing a word of it, all day I kept remembering Renie when I first met her— Oh I don't know! Anyway, I finished up earlier than I expected in Miami and took a plane home to spend the night. Thought I'd like—I don't know what I expected—when I'm away I think it's going to be fine to get home, things will be different, and they never are. I'm on the plane, we're cruising along, say, and everything is quiet and you begin thinking of home, and things are cheerful and bright, somebody's in the kitchen cooking something for you, they're going to be glad to see you, they want to listen to the funny things that have happened to you and you're going to relax, it's the one place on earth you don't have to fight for things— I guess it's a dream. Something I made up way back when I was a kid. For it never happens. And that night—she's easily scared, I didn't want to turn the key and walk in, so I tapped on the door and called to her and she recognized my voice and said, Yes, Claud. Then I walked in and the room was almost dark and the TV going yakkety yak and I stumbled over a stool, one of those damned antiques she has all over the place—and the first thing I said was, *Why in hell can't you keep those damned things off the floor!* Fine way to begin. And she was furious. She had a right to be. And well it wasn't a good time of the month and—anyway she was punishing me for —I won't go into all that. All night I lay there thinking, What does it add up to? what is it all about? what am I slaving myself to death for? Early next morning, Susan heard me and ran in from her room in her pajamas, laughing, she likes·surprises, and I picked her up and hugged her—oh I don't know—she was warm and sweet and soft—and I kissed her two or three times, I don't usually do that, but I had come home and I wanted to find *something* there— I had brought her a present and I let her look for it in my bags. She likes rummaging through things and when she found it she ran back and crawled in my bed and snuggled up and kept saying, thank you thank you. I really didn't have time to take her to school, and she's used to walking—it's only nine blocks and I've always thought it was healthy for her to walk. But I wanted to take her and I did."

On the way, she told him that a man was after her:

—What man?

—Dr. Channing.

—What did he do?

—Followed me.

—Where?

—On my way home from school.

—Where?

—Right along here.

—Here on Arlington?

—Yes sir. I was skating and he—

I interrupted Newell. "I thought she was on her way from school."

He looked at me hard. Said, "I know. I caught it, too. I said, Were you skating, Susan, or were you on the way from school? And she said she forgot, she was on her way from school."

He went on with it:

—What did he try to do to you, Susan?

—He just followed me, tipping behind me and when I stopped, he'd stop and when I walked fast, he walked fast and he got closer and closer and closer and then he said, Little girl I like you, little girl I like you.

Newell was walking around the room. "It drove me wild! I left her at the school, told her to be careful, told her to wait until her mother came for her. I didn't have much time, my plane was due in forty minutes, so I stopped at a drugstore and phoned the chief of police. He was out somewhere. Then I phoned that assistant of his, Neel, and he was out somewhere. So I phoned Renie, told her to pick up Susan after school; and to take her there and go for her every day. I couldn't tell her about Channing. I knew she'd have hysterics. So I told her not to let Susan out of her sight until I got home on the weekend. That I had heard something. She wanted to know what. I told her just do what I say, it probably is nothing, probably just a rumor I've heard, but do what I say! She has plenty of sense, you know, and she said she would. I told her not to mention it; any talk to anybody might endanger Susan; she said she'd be careful. And I knew she would. Renie can be as sensible as anybody I know when she wants to be.

"I drove on out to the airport and parked the car. It's an old Mercury I keep for the purpose. Then I caught my plane and went into Chicago. But I kept thinking about it. I thought once, I'll kill him when I get back, go straight to that lab and blow his brains out. Any court in the world would call it justifiable homicide. I got drunk the next night; the thing had begun to drive me crazy: I began to think there's one chance in a million that Renie told me the truth about that store. If she did— And then right in the middle of my worry about Susan I remembered something Renie had said about Channing last summer; it wasn't much, maybe, but—well, she began talking about his brains, what a brilliant scientist he is, his prestige—as if all that was better than my slogging along selling meat and making ten times, twenty times more than Channing will ever make. It burned me up! Nobody in the world cares more for money than Renie. Who would know it better than me! Now suddenly what I had accomplished was nothing! So I got drunk. There's a nice little girl in Chicago, she's—well, she's a call girl, Mr. Landrum, and I guess you wouldn't understand that kind of thing—but she's got sense. She knows a lot. I was telling her all about it and you know what she said? She said, You kill that man and the courts will let you off. But your company won't. They'll fire you. And then where will you be? where? And I knew she was right. I couldn't kill him but I could have him arrested and let the courts handle it.

"That's the way it happened." He lighted a cigarette. Said softly, "But there's something peculiar going on between those two. Him and Renie. I can't make it out."

He didn't look at me. And I didn't answer him.

He turned, said, "You wouldn't like to believe that, would you?"

"I don't believe it."

"What are your facts?"

"I don't have any. But I happen to know the man you are talking about. He is in love with his own wife and wouldn't—"

He smiled. I got it, all right: How would a one-legged priest know about men and women—real men—red-blooded men— dissatisfied women—

He began to explain—as if he were teaching me the ABC's, "A man can be in love with his wife and at the same time need something that only another woman can give him. A woman he doesn't love is exactly what he wants and must have, sometimes. Sex doesn't have anything to do with love and never has had. Because you are a minister and believe this is wrong does not keep it from being true."

"I won't debate the wrongness with you. We'd have to go too deep into things. But I will question its truth. A man may want— what he needs he's not willing to face up to—exactly what you say: somebody he can depersonalize, use, throw away afterward; or some nice little toy he can play with in childish ways and keep going back to because she lets him be the little boy he really is; or maybe what he wants is not a woman at all but a boy or a man but he's unwilling to admit it, so he takes a woman he can turn into a boy in his fantasy and use—and it never gets him anywhere—never satisfies him and never will—" I stopped. I was ashamed of my anger. He had hurt my male vanity and I had turned and slugged him with psychological facts that are not true, anyway, in this simple form.

He laughed as if he had actually enjoyed my outburst. He was attractive when he laughed deeply, freely, like that. He came over, sat down, seemed more relaxed. "All right. You needn't give me any more facts of life. I spoke in the wrong way to you. And I beg your pardon."

I smiled but I didn't say anything.

"You think I am a heel to bring my wife into this. In this way. A gentleman would never, etc. I know my lessons. Renie began to teach them to me the day she married me. She's plantation South. My folks were—my dad started off poor as they come, then worked up to flagman on the railroad. They were decent, good people—they sent me to college— I am speaking of my wife for the first time in my life, to another man. I'm doing it because I'm angry and worried and scared. I don't know what is happening to us. It is as if— Mr. Landrum, I think what I'm trying to say is this: Something is going on in Renie's mind about Channing. He fascinates her; his brilliance—now I know: I remember what brought it up: he spoke last summer on a health program, on TV, the series the Jaycees were sponsoring. Dr. Abrams had spoken on heart disease; Dr. Channing was speaking on cancer. Afterward, Renie said quite a bit about his brilliance, his brains, that he was amazingly photogenic on television. Yet, she seems to hate him. It is as if— Something is rolling around inside her and I don't get it. When I get mad I say things in the wrong way. There hasn't been an actual affair between those two. Renie wouldn't. She'll do a lot of things—but she has her principles. As far as I know, they've never been around each other and yet he's done something to her. What?"

"I don't know."

"I've thought of everything. I've thought maybe she's a little jealous of them. He's a scientist, his wife is a modern dancer and painter. Renie's heard about those weekly gatherings at Pottle's bookshop. She likes Paul. But he's never asked her there. My wife is a very smart woman—she would like to know artists and intellectuals. She says she gets bored with the talk at the club." He smiled. "Back to the Channings, now. They speak, of course; that is all."

"Your wife is in Windsor Hills' most prominent social group. Mrs. Channing is not a member of Junior League. Your wife is."

"Mrs. Channing is not a member because she doesn't want to be. Renie is a bright girl; she knows that."

This was something I didn't want to talk about. I thought it ridiculous. And anything you can say makes it worse.

"Look—if you knew us—Renie and me, not as we are in public but with each other: we are not calm people. We've fought each other from the first time we met. Sometimes it has been fun. We both have tempers. We both are—well, we are not cold people. But since her father's death. . . . Renie told me she had discussed it with you." He waited for me to speak.

"What?"

"My impotence. That is what she calls it." He laughed so freely that I laughed, too. "She reads things. She told me she had discussed it with you."

She hadn't. She had hinted it; but how could I say this to him?

He smiled. "I've put you in a bad spot. Let's forget it. What Renie seems to have on her mind— Like a lot of other carefully brought up American girls she thinks there is only one way, one nice way, you know. But I happen to be different. There're a dozen ways, maybe a hundred ways. To hear our GI's talk when they get back from the Pacific. . . . But for my wife, there is only one right way. Where she learned it, I don't know. The lady who is her mother would never have mentioned even the word *sex*, to her. The point is, what she has decided is the right way is not right for me. And all this has really got big since her father's death. She flatly refuses my way. Each time I come home, she has another psychology book for me to read. One chapter, I mean. The one she thinks is about me."

We were getting in a swamp.

"But you didn't ask me here to talk about this." He had maneuvered things to a place where I had to say it:

"Newell, what I would like to discuss with you is the warrant you swore out for Mark Channing's arrest. I want to ask you to consider withdrawing those charges, both for his sake and the sake of your little daughter."

His eyes were watching me. I said, "Mark Channing is an innocent man, in my opinion. But even if he were not, I'd still say you are hurting yourself and Susan by bringing this case to trial. You can't win. Suppose you send him to the pen. So what? He'll be in the pen and people will forget him. People's memories are short, especially when they know they may have done the wrong thing. But they won't forget Susan and the trial. They may not talk about it for the next four or five years; but when she begins to date, it will come out again. Debut? It will come out again. Marriage? There it will be. She can live down this spurt of gossip; never a trial. And what will you get out of it? It won't improve your relationship with your wife nor your status in Windsor Hills." I looked at him, I hoped, with sympathy. "Anyway, your status is excellent. It doesn't need to be bettered. Windsor Hills will be on your side during the trial. But afterward—people are fickle, perverse, they will slowly but surely turn their sense of guilt against you; they'll begin asking how people of your class could have let such a thing come to a head; they will blame you and your wife for not having smothered the talk in the first place." I stopped. I'd let him go on from here.

"Channing is obviously your friend."

"The closest friend I have. And I don't want to see him go to jail. And I don't want to see his life ruined nor his research ruined or delayed. That research is on cancer: what he finds or fails to find could be the deciding factor in your life or perhaps your wife's or Susan's, some day, or mine. Looked at this way —but perhaps it is too difficult to look at it from this angle. He's my friend, yes. But you and your wife and child are my parishioners and I am concerned about you. You may not think so but I am. I know how you feel about Susan and her good name and your good name in this community. But when this mess is spread out on the front page of the papers—and a trial will put it there and on TV and radio— Frankly, Newell, I still don't see why you lost your head and swore out that warrant."

"It was his following Susie. I couldn't take it." He was standing again. Walking around the room. "When Renie told me about the store and insisted I have him arrested for attempted rape, I laughed. Laughed! Not because I didn't care but because I know Renie. She's always telling these things. Distorted, fantastic tales, about somebody. Every weekend I hear something. When I met her in Memphis, years ago, I liked her funny stories. They were funny, then. A little stretched and exaggerated but funny; and a lot of them were on her. She could laugh at herself and I like that in a woman. But they've changed, the stories; you can't laugh; if you believed them they'd drive you crazy. So I don't believe them. I listen but I say to myself, That's not true but she has to say it; something in her has to say it. Take it easy. Let her!"

He began picking up things, looking hard at them, laying them down. The same ash tray, same record he'd picked up before. Two or three books. Read the titles, put them down.

"Since her father died, she seems to have her mind too much on him. Worries about her mother and that drunken brother. Talks about her father. Too much. I know when somebody dies, you need to talk about him or think about him—and when Renie thinks, she has to talk. You sort of throw away all the old snapshots and make one nice photograph fit to be put up on the mantel." He looked at me, his eyes were soft, he smiled. "But do you have to *act* like him? Sometimes, Renie talks exactly like old Congressman Addams; one day, I noticed her walking like him. Her mind is on that old place, she loves it; it has its good points, all right, but it's—think of a girl, the only white girl, brought up on a farm where there were a thousand black folks. No wonder they were always talking to her about everybody raping everybody. And yet, as much as she hated that place, and she did, now she talks as if she wishes she were back there." He shook his head.

"When I started out working for the meat packers I knew I had to know meat but I also knew I had to know the men I was selling it to. And I began studying them. You find out a great deal when you concentrate on studying people.

"One thing I found out is that nearly everybody has a word that means too much to them. I began to notice it a year or so after I went out on the road: I'd be sitting in the smoker or club car, talking to two or three or maybe just one—and pretty soon the man I was talking to would use his word. You notice—and you'll find nearly everybody has one word that sets them crazy.

Well, *rape* is Renie's. Stays right on the edge of her mind. I happen to know this about Renie. That's why I didn't believe her when she told me about the store. But when Susie told me—you haven't got a little daughter, you don't know how this sort of thing can tear you up, how it can—" He stopped.

"I don't have a daughter but I think I know how you felt. Any man would."

"It was the way she described it: her looking around, there he was; looking around, there he was, coming closer— God!" He drew in his breath, let it out. Spoke quietly, "Look—I admit there is hardly a chance in the world that Channing was in that store. Or any other man. As I say, I'm not at all sure Susie was there. Those women in that beauty shop could have put it in Susie's head by their questions. Easy. Easy. She could have picked up that cat in the alley. Or in front of the store. Then, when he scratched her—well, I don't know. But I feel that Channing followed her. I don't know why but I feel the truth of it, somehow."

I didn't say anything.

"You don't, obviously."

"No, since you ask me, I don't."

"Then why would Susie tell me? why?" He lowered his voice, tried to talk without emotion, "Look: when I ask Susie anything she tells me the truth. She won't tell Renie. But she tells me. She admits it to me. Trouble is, I'm home just two days a week and I don't want to be fussing at the kid all the time so I try not to get involved. But if I ask her she tells me. I don't believe she's a liar. I don't believe you can inherit lying."

"She's not a liar. And I don't believe you inherit that sort of thing, either. But she is an imaginative child. I mean just that: *imaginative*. And a lonely one. She has a play-like friend named Boody and she and Boody do things together and talk together in her play-like world. Ever heard of Boody?"

He smiled quickly. "Hundreds of times. How did you know? Renie tell you? does she tell you everything?"

"No. Susie told me. She told me quite a story about Boody. She's a fine little storyteller. When I say that, I mean just that. I said a moment ago that she is lonely. She is. She doesn't feel close to people. She sees and hears them but they are far away— it is almost as if they were on TV. She doesn't feel she can actually come in contact with them."

"How do you know this? Read it in books the way Renie does? Renie has the answer to everybody but herself. It is always on page 280 or page 345 or page—"

I ignored this. "Does it seem possible to you that Susie might make up a man following her because she doesn't see enough of the man who is her father?"

He didn't answer.

"Has it ever occurred to you that you and Mark Channing are strangely alike in appearance?"

He drew his breath in sharply. It reminded me of a horse startled by something he hears and can't see.

I stopped.

After a long time, he said, "Go ahead. I see you have a theory about this."

"Yes, I have. My theories are often wrong. But this one is right, I think. Susie has had a great amount of attention from everybody since the store episode. Whether it happened or didn't happen she's been made over by everybody. She has had more attention from you and her mother than she is accustomed to. And she likes it. Naturally. She's human. And she wants to keep things this way. If it takes scare headlines, all right: she'll make the headlines, one way or another. She's always told stories, play-like episodes, to herself. Why not try this one on you? This time, a play-like man following her. She has Dr. Channing now as one of her stock characters, just as she has Boody. She's noticed that he is a character people react to, so why not use him again? Anyway, he looks like her daddy—so she tells you, hoping for a reaction. She wanted you to listen and you did listen."

He barely smiled. His jaw muscles were moving as if he were bearing down on something. He said, "Go ahead."

"Dr. Channing was not following her."

"You don't know this."

"No. But I know the man. His entire life, his personality, morals, interests, purpose in life deny it. I don't believe he would follow a little girl any more than I think you would. You wouldn't, would you?"

He looked at me. Almost smiled. "I never have."

"You never would, would you?"

"I hope not."

I laughed. He laughed. We didn't say anything for a minute or so.

Then I said, "I've no right to say this, but my feeling is that Susan is trying to tell you something about *her*—not about Dr. Channing. There is something she needs and she is asking you for it. But she doesn't feel she can talk to you—"

"It wouldn't be natural for her to. I never talked. I don't think kids do. Anyway, all this is Renie's job. Mine is to make the money and I've done all right. But lately, Renie just doesn't seem to think so."

The phone rang. I apologized for interrupting him and answered it. Jane. She had been calling Boston all evening and still had not got through. She would continue to try. "If I succeed, do you want me to call you?" I told her yes. "Even if it is very late? You've had no sleep, Dave." I told her to call me regardless of the hour. I thanked her and hung up. It bore down on me: Andy in that blizzard right now!—the letter—I felt he was not in the cabin—all day I had compelled myself to be hopeful, even when I was sick with anxiety I still felt hope somewhere in me; and when Jane mentioned the cabin I convinced myself he was there, safe; but suddenly, it drained out—and there were those two in that hotel room waiting—and, as the minutes were passing, the hours, I knew that room would shrink and keep shrinking, pressing them closer closer to each other and yet, now, there was a deep cleavage between them, all that happened last night, all she said—and there was nothing nothing—

I must have rubbed my face with my hands. I don't know. I must have done something, for Newell said, "You have had bad news, Mr. Landrum."

"Yes."

"Can I do anything to help?" Voice warm and kind.

I told him no. There was nothing he could do.

He said quietly that he felt he should leave, we could continue our talk, another time.

I asked him to stay. Said I would like some coffee, if he would. He said he'd be glad to have a cup. I made the coffee.

As we were drinking it, I said, "How is Renie's mother?"

"About the same. Sits there day after day staring out the window." His voice was quiet. Mine was quiet. There was no bitterness in the room now.

"Fifteen years . . . and never a word. I thank God she has a pleasant view. There is a lake on the place and the lawn stretches down to it. And near her window is a live oak. Biggest tree I ever saw. It is almost dead now but the moss hangs there waving back and forth, all day long . . . down at the lake there're the big cypress trees—they green out in the spring— Do you know cypress?" I told him I had seen them in Florida when I went down on fishing trips. "They're feathery and pale green in the spring and she used to like them, they say. There're water lilies and cranes and, now and then, some wild ducks. In front of her window are her flower beds. Renie and I try to keep something blooming all the year round. I must speak to her—she may have forgot to send the bulbs down—" He took out his notebook and wrote a few words in it. Looked up. "We're not sure Mama even notices but as Renie says, if she notices one time it is worth it. The Christmas roses ought to be about to bloom now."

"You feel she has good care?"

"Yes. The old butler and cook were born on the place. As long as they last they'll look after her. They love her. At least, they seem to. And Ronie is there. Renie's twin brother."

I poured Newell another cup of coffee.

"Ronie and Renie . . . Pretty hard on him. I've said, many a time, to have that name was enough to make him take to drink. His real name is Ronald de Graffenreid Addams but you'll never see it except on his checks and vouchers—and his tombstone, some day."

"He handles the business affairs?"

"He paints pictures. Strangest pictures you ever looked at. The things he seems to see were never on this earth. Yes, in name, he is head of the place. When his father went to Congress, years ago, he put a colored man, Mose Addams, in actual charge of things. Mose is old Grandfather Addams' grandson. That makes him and Ron first cousins. But they get along fine. Mose knows his place and he stays there—in the back yard with all the other things Papa and Grandpa wanted to keep out of their sight." Newell half smiled. "Mose went to Tuskegee Institute and learned how to farm the modern way. They have tractors now, use airplanes for spraying—he makes the family a good income. All he asks of Ron is that he sign the vouchers and checks and he picks a time when Ron is sober enough to write his name."

I said, "All this must be pretty hard on Renie. We see it one way; she sees them as the people she belongs to and loves."

"Yes. She worries more than she admits. But you'd think it would make her turn in the opposite direction when she knows what it has done to . . . We never know, do we? I mean we never let ourselves— Since her father's death, she seems to have turned into him. This may sound superstitious to you but sometimes it seems to me . . . you don't think the spirit of a dead man can come back and take up its abode, or whatever you call it, in one of his children? I feel sometimes that old Congressman Addams has come back and is living right in our apartment. I know it sounds pretty superstitious—" He waited for me to answer him.

"Maybe it is safer to say memories come back and swarm all over a person, covering her, so you lose sight of—"

"No. It is more than that. Sometimes Renie even walks like him. But I mentioned that, didn't I? They didn't get along too well while he was alive, they both had tempers—and she was ashamed of the race speeches he used to make in Congress and while campaigning but sometimes now she says the very words he used to say. Well . . . I don't know. But I think a lot of Mama—we call her that, you know; my mother died when I was sixteen. She was like this when I married Renie. She has never spoken to me but I feel she likes me as much as I like her. Sometimes on the plane I think about her all day long. You can see things better when you're flying . . . You feel as if you might be dead and looking back at things . . . down below you . . . sometimes when you're flying above the clouds . . . you look down—you don't feel close, you can see better. I can see that twenty-thousand-acre plantation spreading over that black delta land—and the colored folks . . . then I hear Congressman Addams up at the Capitol . . . I can see him there, he was smooth and got along, a good bargainer . . . making those speeches about the white race and what he called our sacred way of life. And then, I hear Ronie— It was a week after his father's death: Ronie has always remembered the bad things about him—now Renie remembers only the good things. Ron was telling me how his father would take the young black virgins on the place and deflower them, he felt it was his special privilege. Ron said he'd known about it since he was seven years old when he saw his father with one— Ronie was drunk and some of what he said may not be true. I don't know. But after he said that, he began to cry and then he told me about Congressman Addams taking one of these black girls, she was about thirteen, maybe twelve, Ron said, to the woodhouse, not a hundred yards from the house, and well—she must have fought him. Most didn't. But this one must have for he left her hurt and bleeding— And Mama found her there. She may have screamed. Ronie doesn't know why Mama went out there. Anyway, Ronie kept saying *Mama found her! Mama found her!* He said he was lying upstairs in his room reading and Mama came to the door. She was pale and her big dark eyes were full of something he'd never seen and she said, *Ronie, come quick! You must help me!* and he followed her to the woodhouse. He drove the car while Mama sat with the girl and they took her to their doctor's office in town. It was Dr. Jim Guthrie, Uncle Guth's brother—he used to live back home. And Ronie kept saying *She thought I did it! I was eighteen and she thought I did it! She couldn't bear to think Dad did it but she knew. I said Mama, I've never touched one of them, I don't*

*want to go near them, don't you know that! Then who did it? She
kept asking, Then who did it? And I said maybe one of the colored men did it. She looked at me a long time and then she said,
Maybe you're right, Ronie; maybe one of them did it.* And she
tended that nigger girl, Ronie told me, as carefully as if she had
been her own child. And after that, Mama just stopped talking.
She didn't stop all at once. It took her about a month to stop.

"When Ronie finished telling me, he started toward the old
well in the back yard. The colored folks still get water there. A
little nigger came strutting along with his bucket on his head
and had just got ready to draw some water—Ronie had his
whisky bottle in his hand and he hurled that bottle at the well
and it hit the edge of it and broke into a thousand pieces and
whisky and splinters of glass sprayed up and fell into the water.
And the little fellow dropped his bucket and ran and Ronie
laughed and laughed.

"Susan saw this. I was on the steps, I turned and saw her with
Renie standing in the doorway. And then they were gone."

"Does Renie know about her father?"

"She knows and she doesn't know. The way, I guess, we all
know things. I don't believe Ron would tell her. Every evening,
when he's not drinking, he goes and sits by his mother and holds
her hand and they look at the flowers and the lake and the cypress— At least, I hope they do. Now and then he talks to her.
Tells her about what's going on in the world. He believes she
hears him. He told her about the atom bomb. He thinks she
understood because she smiled a little. That's the kind of thing
Ron says. Each morning when he's not drunk he reads the Bible
to her. He lives in fear of her seeing him drunk and he's told
Brooks and Minnie to lock him in his room, if necessary—never
let her see him."

"You've never taken Mrs. Addams to a psychiatrist?"

"Renie wanted her to go. Not at first. She didn't understand.
But later. She wanted to take her to that clinic in Kansas. Or to
New York. And I said, What for? what for, Renie? And she said,
To make Mama talk! But sometimes when I'm in that plane I
find myself thinking, *Suppose Mama talked! Suppose Mama*

talked. . . . I didn't mean to say all this. But when Renie has had such a childhood you'd think she'd lean over backward never to—"

"Maybe we don't know what Renie really thinks. Maybe she doesn't quite know herself."

He stood up. "I beg your pardon for staying so long. You didn't want me to say all this and I didn't intend to. But sometime, I would like to talk to you again." He looked at me rather a long time. "If it is not true what Susan said, or what Renie said, how under heaven's name did Channing get into it?"

I didn't answer that. I said, "I think it would be better to look ahead instead of behind you, just now. It seems to me you have to decide whether you want to send Channing to jail so much that you are willing to ruin Susan's future to do it. I think we can nail it down, just like that."

"Suppose I withdraw the charges. And next week, or the week after, Channing follows her again?"

"If that were to happen, then I'd help you put him where he should be: in a mental hospital. But the likelihood of it is more remote than is the danger of a nuclear bomb falling on Windsor Hills."

He drew in a deep breath.

The phone rang. Once more, Jane said there was no line to Boston open. When I turned around, he was at the door. "It is late. I must go. I'll think about it and call you before I leave town. There will be formalities to go through. God help us all, if I'm doing the wrong thing."

We shook hands and he left.

It was twelve o'clock. I went upstairs. I had stopped thinking. I couldn't put any of this together and didn't try. All I could see now was Grace running up those steps. Grace, outside the phone booth watching me . . . sitting in that plane trying to find the right words to say to her son . . . opening that hotel door and seeing Mark standing there.

19

On Monday afternoon, they found the boy. And on Wednesday, I learned what had happened that weekend. Tom Eliot came down with the Channings from Bratton, we met at the Ryders' home in Baltimore and that evening, after the burial, we talked.

It is difficult to remember that I knew nothing about the clipping until Eliot told me. It seems now I had always known. What would a man do if he were out to hurt you bad? He wouldn't play at it. He'd find the one place in you that you couldn't defend, pick the weapon that could do the job and at the same time leave him nameless and safe. He'd be sure to play it safe. It's the weapon that counts, not the courage. And he didn't have far to look for his weapon. But why he held it ten days after clipping it from the November 5th *Advertiser* is difficult to say. Even if we knew who sent it—and we don't—we might find it hard to follow through that curious interference with impulse which his conscience must have made. Or was he only waiting for the right time? However that may be, his impulse to destroy finally won and he air-mailed the clipping on Thursday, November 15th. Then he probably went about his business in Windsor Hills or The Flats or wherever he lives, joking with acquaintances, or talking politics; maybe helping an old lady across the street at a corner where traffic is bad.

Friday morning, Andy got the letter, read it and went to English class. Everybody remembers him sitting there with the others; his English master noticed that he seemed preoccupied, face a bit pale. He was asked a question twice and did not answer; when it was put to him the third time he said something muddled and vague and everybody laughed because Andy was one of the quick, clever ones; it seemed a joke to the others, this sudden absent-mindedness. He left the room at once when the class was dismissed. No lunch. No afternoon classes. No field practice. No dinner.

Seven o'clock. Tom Eliot, his housemaster, knocked on the door of his room. No answer. Knocked again. Called, opened the door an inch or two. Andy lay on the bed staring at the ceiling. All Eliot got was tight lips, a shake of the head, no words. He felt Andy's forehead. "Are you sick?" Head said no. "Hurt yourself?" No.

"Something has happened. Can you talk about it?"

No reaction.

He slipped his fingers on the boy's wrist: pulse slow. Eyes were dull. "I saw it was shock," he told me as we sat talking in the car, that evening. "Death? house burned? accident? You know how you think these things. But they would have come to the school first. This, obviously, had not gone through official channels." He said he went back through the past week or so, trying to find something that might have built up among the fellows without his knowing. Couldn't pick up a thing.

Said he sat there a few minutes trying to feel his way into the situation. It is hard to talk, he finally told Andy; when things hurt you, words hurt too. "At least, it has always been so with me. Ought not be but it is." He said a little more, told him he wanted to help if he could.

"I didn't get to first base.

"But we had talked pretty freely about things, before, so I kept trying to get through to him. Maybe I tried too hard; don't know."

Usually you can take care of things, Eliot finally told him, but now and then something happens and you feel you can't handle it. You know you are being fought but you can't fight back because there's nothing to fight, except a ghost. It had happened to him once. "Gets you, sort of, when it is like that."

No sound from the bed. Eyes had turned, though, and were looking at him.

"I pushed along. Told him I had been in quite a few jams and had found there's usually somebody who can help you, if you'll let him. I didn't get anywhere with it."

Eliot stopped, offered me a cigarette. We smoked for four or five minutes before he said more. Dr. Ryder had given us a car for our use and it was parked now in the driveway. It must have been close to six o'clock. Dark, and freezing cold. I felt we should go somewhere; we shouldn't just sit there. But I could not interrupt him: he needed to say this and I needed to hear—and I knew he would say it finally, if I would wait.

As the match flared up I saw he looked tired and beat. Letting down now. During the day he had been quiet, easy, feelings completely under control as he helped Mrs. Ryder with the things that had to be done. We had both helped—she was the only one you could help—and I had found myself admiring his nerve, the sheer stamina that could maintain so smooth and pleasant an exterior after all he had been through. I had noticed, too, how naturally Ellen Ryder turned to him: leaning on his small courtesies, responding to his minute witticisms said with such impeccable taste in that sad house. He disregarded her fluff and embroidered mannerisms as if they were a costume and went straight to the real Ellen and the real Ellen responded. You almost felt they were two travelers resuming, after many years of separation, an old and valued relationship.

He lit his cigarette again. I saw the scar: thin line from temple to chin. Korea? Could be. I knew almost nothing about the chap except that the Channings had highly approved of him as their son's housemaster at Bratton. And I had seen a letter or two he had written them about Andy. Discerning stuff, but casual and cheerful. That morning, I had scarcely noticed the not-quite-disfiguring scar. It was his eyes that caught me—and the forelock of black hair that intensified the eyes. He was standing by the piano in the music room and turned as Dr. Ryder introduced us and I thought, *It's been rough on him, all right.*

But as I watched him during the day I began to know, somehow, that those eyes had been looking at one thing for years. And were not, even now, through looking, for they were still focused on it, on something no longer outside him but inside. We hate in this day and time to say a man's eyes are haunted but I think his were. The incredible thing that had happened to Andy had been a strain; and it showed in the fatigue lines in his face. But this other was what I became increasingly aware of during the day and I think Ellen Ryder saw it, too. She sees so much more than we want to believe. It is hard for me, for Grace and Mark and most of our friends, to concede that a woman whose mind behaves like a handful of feathers blowing in a breeze has a deep-layered wisdom that we can't penetrate. Now, two years later as I write this, I see it as partly a biological matter: a female talent for holding on to life. I can't say that she has the male reverence for life (when the male feels such a thing); it is, rather, the female instinct for life (when a female etc.). There are plenty of each sex who don't cherish life on any level, of course, and saying it this way gives it not only a specious tinge, but gives no real insight into Ellen. What I think Ellen does—or her kind of woman does—is meet ordeal not with the mind alone, as men tend to do, but with the whole organism. Everything in her— heart, imagination, intuition, understanding—reaches out and keeps the old wheel turning no matter how many spokes are broken. That afternoon:

We had come back from the cemetery and had gone into the music room, the six of us. Suddenly it was as if we were paralyzed. It hit us, somehow, all at once: the horror, the monstrous unreason— Ten thousand threads knotted around us—

It had begun earlier, of course. All day: everyone had been too calm, too quiet. At the Retreat—as the funeral home was called —in that cold, windy place at the cemetery, there had been no grief in us, no tears.

Only the family had gathered there and their most intimate Baltimore friends, and Eliot and I—and the Ryders' rector. He was reading the order of burial and I was assisting him. He had begun to say those old, hypnotic words of anguished faith: *I am the resurrection and the life, saith the Lord: he that believeth in me, though he were dead, yet shall he live. . . .* His voice was grave, confident, but those words which had never failed me before were falling like pebbles, striking, bruising all of us standing there. They needed—Mark and Grace desperately needed—a new gesture from God. These ancient symbols could not give it to them. I felt it. The friend in me knew the way their minds worked, understood the rhythm in which their hearts moved, and struggled to push the priest in me aside and find for them what they had to have; there must be words somewhere, somewhere in the human vocabulary, that could bring comfort to them. But I did not know them. I knew only these words, these old and beloved words which could not now give these two what they had to have. The rector had asked me to read the final prayers. The time had come for me to do so. I found the place in the Prayer Book, I began to say: *O God, whose most dear Son did take little children into his arms and bless them; Give us grace, we beseech thee, to entrust . . .* I saw Mark's eyes: I could not go on. I could not say what had no meaning for him. I could not force the words out of my mouth—the open grave tilted as wave upon wave of feeling swept over me, an awful silence was bearing down— And then, I heard my voice speaking calmly, clearly . . . *care and love, and bring us all to thy heavenly kingdom; through the same thy Son, Jesus Christ our Lord. Amen. . . . Deal graciously . . . with all those who mourn, that, casting every care on thee . . . Amen.* Their rector whispered, *Amen.* And then, as I closed the Prayer Book, I saw those two stiff figures turning away. Uncomforted. Emptied out. Everything unexplained, every question unanswered. I was trembling, someone was touching my hand, it was the rector and I realized he was trying to shake— I pulled my muscles under control and shook his thin firm hand. Now he was offering to take me to the Ryders' home and I was thanking him, explaining that a friend of the Ryders had planned to drive me and the boy's teacher home.

Eliot and I did not talk to each other while in the car. The friend kept a little conversation going, almost by himself. When we left him, we walked into the house in silence. The others were in the music room and we went there, too. Not knowing what else to do. Six silent people; two slender women in black and the four men. The stillness was complete. The moment had finally come when good and evil had canceled each other out, when the tender the brutal the truth and the lie, death and life, had merged into nothing. Nothing. Nothing. And I, their priest, could not help even myself.

And then it was that Ellen Ryder— What gave her the strength to breathe, to move, to pick up the old routines, the old patterns and stuff us into them as if they were an iron lung, I don't know. But she did it—in such a trite way, too. She laid her black hat, black gloves, black bag in a limp pile on that piano. I see them now, lying there—I shall always see them. Then she suggested coffee. No one could answer her. She turned to Grace and Mark: their faces were drained of color and feeling and they stood stiff and unmoving but she seemed not to notice. She said in a quiet, easy voice that she thought perhaps they would like to rest—and they turned like blind children and went out of the room. Then she picked up the evening paper and gave it to her husband. Then she opened the cabinet and brought out a tray with brandy and glasses and set it on the piano. Then she went out into the hall. She can walk without a sound but she let her heels tap tap brightly across the floor and I heard her say, "Oh Mona," in a calm cheerful tone. The maid followed her to her bedroom. The three of us were left standing there. We had nothing to say but we could not separate. Dr. Ryder, as if commanded to do so, held out his cigarettes. Each of us took one. He offered us the *Evening Sun*. We said no. He went to his usual chair, unfolded the paper and scanned it slowly page by page. Eliot walked over to the window. The early winter dusk had blotted out the garden but he seemed not to notice, he just stood there looking at it. I went to the piano, saw the *Fourth Brandenburg* lying there, opened it. I could not hear a sound in my mind but I kept turning the pages. Then I smelled coffee and toast—heard Mona going upstairs, knew she was taking them the coffee they had felt unable to want. Tap tap tap up the stairs. The movement, the sounds, the smells dropped into my organism —no more than one faint ripple on a becalmed sea but enough to change my metabolism. I felt better, somehow; not much, just a little better. . . .

Then Ellen returned. She stood in the doorway, diminished and muted by her black dress and yet strong and sure. Mona brought in a tray of coffee, placed it on the table. Ellen poured three cups: put one on the table by her husband, one on the piano for me; took one to the window where Eliot stood. I drank the coffee. Dr. Ryder drank the coffee. Eliot drank the coffee. She began to talk gently to Eliot about her African violets; she brought a rare specimen to the piano to show me, after showing it to Eliot. I desperately searched for a word and came up with *remarkable.* I remember those white limp blooms with the crumpled petals, and the feel of that succulent hairy leaf which I must have held rather a long time. Then she spoke softly to Coco, her cocker spaniel, who again, as he had been doing throughout the day, put his paw on her skirt and begged for explanation of this silence and the new strange emptiness he heard in his household. Her words were hardly more than speech automatisms, her voice was thin as a glass bell—it is always like that and irritating almost beyond belief. But she was doing it: she was reminding us that you keep moving, you walk like animal or machine if you cannot walk like a human being or a child of God, but you don't stop walking. There was stern sense in those silent commands she was issuing. I felt the solid rock beneath that whipped cream which masks her personality. Whether she has thought through, even to a small extent, the twisting ambiguities of the human situation, I don't know; she would certainly shun the current vocabulary of existentialism, would be appalled by it, I suspect, and without knowing why; but she understands tragedy: she feels the eternal justice of it somewhere in her and she had more to meet it with that day than did the rest of us—more than her scientist son-in-law, or her surgeon husband or her artist daughter, or her daughter's priest possessed, because— Because she saw it as tragedy, I think now, and by doing so gave dignity to the human beings involved in it, while we saw it more superficially as insane malevolence, irrational accident, hideous melodrama.

Now and then, she looked at her husband whose face was hidden behind his newspaper. She finally said, "Were you going to see Mrs. Heinz, dear?" He came from behind it. I don't think he remembered who Mrs. Heinz was but her face expected him to remember and I knew he would, in time. He went back behind his paper; came out five minutes later and said, I think I'll go over to the hospital; think perhaps I should look in on Mrs. Heinz and one or two others. She said, Yes dear. He left the room. We heard the tires crunch on the gravel as he backed out of the driveway. I said Eliot and I would go out for a bit of air, perhaps for a walk; perhaps downtown—she was not to plan for our supper. She said we might find it interesting to drive around the grounds of Johns Hopkins University, and then she gave me a house key, told us to go to the refrigerator when we came in if we were hungry, and we left her.

As I sat there in the car, I saw the light on in the music room. I thought, She is there, emptying ash trays, straightening the music on the piano, patting her cocker spaniel, moving the violets on the window ledge an inch this way, that, folding the doctor's evening newspaper, reducing this vast disorder to a size she can deal with, making the thread small enough to slip through the eye of her needle. Or, now that she is alone, has she finally laid aside her strength and wisdom altogether and become the little girl that you sometimes see peering out of her eyes—

Upstairs, in the room toward the back, Grace's and Mark's room, there was a light. I was glad. I don't quite know why; perhaps I thought, maybe now they can see each other. All day, I had the crazy feeling that neither had seen the other in a long time—not since Friday night. They had said a few words during the day, of course; each had spoken to me now and then but I could not remember their speaking to each other—and at the cemetery as I looked at Mark—

Eliot was talking. I heard him say,

"Strange . . . way you tell what you said when you don't know what you said. I am not sure what I said to the boy. It is too mixed up with what I wish I had said." He smoked for a while. Deliberately put his voice on a much lighter level, "I'm afraid I still believe words are magic; the right ones." Stopped. "I woke up on the train last night, talking in my sleep. I was saying, *Sometimes when a fellow gets in a tough spot it is better to talk about it if he knows somebody he can trust.* I woke up hearing myself say it." He said he lay there listening, trying to see how Andy would react to it. Everything quiet except for the grind of wheels underneath him and the moan of the diesel's whistle a mile ahead, it seemed, and the rush of air you can't feel— He said he kept saying, *There's always somebody you can trust.* Would say it and listen, asking himself, Is there? answering, no. Plenty of times, no.

"I must have dropped off to sleep for I saw, I guess it was a dream, don't know, but I saw a pale green wet glistening meadow and a thousand wild geese slowly rising out of it in a thick trumpeting smoky-white cloud, and drifting, they weren't flying they were drifting as if caught in an air stream, across a small tidal river and then they began to drop slowly, one, three, four, eight, twenty, a hundred maybe, into the marsh on the other side, each falling with a soft rubbery thud into the marsh— and finally they were gone and the air was quiet and still and I could see their shadows moving in the water and I said, *That is impossible*— Then I woke up and lay there listening to the train whistle a mile off."

But after a while, it began once more: his trying to decide what he had said to Andy and what he should have said—and all the time that box in the baggage car—

"I probably was half-asleep but felt I was awake. Whether I was or not, I kept thinking if I had said it right, exactly right,

Andy would have told me about that clipping and then I could have—" He stopped.

"Clipping?" That is the first I knew of it.

"The newspaper clipping about his father. Pasted on a sheet of paper in that letter."

So that was the way S.K. had done it. Why S.K.? I don't know. I had pinned it on him, that's all. I could see his face: grinning as if he had played a good trick on somebody. He'd say, All I did was address an envelope—nothing wrong about addressing an envelope, is there? It was in the paper—I didn't put it there—all I did was address an envelope. Not against the law, is it?

I needed to say something. I tried. "Seems to me you said about all you could say. I don't believe Andy could have told you about that clipping."

"I don't know. Guess not. Anyway, I felt I couldn't keep pushing him so I stopped." He sat there, he said, looking at that room. "It was like my room when I was in school—and a thousand other boys' rooms, I guess. Somehow it made me feel he'd hear me."

He didn't describe it. He didn't need to. There it was: spread out in my mind much as it had been at home—everything in it exposing a boy's dreams and hopes—and fears. Tennis racquet on wall, initials printed in blue ink. This was his second one—he had outgrown his first. Desk—usually with a pair of muddy shoes on it, or two or three. Three photographs: Mark, Grace, his terrier, side by side. Shelves chock-full of labeled rocks, arrowheads. Andy thought two years ago he'd be a mining engineer, last year he was going to be an archeologist. This year, I didn't know, hadn't heard his plans. Canoe paddle on wall; camp emblems, awards, all the gadgets you have at camp. Bookshelves: stack of *National Geographics* and two or three comic books; a dozen books on Egypt and Mexico. Oboe on top shelf; music rack. Stamp collection . . . Andy had wanted to take everything with him when he went to school. Grace tried to persuade him to leave his rock collection—pretty solid stuff; but he wanted that, too, and Mark had said, Let him take it if he wants to; it's as much him as his fingernails. The boy ended up taking pretty near all his gear, including new ice skates.

Eliot finished his cigarette. Said slowly, "I forgot that other room a boy fills with things nobody ever sees."

He seemed young to be talking like this. Maybe the scar had done it. But plenty of people have scars who don't have insight; he may have been born thinking, talking, feeling like this —he said it as if he had been thinking about it half a lifetime.

Finally, he asked Andy if he'd like to call home. Andy said no.

"All right, let's go down to my apartment and get something to eat. I'm sort of hungry. You're not, I can see. I never was, either, when I'd been punched in the head. How about a cold towel first?"

That was when Eliot thought of it: while he was in the shower room. He said he stood at the sink with a wet towel in his hands and thought the word: *letter*. He remembered he was reading his mail that morning and had glanced up; saw one of the boys with a letter. Dozens of them had letters of course, but this boy was chalk-pale and the letter was pink. And then he had gone back to his own mail and forgot it. Sure, it was Andy: he was standing near the door reading it and the paper looked cheap-pink and his face was chalky. But somehow—you can't hover over them—he had given it no further thought.

He put the wet towel on Andy's head and waited. Let the coldness do its work. Then they went down to his rooms. He gave him a demitasse of black coffee with plenty of sugar and told him to drink it like medicine. Then he told him he was going to ask him a personal question:

"You got a letter this morning?"

Eyes said yes.

"OK. Was it from your parents?"

Andy whispered no.

"Anybody you know or care for wrote it? No? Then somebody you don't know wrote something that socked the daylights out of you. I'd guess it was a lie and a mean one."

He waited. Thought he saw something change in Andy's face. Waited. Said, "Your parents don't lie to you, do they?"

"They never have."

"They tell you the important things?"

"I think so."

"Then what seems important in that letter just can't be. A crank wrote you a lie, see? Because he thinks your family is his enemy. Made it up in his head. These things happen, Andy. They are crazy, unbelievable, but they happen. You've got to tell yourself he would have sent that letter to any fellow here, had he decided that particular family was his enemy. He feels he has an inalienable right to destroy an enemy. So he stays safely hidden and writes you something he thinks will hurt you and your family."

Eliot rubbed his cigarette, threw it out of the car window. "Thought I was doing fine. Told him to turn on the TV while I looked around for something to eat." He opened a can of spaghetti and meat balls, heated it, made a green salad. Andy ate rather more than you would have expected. "He'd look at me; eat; look at me. His eyes—I don't know the word. Innocence, maybe. But innocence doesn't say it."

"He was too sensitive, I'm afraid."

"Yes, but I mean something else. His eyes had no expectation of coming in contact with evil. He believed the world was a good place to live in, a safe place." He stopped. "That may not be the right way to say it, but it left him wide open—for anything." He stopped again. Said with sudden anger, "Why on earth did they shelter him, like that?"

I said Andy had been exposed to plenty of danger and hardship, all his life. Tramping through mountains, climbing cliffs—

"Physical hardship, you mean."

"Yes, but it toughened him. For instance—he saved an older and much bigger boy from drowning on a Scout trip when he was eleven. Swam a quarter of a mile across the lake after their canoe tipped, towing him in; the other kid was crazy-scared and fought him all the way. Andy was scared, too, but he hung on and brought him in. He had a paper route when he was nine or ten— up at four-thirty every morning. You mean something different, I know. But what I am saying is the boy wasn't soft, morally or physically."

Eliot said gently, "I had never thought of him as soft. I guess I'm not saying it very well."

"Nor am I—but let me add this: sex, all that: his parents are modern, you know; and always made a point of being frank with him about such things. He wasn't ignorant or prudish. He certainly knew about deviations and accepted those he knew about without going off the deep end. But when a deviation—and this kind—concerns your father—"

"I don't mean deviation—at least, not *as* deviation. I mean evil." He pressed hard on the word. "He'd never seen evil working close-up in the human race—no matter what he'd heard about it."

The boy—I had a shattering realization that he was dead. *Why do we keep talking as if there is something we can still do! There is,* another part of me whispered.

"I think I am trying to say," Eliot's voice was warm, sympathetic, but persistent, "that Andy thought good people are good and only bad people are bad. He loved and admired his father. *Because he did,* he thought him incapable of the act that was mentioned in that newspaper clipping. At the same time, he found it almost impossible to believe his father would be arrested if he hadn't done it. He couldn't believe what was in that newspaper but he could not believe a newspaper might print something that would ruin an innocent man's life." Eliot's voice was bitter as he said this. "It wound up in his head and unwound, and wound up and unwound. The worst part of it was knowing his father couldn't have done it and yet knowing—for he was sensitive and highly intelligent—that in every man there are impulses, instincts, that may at some weak moment sweep over him and cause him to do wrong. It was this knowing and not-knowing, believing and not-believing, that tore him to pieces. He saw evil close, for the first time, *in or reflected in his own father.* Coming that way—" He stopped, seemed to be thinking about it. Said, "Andy had no idea that evil is in all of us tangled up with the good, that good and evil not only destroy each other, they feed on each other, can't do without each other."

"Did you? at his age?" My voice was full of impatience. What was he asking of the boy—of anybody!

"No. But I wish to God I had."

I fought him hard that night, in my mind. I resisted what he was saying. But now, I know he was almost right. Andy did have a profound need to see the people he loved in pure, uncomplicated terms. They were good. There was evil in the world, sure; but it was far away, almost as far as Outer Space which he had heard about, too. I had felt this in him without putting my feeling into words. I had said to myself, The boy's too innocent, too tender; meaning something I could not formulate beyond these vague words. But that night, I didn't feel up to talking more about it.

And Eliot dropped it, too. Said quietly, "Of course it would have broken up any thirteen-year-old who cared for his family."

He went back to his account: "After Andy had looked at me a long time he told me the letter wasn't signed. I asked him if it concerned his father. He said it did." Eliot then told him his father was in politics in Boston and knew all about anonymous letters.

—My father's not in politics.

—I'm afraid there may be people who don't like scientists, either.

—It is cancer research.

—Yes, I know. And most people are grateful. But now and then, somebody isn't. Minds twist things, remember. There are cranks who think it's wrong to tamper with what they call God's will. Other cranks hate science because some of the great scientists are Jews. They're not all cranks, either. People have good reasons for fearing science, too.

—Why? Andy asked.

Eliot said a little about automation, nuclear weapons, fall-out from tests— People's anxiety—their need to turn their fear on someone—

He felt Andy had something to say. Waited. Andy couldn't say it. Finally, as casually as he could, Eliot asked him if he and his father were friends.

—Of course.

—You respect him?

—Yes.

—Trust him?

Long silence. —Yes.

—Your mother does, too, of course?

Boy swallowed hard.

Eliot pushed on. "Felt I had to." He talked about loyalty. Said, You make up your mind, Andy: a man is your friend—he has his faults, sure; big ones; but the point is, when you once decide you believe in him you stand by no matter what anybody else says. Certainly no anonymous letter written by a coward or crazy person could shake you.

That was when Andy cried. He buried his face on the table and cried hard. Eliot pushed on. —Whatever was in that letter is a damned lie. You've got to realize that the man who sent it is trying to compel you to doubt your father.

Andy couldn't answer. Finally, Eliot asked him when he had heard from his mother. Andy was working hard on himself now —Can you tell me?

—Yesterday.

—Everything OK?

—She said it was.

—Then it is. No matter what somebody wrote you, everything is OK if she said it was.

Eliot turned to me. "I couldn't have made it worse." He was silent a long time. Then he said, "Is there any place we can go where it's warm? Somewhere for food?"

I suggested a German restaurant I remembered from football days, wasn't sure what street it was on. Howard or Park, I thought; below Franklin, somewhere, I thought. Wasn't even sure it still existed. He asked me to drive since he knew nothing about Baltimore.

I was cold, too, and wanted something—but not food. I think

I wanted to move, get away from what his words and my thoughts were building up and tearing down. He had appealed to the boy's loyalty: *You believe in a man therefore you can't think evil of him because others do;* on the other hand, he was saying to me, *What the boy didn't know was, there's evil in every one of us, evil and good feeding on each other—* And both statements were true, of course; but the fine points didn't interlock.

20

I backed the car into the driveway and turned toward the city, into University Parkway, headed for Charles Street. Now and then I pointed out a building. When we came to Mount Vernon Place, I said, "Mrs. Ryder studied music at Peabody, over there." He nodded, tried to look at the Peabody Conservatory buildings. "The Duchess of Windsor's childhood home is just a block or two away." He nodded again. "Off here, a few streets east, is where Henry Mencken lived." Nodded again. That was about all I could manage in the way of a guided tour.

As we crossed Franklin he said, "What I tried to say back there— As I think about it, each thing I said canceled out something else I said." He smiled that quick smile which seemed unable to stay on his face long.

We found a parking lot, went inside the restaurant. He looked at the walls covered with photographs of fighters, actors, etc. Went to the photographs nearest us, looked at them a long time. Came back, picked up the menu, looked at it a long time. I finally said how about some oyster stew and crab cakes and cole slaw?

"Be fine—but I'd like a Martini first, if you don't mind."

After he drank the Martini he said, "Back to that night—or is it better not to talk about it?"

I told him I'd like to hear.

He said Andy walked over to the grate. "I asked him if he didn't think it a good idea to throw the letter in. Give it the treatment it deserved."

Andy looked in the fire for a minute, maybe, but he didn't burn the letter.

"I got to him first, that afternoon. My shovel touched something solid and I knew. I was three hundred yards from the hut, off the path about a hundred feet. I was afraid Dr. Channing might come out—he had gone in to rest—I wanted to save him this. I knew reporters were likely to get there any time. I dug as fast as I could. Pulled the letter out of his pocket, I knew it was with him—it was almost impossible to loosen it—had no idea —did you know. . . ." He stared at his plate. "I finally got it out, and slipped it into the pocket of my jacket. Then I called two of the men to help me. Later, when no one was around, I gave the letter to Dr. Channing. He opened it, handed it to me, without a word. That was when I read the clipping."

"Do you have it now?"

"No, I gave it back to him."

Eliot was staring at the photographs on the wall opposite our table. "That face is familiar. Can't place her."

"Norma Shearer."

"Long time ago, wasn't it. Her era, I mean." He looked at it again. "There was a movie of hers I saw when I was a kid." The waitress brought the oyster stew. We ate it without talking much. She brought the crab cakes and coffee.

Then he told me more about that night when Andy was in his room—as if there were something he couldn't get straight. Said he brought in cake and milk for Andy and coffee for himself; put a new record on, something of dello Joio's— "I knew Andy was accustomed to contemporary music and might like it."

But as they listened to the music he realized he had got nowhere near dead center. The boy was pale, eyes dilated. Eliot sent a message to the infirmary, the nurse came over and checked, she suggested that Andy go back with her, Andy didn't want to, Eliot told her he'd keep him in his rooms for the night. She left a tablet for him to take when he went to bed.

"That was the second big error I made: when I didn't let her take him back with her. If I had let her—you keep going back over it, trying to see where you— Do you mind, sir, if I have a brandy and will you have one, too?" I told him I would like a glass of cognac. He ordered the cognac.

"He was quiet when I left for the headmaster's house. I felt all right about leaving him. Asked one of the men upstairs to keep an eye out. Andy said he'd be OK. He was such a reliable fellow, it never occurred to me he'd—

"And then, when I came back, I found the note saying he had gone out for a walk. He said he'd be back in a little while. And I believed him."

But Eliot was worried. He had noticed on his way home how heavy the snow was. Kept going to the window. Let ten minutes pass then went out to look for the boy. He was surprised at the intensity of the wind as he walked over to the next house. Snow was coming down fast. When he started back his tracks were gone. He called two of the teachers; the three of them went out with their flashlights. They made the round of houses, buildings. "It took us about thirty minutes." By that time, paths were filling, drifts piling—

"We were New Englanders and used to snow, used to winds. We didn't like it a bit. We'd stand there straining to see a small blob somewhere but we couldn't see twenty feet ahead of us.

"To tell you the truth, from that moment, I was scared sick.

"We got two more men and went the rounds of the campus again. The snow was full of wind, heavy-soft. We'd try to push through. Terrific resistance. We'd keep trying. Soft, heavy, rolling over us like a big white cold animal fighting by smothering us. It seemed alive—"

"There's somebody two tables away reading your lips," I said. "Turn your chair a little."

Eliot didn't look up, just moved over to the left side of the table. "We took ski poles. Poked around with them. Then somebody plunged his arm down in a drift—and we all began doing it. There were endless drifts but we kept plunging our arms in." His chin was shaking. I pushed his brandy toward him. He drank it. Ordered another. "We poked, then we'd stand there flashing our lights against that massive blowing whiteness and calling. The words fell to pieces and whipped back across us but we kept calling. We went to the lake. Frozen. No signs. All human signs wiped out but we kept calling. I began to feel I had gone through it before—a long time ago . . . and what I was looking for I had never found, I wouldn't find it this time, either—that's when I began to feel the sweat rolling down me. I don't know—" He stared at me, not looking at me, looking for the words he wanted—

"—primordial memory, terror, I guess it was. What was outside blew open something ten thousand years deep inside and it overwhelmed me, almost. The others, too, I think now. But on the surface we were controlled and sensible in our actions—at least I think we were—except when we'd start thrusting our arms down in those drifts."

Then, in some inexplicable way, they got their second wind, their psychic wind. They slowed down. The long haul was ahead and they knew it. They went inside, warmed up, had a smoke and talked it over sensibly.

"We picked four seniors who could be relied upon. Husky Maine boys. They put on snowshoes. They were to stick together and go everywhere—the campus stretches back a long way; an instructor who is an experienced skier went along with them; they took thermos bottles of hot coffee.

"Then I went to the headmaster's and told him. He asked first thing what Andy had on. I couldn't for the life of me remember: a heavy sweater and his leather coat, probably. Did he have a flashlight? I didn't know. I checked his room. His leather coat was gone; we decided he had it on. His flashlight was gone; we decided he had taken it. It made us feel better. That seems stupid now; how far could you see in a blizzard with a flashlight!"

"He was good outdoors, knew how to manage." I had said it before but somehow I felt compelled to repeat it.

"Yes, but he didn't know snow." He was staring at Norma Shearer again. "Can't think what picture that was—I must have been about eight years old." He left it, stared down at the table. Looked up, said, "I'm not trying to make myself drunk but do you mind, sir, if I have another brandy? And will you?" I told him no but to do what he wished.

He ordered the brandy, then went on with his story.

The headmaster called four of the employees: men who had worked at the school for years. They knew every inch of the place. They went out together. He went with them. There were three searching parties now. "We were headed in different directions but we'd keep meeting each other.

"At two o'clock he and two of the men started to the village to call Dr. Channing; our phones were out; they took the midget caterpillar the school owns and made it somehow; picked up several hunters who know the woods and roads and trails as well as they know their own house.

"At four o'clock he got his call through. That was lucky. It was the last call to go through. Dr. Channing said first thing, Don't you have a hut a mile or so from the school? He said Andy had written him it reminded him of their place in the mountains. He might go there. They told him they'd go see. Told him there was a fireplace in the hut; if the boy was there, he'd be safe and warm.

"The wind was fierce. I still don't see how we found the hut but we did, soon after daylight.

"When we walked inside, I felt he had been there—can't tell you what the signs were but I felt he had been there. It made sense. The only thing that did. I knew Andy hadn't gone off his head. He went out for a walk. The snow made him feel better, excited him, probably. He decided to go to the hut and come right back. I remembered a trip we made in late October; he said then it reminded him of their cabin in the mountains, he seemed to like it. Told me about his trips with his father to their place. He figured he could make it in twenty minutes, back in twenty; probably figured he'd be in my rooms shortly after I returned, and left a note saying so."

"Did he know where you had gone?"

"Not necessarily. He may have guessed it."

"Then they called him—his parents—before you got back."

"I didn't know that."

"Immediately after the headmaster's call to them. His mother told him she was flying up the next morning. That probably did it: He'd either have to let her know he knew they had lied to him or he'd have to think up a good enough lie to keep her from finding out he knew they were lying. It panicked him."

"So he ran."

Back, I thought. Deliberately back—to a place where everything had been good and right. If he could get to the cabin . . . everything would swing around as it had once been and there'd be no newspaper clipping and no arrest and no little girl in a dark store—

Eliot finally said, "What did they tell him? do you know?"

"Pretty much what you said: people who write anonymous letters are cowards, liars, sick people. They told him they had received some letters, too—which they had. For him to try not to worry . . . she'd explain . . . whatever was in his letter was not true . . . hoped you'd bring him to meet the plane, maybe the three of you could have dinner and go to a show—"

"God!"

The fat old man who had been picking his teeth and trying to read Eliot's lips picked up his tab, laid a tip down, pulled at the fly of his pants, shook himself a little, looked hard at Eliot as he passed him, waddled slowly over to the cashier's, paid his bill and waddled out.

I said, "I'd like some more coffee. Would you?" We ordered coffee. When the coffee came, I said, "I know it's not easy—but were you going to tell me about the hut?"

He nodded. "After we got there I kept saying, He's near here. A small fire had burned out in the fireplace. We didn't know that he had made it, of course. The ashes were not warm but the stones of the fireplace were not cold, either. I ran my hand over the andirons. Felt the firebricks at the back of the chimney. They should be cold, if there'd been no fire. They weren't cold. I asked Kurt to do it— Kurt was the one who was with me through all of it. We squatted there in that freezing cold cabin and I said, You feel them, Kurt. He ran his hands over stones, andirons, the back of the fireplace. Shook his head, They're not cold. Wiped his hands on his pants. Said, We're going to find him. And I believed it.

"We began going round and round that hut, calling and poking. Four of us stayed all day Saturday. We'd come inside, sleep an hour, go out, sure each time we'd find him. Each time, we believed it. When the snow stopped Saturday noon, they brought us tools and we started shoveling. Others came to spell us. Sunday was blinding bright. There're clumps of birches around the place. It must have been a wonderful sight—if you could shift gears; I couldn't. What I mean is—well, I'm sure you know: if the most beautiful thing in the world had appeared before us that day I wouldn't have seen it. They scraped the trail; somebody brought us food and dark glasses. News didn't creep out until Monday. Lines were down. They called the student body together Sunday and told the fellows Andy had got lost in the snow; asked them not to talk about it; nobody to talk to, of course, but each other. They must have asked plenty of questions of each other. Andy had the reputation of being about as level-headed as they come.

"Monday afternoon, about three-thirty, I found him. Dr. Channing was inside; we had persuaded him to go in and drink some soup. One of the men urged him to lie down for a while in the adjoining room where the cots were. I think he must have fallen asleep. Anyway, he was there when I found his son." He seemed not to want to say more than that.

I asked him when the Channings had made it to the school. He said Sunday morning. The train was unable to get through so they came by helicopter. I wanted to ask about Grace, but I knew; and it was easier not to have it said.

Eliot stopped. Looked at me in that way of his—it is more listening than looking.

"Monotone. His voice. Sounds like he's drilling through rock."

I nodded. "When he's feeling things. Not otherwise."

"I noticed that." He said he didn't know how to say what happened to them when Dr. Channing got there: "We never spoke again of Andy. Nor did he. It was something we were looking for; something we must solve. The whole problem was depersonalized. In an incredible way, the search turned into research. I can't explain the process but it happened and it kept us steady. He did that; he made us feel that way. He developed a method, organized things, asked for facts: how long had it been snowing when I left the house? snow wet or dry? what direction was the wind coming from? any water around? small, big streams? cliffs? ravine? what kind of woods? We told him a few clumps of birches and maples were near the hut; some evergreens farther back; no real forest. Back of that were fields. No cliffs. No big stream; none wider than three feet and shallow and only two of them—back of the cabin. He wanted a map drawn of school grounds, adjacent terrain, the hut, all the paths. He asked three of us to draw maps separately then check them against the others. Asked about a path leading beyond the cabin. We told him there wasn't any: only the one that led to the school and a short one that led to the latrine back of the hut. He made us drink coffee; then he asked us questions about our maps; then asked us to divide the area around the cabin into rectangles of equal size and number them; told us to dig in one rectangle at a time—we had been moving here, there, everywhere, I'm afraid. He took me out on the scraped path and asked me a dozen questions about the wind that night, its direction, its force, the density of the snow, the temperature. Then he asked me to tell him exactly when I left for the headmaster's and what Andy's note said. Asked me how long it would take you to walk to the cabin from the school in a light snow. He agreed with me that the round trip could be made in forty minutes in ordinary weather. Then he said he'd like to think about it a bit and went into the other room. Came out. Told us not to dig near the hut. Studied the map with the numbered rectangles and told us to dig in rectangle 5, to move from there to rectangle 7, and on to 9. Said the boy was left-handed. Believed he'd veer to the left when the snow blinded him. To forget the rectangles to the right of the path, for the time being.

"We went back to our digging, sure we'd find Andy—in time. And as long as he was with us we kept our nerve. He was cool, certain of what he was doing, no emotion; nothing functioning but brain and muscle, everything else locked out. And we were the same. Until he'd go in that other room to rest—which he never did until we insisted on it.

"Then the thing would begin to heave—"

He looked at me. Said, "I know some people don't like this kind of talk but—I think I mean all that's down below in a man—in his mythic mind, unconscious, whatever name you want to give it; childhood memory, phylum, prehistoric—just pushed through to the surface." Studied the table, looked up, "The fellows there by the fire, drying their boots or resting would begin to remember things: somebody's grandmother had told such and such a story; one of them was about a mad dog: Seems a mad dog crossed a state line somewhere and ran down the paved road; every farmhouse he came to he stopped and bit something, a calf, or milk cow, another dog, a child lying asleep on the porch, then he'd run panting down the road until he came to another farmhouse, then he ran up a lane and got on an unpaved road running on and on . . . but there's no use to tell you about that. Somebody else remembered he was more afraid of a blizzard than of anything, when he was little; somebody else told about seeing a couple frozen in a car, spent five minutes describing their hands in minute detail; everybody remembered a dream or two and insisted on telling it in total recall —there was one fellow who didn't tell anything but would just shake his head at the end of each dream, each story, and mutter, *It's not death, it's how you die—* Then suddenly, our problem would turn back into a boy named Andy whom we'd felt responsible for and we'd begin to feel we were going to crack up. One of us would step out to pee—and lean against the hut and cry like a baby. I say one: every one of us broke down at one time or another, except Kurt. He'd had his—nothing could ever break him again. You see, his mother was a Jewess and was killed in Auschwitz; two of his aunts were gassed; his young sister was experimented on by the Nazi scientists. He happened to be in Switzerland in school; somehow his family's friends got him over here.

"Then Dr. Channing would come out of the other room and we'd get steady, almost at once. He'd stand there looking at us, and you'd feel something pulling at you, you'd wake up from your nightmare. We'd begin to talk sensibly, unemotionally, about all kinds of things—politics, Eisenhower, Nixon, Adlai Stevenson; India, Nehru, science—he told us about the lab in Windsor Hills, what he and his group were doing; told us about the research going on at Memorial Center, other places; Oak Ridge; somebody mentioned World War II, asked if he'd been in it; he said he had been commander of a bomber in the Pacific; based on Tinian. Before that flew the Hump for eight months. His men must have worshipped him. I know how we felt—"

I nodded. "He's a great guy."

Eliot put two teaspoonsful of sugar in what remained of his coffee and sipped it.

He said, "I've read the clipping, that is all I know. Who sent that letter, do you know?"

I told him I didn't know.

He left that. Said again, "Dr. Channing showed me the clipping. Just handed it to me. Didn't say a word."

What to tell him. . . . He deserved the truth and would understand it were I to tell him what Mark said actually happened. Now that the charges had been withdrawn, would it be a risk? That was for Mark to decide.

I began cautiously: I told him a small girl had accused Mark Channing of attempting to rape her in an empty store; or rather, her mother had accused him. Then she changed it to a charge of statutory rape. When the father finally swore out a warrant he charged Dr. Channing with attempt to seduce a minor. "I believe this is right, am not too sure of the legal terms."

"It sounds incredible."

"As a matter of fact, this kind of accusation is fairly common: A smart, imaginative youngster, mixed up, lonely, with no good relationship with her parents, accuses a man of attempting to harm her sexually. It is curious that these accusations are almost invariably made by little girls. I have never heard of a little boy accusing a woman of this sort of thing. Have you?"

"No, I don't believe I have."

"In this case, the child's mother doesn't seem to know how to handle her. They don't communicate very well. The father is regional sales manager for a Chicago firm and is away most of the time. The mother became hysterical when she found the scratch on Susie's arm."

"Scratch?"

"A cat scratched her." I began to elaborate freely: I told him about the yellow tomcat which everybody had seen sleeping in the window of Toni's old store, at the shopping center. It had been in and out of the place for years, apparently. Toni had died or disappeared—no one seemed clear about that. Anyway the store had been closed a long time. It was built many years before Windsor Hills became the fashionable part of town it now is, and was old and ramshackle and people wanted it torn down. The shopping center's clean, horizontal lines juxtaposed to the angular up-and-down building with its odd protuberances didn't make good sense, architecturally or otherwise. Finally, a group bought it for back taxes and began to remodel it to be used as a clinic, stripping off the protuberances, etc. Then, one Monday afternoon, eight-year-old Susan Newell walked in there, prowling around as kids do. "She likes cats and must have picked up the old yellow cat. Anyway, he scratched her."

Eliot did not comment. I went on, snipping my story here, twisting it there. "Naturally it upset her. She ran into the beauty shop next door and told them a man had scared her in that dark place. They asked her who it was. She said she did not know; she had never seen him before."

"But she had seen Dr. Channing?"

"I'm sure she had seen him at church. The Newells and Channings are communicants of All Saints. The fact is, they have known each other for years—not intimately, they don't go in the same crowd, but Susan is alert, she should have recognized him. And yet, she said again and again, in the shop, that she had never seen the man before."

"To whom? I mean who heard her say it?"

"Nella Perkins, the beauty-shop owner. And Duveen, of course —the young operator. The women having their hair done must have heard rather a bit of it, too."

"What time was this?"

"She ran in the beauty shop at exactly five-thirty."

"And Dr. Channing was at the lab?"

"He usually is. But that day he happened to come home early. It was a fine fall day and he and his wife had worked outdoors a while, planting some tulip bulbs. A rare black variety—"
I stopped. I don't know why.

"Black?"

"Yes, but that's irrelevant."

"You don't sound too sure." He was almost smiling.

"I must admit that nothing seems irrelevant, just now. You find yourself dragging every item in, scrutinizing it, feeling it may have a secret significance. Everything seems to be a print of a hidden impulse, a secret sin. If not for you, you're sure others will think so. Of course my common sense tells me those tulips have nothing whatever to do with it. But my common sense also tells me to be careful not to let people know they were black."

"You aren't serious!"

"I'm afraid I am."

He offered me a cigarette, we smoked for a few minutes. He smiled, said, "I'm lost. Mind putting me back on the track?"

"You and I were discussing the possible effect of black tulips on people's emotions. After coming in from planting those bulbs, Mark went down to the shopping center for some Cokes, came back and went out on the terrace to read. He was there at five-thirty."

"He say so?"

"I saw him there."

"Well—that should have settled it."

"By then both Susan and her mother were insisting that the man in the store was Dr. Channing and people preferred to believe her."

"Why did she change her story?"

I shook my head.

"She must have had some reason."

The best in the world, I thought. I was feeling like the liar I was but what else could I say! I went on with it, "She told her mother the man in the store was tall and thin. Dr. Channing is tall and thin, as you know."

"But good Lord—hundreds of men are tall and thin."

"Susan's father, for instance."

"Are you suggesting—"

"He was in Chicago."

"You are sure?"

"There's no doubt about that."

He studied my face.

I went on with my censored account. "When Susan ran in the beauty shop she told them she was not hurt."

"Was she?"

"She was scratched by that cat but I don't think she knew it, until the women saw the scratch on her arm. Then they asked her more questions. Later—well, it seems she hid it from her mother for twenty-four hours. Susie feels safer hiding things. When her mother discovered it, the arm was swollen and red and badly infected. Naturally, she wanted to know where Susie had got the scratch. Susie defended her right to privacy as long as she could then blurted out her story about the half-dark store, a pile of lumber, a man scaring her. And her mother decided she had been raped."

"Had she?"

"Their doctor told me she had not been touched."

Eliot waited.

"It came up in an odd way: you see, I had been scratched by a cat, too."

"Same one!"

"No. My cat." Eliot looked solemn. Then he began to laugh and for some unaccountable reason it set me off. It was not ordinary laughter; the kind, rather, that seems to be forcing itself out of a sealed-up place; once out, it is not easy to control. I sobered up as quickly as I could, said, "Ali Baba; mean, no sense, no training, can't be trained. I'm rid of him now."

"Where did he go to?"

"Susan has him." I did not look at Eliot. "I'm going to get me a Boxer—in fact, I have a puppy but he's not big enough to take away from his mother. Maybe in two or three weeks— But this is beside the point. I dropped in to see Dr. Guthrie because my scratch was infected, too. While he was cleaning it up he happened to mention that he hadn't treated a cat scratch in a year but had had three, that week. He casually mentioned Susie's scratch. I said something, he said something, then I told him the police had questioned me about the Newells and Channings—"

"Excuse me—who got the third scratch?"

"I have no idea." That stopped us for a few seconds. Then I picked up my story, "The doctor had not heard this. Then, I don't know why, he told me in rather more detail than he needed to, about Mrs. Newell's call to him and her insistence that he examine Susie. He explained that Renie Newell is the daughter of an old friend of his down in Mississippi, he'd known her since she was born, had brought her into the world, et cetera. But the point I am making in this circuitous way is that Mrs. Newell accused Mark Channing of attempted rape *after* Dr. Guthrie had checked Susan."

"Then, of course, she was out to get him."

"It's simpler to say so but I don't think she was. If she was out to get anybody, I think it was her husband."

Eliot stared at Norma Shearer, turned back. His face was drawn with fatigue and his eyes were hard to look at. He said slowly, "If a woman wanted to break a man this would be the way to do it, of course. Medea . . . eternally bent on her revenge. What is there in us that enrages this kind of woman?"

"Too much Jason, I'd guess."

"Maybe." He smiled. "And her name, this time, is Renie. Doesn't quite fit, does it?"

The theory didn't fit, either. Renie's smiling, handsome face flashed through my mind: I saw her at the country club, casually friendly, making her good-humored critical comments about people and events; oh, a little nasty, maybe—these comments; a little dishonest: you'd admit it if you ever gave them a close scrutiny; but funny, and people laughed and liked her. I saw her driving down the green . . . at the shopping center, considerate of the employees in the stores . . . saw her in her Gray Lady uniform at the hospital, doing a thousand kind deeds—there was no one I knew who had done as many thoughtful things for people as Renie.

"You'd never cast her for the role of Medea, once you saw her." And yet, as I said it, I heard Claud's words as one hears the street noises when one is whispering to another in a room: *Renie did this deliberately to shame me . . . she was after me . . . she didn't give a thought to what it would do to Susan. . . .*

"Then what was her motivation? A woman of her social class doesn't drag her little daughter through the mud without some reason, some provocation."

"It's not simple, whatever it is. How can we abstract one reason, one motivation? There're probably a hundred. I said she was out to hurt Claud Newell because it is true, I think; but, in my opinion, it is only a small part of the truth. I don't know why she picked on Mark Channing. Unless— He is curiously like Claud Newell in appearance and yet, completely different from him in personality. Perhaps she feels drawn to him and at the same time, repelled. I don't know. Perhaps she thinks things that arouse her guilt—that cause her to feel *somebody* should be

punished. There're a lot of people who want somebody punished, nowadays. She isn't alone in that."

"So she told her husband a twisted lie and he had Dr. Channing arrested."

"Not then. A week later."

"Why a week?"

"Newell didn't believe his wife about the store. He swore out
the warrant when Susan said Dr. Channing had been following her from school. That was the push-over."

I plunged back into my analysis of Renie. "She's driven her
husband into making money and nothing but money. Now that
he's giving his entire life to it, she finds him boring. She's a
woman who reads many books which I fear she doesn't understand. Psychology, for instance. She's bright enough; it's just
that her memories won't let her see clearly what she reads; she
sees a tenth of what she reads, I'd say. That can mix you up.
I'm going in deep now—and remember, I don't know much
about her. Actually, I'm stringing along a bit theoretically, just
here." I stopped. I was remembering the old doctor's words, and
Claud's; Renie's mother . . . her final *there is nothing more to
say*—sitting in her room with her lace shawl around her shoulders
in the sweltering heat—twilight . . . that pan of okra . . .
black hands reaching—Renie's dream of the empty rooms and
no one in them when she opens the doors—Ron, her twin
brother, with his whisky bottle, walking stiffly toward the well
in the back where the colored folks get their drinking water,
crashing the bottle against the brick rim of the well, glass and
alcohol splintering up in a shining blinding spray and falling into
the dark water below while a small Negro boy waited with his
bucket—

As impossible to create a whole Renie as it would be to gather
up that whisky and those fragments of glass and synthesize them
into what they had once been— Why try? I said, "The word
rape holds half of Renie's world. Symbol or sign: I don't know
which. Both, maybe. It holds all she fears, all she dares not understand, all she wants that has been forbidden her, all she hates

in those she loves. In this one word these ambivalent feelings meet and overlap. And yet, side by side with this or maybe interwoven with it, is so much in Renie that is valid and even good and sweet. How to untangle it . . . I don't know. I have tried to understand what the word did to her when it was linked to her child—"

"She did the linking, didn't she?"

"Did she? You see, I'm not sure. Something in her did it, maybe. But if it did, this made it worse because something else in her did not want it: it acted like powerful enzymes, expediting, accelerating the destructive elements of her nature— She loves Susan even as she hates her; loves and hates Claud, loves and fears her mother, loves and hates her dead father, and Ron, her twin brother. That's the family picture. But get Renie out of her family and into the community and she is calm, cheerful, and, as I have said, rather witty and most kind, most helpful, efficient—"

"But no love. Kindness is not love."

"Love has kindness in it. No, I guess you're right: it is not necessarily love."

"She sounds like one of these split-level personalities."

"Aren't we all?"

"Yes, but you are suggesting, aren't you, that she didn't know what she was doing?"

"I think she was aware of what she was doing, but only one step at a time. She never saw the curve of the path she was walking on. She didn't know why she took each step, and she didn't see what its consequences might be."

"And that is why you couldn't see her as Medea: because Medea knew. Knew everything. And then, deliberately did what she wanted to do. But Renie flies blind through moral space— and with no instruments. If she crashes into someone she thinks that someone crashed into her." There was a question in his voice.

I couldn't answer. My feelings had dragged me beyond words, for a moment.

He said softly, "I suppose Renie is not equal—to Renie."

"She's not equal to Renie and all her invisible collaborators. That's why it is difficult to find one person to blame."

"But she killed Andy."

"She helped kill him. She created a background, a situation. The letter did most of it."

"Could she have sent it?"

"I'm not too sure of anything, tonight, but I'd say no. I believe each of us has our own personal way of doing evil just as our bodies are susceptible only to certain diseases. Here's a man, for instance, who has tuberculosis: his brother has diabetes: each has broken under too much strain, but the strain expresses itself in a different disease. Evil works in us the same way. Or I think so. We are not capable of all sins nor of all virtues. To send an anonymous letter to a child, or to anyone, is not Renie's way. There're many reasons for this; some I think I know; others I don't know. One is, of course, that Renie's crowd, her class, wouldn't do this sort of thing. And Renie's conscience conforms to that of her group."

He smiled. "You don't talk much like a clergyman."

"I don't know how a clergyman should talk." I meant it. "I keep trying to find out—I just don't know, so I have to talk like myself."

"I'm sorry. It is so easy to build up stereotypes. I was reared a Catholic. I had from childhood a picture of what a Protestant clergyman was like. And what a Catholic priest was like, too. Then I gave up my church. I've fought my childhood beliefs hard—too hard, you'd think. To keep my doubts down I've set up over them some pretty stiff dead figures, I'm afraid, of what the church, its body of beliefs, its priests, its purposes and so on, are. Catholic and Protestant."

I was silent.

"The letter. . . . Do you mind if we go back to it? Somebody sent it. Have you any idea who?"

"I don't know. The janitor at the lab may have. I have no way of communicating my reasons for thinking so: therefore I probably don't have any. Just a vague hunch. All I can get at is: he is an ignorant man and I don't think there is much pity in him. He is afraid of what goes on at the lab: talks to the mice as if they were his contemporaries, hates the monkeys; thinks cancer is contagious; is always washing his hands; warned me, once, to wash mine after leaving the lab. At the same time, it fascinates him. About a month ago, Dr. Channing found him looking at the tumors in the museum jars; he was concentrating on the breast tumors, rocking the jars back and forth, sort of. You can imagine what was going on inside his head."

"I don't know about *his* head: I know what's going on in mine and it's pretty gruesome."

"That's the point. I don't actually know, either. I have an idea, though, that what is in my head is closer to what S.K. would think than what Mark Channing would think—about those jars. That's as near as I can get to it."

"But to send that clipping—"

"He'd worked up a pretty stiff resentment. He didn't think about the boy—the boy was just a *thing* he used to injure the boss with. Here he was: a janitor whose job is to clean a building: a normal building, see? But the way he saw things—it was like cleaning an abnormal chamber of horrors." Yet he liked it, I said. We couldn't forget that. He liked the animal room, feared it and was drawn to it; liked watching malignant tissue grow, and yet was afraid he'd catch cancer; was terrified by the radioactive material, he had been warned, you know; and yet he was drawn to it, too. You need somebody to take it out on, when you're mixed up like this. The boss, of course: the one responsible for causing you the anxiety. But Dr. Channing in that lab was the symbol of prestige, power, importance. S. K. didn't dare —until Mark was arrested and the talk began. After that, he felt morally superior; why not? the big scientist had been arrested, hadn't he? and for a dirty low-down act with a nice, pure, helpless little girl. S.K. felt as free to hurt him as a caste-ridden Indian would feel free to hurt an Untouchable.

"Or certain whites might feel free to hurt a Negro."

"Yes. I used the other because I think S.K. felt Mark to be *unclean*, in the special sense of the Untouchable." I stopped;

thought about it. "Anyway—it became even easier after they began calling him Communist and nigger-lover."

"They are doing that?"

"Some are. The anonymous letter-writers are—those making the telephone calls are."

"And this is the work of hoodlums and people like S.K.?"

"I wish I thought so. But I don't see it that way. Our senior warden at All Saints gave it the first push-over when he took Dr. Channing off the TV cancer program. I gave it the second when, instead of refusing to go along with him, I acquiesced for the sake of harmony." I sketched in a few details.

"But you protested."

"Yes, I protested. But I went along."

Silence.

"After all, what else could you have done?"

"I don't know. There is a better way but I don't know what it is."

"Then you just have to submit, don't you? and try not to worry too much?"

"A free, responsible man wouldn't. We clergymen don't search much for what is good and right. I think sometimes: suppose the scientists had let well enough alone when the polio scourge was on us. But the point is: they didn't. They kept searching, thousands of them did nothing but search. We preachers submit to a moral fate that is not a moral fate, with no real effort at searching. We are not free, responsible instruments of God: we are instruments of the community."

"You are blaming yourself too much, I think."

Maybe. But Andy is dead. And I hadn't seen much farther ahead than Renie had.

He said, "I have an idea most preachers know something that a lot of them don't admit even to themselves."

"What?" But I knew.

"Evil. Unconquerable evil in man. You get rid of one form of it, it bobs up in another form. In a sense, why work at it so hard? Why not just count on God's forgiveness of man's frailty and rock along."

"You know, of course, I don't believe that."

"Yes, I know." We looked at each other gravely. He said softly, "And I don't believe it, either."

We had talked ourselves into a dead end. There was nothing more I wanted to say or he wanted to say. We left the restaurant and I drove home. I don't think we spoke until we had left the city and turned into University Parkway.

Then I said, "Claud Newell has withdrawn the charges against Dr. Channing. He did it on the day you found Andy's body."

"God . . . have you told him?"

"Not yet."

Five minutes later, he said, "I don't want to seem morbid or a masochist, but we both know something we've been tiptoeing around: had I let the nurse take Andy with her he would be alive right now—regardless of the item printed in the paper, regardless of this Renie Newell, regardless of Susie, or that anonymous letter, regardless even of the existence of that damned store. I made the big mistake—why don't we admit it!"

"You did what you thought would help a boy who was in trouble. You are human: you didn't know about the clipping; you knew nothing of the context out of which that letter came; you couldn't have foreseen the boy's need to go to that cabin. You had good motives."

"Who doesn't! Who, today, would admit he had bad motives! He'd explain he is just a sleepwalker and didn't mean to; or he'd blame it on his childhood, his parents, or on the teacher he had in the first grade, or on fate, or the human condition— How can we know? I mean it," his voice was almost a whisper now, "tell me, *how can we know?*"

The agony in eyes which I could not see in the dark had filled the voice. I said slowly, "We can't. We have to have a little faith in ourselves, now and then, as well as in others. You can't keep a secret agent sniffing around inside you, all the time." He didn't answer. "To blame yourself now would be a cruel twisting of human responsibility."

I drove a half-mile before he said, "I see it with my mind."

"With part of your mind."

"Yeah . . . guess so."

I tried again. "We have enough shameful motives without turning our decent ones inside out. You felt only compassion and concern for Andy. To turn the finest feelings a man can have into something evil is like smelling the manure that nourishes the rose—instead of smelling the rose. Will you go along with that cliché?"

"Yes. That is, it sounds sensible, even wise, when you say it in that deep relaxed voice of yours." He looked at me, at least I felt he did, and I felt he was smiling. "And the clerical collar, knowing you have it on, brings back things . . . I feel I'm about to make my confession."

I couldn't reply to that one. He said, "I beg your pardon. I have shaken loose inside. I had no right, and no desire, to say that." We were nearing the Roland Park section. He said, "You see, it has happened before. We were in my car, I was passing a truck, and she was killed. Everybody said it was not my fault. Everybody! But I'm not sure they know—or I know—and she is dead."

I slowed down. I knew he needed to say more. He didn't say it.

When we got to the house, the light was on in the music room. There was a note from Ellen on the piano telling us there were sandwiches and fruit juice in the refrigerator. Neither of us wanted anything to eat. A terrible hunger was gnawing at us but it was inside our souls. We turned off the lights and went upstairs. In front of my door, we paused. He whispered, "I'm leaving early on the six o'clock plane. Dr. Channing is taking me to the airport. I won't see you in the morning. I hope very much we shall meet again. Somewhere."

21

I tried to sleep. But we had talked too much. Left too many doors cracked and the wind was blowing a gale down there.

I tried to figure Eliot out: I would put that face together: place the scar where it belonged; those eyes with that look of the damned in them; the thin sensitive mouth; quick-fading smile; add his startling insight—startling that is, for a man as young as he looked—and his compassion, his talent for candor; add his thin wiry body to all this and the moral and mental energy you felt in him—then bang! it would hit that last sentence about the girl or woman, whoever it was, killed in his car— I'd get as far as to tell myself: *the scar must have come from that accident*—then the whole thing would blow up in my face and I'd lose him. I could not see him as the kind of person who goes around killing people by means of his bad judgment. Whatever made sense about Eliot, this didn't. This was a lie he had branded himself with. Why did he need to?

That was one thought, or cluster of thoughts, in my mind. But others came and stacked up alongside; or piled up on— I don't know. It is difficult to use visual images to describe what is happening inside your mind when everything: your memory—everything: imagination, emotions, beliefs, the ABC knowledge you know is ABC, all of it seems to have come unhinged or to have turned into a liquid or gas that is streaming—I'm mixing metaphors, all right, but why not? Mixed metaphors may feel pretty comfortable down in those catacombs where a man's experiences huddle around burnt-out fires whose ashes feel like ice—that open grave—flowers blowing—Mark's face, her face—

I pushed it away. It came back. I pushed it away, I couldn't deal with it. It went too deep. But it stacked up along with the other—there is something to say, something those two can hear, and you have failed to find the words—

Meg . . . I wanted to talk to her. Would she understand? She can be the most unreasonable sister in all the world but sometimes her heart gentles and when it does she sees beyond what I see. She can say the right word—she did long ago when the horse was cropping the grass—strange how it comes and goes, comes and goes, when it happened so long ago: a boy is running, panting—the other lay there asleep . . . he's just asleep, isn't he? isn't he?—and people saying we'll send him to camp camp is fun he'll have a good time playing swimming overnight trips he'll forget playing tennis he'll forget—why, son, are you crying? it's been a long time two weeks why? why? I don't know why I don't know why—and then Meg's voice: Death is what happens to all of us, Davey; it just happened sooner to him a little sooner just about fifty years sooner, that's all—voice so sure in its eleven-year-old wisdom, hand so firm as it pulled me behind the chicken house—whispering the facts of death as she had whispered the facts of life: Davey, I've told you! you've got that little thing hanging down on you and I've got something inside me I don't know what but it's something—I told you I can't see it but I've got it and it's different from yours, yes it is, too, and I've got it even if you can't see it, but *everybody has a navel,* don't they? sure they do! everybody! well *everybody dies* —see? it can't be bad because it happens to everybody, see? here wipe here on my dress, sure I don't mind you wiping your nose on it—why him and not you? because his horse threw him and yours didn't throw you and his head hit a tree now wipe your nose—why it didn't throw you? because silly! you ride better— yes you do! all right then you don't then his horse was meaner, that's why—come on now I've got something nice for you it's a chocolate bar and you can have it all sure you can!

Stacking up beside the other—no sense, no reason—

S.K. tiptoeing . . . wash your hands, better wash your hands Mr. Landrum—and a woman flying out to sea bound in a package of pulsating aluminum and steel that took her out out out from—no gas—tell him it is OK tell him I think—and a small boy stands there listening as his father says take those damn things off your head—

Stacking up beside the other—no sense—no reason—

—Andy . . . their son . . . searching for a father who never existed not as he dreamed him, no; not as I dreamed—have I stopped searching—have I? is that why I have nothing to say? because nothing exists as I dreamed it not even God as I dreamed Him am I turning away because He is speaking a new language no one on earth has learned—is it because I cannot learn it—

I got up. I'd go downstairs, get me a glass of milk or something. Eat a sandwich, maybe. Anything to stop this.

It seems to me, now, as I write it down, the final, the absolute humiliation that a tortured man—anguished by memories of the Close and the Far Ones who have helped create him and helped destroy, uncertain of his own destiny and the destiny of the human race, torn not by his idea of God but by his not understanding why why he loves Him, knowing he does knowing he must but never quite understanding—can stumble through one hole then another hole and another of mystery and confusion and despair and then suddenly feel not that he has seen a vision—no! but that he has found security: in a small, warm, lighted room with the kettle purring, maybe; or slipping into Noah's skin, as every one of us does again and again, can feel safe safe in a watertight Ark on the raging seas; or can find surcease from unanswerable questions and unrequited longing by turning on the light and drinking a glass of milk or eating a sandwich, or maybe, having a cc. of something shot into his arm—

I got up, almost as a reflex defense against my thoughts, and went downstairs. As I reached the kitchen I saw a light through the half-closed door. It was too late: I had to go in for whoever was there had heard me.

Mark . . . sitting at the kitchen table with that newspaper clipping in his hand.

I sat there with him until the dawn came. After three hours of silence, I said, Mark?
Yes.
Will you give it to me?
He handed me the clipping. I struck a match and burned it.

22

I took a plane home at noon, that day. Found a stack of telephone messages waiting for me on my desk at the church office —among them, urgent calls from the architect, the interior decorator, and the Musgrave Electric Company. Things, obviously, were not moving too smoothly at the new rectory. After meeting these men, I went back to the office, and four hours later had got down to the last two calls: Miss Hortense and Mrs. Riley.

I couldn't tangle with Miss Hortense—not until after a shower and a night's sleep. But I called Mrs. Riley and settled back without the usual dread for our thirty minutes of chitchat. I had not given Sunday's vestry meeting much thought since we walked out of the church office—I had suggested that the meeting be held there and not in the Snyder home—for before I reached my car, that late Sunday afternoon, I was called back to take a long-distance call from the headmaster who told me there was no chance that Andy would be found alive.

But now— Yes. I wanted to talk with this little woman who had dared stand up to Dewey Snyder, and had won. After her few words, the vestry had voted to table Snyder's motion requesting Mark's resignation. I had said what I could and said it plainly but Mrs. Riley won the moral battle for us.

As I dialed her number and waited for that vague voice to answer I was remembering what we all knew: that Snyder's bank held her note and a mortgage on her home as security, that she was having great difficulty meeting her payments, and yet she had dared— She was answering the phone: She always begins when you call her by saying *yes yes*. . . . And she said it now. Then, as if suddenly remembering why she had asked me to call her, she said she wanted to tell me of her distress and concern for the Channings and to ask how they were. She said she also wanted to tell me she had put a bowl of red roses on my desk—had I found them? I explained that I had not, as yet, gone to· my rooms. I congratulated her on what had happened at the vestry meeting. "You did a remarkably courageous thing."

She said, "I did only what was right to do." Then she laughed and told me Katie had warned her in time for her to prepare for it. "I don't know why I thought of what I did. So many years ago. . . . But lying awake, Saturday night, I went through all the arguments about a man's innocence until he is proved guilty, all the arguments about justice, all that. It wouldn't work with Dewey, I knew. And then I saw the young Dewey—it was almost as if God had led me back to that old schoolhouse—I could see Miss Nellie, our teacher, and Dewey was saying his Friday afternoon quotation; he was a timid boy and studious, and wanted to be what he called 'a thinker.' And suddenly I heard him: *The quality of mercy is not strained* . . . I was afraid I was wrong, afraid I had made it up; so I got out of bed and went down to the cellar and looked through an old bookcase that has my childhood books in it and my old school books—and there, in a diary I had kept that year, in a ten-cent blue composition book, I found the quotation written by Dewey and after it, *This is my favorite quotation. D.S.* I didn't know that it would work. I know people sometimes do wrong because of their bad memories; I asked myself, do they ever do right because of their good ones? I decided to try it and I prayed every time I waked up during the night, and that was very often." Then she said, "I am sorry my voice trembled. It seems to do it if I stand on my feet to speak."

It had worked. She usually looks at you as if she sees only half of you but she saw all of Dewey, that Sunday afternoon. She asked to speak after he had made his statement about Dr. Channing, the need for his resignation, etc., the harm it was doing to the church and so on. She stood up and faced Dewey. Her voice was trembling and there was a spot of red on each cheek. She said, "Dewey, do you remember Miss Nellie in the Old Windsor high school who used to teach you and me?" He nodded. "Do you remember that she required us each Friday afternoon to give a quotation?" He nodded. "Do you remember your favorite quotation?" He wasn't sure he did. "No," she said, "you have so much on your mind, so many responsibilities, but it was from Shakespeare and I am sure you have not forgot Shakespeare."

We were smiling now.

He told her of course not.

"But you do not remember your favorite quotation? Let me start you off—" She smiled at him in complete friendliness, "I think it will come back to you: *The quality of mercy is not strained, It droppeth as the gentle rain*— Will you finish it, Dewey?"

He looked at her, through her. There was no answering softness in his face but his voice picked it up as if under hypnosis: "*—from heaven upon the place beneath. It is twice blest; it blesseth him that gives and him that takes. 'Tis mightiest in the mightiest;—*"

"Yes," she nodded at him as if she were Miss Nellie, "*—consider this, that in the course of justice none of us should see salvation: we do pray for mercy; and that same prayer doth teach us all to render the deeds of mercy.* I remember you said to me—we were fourteen—you said you thought *mercy* was the most beautiful word in the English language. It still is, Dewey. Let's keep it so by what we now restrain ourselves from doing."

That was all. She sat down. We were as quiet as if at a meeting of Friends. Ben Jordan looked at me, at Mrs. Riley, at Dr. Guthrie, at Dewey. Mr. Esteridge's face turned brick red but he did not speak. Nor did Dewey. The faces of the others were hard to read. Ben stood, looked at Dewey, and quietly moved that the motion be tabled. I hoped Dr. Guthrie would second it, I hoped he would think of Arundel and do this—but wherever his thoughts were, they did not find their way into words. We waited. Finally Mrs. Riley said, "I second Ben's motion." Dr. Guthrie then said he felt, for personal reasons, that he must abstain from voting. Esteridge voted against the tabling. The others voted for Mrs. Riley—it was for her, I think; they felt her courage and courage is a miraculous thing: only a rare person can resist paying tribute to it.

I think of her often. She died last year and the bank, after her death, took her home as it had full right to do. I doubt that she ever thought of herself as running a risk when she stood up to Dewey at that vestry meeting. Moral courage is not nourished so near the surface of a life: its roots go deep and are firmly embedded in what a man or woman values most. The truth about Gertrude Riley is that she valued what she believed was right more than she valued her home. I believe it is as simple, and as complex, as that.

The week that followed my return was a busy one and I was glad. A dozen committee meetings; calls on my parishioners—it seemed as if half of Windsor Hills had influenza—consultations about the rectory which the altar guild wanted ready for the house-warming on Christmas Day. I saw Neel at the Mental Health luncheon but we had no time to talk; had dinner with Jane one night and went to the symphony with her, afterward. Every time I looked across the street at that closed-up house I could see Mark and Grace as I last saw them but I pushed away from it.

Finally, I decided I must talk to Katie and Syd. They deserved to know about the anonymous letter because they loved the boy. It was a difficult time for the three of us as I told the little I felt I must tell. But Katie listened quietly as I knew she would, and though she was trembling as I went into the hard spots, she kept her composure. Syd asked only when Mark would be back. I told him I did not know—I had urged him to stay as long as he could. Katie said, Thank you, Dave, for trusting us. And they left.

Mark might have stayed longer in Baltimore had Miss Mabel and S.K. not succeeded so well with their liberation project.

An hour after the opened cages were found, the director of the Laboratories called him. On one level, the disturbing news must have brought him profound relief for now he had a problem he could do something about. He flew in late that afternoon and went directly from the local airport to his office where his secretary, two technologists and two of the doctors on the research staff were waiting for him. They were in process of piecing it together:

The empty cages had been discovered by the day janitor around seven o'clock, that morning. He had come on at six-thirty and shortly afterward had gone to the fourth floor as was his custom. When the elevator door slid open, he almost stepped on a hamster. Then about twenty feet away he saw a duck. And about the same time, he saw the door to the animal room open. He said he went straight there and was so dumfounded by the empty cages that he didn't do a thing, at first. Finally, he closed the window. Then he went into Dr. Channing's office and telephoned the night watchman who had left the building about five minutes after the day janitor came on duty.

The old man was just getting to his breakfast and didn't like being kept from his coffee. Also, he didn't like the day janitor and wouldn't try to understand what he was telling him. Did he see anybody besides S.K. in the building during the night? Of course he didn't, he rasped out. If he'd seen anybody he'd have given the alarm. Go into the animal room? No, he didn't go near it; he wasn't supposed to go in there, he was supposed to check the doors, that's all; no, he never heard a sound on that floor. Not a sound anywheres. Nobody had been in the building, nobody!

—Well how you think the animals got out? you think they just opened their cages and walked out?

—It wasn't my business to know.

—It's your business to keep people out of there.

—I tell you nobody was in there. It was so quiet all night I could have heard a mouse—

—You didn't hear fifty and four monkeys and no telling how many rabbits and those other things racing out the building. You fell asleep, that's what.

—In my forty-two years as night watchman I have never fell asleep. You ask anybody and they'll tell—

—Nobody knows and nobody cares. All I want is where is those mice and monkeys?

—You think I got em right here, don't you, eating breakfast with me!

—Yeah yeah—that's what I think. I think you got em, maybe you fried em for breakfast, maybe you all playing in the trees together—

He lost his temper with the old man. And then he lost his head and ran up and down the stairway looking for scurrying shadows until he was winded. Finally, it occurred to him to call the director of the Laboratories.

The director arrived in twenty minutes. He called Mark's assistants, called the rest of the staff, the technologists, the County Public Health Department, U.S. Public Health.

"Since I live right around the corner I got there first," said a technologist. "What we couldn't understand was the fact that seven cages weren't tampered with. They went through every tier of cages in both sections of the room—even the cubicle where Jim has his rabies mice. But seven cages down at the other end were left unopened."

"I think they heard something," the secretary said. "The night watchman, perhaps. Or Miss Mabel got scared when the mice began scampering over her feet." The three girls, tense and tired after a grueling day, began to giggle hysterically.

Mark asked how Miss Mabel got in the picture.

Nobody knew. At least, not how it started. Two of the doctors went for S.K. who had left the building at his usual time of two A.M., so the night watchman said. They brought S.K. to Dr. Channing's office and fired questions at him. He denied everything. He declared he had cleaned the rooms and hadn't heard a thing or seen a thing. The day janitor had reported finding the mop on the floor of the corridor and a bucket of cleaning water in Dr. Hassler's office. S.K. said he put everything up where it belonged—if a mop was anywheres the day janitor put it there.

More questions. More denials. But it told on him after a time, and he turned red in the face and began waving his long thin hands around and sucking in deep breaths of air as if he couldn't breathe too well. Then Dr. Hassler said, "We found her bag in Dr. Channing's office so you may as well tell us who she is. If you don't, we'll send for your wife and ask her what woman comes in here at night with you."

"The bag?" Mark asked.

"Yes."

The three girls were off again. Peals of laughter. The secretary sobered as quickly as she could and told him they had found her bag in his office. It had one of the mice in it. Miss Mabel was probably going to make a pet of it.

"Out of which batch? or do you know?"

They were not sure, the technologist said, but Jim believed it was one of his rabies mice. He was running tests on it now. Eight of them were out. They felt they had to find the owner of the bag, under the circumstances. That is why they put so much pressure on—

"I had just come, Dr. Channing. They hadn't phoned me and I didn't know what it was all about but I got my pad and pencil and took down every word I could. The record is here, if you need it. The bag was a knitting bag, that type of bag. Pink and white and black, with flowers worked in *petit point*. They brought the bag in and showed it to S.K. Even then, S.K. wouldn't talk. He looked at it and his face got very red, that is all. Then they told him they'd send for his wife. This finally broke him down and he said, It wasn't no woman—it was just Miss Mabel."

"Who is Miss Mabel?"

The secretary briefed Mark: Miss Mabel was active in the Society for Prevention of Cruelty to Animals. She lived near the lake in a small gray-shingled house full of antiques. "She's that little woman with dyed red hair who always wears a coat in July and August." Mark shook his head. He didn't know her. "She goes to Mr. Pottle's bookshop and browses around the books quite often. You may have seen her there."

Mark didn't think so. He asked if she could possibly be one of the letter writers who protested the use of the monkeys.

"Yes sir. She was. Her letter was printed in the paper; it said we were giving offense to the Hindus by using the monkeys in experiments. She has been to India. She travels a great deal."

"Had she handled the mouse? was she bitten?"

She had refused to say. They told her they would be compelled to send her to the hospital if she didn't tell them. They explained that the mouse happened to be sick with a virulent disease, a bite from it could be fatal.

She said she didn't believe the mouse was sick, she didn't believe in disease, she did not like the word *fatal*, and it was none of their business whether the poor thing had scratched her a little or not. Nevertheless, the hospital threat seemed to shake her and she finally let them look at what she called the scratch. It was a nice nip from a tooth. The bag had been taken away from her and the series of rabies shots would be started immediately, Dr. Grayson told Mark.

The girls continued their story:

Two of Mark's assistants had gone that morning for Miss Mabel. They found her at home in a green dressing gown feeding her parakeets. One is blue and one is green and blue. She has taught them to speak and one of them says *pretty Miss Mabel I love you* and the other says *to be or not to be . . . to be or not to be*—and then Miss Mabel says *kiss me kiss me kiss me* and the parakeets hop on her shoulder and pop over and pip her mouth.

Well, she was feeding them and talking to them and they were talking to her when in came the two staff workers in their white coats—they had forgot to take them off. Miss Mabel paid no attention to them because the parakeets were talking to her but after the blue one responded to her overtures and kissed her, she turned and asked where the ambulance was. They told her there was no ambulance. She said, Why not?

Then George said—he is the biochemist just down from New York—"I thought I was in a psych ward at Bellevue. She told us to go right back to our ambulance and find that poor hurt soul who needed us and didn't we see she was busy giving the parakeets their breakfast? Then she threw the seeds on us. When she did that, I was pretty sure she was hiding behind a screen of pseudo psychosis. I felt she knew exactly why we were there. So I said, Come along Miss Mabel: we have your bag over at the Laboratories and we know everything; the janitor has told us everything. Then she turned quiet. She carefully lifted the parakeets off her shoulders, put them in their cage, covered it with a cloth just as if it were nighttime. Then she said calmly, Certainly I'll come. But not like this, not dishabille."

She went into her bedroom to dress. Jim watched the window and the back door from the side entrance and George listened for sounds inside her room. When she came out, she was dressed in a black dress, black coat, black hat and black gloves. She stood there looking at them with immense dignity. Then she told them she wanted them to know before they took one step out of the house to get in that ambulance—she never noticed that they put her in a car—that what she had done was right. "I let those poor suffering animals out of their concentration camp and I am proud I did it. Proud as can be. No matter how you punish me, even if you put me in prison, I shall remain proud to the end because what I did was right."

They brought her up to the office, the director of the Laboratories introduced himself and asked her to please sit down.

She said she preferred to stand but suddenly her face turned green and she sat down. She folded her black-gloved hands in her lap, pressed her lips together, touched them with her handkerchief. Then she told, in precise detail, what had happened:

S.K. had waited for her outside the building late that night. It was exactly one-twenty, she said, when she arrived. She told how she took a cab half the distance and got out and walked the rest of the way because she was certainly not going to have a cab driver spying on her. When she got in the cab, which she had phoned for, she distinctly saw a man spying on her behind a tree. And while she was walking to the Laboratories she saw two spies following her but she eluded them by running around three trees twice and waiting, then crouching behind a privet hedge and walking hunched-down for fifty feet and when she finally stood up, they were gone. "I am very good at tricking them," she said with real triumph in her eyes. Then she told how S.K. had warned her about the night watchman; and how he tipped on his toes down the corridors and how she followed him.

"That man of yours," she called S.K. so throughout the interview, "turned and whispered, Can't you walk without so much clackity-clack? The night watchman will hear you. Can't you walk on your toes?

"I said, I cannot; I have bunions.

"And he said, Well can't you keep those heels from clacking?

"And I said, I cannot; I didn't make the shoes.

"We went to the animal room and he opened the door and turned on the lights and when he turned on the lights I saw the poor little mice's eyes shining and I knew they knew—for animals are sensitive and feel things—that I had come to rescue them. And one of the monkeys reached its hand out and I shook hands with it, *Welcome to America*, I said. And then I told that man of yours, *Now I am to open the cages*."

She looked gravely at the director. "For years it has been my paramount desire to open every animal cage in the world and liberate all the poor imprisoned creatures. What a wonderful place this earth will be when the animals are free! Nature intended it so and beyond Nature I am sure the Higher One intends it so. Only—I can't quite see how I can free the canaries and parakeets, they have to have cages, if I took their cages away they'd—"

She faltered. Then she said, "Cats . . ." and looked at the scientists listening to her and every one of them, the secretary said, nodded in grave agreement.

"Then I said, Now *I* want to open the cages."

She said S.K. was real nice and told her to go ahead go ahead go ahead! And she told him not to talk so much, and he stood there real quiet and let her open the cages, one by one. But nothing came out. She called, Come out, creatures! But none came out. That is, at first. A mouse ran to the back of his cage and looked at her and she called to him, Come out you poor tortured creature, come out of your prison! But it just ran to the other corner. She said she kept calling it and finally it crept out and ran up the outside of its cage and crouched there and she reached over and picked it up and put it in her bag. "Because it was the first. And I knew it required a great amount of courage to be the first. So I thought I'd take it home with me—"

Suddenly, they were all coming out: hamsters and mice and rabbits, racing up the tiers of cages, racing out the open doors, racing around and around the floor, jumping across each other. Miss Mabel had now opened the doors of the duck cages and four ducks waddled out of the room and down the corridor and then she freed the pigeons and they flew across the low partition to the monkey room which proved too much for the monkeys. Out the monkeys marched, en masse, and one of them leaped on S.K.'s shoulder and began drumming on his head. S.K. screamed, Get off me, get off me, and fought it until it lost its balance. Then he ran out for his mop and came back and began waving it at the monkeys and screaming *scat scat* and trying to push them back in the cages, any cage he could get them in, and then a duck waddled between his legs and he fell and Miss Mabel told him to behave himself! But one of the monkeys had started toward him again and S.K. struck it hard with his mop. This was more than Miss Mabel could endure. She said,

Open the windows, you fool! And he did. And two of the monkeys got up on the window ledge and swung over to a tree—

"—there must have been a tree." She pondered this. "Certainly the monkeys jumped somewhere. Then I ran out because—" She seemed unable to complete that sentence.

And S.K. followed her, she finally said, and she scolded him for being so cruel and he called her a batty old—

"I won't repeat it. I said, Find me a chair to sit down. This minute! He brought me in here, I think it was here, it was a place similar to this room. I didn't like the way that man of yours looked at me, so I said, I am going home. And he said, Go home, you batty old witch, go! And I did. I ran down the corridor looking for the stairway and I heard him say, The old dunce don't even see the elevator. But I don't approve of automatic elevators and I was afraid he might get in it with me—" She pondered this. Then she said, "Yes, the stairs were much better. I ran because I didn't trust the look in his eyes, and frankly, his hands are long enough to loop around anybody's neck, easily, easily. He had the mop, too, and I knew if he'd strike a monkey he'd strike me, so I hurried out and that is why I forgot my bag."

"Did you walk home?" asked the director.

"Certainly I walked. What else would one do?"

Miss Mabel said that she had thought it over during the night and had decided the janitor was not a bad man. A little stupid and excitable but otherwise a fine man—at least he was willing to run a risk in order to give the captive animals their freedom. She said she had never understood people becoming upset over those slave camps in Russia or those dreadful concentration camps in Germany when we have these cruel concentration camps in every laboratory in our country—where the poor animals undergo dreadful ordeals.

Mark asked the girls if S.K. had been given his first shot. They said no, he had refused to let them give it, although he admitted that something had bit him. Where? On the back. Then it was probably not one of the mice. Dr. Grayson said he doubted it, too. A mouse could have bitten him, of course, in the scramble.

It was not possible to identify the mice. Thirty in all escaped—eight of them Jim's. The director felt it unwise to tell S.K. about the rabies mice until he had discussed it with Dr. Channing.

"Quite probably he was bitten or scratched by the monkey," said Mark. "Has he been examined?"

"No sir," said his secretary. "S.K. is mad with all of us. He won't let anybody touch him. Perhaps the Public Health men could manage it. I'll see about it, sir, if you want me to."

Mark stayed at the lab all night, checking with the veterinarian, various members of his staff, the County Public Health men, and the men from the U.S.P.H. who were assisting in the search. The police department had been asked to help, and eighteen mice had been caught by midafternoon the first day, before Mark had arrived—within a few blocks of the Laboratories; two more were found in the basement. Five hamsters were in the basement, one was found on the back stairs, another near a garbage can. One monkey was found sitting on the hood of a parked car, down in the south section of the city. Several children had found rabbits. One had hopped into a schoolroom—"the one we were treating with cobalt." All night they were picking up mice, hamsters, ducks, pigeons. The church janitor found a monkey early the second morning, in the First Methodist church downtown, sitting on the pulpit.

And Duveen found a mouse when she opened up the beauty shop the morning following the Great Liberation. When she walked in, she opened the blinds and saw a white unmoving something on her manicure table. She went over to see what it was, saw it was a white mouse and was about to pick it up and cuddle it—Duveen loves little things, especially white mice—when she noticed it had a curious hump in its back and a small plastic "house" over it. And Duveen—it's because she's read so much, said Nella—knew something was odd about it, very odd indeed; so she called her husband at the filling station to come over she had something to show him, something queer. It's really queer, she told him. Johnny didn't want to come, he was sweeping up the office, but her voice was trembling and he decided he'd better. So he went over to Nella's shop. He picked up the mouse and examined it and said it was bound to be a mouse used in an experiment. "They're growing something on it or in it." He called the Laboratories and one of the assistants came over at once and got the mouse. They asked him not to talk and I don't think he did, at least not much; but, by now, Nella was there, and her first customer had just come in early for a permanent. And of course news of Miss Mabel's coup was leaking out in a dozen different places by noon that day. And that night, the local TV news commentator did quite a story on it, urging people to call the Laboratories or the health department if they found any strange rabbits, ducks, hamsters, pigeons, or monkeys or mice and to report at once to their doctor or the health department if they had been bitten or scratched, for a few—only a few remember!—had virulent diseases some of which would cause death in a human scratched or bitten by the sick animal but try not to be alarmed there is no need for panic none whatever—it is true there is one white mouse with rabies still unaccounted for and it is likely to be in the north side of the city so keep alert and don't handle it yourself and do not let the children handle it but call the Laboratories or the Public Health office or call this station take the number down please Ivy 6-1234 did you get it? If not here it is again Ivy 6-1234.

After the six-thirty news broadcast, the station received more than a hundred telephone calls: some of them denouncing the Laboratories for being negligent, six or eight commending them for the efficient way in which the debacle had been handled, twenty or more protesting all laboratories everywhere, fifteen condemning experimentation on animals, five condemning all science, ten stating that the Governor should look into this undoubtedly the whole thing was the work of subversives, two saying it was because the Republicans had been in office too long, three saying it was because the Democratic party had got into the clutches of the leftists, one said the cure for cancer had already been found—everybody knew Krebiozen was the cure, everybody but the A.M.A. which was deliberately holding out on the people—and thirteen calls were from people who said they had seen the white mouse with rabies it was right now in their house somewhere and please send somebody at once to catch it—

The next day, there were still six mice missing, one of which probably had rabies virus in it; one monkey; two ducks from the leukemia experiment and a rabbit.

The following day, Mark called S.K. into his office. They had a long talk but Mark did not discuss it, afterward, with me except to say he had told the director the man must go. The director thought he should be turned over to the police and was somewhat insistent about this. Mark asked him to talk it over with Kelton Neel, first. The two of them went down to police headquarters, had a talk with Neel and the Chief, both of whom advised against arresting S.K. The old Chief kept saying, "All I'm doing right now is trying to keep the lid from blowing off. Arrest this man—" he shook his head instead of completing the sentence.

The director of the Laboratories is a brilliant, fair-minded and courageous man but he has a disquieting habit of completing his sentences and expecting everybody else to do the same. He said, "Chief, exactly what would happen?" The Chief rubbed his hands over his tired old red face—Neel told me afterward— sighed, looked up and said, "I don't know. What's more, I don't want to know. But it'll sure happen. You can't afford to keep that janitor at the lab. But remember: we can't afford to keep him in jail, either."

"Then he should be sent to the State Hospital. He's a crazy man."

"No crazier than a lot more on the loose."

So: S.K. was hanging around the Flats where he lived, part of the time; and part of the time, up at the shopping center in Windsor Hills which was not too far from the Laboratories: talking. He had his severance pay and he had his story to tell and he seemed content to stand around and tell it. It worried Neel. He tried to help him find another job but S.K. seemed satisfied with the new one he had. This worried me, too, when I heard it. It came to me, all of it, in dribbles from Neel, from

Jane, who knew the secretary well, a little from Mark—and later, Johnny told me more.

As for Miss Mabel: eccentric, yes; head full of confusion; but she came from one of the city's oldest families. It was impossible to think of anything better to do about her than to push it out of everybody's mind by never mentioning her again. Not once did her name appear on broadcast or in newspaper.

It is easy to look back on something after it has happened and see it building up; almost impossible to hear it coming toward you. We human beings probably have a built-in radar system but we've buried it deep inside us along with other good psychic equipment that we used to call prophetic dreams, intuition and so on.

I had rather enjoyed Miss Mabel's freedom-for-the-animals coup. It was something to laugh about. And it was good to have Mark home again and to know his mind was now on mice and monkeys and ducks and Miss Mabel. The lines were deep in his face but he had smiled when he told me about it, had laughed a time or two. This relieved me. And I was also relieved to learn that S.K. had been fired.

I believe now that Johnny meant his words as a warning, vaguely, without acknowledging his intention. I didn't think so then. I thought it was just more talk. Johnny's a great one for finding out everything and telling it, and twisting it a little.

I had stopped by, for gas. Johnny came over to the car while the tank was filling and said, "Look Reverend, there's a lot of talk going round."

He left to turn off the hose. Read the meter, came back.

I said, "What about, Johnny?"

Johnny gave the windshield a swipe or two before he said more. "That janitor they fired at the lab. Maybe they shouldn't have fired him."

"You know why they did, don't you?"

"I guess so—the mice, wasn't it? and all those other things? He let them out, didn't he?"

"Yeah, he let them out."

"Well, after all, they've got them back now. To make a man lose his job because of a few mice and things—some folks can't understand that. See? So they get resentful. See? They think S.K.'s had a dirty deal. He's sixty-two years old—what kind of job can he get now?"

I said, "Johnny, I don't know much about it except that those mice weren't ordinary mice. People went into a panic about the ones with rabies, of course. Naturally. But the lab is using the mice in various experiments, as you know. Dr. Channing's experiments have to do with cancer. Some of those mice have been implanted with malignant tissue. Others are of the twentieth, perhaps thirtieth generation, grown under controlled conditions. They're studying resistance to cancer: trying to breed it in and breed it out. You studied chemistry in high school, didn't you?"

"Oh sure."

"Then you understand that it wasn't simply the fact of turning the mice loose or even that a few had dangerous viruses in them. The real point is: the loss of those mice might have destroyed that entire experiment. Years of work wasted. The same is true of the other animals."

"Yeah, guess so. But they caught them all, didn't they?"

They had caught most of them. One rabbit was still out; several mice in the hormones experiment; and two ducks—

He said, "I'm sure they've caught them. They caught the last monkey yesterday. I heard it was up in a tree and went over to the park to watch. You hear about their catching it?"

I shook my head.

"Well, I'm telling you I never saw such a sight! The little devil was way up on a limb of an oak, sitting there throwing twigs down on us. And talking her head off. It was a she and was she mad! They had a big net—" He told me the vet from the lab and two others from Public Health had climbed a tree back of the oak and had asked the crowd to keep talking but to talk real easy. So everybody was talking to her. They called her Marilyn and sort of kidded her and each other along. And she kept chattering and throwing twigs at them. "We must have sounded like those United Nations," Johnny said. And all the time, the vet and the others were easing up that tree behind her with their net, closing in on her, and the crowd forgot to talk now—they were so intent on how the vet and the others were going to do the trick. The vet eased from a limb of his tree to a limb of her tree, then one of the Public Health men motioned to them to keep talking.

"I had a piece of the net ready to jerk," Johnny said, "and three or four others had a piece. Then the vet threw the other end of it in a slow loop over her, then we began to pull it in quick but easy, kind of. And that monkey when she saw they had tricked her cried like a baby, put her hands over her face— golly, I'll never forget it—and we all looked at each other like crazies and Bob—you know Bob over at Matthews? well, Bob said Christ I'm leaving here—excuse me Reverend—and he left. I felt sort of sick to my stomach, myself. But the vet and the others just kept easing in, easing in, and one of the doctors began to talk to her like she was a baby; and he got to her and picked her up and patted her and she looked at him with the tears rolling down her face and her lips shaking. Gee, I didn't know which was us and which was them, I mean which was human and which was animal and which was—"

Johnny went in for my change.

When he came back, he said, "Now it's all over and no damage done, why can't they let the old man go back?"

I suggested that if a janitor would open the cages, he might do other things. I reminded Johnny they were working with radioactive isotopes at the lab— "Suppose he decided to mess around with that stuff? Let the tracer atoms out, say? Suppose he and Miss Mabel decided their next duty to the world was to free all the radioactive material?"

"They ought to keep it locked up."

"They do. In lead boxes. But a man who disobeys orders in a lab can be pretty dangerous."

"Yeah. But he sure is shootin his mouth off."

"What about?"

Johnny gave the windshield a few more swipes. Wiped the corners of the glass, squirted more fluid on, wiped the corners again. "Oh . . . just crazy stuff."

"Like to know, if you'll tell me."

"He keeps saying that Dr. Channing had niggers at the lab. Said they came from that medical school in Nashville—a bunch of them to study the experiments. And they had sandwiches and coffee and white and black sat down and *ate together*. That wasn't all. He said Dr. Channing's wife used to dance up in New York. Claims he saw a picture of her and those dancers and there was a black one in it. I told him it wasn't so, it couldn't be! They're decent folks, I said, fine people; they'd no more do that than I would or you would. Then S.K. got mad and began waving his hands around. You know how he does." Johnny spat. Looked at the spittle, looked at me. "What makes him walk with his heels off the ground?"

"I don't know, Johnny."

"Well—that is when he told it. Right out. Before everybody. About the doctors and those technicians." Johnny looked at me, looked at the cleaning paper in his hand, squashed it up in a ball, threw it in the wastecan.

"What did he tell?"

"Oh . . . I don know. Said they were doing something together that wasn't fit to say out loud."

"What do you think he meant?"

"I be damned if I know. Excuse me, Reverend."

"Now let me get it straight: the men biologists and chemists and doctors and the women technicians were—"

"Seems so."

"What on earth were they doing?"

"Well, seems they—" Johnny was looking intently now across the street as if watching a dogfight or something. Turned back. "But it was their doing it together that—"

"Doing what, Johnny?"

"Castrating those mice." He grinned. And I grinned, too, of course.

"Back up to the beginning, will you?"

"There's not a beginning that I know of. Seems they'd been castrating some male mice, then feeding them something that turned them into females. See? Or almost into. Both men and women doing it. Did you ever hear such a—" Johnny was watching me carefully now, pacing his words to my reactions. My face must have sent him the message he wanted for he suddenly laughed. "The fool! Biggest fool in this city—and we sure have our share, don't we? Of course anybody with a grain knows whatever those scientists were doing, it wasn't that. Or if it was, they had their reasons."

"Was it their doing it together—I mean their working on the experiment together, that seemed to bother him?"

"It was everything. He said, You see what is in that man's dirty mind? He'd hurt any little girl he could get his hands on."

I didn't know what to say. But I knew I'd better try. I said, "Johnny—" Then I stopped. What was the use! But I knew I should try, so I said it this way, "Dr. Channing and his staff are studying, among other things, the endocrine system. Watching the effect of certain hormones on the growth of normal cells and cancer cells under all kinds of conditions. Researchers the country over are working on this problem. A few years ago, a doctor doing research found that cancer of the prostate gland in men could sometimes be stopped or the growth delayed by castration, then giving the patient estrogen which is one of the female hormones. It seemed to work and it gave the researchers a new lead. They have gone a long way since then."

"Yeah," said Johnny, brightening. "Believe I read about that in *Time* or *Newsweek* or somewhere." I could see he felt better.

"It's a tricky business, apparently." I knew I didn't know enough to be giving Johnny a lesson but I said, "It didn't always work. Sometimes hormones caused a tumor to grow. It was difficult to determine whether the growth was caused from giving the hormones too soon or too late or whether there was something in the hormone that decreased growth and something else that speeded up the malignancy. So they began splitting the hormones and extracting certain elements or constituents, recombining them, and trying them on tumors in mice. Then they began feeding or injecting certain vitamins to try to discover whether the vitamins built up resistance to growth or stimulated growth. To tell you the truth, Johnny, I am on the Cancer Committee but about all I know is what I read in the papers. I ought to know more but I don't. What I do know is: they're trying to find out what causes cancer so you and S.K. and I won't die of it."

"Yeah. But you see, Reverend, S.K. thinks they're turning boy mice into girl mice. And he says that's against God's will. He says they're just turning boy mice into girl mice for the fun of it. Says there's already too many females cluttering up the earth, as it is."

"Anybody else hear him?"

"Sure. The ones in there, playing checkers."

"What was their reaction?"

"Didn't have one. And it made S.K. mad. See? Because they didn't notice him. So he said a lot more."

"What?"

"Oh . . . I don know." Johnny came over to the door of the car, lowered his voice. "You ever hear anything about the lab keeping breast tumors in jars?"

"It is possible. A lab sometimes has a shelf or two or table or two of museum jars with specimens in them. For use in lectures to medical students or to civic groups."

"S.K. says they did. He says the night he let the mice and monkeys and ducks out he dumped those tumors in the garbage cans. He said he'd show them. You know: what they could do and what they couldn't do in that lab. Said it made him so blazing mad when he thought about big black —— (don't reckon you want to hear those words, Reverend) looking at those breast tumors . . . he decided he'd show them, he'd show them and the Supreme Court both who was boss in this country. Said he would like to've throwed that Supreme Court out with them tumors. Pitch em all out together in the garbage, he said."

I don't know how long Johnny and I stared at each other. I could see it mushrooming in S.K.'s mind, growing larger, larger, larger, larger. . . .

"Then he said he had other reasons for being absolutely sure it was Dr. Channing in that store."

"Do you know, Johnny, that the Newells withdrew the charges?"

"I heard so."

"They made a statement to the police that in their opinion nobody was there. The child was confused and just thought she heard somebody. The case was closed. You understand the child was not hurt?"

"Her arm was scratched, wasn't it?"

"Yes. A cat scratched it. That old cat in Toni's. You've seen it, haven't you, lying in the window?"

"Oh sure. That is, I used to see it. Nobody's seen it since the day that kid went in there. Duveen used to pet it all the time. An old yellow cat, wasn't it? You suppose that little girl put a hex on it?" Johnny stared at the gas tank. Went up, read the meter—I had already paid him—came back, said, "I'm gettin where I need glasses.

"Who started it all, anyway, Reverend?"

"I don't know, Johnny."

"Have the Channings got enemies here?"

"Not that I know of."

"They've sure had a lot of trouble. Too bad about their little son. How did *it* happen?"

I couldn't answer.

"He went out in the snow, wasn't that it—and got lost?"

"Yes."

"What you reckon made the kid do a crazy thing like that?"

"I don't know, Johnny. He had never seen a big snow before.

Maybe he just thought he'd take a walk in it . . . there's something about snow. . . ."

"Yeah. . . . Gee, I was mighty sorry to hear about that."

24

In the late afternoon, Charlie dropped by to talk with me about the Christmas carols program. It would be televised at All Saints, at five o'clock, on the Sunday before Christmas. He was planning to use a shortened version of Britten's *Ceremony of Carols,* the brief Scriptural readings would be done by one of the acolytes—I was to give the closing prayer. The choirboys were singing well and with a little more practice would do all right; Billy, the youngest of the sopranos, one of the boys we had brought in from the Flats, was trying his first solo—he needed training, lots of it, and discipline, "the kid can't sit still, digs his elbow into the others, cracks his knuckles, but the voice is superb. Lately, I've been visiting their families," he looked at me, laughed. "I am just about twenty years late catching on to bad housing and all that. But it's more than bad housing—there's nothing down there for their minds to live on—it's a cultural junk pile." He said slowly, "I didn't come here to talk about the choir or the Flats. Do you know about that picture of Grace? Taken years ago with a dance group in New York. There happened to be a Negro in it. A man."

I said I had heard about it, yes, some time ago. Just before Andy's death.

Katie had told him yesterday, he said, that her father had used the picture at the time he was trying to force Mark's resignation from the vestry. She'd had no intention of telling him, hoped the awful business was done with, but she was worried and scared because she had just found out that others had seen the picture besides the vestry. She had been at the Club the day before—one of her friends mentioned it—had seen it—her brother showed it to her.

"Does Katie have any idea how widely it has been shown?"

She wasn't sure, Charlie said. Her friend's brother was working very closely with M—— in his campaign for governor next spring. "Katie is afraid it is going to be used as Exhibit A in M——'s race hate shindigs. It is not beneath him."

"No, I guess not. Who is this brother you were speaking of?"

Charlie told me his name. I had never known him. Apparently he was slated for a good post in the state government if M—— won. "I've known the guy since we were kids. He loves slime. Would do this sort of thing free, just for the fun of it. It is all strictly anonymous, of course. You'll never be able to prove that M—— or any of his henchmen had a thing to do with it."

"You think Snyder gave him the picture?"

"He must have."

"Then he's backing M——'s campaign?"

"Oh sure. M——'s a capable man, efficient, honest with money, and thoroughly unprincipled in his fight against integration. That is what Dewey wants."

"What is he after? I mean, in a big way? You've known him a long time, Charlie. He isn't doing it just to maintain segregation. Is it to hurt Mark and Grace? Is it something else? I've thought about it ever since he took Mark off the TV show. What hole inside him is he trying to stuff up?"

Charlie smiled, shook his head. "I don't know. Ever since K-k-k-katie t-told me—" He had begun to stammer. I hadn't heard him do it in a long time. He stopped, stretched out his long legs, looked down at the floor, then at me, through me, said, "I've been thinking about something that happened when I was a kid. I don't trust my memories too much. It may not be true. But if it is—" He pulled his legs up against the chair, sort of hunched over himself, "I just don't know, Dave. But this thing, this memory, keeps coming back to me. Ever since yesterday." He was speaking slowly now. "I am in a small cottage . . . I think it is down at the Island because it is cool and the smell is salty—my grandmother used to take a cottage there every summer; so did the Snyder family. Grandma has gone out somewhere—to the store, maybe, or to a friend's house . . . and a face is bending over me . . . I am lying there . . . I am not sure where I am but I am naked, I feel I am naked, and this face is bending over me. I can't really see it, not clearly, but I seem to know the face is Dewey's. And there is an old crumbly brick fireplace painted white—I remember that, I see it clearly, and the waves are pounding. . . ."

He stopped. "It sounds like a dream, doesn't it?"

I nodded. It did.

"But it isn't. It is a memory."

"You think something had happened?"

"I think so."

"But you don't know."

"I've remembered it all my life—that is, once a year or twice, it crosses my mind, it doesn't stay there, just floats through. But I don't know. I could have made it up, I realize that. It is even possible that I wanted something to happen, then remembered the wish as if it were a real scene."

"How old do you think you were?"

"Six, maybe. I am not at all sure. I never see myself old or young in my memories or dreams. But I often think things happened when I was six."

"Did it happen again?"

"I don't know. It is sort of—dead. I mean by that, I don't see it as a story that moves from here to here to here. The image is just there and very still. I remember feeling weak and unable to fight back. I felt I had nothing to do with it, in a way. I am not sure about this, but I think it now."

I asked him if the families were old friends.

"Yes. Both families had big farms before the Civil War; and both moved in to the small town of Old Windsor decades before it became part of the city."

"You can't remember anything else?"

"The scene as it comes back to me is motionless and still, as I said—like a painting. Except for those waves pounding. Everything is dark around it—just this one spot is lighted up: the white crumbly fireplace, and me lying there, and his face. I'd believe it had never happened, that it was a fantasy or dream or even something I'd read in a book and sort of claimed afterward —if it weren't that I still have the little sailboat."

"Sailboat?"

"The one he gave me. I think he gave it to me."

"But you're not sure?"

"Someone gave it to me but I am not sure, no."

I felt I had seen it; I couldn't remember where but I was sure I had seen a fine little three-masted clipper about fourteen inches long. Beautiful workmanship. But where? I was trying to remember. Of course everybody has seen little clippers—yes, but this is his and I've seen it. I tried to find it: on his mantel? maybe. Yes, in the bedroom. —Now I knew: it was the night he tried to take his life. After he phoned me, I hurried to his apartment, turned on the light in his living room, saw nothing there but the piano—there were plenty of things there but I saw only the big shining Steinway as I went into his bedroom. It was right after I emptied the gun—I was remembering it: I put the cartridges in the bedside table and the .38 in my pocket and just at that moment I happened to look at the mantel and saw the little clipper. I remember some manuscript was lying on a chair, ten or fifteen pages of music written in pencil; I thought I'd better put it up for him, and as I opened his top bureau drawer to lay the music in, I saw a dozen or more clean white handkerchiefs in two neat piles—

I felt I was being dragged— It was a most curious feeling: a few small concrete facts: a little clipper, the pages spilling out of the chair, the handkerchiefs, the smooth weight of the .38 against my palm, were compelling me to believe what he was saying was true, even though I knew perfectly well that someone else might have given it to him—or it could have been a gift from a generous young Dewey Snyder to a lonely orphaned kid who lived next door with his grandmother.

I said, "And you think this experience, perhaps completely forgotten by him, or half forgotten, is driving him to persecute the Channings simply because Mark was accused of something too much like what he had done? Isn't this making things pretty simple? Our motives are seldom so clean-cut and all of a piece, are they?"

"I don't think one experience, or memory, could do it, no. You don't become a witch hunter—or a coward, either—just because you'd had one bad experience."

"But you think it may have something to do with it?"

"Something, yes."

Charlie's face was thoughtful, he was searching, not accusing. "I think this affair of Susan and the store may have aroused something in him, dread, maybe; and he's turned it against Mark. I can be wrong. All day, I've thought about it. Of course, it may be my part in it that I'm really thinking about."

"How old was Dewey?"

"About eighteen. If I was six."

"Then he was not a child."

"No."

"We all have some pretty bad memories, Charlie. We've done things we don't like to think about—worse things, perhaps, than this."

"Much worse," he said softly. "You know I'm aware of that."

"Then why aren't we all witch hunters? It is too easy."

"Yes, I suppose it is. It is strange though how I keep thinking of it. It seems important, somehow."

We looked at each other a long time. Charlie and I had been through a lot together. He finally said, "That photograph business has sort of— He's from a good family, you know. You think of hooligans doing this sort of thing, or the 'wool hat boys'—ignorant people—"

I interrupted our talk to make us some coffee. And while waiting for the water to boil I asked Charlie about the opera. He was in the middle of the last act, still having trouble, he said; approaching the final scene, "with no idea what is going to happen there." He left that, and talked of the staging of the first act, told me of his ideas, the technical problems involved. I rather hoped we might pull out of our analysis of Snyder. It is too easy to draw this kind of map of a man's motivations, as I well knew. And yet, I had begun it. I tried to stick with the opera but when we settled down with the coffee, we were back on Dewey. Somewhere along the way, I asked Charlie how he felt about him.

"I don't remember much about the young Dewey or about myself, either. But you mean how do I feel now?" His hands played five finger exercises on the arm of the chair. "I don't have any resentment of what happened so long ago—if," he smiled, "it happened. I don't think it made me what I am. It may have given me a little push in the direction I was going, anyway. I don't know. You remember I told you Grandma taught me to crochet and a lot of other things, like that. She'd never had a boy in the family; she knew only what you teach girls. And the kids laughed at me, of course. Of the two experiences, I suspect Grandma's twisted me more. I've always known Dewey and his family—and Connie, long before she married him, was my close friend. She noticed me when I was about fourteen: heard me play and immediately decided I had a special talent. She sent me to Juilliard, as you know. And when I came back home a few years ago, Dewey offered me my job at All Saints. Katie seems like a little sister to me. On the surface, everything is friendly and impersonal."

There were long silences during our talk. He'd say something, I'd listen, of course; finally, I'd say something. I was deeply disturbed about the photograph—I wanted to get my mind on what to do about it, if anything could be done; and yet, I was caught in Charlie's mood—

I said, "It seems to me that the same tangled relationships and problems which caused him to go to you in that beach cottage may still be operating on other levels. Not so much the old memory as the same old urgent need. Still unsatisfied, still wanting something. And we don't know what he wants, do we?"

He smiled. "I guess not."

"Once, he thought it was that experience with you. He craved it and he let himself have it. He's thought it was segregation—still thinks so—still feels he can't do without it, as an alcoholic thinks he can't get along without his whisky. So he tries to hold on to it by any means. He thought it was money—he got it, and he finds he still wants something. Now he thinks he wants to hurt Mark. The symbol keeps changing, doesn't it?"

I thought about what Katie had said in my study that night, weeks ago. Something came into Charlie's eyes and I felt he knew of Dewey's feeling about the friendship between Mark and me. He wouldn't mention it; I couldn't. Finally, I said, "Where are we?"

"I don't know."

"I mean, what should we do, Charlie?"

"I don't know. That's why I dumped it on you. Can you talk to him? you're good at it, you know."

What part of him would I be talking to? What could I appeal to? This senior warden of All Saints—what did he love and cherish and dream about and believe in—

"Dave . . . this memory business: I know we want things and we don't know why, or what it is we want. And we keep thinking we've found it but the wanting comes back after a little and hurts more than ever. —I'm not forgetting what you said."

I felt he was now thinking about himself. There was something he was trying to get at.

He said, "And I know you think beliefs, values are more important to a man than his memories, and I try to think so, too. Trouble is, bad memories seem to have a thousand times more influence on you than good beliefs."

"Only the ones we don't take responsibility for. Or can't, because we've forgotten them."

"But even when we remember," he was looking through me and the old, terrible look had come back on his face, "and want to take responsibility— We say this but what do we mean? How can I take responsibility now for what I failed to do, long ago! God knows I could never forget what I failed to do. But how, Dave! How can I? I can't change what happened—I can't go back to that cliff and—" He stopped. His voice became quiet, easier. "I know what you are about to say: that God forgives. It is a beautiful idea—but for me, it is uncreated. I mean, I don't feel it or hear it, yet. I tell myself I must just go ahead— It sounds reasonable but what does it mean? Go ahead—where! I feel I only go round in a circle. The circle, maybe, gets bigger but always the cliff appears. . . . I hoped doing the opera—it's not therapy, don't think that, it is what I want to write, the music has come because it had to come, and it's good, I think it's good—"

"Katie thinks it is superb and she knows a great deal."

"Yes, she does. And as I've said before, she has a fine gift for composition, her talent is more real than mine, deeper—"

"I like what I've heard, too; I'm no expert, but I have heard my share of music."

"Yes, and I value your opinion. The music—I've said it a hundred times—it's all right, it is still flowing, but I can't resolve the Coward's life, I can't find a way out for him. When the big moment comes and he has to do the right thing, the courage has to flow through him so he will do what he must do— But what is that big moment going to be? what is going to make his courage flow. . . ."

I thought the word *love*, I could not say it. He would not want me to, he had to find it in his own way. I said this, "Sometimes people call physical confidence, courage. But it isn't. For instance, with me: I was trained from the time I was three years old to be an athlete, to use my body in ten thousand different ways, fight through the competition, outwit the hazard; and so on. And I ended up with a lot of physical confidence. But that's not courage. I found it out when I lost my leg. Most of the fellows at college thought courage was tied up with sexual potency. I doubt there's much of a tie-up; look at the frigid little women who have courage to do what would scare most men into the jitters. There're people who do risky things, fantastically dangerous things, who have little courage—they just happen not to have imagination. They don't know what the danger or risk involved is. I don't have the answer but I think whatever courage is, it's a by-product of something else we want to do very much, or feel compelled by our image of ourselves or our beliefs, to do."

He listened but did not answer.

He said, "Mark and Grace need it now."

"All they can get hold of."

"Can they stay? can they stick it out?"

I told him I thought Mark could. He'd concentrate on his work at the lab and push everything else away. But it would be different with Grace. At least, Mark thought so.

"The Laboratories want him to stay?"

"The director does. Whether he will be kicked out later by the board, I don't know. I suppose there're all kinds of pressures."

We swapped a little of the talk we'd heard. I told him what Johnny had said. He had picked up things from the choirboys who repeated, of course, what they had heard down in the Flats. Something about the Channings having "et with niggers," according to Billy. Other things. Charlie thought the real reason for Andy's death should have been told. The truth might have shocked people into some sense: or satisfied those who, for their own dark reasons, wanted Mark to suffer. Decent people did not know what to do or say about the store episode; but they would have known what to say about that letter to the boy and the speaking up would have done them good and the city good, too. "I'm not much of an intellectual, Dave; everything has to come from my feelings, my intuition. But I've thought plenty about things—and it seems to me the trouble with the whole world today is that nearly everybody wants to find somebody more cruel, more debased, more of a moral sleepwalker than they are. We are comparing ourselves with the worst, not the best. The way everybody jumped on Mark: Here was this fine, quiet, smart scientist, see? and all the time he was nothing but a nasty, dirty pervert who ran after little girls! They say it and feel relieved. Whatever they've done that's wrong or cheap or cruel or blind can't be as bad as what Dr. Channing did. It leaves them feeling purified. Almost forgiven."

"And they want him punished."

"Sure. Until he is, they can't be sure he's guilty, see? The trial being called off—they were counting on that: it would have drained off so much anxiety. They feel there was something crooked about the whole business." Charlie laughed. "This city is still just a big overflowing scared country town."

Quietly, after a little, "Grace will find it terribly hard to live here. Always wondering who sent the letter . . . It can never be home, again, for her."

Another long silence. "With his prestige, Mark won't have trouble about another job, will he? If they leave?"

"I just don't know, Charlie."

He was standing. I said, "Katie told me the good news."

"About the City Center?"

"It's fine that they want to put *The Coward* on."

He told me he had sent the first two acts to a friend on the faculty at Juilliard. The friend showed them to a few people connected with the City Opera Company. If the third act measured up, there was a big chance they'd put it on. He was trying not to count on it too much but— "Say I get one good review. Just one." He laughed and I laughed with him as we walked to the street entrance. I stood watching him as he went to his car, parked near the corner. As he passed under the street light, his blond hair lit up in the brightness, then I lost him in the foggy evening. I heard the car start, move down the street.

Things can bear down. Charlie . . . Grace's photograph . . . Dewey . . . Katie . . . talk to them, try to say something, talk to them— Why do they think you can talk to everybody!

I left the study and walked down Arlington, past the Newell apartment toward Pottle's Bookshop. I needed air, exercise. On my way back, I saw Susan sitting on the steps of the apartment building with Ali Baba in her arms. I said hello, and she hopped up and walked along with me for a block. Then I sent her scooting back home. It had suddenly occurred to me that sharp eyes might be watching.

25

As I remember it now, those calls came about this time. My phone began to ring: every night, two o'clock, a different voice. The first one said folks didn't like preachers in their city who took up for Communists and dirty perverts, "Go home, preacher, where you come from." Phone clicked. The next night, "If you preach again on mixing the races we'll mix you with—" and there followed an incoherent paragraph of obscenities which was rounded off with, "—and get this straight: we're going to have decent, moral people in this city and we're warning you!" Two or three nights later, came something almost unbelievable: The phone rang as usual, at two o'clock: I was awake and waiting for it. As I picked up the receiver, a voice screamed, *help help help help!* I gave my name and asked who was calling and the voice laughed and said, "You made a mistake, preacher; that's *your* voice calling for help."

My reaction to the first calls was mild. After all, you can't take this sort of nonsense too seriously. But that last one, I admit, left me feeling that somebody was on pretty shaky ground and it could be me. I lay awake quite a while, afterward. Finally, I got up, smoked a cigarette, told myself there couldn't be many like this one around; knowing it had taken only one to kill Andy, yet saying it, hoping, somehow, to shrink its uncanniness down to something I could deal with.

But after I had my coffee, next morning, my sense of balance, humor, whatever, was functioning again. I thought about the call, yes; but I didn't let it get on my mind. I picked up Karl Jaspers—I was doing a paper in February for the bookshop group on "Existentialism from the Christian Point of View." Read a chapter carefully, even critically; made notes, marked phrases. Then Johnny's voice began: *"But you see, he thinks they're turning boy mice into girl mice.* . . .

Mark . . . I had heard him, this morning, trying to start his car. The temperature was below freezing and the car was old and its battery, too, probably. I turned on the light when I heard him struggling with it, saw it was six o'clock. He was going to the lab earlier and staying later—as if the house had become unbearable. He had been here, with me, only twice. Both visits were shortly after Miss Mabel's escapade. Now and then, I had run into him at the shopping center. But no time for much talk. What kind of calls was he getting and paying no attention to? how about the lab? were they getting threats over there? The man who sent that clipping to Andy would do anything! Would he? Not necessarily: he might have wanted only to hurt a young boy. My mind drifted with this. . . . I pulled it back to the Jaspers book. Read another chapter. Then suddenly, could read no more. All kinds of grim possibilities had begun to race through my mind. I rejected them almost as quickly as I thought them, killing them off with *fantastic, incredible*—I realized that phone call, last night, had been heard by other listeners deep inside me: as if on a party line, receivers had been eased off the hooks—

You can't keep thinking this sort of thing. You do something. I dialed Neel's office, told him briefly about the calls. Was surprised to hear myself making it all rather funny as I told it. But he listened seriously enough and we arranged to see each other the next day. Then I called Mark at the lab and suggested that we get together soon, for steaks. I had missed him. How about tonight? Good. He suggested that I come to his house. I agreed. His voice was relaxed. I couldn't help but feel that things were better with him personally, at least—and this relieved me, some-what.

I could think of nothing more to do about the matter, so I checked my appointments for the day and made a few routine telephone calls. Every person I talked with sounded calm, ra-tional, cheerful. With one, I discussed the Cerebral Palsy Com-mittee's drive for funds; with another, the speech clinic our par-ish has a special interest in; with another, the series of mental health programs that were to be televised in the spring on Sun-day afternoons. Mrs. Riley called about a pot plant she was bringing over to brighten up the study. I called old Mrs. Nixon who is helpless with arthritis: her voice was chirpy as she told me a very funny story about two friends of hers. I called Judge An-drews who is recovering from a coronary thrombosis—he said he was reading, at the moment, a volume of Justice Oliver Wendell Holmes' decisions and would like to quote one para-graph— And as I listened to his modulated voice reading those wise, discerning words, I felt his tempered generous spirit, his disciplined intelligence, and was profoundly reassured. I thought, These are the ones who count, who give the community its quality—not the hoodlums, the crackpots, the haters— Was I playing that old magic game of numbers? One good man equals one evil man: Judge Andrews cancels out S.K., Mrs. Nixon's bright courage cancels out M——'s sly henchman—surely there are twice as many, ten times as many— Of course, it makes about as much sense as saying, Here are two, four, ten thousand healthy people: why worry about the one or three or five walking the streets with smallpox! But I did not struggle to clear up the confusion in my mind. I was too close, too shackled to the others. As I now try to recover that morning, I remember only the ach-ing oscillation of my feelings from *this is small* to *this is too large to deal with.*

I went to the church office for a few minutes and shortly after my return, Dewey Snyder called. As he said Good morning, my friend!—his usual greeting to me—I could hear Charlie's slow stammer . . . and, suddenly, a little schooner was bouncing on the sound waves set up by those two voices relentlessly moving against each other—and I was having trouble making relevant replies, as Snyder told me about the Constance Snyder Fund he was setting up for art students. He had spent last evening reading old letters of Connie's . . . she had written them from Florence the winter before her last illness—he thought I might, perhaps, like to read a few of them, sometime. His voice was warm and gentle. His words and mood seemed completely sincere. Would dinner, Friday evening, be possible? at his house? Katie would be there, too. He was setting up, he said, only a small fund to begin with: a half-million. But in two years he would add another half-million, perhaps more: this, he would like my opinion on. The Fund had been Connie's dream; he felt now was a good time to launch the project. He hoped I'd serve on its board of directors; he would, of course; and Katie, and others to be selected. Perhaps we'd find another young Marin or Knaths whom we could put on his creative feet, etc. I told him I'd like to work on the board. And as we talked, I was thinking of Grace, of her wisdom and awareness of the world of art, of the distinguished contribution she could make, while I—

Afterward, I had a curious feeling of unreality about him. The pieces would not come together. A little schooner . . . Katie's voice . . . the dossier . . . Grace's photograph . . . Connie . . . the Fund . . . art gallery . . . Cancer Committee—all this, yes; but where was Dewey? I couldn't find him. A trackless desert stretched between that photograph of the dancers and a fourteen-year-old boy's favorite quotation about the quality of mercy. . . .

I left the study and went for a walk. I was lost in a moral fog. Lost in the intricate twistings and turnings of this man's life, of mine, of everybody's. We know so little. We see so dimly. Our awareness is no more than a dot in a great void. What do we know about the human brain? the mind? how can we talk about the soul when we cannot define even those two words? Things are smooth: all seems well—and then in the darkness an iceberg of an old terror, an old memory, rips us to pieces; or an extra drop or two of a powerful chemical in our bloodstream turns our mind into a raging hell; or a different chemical, it may be, drags us out of our deep sense of alienation, our wretched anxiety and makes us feel secure and calm and close to God. How can a priest come to terms with these facts! Not by denial, no. There is a door somewhere, hard to open but it must be opened. A new way to think about man and his relationship with God. A way different from the scientific mode, closer to the way we think about a great painting or great music or poetry. Perhaps we cannot think about God: we must feel. But feeling is not enough, there must be an awareness that the intellect will bow to. A new dialogue—yes, yes, yes! But how do we find it! And in the meantime, how can I talk with honesty about human responsibility when I do not understand what I am saying! I know only that we are responsible. I know it, just as I know I must feel love before I can be a human being or a child of God. And yet, what is love? how do we define it? this love we must have to survive but which, when we feel it deeply, will urge us on to give our life for another!

And now, suddenly, I was thinking of Susan . . . Renie . . . those tulips . . . the Cokes . . . Andy . . . Grace . . . no, I couldn't bear to think about her. I was hearing Charlie: that memory, if true, seemed a small, pitiful, sick mistake in Snyder's past. Set it against the monstrous evils sweeping across men's minds today and it seems too small to notice. But the dossier: the photograph: this was calculated evil, germ warfare. Here is deliberate cruelty, deliberate incitement of hungers and fantasies and dreads of confused people. A curious irresponsibility. Are you going to ignore it? are you going to try only to understand, to feel compassion, and do nothing? I said, No! I felt I was shouting it at myself. My impulse was to go to his office immediately and talk it out with him: confront him with the facts, compel him to discuss all of it with me.

Then I remembered his eyes. I knew I could not go through with it. Not because of fear. I had no fear of this man. But because I had not forgotten Katie's words, and my feeling for Mark and Grace went so deep—we'd be unable to talk it out with reason and good will—I was afraid of myself—my anger once aroused can get out of control. I did not feel compassion for him; he was not, at this moment, one of God's children whom I as priest must care for. I should be thinking of this man's redemption—and all I could think of, suddenly, was Grace's body stared at by dirty wet-lipped men who would look at it and then at the Negro dancer's body weaving out of the two images an obscenity shaped to fit their own hollow hearts. I tried to push away from this, tried to find a reasonable way of looking at all of it. I finally told myself I knew nothing about the photograph save what Katie had said to me, and to Charlie. Were I to quote her words Charlie would lose his job, immediately. And it wouldn't make things easy for her, either. Once taking this step, I'd have to take the next and the church would be thrown into turmoil—the entire city would be shaken by it— And what would come of it? The damage had been done as far as Mark and she were concerned. Yes, but how about the rest of us? I didn't ask that.

I got back in time to go to the Yacht Club for a luncheon meeting of one of the committees I had involved myself with. Then back to the study, about mid-afternoon. I pulled out my sermon—

It was the season of Advent and I wanted to speak of love and hope, and of Jesus as a symbol of the complete person. . . .

And then, Miss Hortense called. She was gay and excited. She and Phelia and those barking ghosts of hers were on a merry chase after Communists: she was going through the phone book, she said; she had membership lists of several so-called liberal organizations, and the NAACP—at least, she had their letterheads which amounted to the same thing. She believed she was going to find at least fifty people right here in Windsor Hills who would bear watching—and no telling how many on the other side of town where those union members lived. She was sending the names to the Un-American Activities Committee and Phelia had had a splendid idea: Phelia thought it would be clever to use the letterheads of the various boards she was on, the Congressmen would give such a letter more attention. Didn't I think Phelia was right? I said, Yes, I thought Phelia was right; certainly if those names were sent in on the letterhead of the First National Bank, for instance, I'd think they'd read it with care. But did she think the bank would approve of this? Now my dear

Father Landrum, how absurd! Of course, the bank would approve! She was its largest stockholder and had known those boys running it since they were born how ridiculous they are loyal Americans aren't they? you don't seem enthusiastic, Father Landrum. . . .

"I am not," I said, more shortly than I had ever spoken to her.

"But surely you don't approve of Communists, Father Landrum!"

I told her I didn't. I began to try to tell her why I felt her plan was unwise. Then gave up. What was the use of talking to this mad woman on her own terms!

After that was over, I worked three hours on my sermon and finally crumpled the sheets and threw them in the waste basket.

At seven o'clock, I went over to the Channings' house.

I walked through the living room, saw her blue sweater on the arm of the sofa where she must have left it that Friday night before she went to Andy. Her sketch pad and pencil were lying nearby. She had drawn one thin curving line— Three library books were on the end table. I picked up one of them: long overdue. Her thimble was there, and a threaded needle. Dead flowers in a bowl, a half-rotted apple on a plate. The room looked abandoned. Apparently, Mark had used it only as a passageway since his return. I stood there, thinking of her—

He called me to come on in the kitchen. He was trimming the steaks and had them about ready for the charcoal grill which he had brought from the back terrace and set in the kitchen fireplace. There was a loaf of Italian bread lying on the table, and some butter. I offered to make the salad and went to the refrigerator for the lettuce and water cress. As I washed and dried the greens, and looked over Grace's seasonings, pulling out a bottle of this and that, hunting garlic, vinegar and so on, he worked on the burner, finally had the coals the way he wanted them and laid the steaks on the grill. It was the first time, since the afternoon Susan went to the store, that we had been together in the old, casual way. He seemed relaxed—or I tried to think so. He was working easily, cheerfully, handling everything with the precision and neatness which I used to kid him about. Now, I was as glad to see it as if I had found something of great value which I thought permanently lost.

He went in the living room for the drinks. I walked around opening drawers in search of a fresh dish towel. Noticed the kitchen laundry had not been sent out—the hamper was overflowing. I was looking at everything. On the paneled walls were four reproductions from Matisse's late period. I had always thought it a fine idea to have them here with the brass and copper and her white dishes. The place looked cheerful in spite of dusty shelves and foggy glasses—and smelled good, as garlic and tarragon and cut lemon and vinegar and smoke from the broiling meat mingled and floated in slow streams through the room. Saw her apron hanging on the closet door knob—

Mark brought in the drinks and we sat at the kitchen table while the steaks broiled and I worked on the salad. We didn't say much but the old feeling between us was right. My brain knew better but I felt, Things are going to be as they once were; somehow, this other will level off; we'll talk again as we used to—and some day, Grace will sit here again listening, looking at us, feeling with each of us. . . . I remembered that we had always talked at our best, and now and then even with eloquence, when she was listening. Or perhaps her being there made it seem so—just as everything else acquired quality and meaning in her presence. —It was a stabbing memory. I was stirring the dressing in the salad and we must have stopped talking—for how long, I don't know: when I looked up, he was drinking his bourbon and staring at the floor. His face was worn and strained and I realized how thin he had become during these weeks. The fine glow had lasted about twenty minutes. Now, once more, the present clamped down on us.

I finally asked if we should look at the steaks. With what I felt was a push of absolute will power he got to his feet and walked to the grill. He lifted the meat: it was well browned. I took the plates over, and in a moment or two we were back at the kitchen table, and I was serving the salad.

The steaks were excellent and I said so, but we ate them with no real pleasure. Between old friends, small talk can become an impossibility. I struggled for words but none came. I don't think he tried. Even now, I see those steak knives cutting through the meat, forks lifting, knives cutting—no sound except a thin *scrape scrape* of metal against plate.

I poured the coffee. All I had planned to tell him, ask him, went out of my head. I couldn't put anything else on this man. He would dismiss phone calls as unimportant; the circulation of the photograph—no, I couldn't tell him this. All he wanted was to be left alone with his work—to have a little peace of mind— And with him, in this kitchen, the talk, the threats had grown small. A foolish fear. What he needed was to settle down—

I was about to say, Look Mark: since there is to be no trial and all of that has been settled, wouldn't it be good for Grace to come home and get back into her teaching and theater? wouldn't it be better for both of you to go ahead with things just as you used to do? It would be hard at first but—

Before I could find a way to begin, he said, "I have a new job." Smiled. He was going to keep the emotion out of this. "An administrative post. I'm not sure what kind of administrator I'll make but the research institute is small and maybe I'll do all right."

In Illinois, he said. "It's quite a ways off and they know nothing about my arrest."

Mark not doing research— I tried not to show my concern too much. I said, "I'm sure you have investigated other possibilities thoroughly."

He said he had. Something might open up later, of course.

"The National Cancer Institute is out of the question? You have many friends there, don't you?"

I wasn't making it easy for him, I'm afraid. I was simply expressing my reaction to this monstrous situation.

"I have friends but security regulations make that impossible."

"You were cleared by the FBI, when was it, last year? when you were at Oak Ridge?"

He reminded me that he had not at that time been arrested on a morals charge. It was impossible now to get a government post. There was no use even to make inquiry.

I said, deliberately, "Why are you leaving? The director wants you to stay. Then why not stay? Ignore everything and stay. Things will die down, they always do. Our city will have a cleaner conscience if you stay."

He smiled, he was feeling this deeply and knew I was. He said he realized that the director had gone out on a limb for him. Both of them could lose their jobs if certain members of the board were antagonized. And he knew that pressures were being put on even those who lived in New York and the Midwest to get rid of him. "This is part of my decision to go. The rest of it is Grace. She can't live here now. It is impossible."

"Why?"

"You know why, Dave."

"I'm not sure I do. I think she has more fortitude than you are giving her credit for. You need her. She needs to be needed. She knows what your work means to you. It seems to me you may be forgetting that she understands this. Her friends are here, the work at the theater, her classes—all this means a great deal to her—"

His eyes were tortured. I couldn't keep on with it. After a moment or two, I asked him when he would be due at his new post. He said by the first of the year. They would go up earlier to find a place to live, etc.

Then Grace would come home soon, to see about things? The packing, the numberless matters relating to school, theater, dance classes—

"There's no need for it and I hope she won't." He meant it. He didn't want her here. I remembered that day in Baltimore—

I swung away from it and mentioned an article I had read recently, asked him to clarify a statement or two in it concerning the virus theory. He was aware of my lack of real knowledge of his work but he had always talked to me as if I knew more than I did. He began now, slowly, tentatively, as if pulling his mind back with difficulty. But in a few minutes he was deep in the subject. And as he talked his face gradually came alive, his eyes filled with the old light.

I poured us some brandy and listened as he explained in technical detail the virus theory I had mentioned and the specific investigations they were making here at the lab. Then he went into the theories that involve the cell's nucleic acids; then he was, somehow, on the subject of properdin, a body chemical Sloan-Kettering researchers had made a vaccine of and which seemed to give mice protection from one of the experimentally induced cancers. And on and on. Then he swung into the theory of genes and oxidation, and the possible relationship this might have to normal and abnormal growth—and from there he went into a description of specific experiments at a research center in California which he was especially interested in. . . .

Actually he was not talking to me, at all. He was only repeating the words, symbols, concepts, hopes which gave his search, and that of his fellow-scientists, its meaning and mystery and purpose.

And all I could say was, This is extraordinarily interesting. It is important for you to stay with it as long as you can. You must.

And then he grew silent and the hope drained out of his face. And for a terrible moment, I knew he knew it was futile, his staying on, even for another day. These projects were the work of years, not weeks. If he was going to leave, he might as well go tomorrow. And then—something slid across that bleak knowledge and the life came back in his face and I knew he would stay on as long as he could.

I said, "Mark, you don't have to go. These experiments are yours, you should see them through. Think about it some more. Don't make your final decision yet."

And once more he said, "I can't possibly ask Grace to go through what it would mean to stay." He pushed the words out and I felt he hated her name as he said it.

When I left, I took the books with me, telling him I would return them to the library.

My talk next day with Neel added little to what I had already heard. He knew nothing about the photograph. Thought it serious but believed it would be saved for the spring political campaign and would not be shown around too much at this time. He also believed it might boomerang on M—— and his legal advisers might have something to say to him, too, about the use of the picture. "I admit this is the optimistic view. But let's go along with it for the time being." What bothered Neel was the fact that somehow Mark had become a symbol to so many different people who could not control their anxieties. "He's sort of radioactive," he smiled. "They're aching to hurt somebody, to lose themselves as individuals, to merge into something big and anonymous—the reason for doing so can be pretty small.

"They need a God to believe in, Dave, and they don't believe in the Christian God. They just pretend to. They need something bigger than Outer Space, something that means more than their political party or their skin color, and they haven't got it. They may go to church but the god they worship is the image of themselves. Anyone who differs from them in looks or beliefs is 'the heathen.'" He laughed. "We've gone into hassles over this one before. This is hardly the time to do it again."

Then he added one small bit of information. He said a guy down in the Flats, named Gus Hestor (he had mentioned him to me before), had made a list of the kinds of people who should be run out of the city. Neel had not seen the list, but would try to get hold of it. When he did, he would call me. "Hestor is boss of two of the worst gangs in the Flats, has a police record a mile long. But so far, we haven't been able to pick him up for this kind of thing."

Neel pulled out some racist leaflets that had been scattered around at the State Fair in the autumn. Gave them to me. Told me of others his men had picked up in alleys, back streets, in pool rooms, cafés, around public schools. Virulent stuff.

We discussed Mark's leaving. I told him of the letter sent to Andy. I had not told him before. He listened without comment; only his eyes changed as I talked. He seemed to lay it aside, as if it were something he would think about later. We smoked for a while without talking. He finally said, "Perhaps Dr. Channing should leave, now. It might save the city a great deal of trouble." He looked up. "I am speaking as a policeman, Dave. A riot is a bad thing—or a dynamiting."

I said I felt we couldn't let them blackmail him. With their threats and sticks of dynamite they are blackmailing all of us, the entire community: You conform to our ways, they are saying, you get rid of the individuals and the ideas we don't like, smother them or drive them out—or we'll blow your homes and your labs and your churches and schools to pieces; we are the Philistines of the nuclear age, we hate intelligence, we fear new ideas, we dread the creative imagination, we cannot endure human excellence, we worship only what is made in our own image: you read our four-letter words and heed our telephone calls—or else! *Go home where you came from . . . go home go home!* You hear it round the world: but it has a cold mean sound when you hear it in your own neighborhood. All this and more I said, or he said. We basically agreed. We differed only in our feelings about Mark: I felt for the sake of his mind, soul, he had to stay as long as he wanted to, he had to make his own decision, and Snyder and M——'s henchmen, S.K. and these hoodlums at the telephone could not make it for him. "After all, most of these threats amount to nothing. Isn't this right?" Most, he agreed. But now and then, one was valid. What the calls did was give you the irrational temperature of a community, and the moral pressure. "Obviously, the pressure is pretty low, at present. The police department can do nothing about that, of course."

As I was leaving, he said quite casually, "That organist of All Saints should watch his step. Hestor resents his work with the choirboys. Some of them were good material for one of his junior gangs. He resents his going down to the Flats and visiting their parents. I've picked this up from my boys. Perhaps you should warn him to be careful."

I said I'd talk to him.

My talk with Neel was in many ways reassuring. He didn't feel the community was near a crisis; things were restless, yes; would

be, even had the store episode never occurred; the restlessness
had definitely focused on Mark, yes; but if he left soon—

Nevertheless, I was deeply disturbed. Troubled over the failure of my sermons to shake the complacency of my communicants; troubled about the lack of leadership—troubled over the
growing anonymity of our activities: it wasn't just anonymous
phone calls and letters, more and more of the community's activities were slipping behind the anonymous mask of "the committee," "the church," "the political party," "the newspaper," "the
board," and the masked ones "Upstairs" who make decisions affecting so many lives without ever divulging the identity of the
men behind the decisions—what does this creeping anonymity
signify? have we already lost the human being, the man with a
name? is he archaic? is this *our* form of totalitarianism? who are
making the cultural and moral decisions of our times? these
nameless ones? this mob made up of the highest and the lowest
—made up of every one of us when we refuse to assume our
identity and our responsibility? When the individual no longer
dares to state his name and his belief, when he no longer dares to
walk in the open as a man with dreams and hopes and memories and aspirations, when his insides have been hollowed out by
a powerful fist and restuffed with the Boss's orders—when this
happens, does it matter who the Boss is?

All day long, as I went about my work, called on the sick,
prayed with the worn and miserable, listened to the lonely who
once having attached me to the other end of the telephone line
hung on and on and on—I asked these questions, and more and
more. When is evil a contagious disease and when is it not? how
is resistance to it built up in the human mind? how do we deal
with the mythic mind of man? this great cauldron out of which
comes the raging mob and the mad hysteria but out of which
comes also the dream of God and beauty and love and poetry—
Why our inertia and lack of leadership? why don't we protect the
community from these carriers of infectious hate and fear? Why
is the demagogue permitted to use germ warfare? why can't Gus
Hestor be picked up for distributing these leaflets when he can
be picked up for stealing two dollars? And mingling with these

questions which I was asking as man, as priest, were questions I was asking as the friend of these two whose lives were so intertwined with my own. Why had they grown apart from each other at the moment they needed most the love which they felt on such deep levels? Suspicion? too small, too sharp a word to fit either of their minds. All of this, the abstract and the specific, things close and things far away had meshed together: I felt deeply torn, profoundly confused.

On sudden impulse, I decided to go up to Jane's place in the mountains. I had planned to go, sometime soon. Why not now? Away from people, from the pulls of my duties, the tortured look in Mark's eyes, Charlie's words, and Snyder's, and the sound of Neel's quiet, reasonable voice—perhaps I could get a clearer view of things.

After two hours of rearranging my schedule, making necessary phone calls and loading the church secretary with more work than I had any right to ask of her, I found I could manage two nights and a day on the mountain.

By three o'clock I was on my way. I enjoy driving; I like hills, rocks, winter trees and half-frozen streams, and bare contours of leaf-thickened ground curving, falling away, rising. And for a long time, I looked and drove and nothing stayed in my mind long enough to be remembered. About eighty miles later, I stopped at a store along the way and purchased a few things for supper and the next day's meals. My spirits had lifted; I was feeling good when I pulled up the steep road to the crest of the mountain and parked below Jane's rock house which is almost hidden by rhododendron. I soon had a log fire going in the library and the heat on in the guest room; then hunted around for blankets and made the bed and fixed something to eat.

After supper, I settled down in the library. It is a fine old room to be alone in. The rafters are great poplar logs put up long ago and with the bark still on them. The bookshelves, which cover the walls, are split logs. The room is full of simple handmade things and deep comfortable faded chairs. I had brought along three books to read. My vague plan had been to read Denis de Rougemont after supper—and leave my problems until the next day. But after supper, I was too relaxed to read. I did nothing but smoke and drink a little of Jane's cognac, and look in the fire. Slowly it began to come back . . . all that had happened to us since October: One Monday afternoon, a little girl named Susan had gone wandering and had entered an empty, half-dark old store . . . and Mark, who happened to be a brilliant scientist, had walked over to the shopping center for some Cokes and had gone wandering, too . . . and their journeys had crossed in that lonely dim place where only a yellow cat had seen them—and then Renie sent Susan on a terrible errand—

It sounded like a fairy tale. —Except that Andy was dead. And Mark was under pressure to give up the research that meant more than life to him. And Grace—

I was remembering only her, now . . . her voice in the car . . . her losing her glove at the airport—strange how this infinitesimally small thing had stayed with me . . . our talks—different from those I had with Mark, and rarely carried on in his presence, for when he was with us, he and I did the talking. They were always—my talks with her—about specific things: a play, a book, someone we knew, Andy's problems of growing up; her problems when staging a new play . . . thinking now about our long, relaxed, and far more frequent silences . . . Grace, making me go through those sweating, aching hours at the bars . . . finding for me a little of the courage I had lost . . . Grace, seeing to it that I read more than books on theology and religious mysticism: leaving one of her art books on my desk or a new record of contemporary music she thought might interest me, or a book of poetry . . . Grace, dancing . . . the strange and fascinating way she moved . . . her curious mixture of sophistication and that archaic something in her—hard to get at: you felt part of her was fifty thousand years old. I was remembering the night she finished planting those tulips: I had gone over a few days after Mark's arrest to see how they were making out and had found her in the living room, sketching—or trying to. We had talked very little, but after a while she took me outside to show me the tulip bed. "I planted the rest of them that night." When

Mark came home from the police station, they had finally got to bed, and after she heard him breathing steadily, she had slipped out, and with a flashlight to see by, had dug in that dark soil and pushed a bulb in, then another and another. . . . "I felt if the rest of them were planted, maybe they'd come up together in the spring, and if they all came up in the spring maybe we'd be here and if we were here, it would mean none of it had happened." She smiled as she said it but the tears were close. "I couldn't tell Mark about my little ritual. It would only have puzzled him." We talked quietly, afterward, about Susan and Renie and the rest of it; and though she did not say so, I knew she felt that even were he acquitted of the charges his future here was gone. That was in early November. It seemed, now, years ago.

I looked in that slow-burning fire, letting the memories come and go. . . . And now, Mark did not want her here with him. I remembered what she had told me in the car. What we had said in my study, that night; his sudden, *I'm not sure she does have confidence in me.* And that question in the car, *You don't think he did anything, Dave?.* . . . In that hotel room in Boston waiting . . . where were their thoughts? where had each gone during those endless hours? not always to their son, no; there must have been moments when they trembled with dread of each other, when their agony sank into heavy-dead doubt, when they wished everything you wish and don't wish. . . . What had she thought since? or could she think? what rearrangement of memories and hopes and terror and love had she been able to make? Was she staying away because she could not bear to come back or because she had guessed he did not want her? couldn't he see— No. You don't see. You tunnel in, hoping you can stay there, hoping you'll never see more than that one small point of light at the other end—only his work, pushing out all feeling— She *was* feeling. And he couldn't endure it. Only by depersonalizing his life could he now live it. I knew I was thinking bluntly about a relationship that was made of ten million subtly interlacing experiences and memories that drew them close and pulled them apart and there was no way I could understand, and no way they could understand what was happening. But I thought I knew Grace well enough to foresee the outcome. Here was one corner I could see around. She could not block feeling out of her life. What would be left? work? It is the same word for all of us but it has a thousand meanings. She loved her work, yes; she would have told you so, and her eyes would have been full of those amazing specks of light, and you would have believed her. But the dance, painting, the theater—these interests, absorbing as they seemed to be, were not what she lived for: the thing that kept her breathing was her love for those two. I could not conceive of her except as I had always known her: giving to them, needing to, wanting to. There was even a little left over for the rest of us. This desperate necessity to give what someone she cared for needed, may be rooted in another soil than love, I am not sure. But it was necessity to Grace, wherever its roots might be buried. I was suddenly angry. With whom? I would not face it. I loved him, too.

I picked up the *Presence of God* and compelled myself to read a few pages; then went to bed.

26

That night, I dreamed of her:

She was lying on the top of a mountain, in her leotard, on a smooth gray rock surrounded by clumps of rhododendron. It must have been cold for the leaves of the rhododendron hung drooped and rubbery as they do when it is below freezing. She was lying there bound not with chains, as I first thought—I was looking down as if from a plane—but with a black vine made of words. I could see it quite plainly for suddenly I was on the ground, but the words were blurred and the wind was blowing hard and I could not hear. Everything slowly turned: a small gray-black bird was on a limb close to me, watching her, his head scrunched deep in his feathers. I thought, He has so much compassion. —And that seemed absurd. —And then it seemed dangerous to be thinking it and I was suddenly awake and saying to myself, I got here just in time—and I was breathing hard as if I had been running.

The breathing subsided; the bird had gone but the image of her lying on the rock would not go away, not quite.

I turned on the light. Yes, I was in Jane's small guest room; across from the bed was the chest of drawers made of spruce, the big knobs on the drawers exactly where they should be; the floor was blue, the walls paneled in pine, the window ledge full of books—all as it had been when I went to bed last night. I looked at the bedside table: my cigarettes were lying on it and near them, the book I had been reading, *The Practice of the Presence of God*. I had slipped a pencil in where I was reading and it was there. I was fully conscious now: the feeling had not gone away, not quite, but I knew it had been a dream. I felt for my crutch, went to the toilet, came back, picked up the book, read a paragraph, two, three, blurred on the fourth, turned off the light and pulled up the blankets, felt the wool against my face, felt myself drifting back into sleep . . . then I heard her say, in that quiet way of hers, *You see, this is why I cannot come back; you understand, don't you?*

That did it. I turned on the light, pushed up the thermostat and went in the kitchen to make some coffee.

It was three o'clock. The kettle had not begun to boil and I sat at the kitchen table, waiting. Staring at the salt and pepper shakers. Wooden. Smooth. You grind the pepper as you use it— That made me think of eggs, I suppose; anyway, I thought of eggs and went to the refrigerator and took two out and laid them on the table. I got out the bread and laid it beside them. I glanced at the electric clock on the wall: two minutes after three. Grace . . . she was looking at her watch . . . she had turned on the light and was looking at her watch: *two minutes after three*—beyond mountains and rivers and hills and farmlands and Virginia Baltimore Roland Park she was lying in her bed in her parents' white brick home thinking, *two minutes after three . . . it was only a dream . . . I'll be awake in a moment. . . .*

The kettle piped up. I could not see her now. I poured water on the coffee, listened to its slow drip drip drip . . . watched the steam lift . . . curl . . . feeling: *this happened! this is an event, not a dream.* No more real than the dream but of another quality of experience—what was it? closer to me than the dream yet it did not go as deep— I was in this kitchen, staring at its old electric stove that from the looks of it must have been here thirty years, touching the handle of the kettle, smelling the coffee—and yet, I saw her look at her watch. . . .

Extrasensory perception: the phrase came into my mind. Maybe this is it; but my senses seemed completely involved in the experience: I felt *I had been there.* I tried to think about extrasensory experience as an idea, a theory, tried to pull back the little I had read about it which was not much because I had always shied away from it; had preferred not to believe: for if it is true, I'd tell myself, it opens up an outer psychic space that is too much for the human heart to deal with; the mind, yes: it seems able to cope with more and more and more and still more knowledge; but the human heart has its limits. I slid away from that thought: I was not thinking clearly, I was trying—which is a different thing—trying to pull back to that safe spot in the brain where we reason and think logically. I finally settled it this way: Even though I was awake I had dreamed it—you're not afraid of dreams, are you? sure I'm not; all right: then, you can accept that you dreamed it; part of you was still in your unconscious dreaming and part of you was here dripping the coffee; don't you smell the coffee? sure I smell it; all right— And now I could see her lying on the rock bound by—and I pulled out of that, thinking consciously now about the meaning of dreams as a part of the total human experience to keep from remembering *my* dream. I thought about dreams in the Freudian sense and Jungian and Old Testament sense; and then I found myself re-

membering tales my grandmother had told me about people separated by distance who had come together when they needed
to, in their dreams—could it be—was this—

I pushed that thought away. Went to the sink and turned the
cold water tap, filled a glass, put it on the table. Sat down, waiting for the coffee to finish dripping. Dreams . . . I was caught
by a sudden vision of all the people of the world, sleeping and
dreaming half their lives away—each night, reaching back into
the past a thousand ten thousand fifty thousand years, maybe,
for their dream or reaching only to yesterday, or maybe to their
young years where words still float with butterflies and leaves in
a swinging bright world outside them but the image sleeps close
by the crib and the Eternal Ones of the Dream are always near
enough to come on the stage of the mind and make a dream with
you. . . . And now dawn would soon come, and some of the
sleepers would awake, sweating and gasping because of what
had happened in their dream, and would begin to dread the day
ahead feeling too weak to meet it; and others would turn over
slowly and stretch and whisper, *I've had a good dream*—and they
would feel strong and hopeful although "reality" was for them,
today, just what it had been yesterday and yesterday may have
seemed the last day they could endure—

Mark . . . what was he dreaming, this night? in that lonely
house? At the lab in the day he was safe; he was in deep mental
ruts where only reason and facts and controlled experiments and
statistical tables were allowed, but at night—

The wind was roaring on the mountain above the house. Not
a tree stirred down here but above the roof, a few hundred feet
above, things were angry and chaotic and I knew the temperature was falling. It would be a cold morning. I cleaned up things
and made a big log fire in the library and picked up the *Presence
of God* and read it to the end. I closed the book—feeling, as I
have felt each time I have read it, his simplicity and faith: this
Brother Lawrence of the seventeenth century who went about
cooking and cleaning an old flagstoned kitchen in a Paris mon-
astery, thinking and dreaming of God: calling Him to come
and let him feel His Presence because he could not bear loneli-

ness, otherwise; believing with humble faith that God would come because he loved Him and longed for Him. —And God came. Day after day, year after year, Brother Lawrence called and God came to that kitchen and pushed the aching loneliness out of his heart and filled it with His Presence. And after a time, the monk's Superiors heard of it, and other famous men heard, and they came to ask Brother Lawrence how he practiced the Presence of God. And Brother Lawrence told them in letters and talks, and there is poetry and, therefore, truth in his honest and naive explanations. I read the book every year or two. The earth is no longer the Center of Everything as it was in Brother Lawrence's time and God is billions of light-years away from most of us, I'm afraid. How could it be otherwise! For between Him and us are the Milky Way with its hundred million planetary systems and beyond the Milky Way are nebulae after nebulae larger and more complex than the whirling cosmos of the Milky Way, and as we think about it our brain refuses knowledge and our imagination grows numb and shrinks into a hard knot and our heart grows ashamed that it once dared to dream that God could hear a human whisper across that inconceivable Void. But Brother Lawrence was so sure. And when I read his words—so powerful are human faith and the love of a man for his God—I feel he is right; I am sure of it, although I do not know why it is so, or whether I shall ever find the words that will convince my mind, with its vague scientific orientation, of this truth.

The first time I read the book I must have been about nineteen. I had just won another tennis match. I had worked hard at it not wanting to win especially but I worked hard at it, partly because it was fun, partly—maybe I did want to win, a little. Anyway, I won. And afterward? Well, I felt emptied out and lonelier than I had ever been in my life. Another cup had been won, that was all; and instead of enjoying the pleasure in my mother's eyes I resented it. She put the cup on her sideboard with all the other cups I had won and every time I went in the dining room I felt angry and baffled and once or twice I had the impulse to go up to the little lady and shake her hard, I almost wanted to hurt her and this worried me, I was afraid of what I felt for those words don't say it, I felt some pretty rough impulses inside me. One evening, I went to the public library to look for something to read, a novel maybe, a book of travel—and the gray-haired librarian who knew books and much more than books, I think now, asked me if I had ever read *The Practice of the Presence of God*. I hadn't, of course, and didn't want to. But she gave it to me, wrote down the numbers and the rest of it, before I could tell her I didn't want it, and I walked out with it under my arm. That night, I read it. And this book is one reason, among a hundred, why I entered the Church: hoping to learn what Brother Lawrence had learned in the seventeenth century.

There are two or three thousand books in Jane's library and always I find a few interesting ones I have missed on other visits. I walked around the room, looking over shelves of poetry, novels, history, psychoanalysis, drama— And then, near the cabinet, I came upon some old camp brochures. I figured quickly: Grace must have been here in 1941 or '42. I searched through the pile until I found booklets of those years, and turned the pages of pictures hoping to find her. There she was, dancing: the pose so characteristic that I spotted her before I recognized her face. Young and sad—hair long at that time and hanging loose and her eyes were large and brooding—and then I found another picture of her on the tennis court and there she was gay and sure as if nothing in the world had ever troubled her. Another Grace. Always another and another. Young one day, terribly old the next; dreaming . . . painting . . . kneeling and talking gravely with her young son . . . and then again, dancing with a wild and terrible strength as if her energy could endure forever . . . or at a party, after the drink she should not have taken, telling her wacky stories, very funny and very sad; and then another time, quiet, thoughtful, letting you see her well-informed mind, talking of important concerns; or again, off somewhere, in that imagination of hers, forgetting to wash the dishes, stacking them up, forgetting—until you wondered how Mark put up with it.

One day, during the trouble, I went over to see her. Returned a record, I think, or a book. She was in the living room, standing near the glass wall that faces the trees and ravine below. Near it, on the narrow terrace, they had planted those tulips. She turned when I called to her and I joined her at the window. We did not say much. We talked about the old beech down below, which had lost its leaves early this year. Then I said, "Grace—I keep trying to see its beginning; how it started, how it built up to this. Mark thinks I'm wrong to ask; he sees it as sheer accident; do you?" And then, she had looked at me gravely, it was one of her "old" days when she seems a million years old. "We caused it," she said. I asked what she meant by that. "There is something in us, Dave, that caused it; part of it; not anything Mark did but something we are and may not know we are." I felt she was wrong and said so. But now, as I remember it, as I see all that happened from that first day, that Monday afternoon, I think she was right, if by "we" she meant all of us.

I went out for a walk. It was too cold to enjoy it and I soon came in, still thinking of her. I could move an inch or so from the dream—the two dreams if they were two—but I could not get away from her. I did not want to think of her—it was Mark I had felt concerned about two nights ago. But now . . . well, she went along with me on that walk. And I let myself remember: her face in Baltimore, the agony I had felt when I could find no words to help them; and the next morning when I went out to tell her goodbye, in her mother's garden: She was standing by a shrub staring at it, and when I drew near she looked at me without changing expression. I could only say her name; and then I kissed her forehead and held her cold hand for a moment and left her, and joined Mark who was waiting in the car to take me to the airport. When we arrived, the plane was in. We had little time to talk more—we had said nothing on the way except the most superficial of comments—but now I asked him when he expected to be back in Windsor Hills and he told me he would stay in Baltimore a few days longer. "I need to get back to the lab," he said, "but I am not sure when I can leave." And Grace? "I don't know. I don't see how she can come back. She can't possibly go through the rest of it." Then I told him that the

Newells had withdrawn the charges, last Monday, and there would be no trial. They were pushing the passengers along to the plane, and we were suddenly separated, and I was glad, for I did not want to see his eyes after I said it.

The whole place was full of her! She had spent so much time here. After Mark returned from the Japanese prison, they had built their summer cabin less than a quarter of a mile away from the camp. They and Andy had come up hundreds of times, going back and forth from library to cabin to tennis courts, to the pool, up to the peak, down to the gulch where Andy would spend hours searching for quartz and amethyst crystals for his rock collection. She had often sat in this library reading, or listening to records— And it was here, on one of these rugs that she lay that day weeping, after the Woman's plane had crashed, while memories rolled over her like a tidal wave.

She had told me of those memories long ago. One April afternoon when we were both in a quiet, retrospective mood:

I had been working on my sermon and had grown restless. I had chosen a tough theme: *Man's encounter with inner space* —one of a series I was doing on Religion and Twentieth-Century Science. —Not so much to bring insight to my congregation as to find some kind of intellectual clarity for myself. I left the typewriter and went to the window. The dogwood on her lawn was blooming, the forsythia and tulips near the rock garden were blooming—and it was raining. I suddenly wanted somebody to talk with, not to preach to. And in a moment, I saw her car turn into their driveway. I thought, I'll return a book: you can always do that. I picked up a book of theirs, I don't remember what, and went over. She was in the living room unpacking two records her mother had sent her: the work of a young composer whose name I had not heard before. Would I stay and listen to them? Andy was at Scout meeting—she was not going for Mark until five-forty-five—we could have some coffee—

She went to the kitchen to make it. I intended to follow her but as I walked through the dining room I stopped and looked at the fresco. I had often looked at it: its giant smoky shapes and curiously unstable planes had a way of holding you. And I asked her to tell me, if she would, why she had called it *Lost Memory*. It was a phrase which held meaning for her, I knew, for she had used it, also, as the name of a dance.

When she came in with the coffee, she sat on a stool near the fire and told me about her and the Woman. Relaxed and easy, most of the time; tense, now and then, as words brought back old feelings, and at these moments she would stop talking and push her shaggy hair out of her eyes and rub that left hand the way she does when fear is sliding through her veins. Then she would look at me and smile: and it was exactly as if we had eased one door shut and opened another.

"She was tall and beautiful—and could do everything: swim, ride, shoot, paint. . . ." Grace smiled. "Saying that is saying nothing. I know. It was not her skills, nor her beauty. It was her quality of imagination that made her extraordinary. Perhaps I am wrong here, too. I won't try to analyze her too much, nor me. What draws you to another human being? I don't know. It is like asking, What makes you want to look at a painting hour after hour after hour . . . she was not real, in one sense—as music is not real—" She drew in a deep breath. "I won't try it any more. She opened up the world for me, I'll leave it at that. There was an old trail at camp: I had hiked down it a hundred times but I had never seen it until the Woman showed it to me: I had never felt a rock becoming a rock through a million years changing changing . . . I had never felt time before . . . a scarlet branch of a sourwood tree—I had never seen what light could do to it. There were Indian pipes creeping out of the ground and once she knelt beside them and whispered, Come! And I knelt by her and looked at those smoky, translucent things —I didn't know what they were, not flowers nor plants, not mushrooms, not lichens—they were just themselves and they seemed miraculous. Everything had just been born: clouds, thunderheads—we'd lie looking up into them and once she said she wanted to fly through one, sometime; and I said, Wouldn't it be too dangerous, could she do it? And she had smiled and said, The trying is the fun. And I knew she was not afraid of death, that she never considered it, and it seemed to me that maybe she had come from somewhere else and didn't belong to the human race, for all of us were afraid of death. Caves . . . she loved to tell me about the caves of the world so many of which are full of man's brooding paintings and sculptures. People see so little, she'd say, in the bright light but there's a dark rim: everything has it, everybody has it, and that is where the strange and the wonderful happens. And the other: I learned from her about tenderness and passion."

And then camp closed and Grace went back to school and a doctor came and told the girls about the facts of life. And she learned during that lecture on "normal love" that this amazing creature who had seemed to her to have come out of a myth, who did not quite belong in the ordinary world, was nothing but a homosexual. "I struggled to hold on to my image of her, to cling to the validity of what I had experienced, but I couldn't. I fought that word the doctor had used, but it whipped me after two or three weeks, lying awake at night looking, listening to Her, then remembering what the doctor had said. My father was a doctor, too, and I felt this one must know; if he said what he said, it must be so. Things fell inward on me, I suppose I was ill, I don't know. Anyway, Mother and Dad decided Key West might be a good place to go, maybe I needed a change. We played on the beach, Mother and I, and fished; she was very sweet; if she knew what was happening inside her daughter she couldn't talk about it, nor could I. So we played together, took sun baths, and all the time I kept thinking of Her . . . and of the old trail, and all she had told me and it seemed good and true and wonderful, then in a split second, it seemed ugly and dirty and horrible. It would zigzag like that, day and night, day and night—

"One morning we were on the beach. I began to wade through the seaweed—hating the slimy stuff on my legs but you had to go through it to get to the good part of the beach—the water was deep deep blue and warm and there were fishing boats, some near, some far out . . . a white cruiser was out farther than the others and I kept looking . . . looking . . . it was moving . . . out to sea . . . growing smaller smaller smaller . . . and then, it was gone. And all this was gone, too."

"The memory?"

"In a sense, yes: the conflict, the knowing and not-knowing. The shell lay there in my mind—I could have told you her name, that she had been a counselor at camp, but the living part of it was gone. The pain had left, and the wonder of it; the mystery, the ecstasy were gone and the love I had felt. The new way of looking at Indian pipes and caves and thunderheads and rocks and poetry stayed, but I forgot who had opened my eyes so I could see. I existed, she existed, but the relationship did not exist."

She looked in the fire a long time. "Strange . . . two people make something, create it together—and then, it is gone and they are still here."

"And that was all?"

"Not quite. Years later, I went to Annapolis to a dance. My date and I dropped in somewhere for a drink. I saw this marvelous-looking woman with an officer from the flying field. As I passed her, I recognized her. I don't think she saw me. I didn't feel anything—I vaguely knew she had been a counselor at the camp I had gone to and I had had a silly sort of crush or something, but though this much came back, nothing else came—no feeling, no real remembering. But I saw the men and women around her reacting as people had done at camp.

"After college, after studying in New York, I came down to be a counselor in Jane's camp.

"Then it happened: I picked up the newspaper and saw Her on the front page. She was standing by a plane. Not the plane that crashed, of course; but a plane she had often taken up. Below, was the story of her going down at sea. I was on my cot in the cabin with the children. It was Quiet Hour: six of them on their cots, reading, wriggling, writing letters, trying to make each other talk and laugh. I eased off the cot, slipped out and began to run—I didn't know where I was running and didn't care, I was just running— And then a hand caught my arm. It was Jane. I was at the end of the hill. She must have been walking out there. She led me to the library and told me to sit down. She gave me a cigarette.

"And suddenly, I was crashing through to age fifteen again: back to the magic and mystery and terror and ecstasy—and the horror and the cruelty and the sweetness and beauty. Crying, as memories pushed back on me.

"I don't remember what I said to Jane except I told her I had loved this woman and it had seemed a wonderful thing to me—until I discovered it was evil and that I had been seduced; and then I had forgot it and now—

"I remember lying on the rug in front of that stone fireplace sobbing like a child, and Jane talking: I didn't hear some of it but finally this came through: she was saying, It is the quality of a relationship that counts; easy to paste a good label on something spurious and cheap, easy to paste a bad one on something fine and delicate— When she said this simple, obvious thing it burst on me like a revelation.

"I hushed my sobs and listened. She was saying: Not one incident, not one point in your life but the whole structure is what counts: what you are moving toward and away from— what you are forming altogether; not this mistake or that sin or virtue but your whole way of looking, the depth of your longing, the vision you hold to—"

"And I lay there, seeing the twisting trail and dreamlike rocks and gray translucent Indian pipes pushing out of the ground and the thunderhead in the sky and the scarlet sourwood—and all of it began to come together, to find its form: the harsh and tender and good and evil, and my heart was breaking because I could not tell Her now what it meant to me."

I gave Grace a cigarette. She smoked for a while and then she said, "And so, one day, I began to paint *Lost Memory*."

"You painted it then?"

"No. While the real memory was lost. The year before she killed herself, I did the first small canvas. And, long afterward, when we built this house, I did the fresco for Mark because he asked me to."

Mark. . . .

I was remembering that evening when they first knew they were in love and she had felt she must tell him about it. Suppose each of us told the one we loved about the far-away memory that means most to us . . . what chaos! And yet, the memory is there—even though we may have pushed it far back—and sooner or later the ones close to us, and sometimes those far away, will collide with it. It is inevitable. For memories don't stay where we push them; they are travelers who are likely to appear anywhere, any time, speaking a strange language. (I tried to amuse myself with the thought but I was not amused; I saw too plainly, suddenly, how I spend my life colliding with memories and dreams—my own and those of all the others: collision after collision—)

I was staring in the fire now, not seeing much there and certainly not thinking: in that relaxed, unconcentrated mood when images . . . memories . . . ideas . . . float across your mind much as they must have done when you were a child: Brother Lawrence in that kitchen cleaning and praying and feeling the Presence of God within him . . . Grace holding tight to her fifteen-year-old memory as you hold what you prize and yet, not sure she is right, not sure, even now— She had learned the trick of pushing something that hurt her, back back back—and she had learned how to accept it again; two technics: which was she using now with Andy? I was sorry I had thought it.

I got up and brought in another log. Poked the fire and swept up the hearth. Mark: would he go to his new job soon? or was he pushing everything out and holding to those experiments? Strange . . . he had never talked to me about his years in prison camp. How well did I know this man whom I loved and believed I knew so intimately? I wasn't sure . . . I saw him in my study; pressing out that cigarette . . . saw him with Eliot and the others at the cabin—

. . . Now the Woman . . . coming back . . . walking along that old trail I had never seen but which I saw now— She had begged the sea to open for her so she could be lost forever, and it had opened and closed again and there was no trace of her left. And yet, she was here in this library, with me whom she had never known. . . . I tried to see her, to understand this girl Odysseus—she seemed like that to me—who had left home to discover the dark Rim of Things—dark not with evil but dark because human eyes close when they glance that way, for mystery and wonder are dazzling and most eyes cannot bear to look. The Wanderer . . . and then, after wandering so long, after looking in caves and thunderheads and all the rest of it, did she grow a little homesick for the ordinary and the "normal"? was that why she tried to fall in love with someone who meant Coming Back Home? We shall never know. Tried to come back —and crashed, saying "tell Bill he has been wonderful," crashing gallantly. And then, this twentieth-century idea came to me: Couldn't a psychoanalyst have straightened her out? couldn't he? Would you want her "straightened out"? would you? —And now I was thinking of Jean . . . *You know how normal I am, Dave . . . the abnormal frightens me so . . . you know this, Dave. . . .*

. . . remembering Grace's painting now: the miracle of it: coming out of the same part of her where the stricken memory lay; feeding on its death and returning to earth as its resurrection. And now I was thinking—as the Woman must have done so often—of that enormous place we call the unconscious whose dimensions never end. I try desperately, sometimes—maybe all of us do—to shut it off because I see a stiff graveyard down there whose corpses never quite die and this frightens me, although it shouldn't. But it does and I pile everything in the world against the door sometimes, forgetting all the rest that is there: the uncreated paintings and sculptures and music, the unsaid poetry and undiscovered ideas—the billion seeds swelling in the darkness . . . ready to sprout, ready to grow—

I stopped my vague thoughts and went to work on Niebuhr's *Beyond Tragedy.* I was determined to read all of it while up here. And I did; carefully marking sentences, paragraphs, here, there, searching for one on which I might build a sermon. After three hours of this almost grim concentration, I fixed

something to eat. And afterward, I hunted through the records
Jane had left at camp and found Brahms' *Second* and played
it on the portable. Then I drove to the small town near the camp
and got gas for the car and some fresh rolls and a newspaper and
talked to two or three people, and then went back up the mountain. I had not solved anything. No. I had only become more
aware of the uncounted levels, the twistings and turnings of
a human life.

On the way back to Windsor Hills, next day, I could not think
of Mark and Grace together. I'd begin to—and then something
would separate them: Mark in that lab. And Grace? The dream
hung over me; I couldn't see beyond it.

A week later, she came home.

She arrived on a late afternoon train. Mark met her, of course.
Around eight o'clock I went over to speak to them. They should
be a bit squared away by now, I thought.

I opened the door, called out in my usual casual way, "Hello,
may I come in?"

She and Mark were standing in the living room. As I walked
toward her I thought, She looks quite well, actually. She had on
that pale blue tweed skirt she wears so much and a sweater and
had changed to her flats: her way of dressing. It reassured me.
Her black hair was shaggier than usual, perhaps; no nail
polish on but she does not always wear it; face thin—yes, but
why not? I was casing the situation, taking too many notes—any-

one with half an eye could see me scribbling them down in my mind. I realized it, tried to relax.

She came toward me and I saw how constrictedly she moved. Before I could react to this, she had put her hands on my arms and I was kissing her forehead. I said what you always say about a trip; I said, It's good to have you home, etc. As I said these things I searched her face for news of her. All I saw was the intent absorbed eyes. Mark was standing near the fireplace, smoking, looking at her, at me. His face was not open; his guard was up, all right; but I felt he was glad I had come. He had already said, Hi Dave.

She sat down. Again, I saw it: the extraordinary stiffness. She moved as if she might break in two. She was looking at me. After a moment, she smiled politely. I had the odd notion that she was struggling to remember more about me and so far could find only a shred, a string or so to hold to. It shook me. But I shoved the talk along, the way you do. Asked about her mother. Asked about her mother's cocker spaniel. Sorry I had done it for it brought Andy's pup to my mind. Went on, as if there were no stopping. Fingered through my memory for that cocker spaniel's name and came up with it: Coco. I said, How is Coco? Then I asked about the maid, How is Mona? Made rather a point of it, as if for some reason we must be excessively careful not to omit one name from the Baltimore household. I asked— You can't remember such talk. When you try you only make up new and worse talk. But it must have been pretty bad. I tried again. More casually. Mentioned politics: something the Secretary of State had said. No reaction. There had been a collision of jet planes that day; civilians hurt, etc. They had not heard. I began to tell them. Saw their faces were strained and at the same time uninterested. Slid off that. Then I told her about Jane, Katie, Berney, the others at Paul's bookshop, last week. Paul had showed his film of Kabuki dancers, the one he made in Japan a few months ago. He had gone to Japan full of Zen Buddhism and tea and flower ceremonials and Noh plays; he had come back talking about the new school of folk artists, about a new Japanese novelist; then he had told us—Paul, who is afraid of all women, told us with a kind of flowering ardor of the delicate reticence of the geishas, and so on and on. But they knew this; after all, Grace had been away only three weeks. Everybody knew Paul's love affair with Japan. But I told them. Then I began to describe the film. . . .

Maybe it was not as asinine as it seems now. Perhaps the only thing wrong was: the talk was completely unreal. My talk. Nobody cared in the least about what I was saying.

She interrupted me in the middle of a sentence, said, "Will you have a drink, Dave?"

I said no.

She walked to the cabinet, poured a jigger of Scotch, drank it. Poured another. Mark joined her and poured a small drink for himself. He said, Maybe Dave would like some coffee. I said no, I must be running along in a moment.

Grace came back to her chair. Again, I saw the rigidity. Mark was standing near the bookshelves. He picked up a book, I thought he was going to mention it, he laid it down, looked at me as if I were saying something. I wasn't but I tried to. The two of us batted a few words back and forth. Grace sat there, holding her glass, turning it round and round. Then she saw me looking at her and drank the stuff quickly as if a nurse had ordered her to take her medicine. When Mark and I talked she stared at Mark. When we laughed—and we did, somehow you can always manage a laugh or two—her face reflected the laughter as a small child's face reflects the uncomprehended mood of the grownups.

She poured another drink. This time, Mark let her do it without his help.

She came back. Sat down. Stared into the glass. It was suddenly empty. She began to talk: She asked me how my mother was. She said, "Have you seen Paul and the others lately? or Berney?"

Mark looked at her, turned to say something to me, did not say it.

I said yes—as if I had not already told her. I began, once

more, to talk about that film. The needle had stuck and the sentences were compulsively repeating themselves. She was not listening. She was rubbing the fingers of her left hand and looking down at the floor. Her black hair had slipped across her temple and a streak of shadow pulled at her chin and throat. I watched it a moment: black hair, shadow; watched it pull her pale face into two overlapping faces; then saw such agony stamped there that I could not bear to look. I turned to Mark, finished my sentence, said I must run along.

He followed me to the terrace. Down the steps. Into the dark. I could not see his face. He said, "This coming back is rough."

"I know."

"She shouldn't have come."

"She had to."

"Why?"

You have to. Of course you do. But how do you say it? "To pack—for one thing."

"I don't think so. I think it is bad for her. Whatever she has to do, packing isn't it."

What to say? I didn't try.

"Johnson's could have handled the whole thing. And much better. It is one hard thing she didn't have to subject herself to." There was impatience in his voice. I felt he was covering his fear—something else, too, maybe.

He was certainly talking out of character and he knew it. He wanted me to argue this. I knew that, too. Wanted me to push him back into his ruts. It is a curious thing: how we bounce out when trouble comes, how pain strips us down, cleans off our individual qualities: Mark was not Mark talking now; he was any man in trouble, any man who is angered and terrified to feel a new trouble rushing toward him. He felt it all right—and I did too.

All I could manage was, "The packing is important for her."

"For God's sake, why?"

"She'll be different, afterward."

"I don't see it."

"She's got to tie it together, somehow. With all that went before, all that will come afterward. I don't know why, Mark; you just do."

"I don't think so. A clean break is better. She's brooding too much—you can see that. It would be much better if she could get her mind on something else now."

What? You expect her to dance? You expect her to paint a picture? Then, sensing his misery, I wanted to say something more, something better; use words he could accept more easily. Say something impersonal, abstract, so his mind would feel comfortable with it. But I couldn't.

We stood there looking out into the night. Back of me, in my childhood was a grandmother who had misunderstood many things about life but she understood a few things about death— at least she understood the human need of ritual when the cleavage comes. Your reason tells you to begin again, to make a clean break but the rest of you won't go along with it. And Grandma knew how the things that are left behind reach out and pull you back unless you stop and let life and death meet and divide up things. And she had talked to me: fumbling for words, often she was just an old confused woman rambling through her memories, but now and then she talked with sudden clear perception, with startling insight and I knew she was right.

I remember, it was long ago, I was just a small boy, she said, "There's a final conversation you must have with a room when someone it is used to goes away and is not returning." This was when my grandfather died on Eastern Shore. She said, "Come with me, boy." And I followed her, a little scared, sure; but I followed her down the wide hall, past the old chest of drawers that jutted out so you had to step aside for it; I remember there was a pier glass at the end of the hall and as we walked I saw her image in it coming closer closer closer as we walked on and on past the stairway, closer as we passed her room, and when she stopped at his door, the woman in the glass stopped, too; she leaned down as my grandmother leaned down to unlock the door, and the two of them together unlocked it. It must have been a heavy door, I thought. But it swung open, quite easily, and we walked into his room.

She spent long hours there, day after day after day; and I spent them with her, standing silent and bewitched as she opened bureau drawers, lifted things out; as she opened his desk, lifted his ledgers out, and boxes of records and papers, and speeches he had made. He had been in politics and seemed to have made a great many speeches. The speeches she put in the wastebasket. She tilted the box and they tumbled into the wastebasket, rattled and hissed and sighed and lay still. Then she took down the pictures, leaving two or three, putting the rest in a dark closet. Then she laid aside things to give to the right people: this for his sister; that for his brother; this for someone I did not know. . . .

One morning, she went to the trunk in his dressing room. She unlocked it and lifted the lid. I edged nearer. The first tray was filled with collar boxes, and shirts, and ties, and small boxes of cuff links and a pair of yellowed suspenders and one or two odd things, half like toys, Chinese toys, maybe, I wasn't sure what they were; and three or four old faded pictures. She took the tray out. There lay his old Prince Albert in moth balls. She lifted that tray out. The rest of the trunk was filled with letters. She lifted them out: packet after packet. Now and then she opened an envelope. Once she smiled as she read. Once she looked up at his father's portrait on the wall and studied the old face, then returned to her reading; she folded the letter slowly and slipped it into the envelope. Once she frowned and said *tch tch tch*, tore a letter across, dropped it in the wastebasket. Then, finally, she stopped reading. She said, *Ah . . . dear God.* She looked at an envelope without removing the letter. She looked at it so long I thought she had gone to sleep so I went to her and shook her and whispered *Granma . . .* and she stared at me as if I were a part of a strange unborn future that had not yet come to her: She did not know who I was and I knew it, and my heart almost stopped beating. I sobbed and whispered her name again, and hushed. It was as if an old wisdom I could not have experienced put its hand on my mouth. I somehow knew I had taken a step into a magic circle where time never comes; where everything stays green forever; I did not quite know but I knew; and I knew I was not expected to understand and I did not try. I stood there, the small stranger not yet born into her awareness, and watched and waited and watched as she rearranged her life and his, as she separated, destroyed what must be destroyed, kept what must be kept. And then—I suppose I had stood there too long—I needed to relieve myself but I could not bear to leave, I was not sure she'd be there when I came back so I stayed and held my legs tight together, moving this way, that, holding them tight wiggling with discomfort but determined not to— And then, she saw me. Someone saw me, and I watched Her, this Someone, move down down the years toward me, coming closer and closer and closer—what did a ten-year-old know about time!—but I felt Her coming toward me: that Ancient Dark Mother of us all who never forgets to clean and spank and nurse and push and pull and crush and heal the sons of the earth—closer and closer she came and I knew she was about to recognize me as belonging to her, and she did: she turned and said, "Go to the bathroom, David. At once!" And I went, feeling safe again, secure again, knowing I was once more in her terrible and comforting and ever-present care.

Those few days . . . I must, in memory, have put my whole life in them, somehow. But I remember this clearly: I knew, furtively, yes, as if it were a secret, but I knew his big walnut bed was watching her; and his old reading chair watched her, too. I remember she looked at the chair, one day, for a long time; she stood facing it, her thin tall body keeping distance from it. And I knew she hated it and it hated her, and I knew the two were saying things formally, coldly, that must be said and finished with. Then she picked up the reading lamp and took it away from its old place beside the chair. And I felt with my bones and muscles and in the pit of my stomach the immeasurable width of final separation. I knew, somehow, that a design had once had meaning and now the meaning had left it. Therefore—but I had no words after *therefore*. I was only a mute wondering ten-year-old leaning over the edge of what remains after death takes its share.

Had I remembered this, that evening, I could not have spoken of it to Mark. Not then. Perhaps not ever. But nothing came back to me of that time long ago, as we stood talking on the steps, except the feeling, the urgency of Grace's need. I knew she had to go through it. She must settle things forever with Andy's room. But more: with the whole house which they had dreamed and planned and built and worked for and lived in and now were leaving. There were deaths within deaths to come to terms with. But all I could manage was to repeat what I had said, "She can't throw the past away as if it had never been. She's got to tie it up with where she is now or it will pull her to pieces. Let's call it her need of liturgy."

"It won't tie, Dave. God knows she's tried—I've tried—"

She was at the door. She said, "Mark? oh . . . I thought maybe you had gone . . . with Dave."

"I'm coming, darling." He said to me, "Drop in to see her, won't you? As often as you can?"

I said I would.

I called good night to her, looked at Mark; hoped he could somehow guess how I felt about him and her. He put his hand on my shoulder and we stood there in the dark. We didn't try words. Neither of us knew any to use. He finally said, "Night, Dave," and followed Grace inside. And I crossed the street. Andy's death had taken a lot from them besides himself. I began to see it, that night. And I knew they didn't know what to do about it, where to begin again. Nor did I.

28

The next morning I dropped in to see her. She had pulled out a carton and set it in the middle of the living-room floor. The kind of box in which a dozen pillows might have been shipped, say from Altman's or Macy's or Sears, Roebuck. I said, "That's a fine box. Now what shall we put in it?" She said she hadn't decided. She had put half a dozen pairs of shoes in a chair, a jug and two small flower bowls in another chair, a pile of toilet things—brushes, hot water bag, syringe, jars—in another chair. There was a crumpled piece of wrapping paper near the box, a wad of string, a hatbox. A chair from the dining room was in the living room near the door. She must have been standing on it to lift something down. The disorder reassured me. At least she's begun on something.

"Maybe all this stuff?" I said.

"No, I don't think so." Her face was absorbed and at the same time distracted. I had seen her like this, now and then, when painting or working on the choreography for a dance. She's working it through, I told myself: let her be.

We talked a bit. Not much. But she seemed less in a state of shock or whatever it was that had troubled us the night before. Less frozen. And she seemed glad to see me and certainly I was no longer that stranger with a familiar face.

Next morning I went over again.

But as the days passed, I began to know she did not want me there. I'd call out, "Grace, may I come?" and walk in—and she'd look as startled as if I had torn the door from its hinges. Usually she was pulling things out of drawers or kneeling by an open box. Sometimes, when I came in, not always, a quick distaste would slide over her face. Then she'd say pleasantly, "Hello, Dave." And I'd stand there, speechless and awkward in this new role of intruder. Yet I'd doggedly go back next day, feeling I must not let her have her way. I'd stand and watch her move stiffly from this to that. Grace, whose body had been so fluid, so flexible— One day, I knew: she was in the snow: she had become that lost boy and had assumed his suffering.

I began quietly to talk to her about the old crowd who gathered in Paul's bookshop. They didn't go as often or stay as long as when she used to be with them. Grace had been the enzyme that speeded up the talk in the old days, the plans, the ideas, the gaiety. I told her about Berney pinch-hitting for her at the Red Bank theater. How he laughed at himself as director and yet—well, he's pretty good, you know. But the Red Bank group was no more to her now than any city's group of amateur actors. I knew she did not care but I tried to make her care. And she listened but she did not say much. Her dance group: they would like to come and say hello, one by one or in small groups —if she felt up to it? She said of course she'd love to see them sometime. And that was that. I'd say, Let's try a little music. Let's play a little Bartók. How about the *Third Concerto?* No? Then let's listen to one of the *Brandenburgs.* And she'd shake her head and say, "You mind helping me with this box, Dave?" She was poised, she smiled vaguely, she even touched my arm now and then but as casually as she might have touched a chair. She was not connecting. Not with any of us. Mark or me or Jane or any of us.

Slowly, dimly I began to see what was happening. She was closing up everything in her but one small place: the way you close up an enormous ancestral home and live in one room and the kitchen: then, one day, there is too much of that and you put a cot in the kitchen and live there. . . . Her old enthusiasms, work, plans, friends—everything was covering itself with dust-sheets.

I felt this. Yet a day came now and then when her world seemed to be opening up again and I could say to myself, You see, you've been imagining things.

But next day, it would be shrinking fast. And I'd walk around saying to myself, *Think of something to do!* But I didn't know what to do—except keep going over. So I went every day, talked with her, shoved boxes around, made her drink coffee with me even when she did not want it, hoping the coffee would cut down those furtive persisting trips to her room. For now she no longer openly poured herself a drink while I was there; instead she slid into her room, stayed a few minutes, slid out again, making like she had never left me. I had the feeling she was fooling somebody—but who?

A week went by. Perhaps more than a week. I'm not sure. The piles of things spread from chair to chair to chair to chair. Every room was disarranged, except Andy's. That door was closed. But things were piled up, pulled down, stacked in new disarray everywhere else. Yet nothing got packed. More things were taken off coat hangers and laid across tables, more things heaped up on the rugs. I would wonder if Mark saw what I saw. If he did, why on earth didn't he *do something!*

One day I said, "Sit down and rest. We'll have some coffee. Then I am going to put on a record. Stravinsky? The symphony, maybe? No? A Beethoven quartet? *Fifteenth,* maybe? Let's try it." I could hear my voice wheedling and I was ashamed but I was desperate, too. But when I came in with the coffee, she was pulling at another box. She said, "Help me, won't you Dave, with this?" And I helped her, of course. Glad she could still ask me to do things. Shaken to my roots. Irritated, too. I felt, You can do better than this; after all, other people have lost, too, some have lost everybody in the world they cared for and everything and yet they go on. You can't do this.

But if you love a woman, you don't say it; and I loved her.

Another day, when I walked in, I saw a dozen white cups piled up on her desk. They had not been there the day before. And all the cabinet doors in the kitchen were open. But the big carton was still empty. No. There was a brush in it. One hairbrush. One clear plastic hairbrush. That did it: I began to know we were under a spell: I began to understand that there was someone involved in this, a Grace I knew but not well enough to speak to, and she was outwitting my Grace. Everything Grace wanted to do the Other One kept her from doing. Outsmarted her. It wasn't clean-cut; it never is; but that day it seemed so; that day, the Other One cast a young shadow. I said sharply, not knowing which Grace would hear me, "Come, let's fill up a box or two; let's leave the breakable things for the packers but how about all this? hmmh? let's fill up a few boxes. The place is a mess, don't you think? let's begin somewhere."

But somehow we didn't. We began, yes. Then Grace said (or that Other One said), "Dave—would you mind helping me here?" And I helped her lift another box. I suppose it was a box—heavens only knows what it was I was actually helping her with. Then she sat down on the floor and the routine began. She went through it, thing by thing by thing. Slow slow slow. Laying each thing on the rug. I lit a cigarette, stood there and watched her. Then suddenly she was on her feet. She started toward her room, came back, angrily threw all of the things in the box and left the room. *Angrily* is the word, I think. But I noticed that in her anger she moved freely.

And then, one day—in my memory I seem always to have stood there, smoking, and helplessly watching her as she knelt beside a box or drawer—she was taking things out: thing by thing by thing in that slow way. She seemed different. She did not move stiffly. She moved with ease and certainty. She seemed more the old Grace. Her eyes were big and soft, the gray flecked with yellow lights—all of us who know her have seen her eyes like this, at times. Face thin and tired and too gentle. Her shaggy soft thick hair holding its place against her head. I watched her body bend, unbend as she took something out, laid it on the rug. This day, I was fighting my fear the bad way, trying to extricate her from her trap by pretending there was no trap. I was thinking of her, not of the trouble she was in. I loved her. I knew it that day. I had known it a long time, but I dared not measure it or think it in words. All the words I had now were, Doesn't Mark care? doesn't he care enough to see how she needs him? Why does he stay at that lab all day and half the night? doesn't he care?

She stopped. She began to rub the fingers of her left hand, the way she does. She seemed to be listening; she seemed to be looking at something I could not see. Then she picked up those things and hurled them into that box.

Had she screamed, it could not have been more plain. She was begging for help. I knew . . . yes, at least I knew that much. I knew the more you need the help, the less you can ask for it in language others speak. You fall back on your private language, you live in code, begging them to decode the message, praying to God they won't be able to.

I knew because I had done it. After the leg trouble I hadn't talked for a month, except to say yes and no. But I had my sign language: I broke things, misplaced things, twisted and ruined things. I could not curse and blaspheme because I was a priest but my muscles and tendons and bloodstream cursed and blasphemed for me. I would have wrecked the whole world had I been able to get at it. But I was flat on my back on that hospital bed. And all I could do was lie there and let my hands furiously destroy for me. I did not say an unpleasant word. No. I couldn't. You've got to be pretty cheerful to use words; there's got to be something to hold them together, something firm inside you; when you're hopeless, scared, words just fall everywhere and are lost. All I could think of, that time long ago, was the leg: I wanted it back; I wanted only it; I must have it; without it, the rest of me was nothing, nothing. A blank . . . no image— For a moment the old terror sloshed over me, the pain, the hopelessness. Then it subsided. The hospital ward slid into that dim place where it stays, with the broken plane and the tangled parachute and the war and the rest of it. And now: I was back with Grace; I was hearing her language. I did not know what to do—but I knew I would not prod her any more. Give her time. Nobody can help you jump that chasm: you do it yourself or you don't. They can help you find a narrow place, maybe, to make your jump; that's about all; or now and then, they can help you want to. I tried to believe this.

But I was scared. For her. For Mark. For me. She was so still. After those sharp quick movements, she sat so still. There seemed a vast space between her and me. I felt no matter how many steps I took I could not reach her. She was listening to a long-drawn-out colloquy . . . it might never end, for it was as if all the clocks had stopped in her mind.

She needed Mark. But I knew now he could not come. Those cells: that minute complex whirling universe you cannot see except under powerful lens had stretched wide and enclosed him; he was inside it, safe and secure as long as he stayed there, watching his viruses, analyzing them, untwisting nucleic acids, counting, measuring . . . and he would stay.

I stood up. Grace stood, too.

And because I loved this girl and wanted desperately to help her I took her in my arms. She clung to me the way a kitten does and I had to extricate her from me. I patted her shoulder and pulled her black hair back of her ears as if she were my kid sister, and said, I must go now. Her eyes were blazing. Not with one feeling but two three four five feelings that embraced and fought and pushed and implored— There are no words for what I saw in her eyes. I said once more, I must go now; I'll drop in again this afternoon.

But I did not go. I took her in my arms and kissed her on the mouth, again and again, and I knew she wanted me to, and I knew I had to. For months, years, this moment had been moving steadily toward us.

I held her a long time. Then I let her go and turned and left her. I was trembling as I walked across the street: there were tensities of feeling in me that I dared not label.

29

I walked in my study, sat down at the desk. Don't know what I thought. Nothing probably. What had happened had washed away my mind.

I loved her. I had loved her a long time. But I had never permitted—its shadow, yes; the half-knowledge, yes; now and then; for a moment; sometimes, when I had kissed her on the forehead, as a brother sort of, as her husband's friend, I had cheated, yes; it had meant more than I pretended; but even so, I was aware of the barriers and I had not crossed them in my conscious mind. What I did in that dark part of the mind where we play the tricks on ourselves I don't pretend to know. Now she wanted me. . . . I sat there swept by feeling; all kinds of chemical changes were taking place inside me; and in one sense, I suppose I was completely at their mercy. I don't know much about those things. All I knew was that I felt free . . . released . . . sure . . . triumphant . . . strong—

And then—

I saw his face—eyes—white gown—hands: fragments blown off him. I could not see Mark, my friend. I could not see or feel him as a man, could not respond to him. Just saw, felt fragments blown off him. But it was enough. Mark: I had loved him, too; my feeling for him had been deeper, or I had always thought so, than what I felt for her; my relationship with him had sunk a shaft a long way down in me and in a curious sense it had been a protection from the other, the feeling for her. I was not sure how he felt; you're never sure what Mark is feeling, you are not sure he knows his own feeling; but I had felt this way about him and I had tried to stand by when he needed me, not with too much skill or sense, maybe, but I had tried—

His hand lay on my mind: strong, long skillful fingers rubbing the side of that slide file in his office, then I saw the hand turning a pencil round and round, then I saw it lifting out a mouse, examining it, taking a smear or something, then I saw it writing words down, then I saw it putting a record on the hi-fi, then I saw it holding a dead cigarette, then I saw it trembling as he told me about Andy. —God!

I had broken apart inside: love for him love for her slashed at me canceling each other out— Slowly I became angry. I began to think: this thing, this thing happening to us: Mark had asked me to go see her; as often as you can, he'd said, and I had done it as much for him as for her; but didn't he know that something—this: this day after day watching her loneliness, watching her mind staring at the snow looking for tracks . . . watching it go on that pitiful search, again and again and again— watching it become that boy—and not daring to mention it; day after day feeling powerless to help, knowing she was drifting dangerously near the edge of—it couldn't go on as it was—how did he expect—never seeing her—coming in late at night, leaving early in the morning to go back to those cells, those mice, all that nucleic acid stuff whatever it is, virus, all that, peering through that microscope at—why doesn't he turn that 'scope on his own life a little, look at what is happening in her heart and mind—whatever is about to happen is his fault, his. All right— I'm to blame too—but he shares it—he pushed us into—not intentionally but . . . maybe he wants it this way . . . not consciously . . . nobody seems to want consciously what he goes after or lets happen—but maybe . . . I know this: she has not been loved for a long time, her body is . . . I felt this—when I held her in my arms I knew it—he has not—maybe he is unable to—maybe we've looked at the thing superficially: it may be—it is possible that something has made it impossible for him . . . maybe she was right that time . . . going to the airport she said things may have broken up in him—you can be too reasonable, too— That store. What happened in that dark place? what? do we know? does anybody? even he doesn't know—he said he was not there then he said he was there then he said he did not touch her he said nothing happened but EVERYTHING HAPPENED— can't he see?

His eyes: their quiet clarity when he talks about the people he cares for; their glow when he talks about his work, his research, what he is looking for in that cell. . . . They exonerated him completely and I could not endure the memory of them. I began to get cagey with myself: I said, She is like a sister to me; suppose Meg were in trouble, wouldn't I want someone to be concerned? I have been concerned, that's all; deeply concerned about her since the night she came home; she is lost, she has no defense against what she feels, sees inside her, somebody has to help her—that is all I wanted to do—don't keep lying: all I wanted to do until I felt her lips, body—don't keep lying: you've loved her for years and you've wanted her; you feel exactly as any man would feel who had loved a woman a long time but had been chained away from her by—and then found one day that she wanted him and needed him and had snapped the chain in two— Yes. That is the truth. But— I am not just any man, I am— I made a wrenching effort to get on my vestments: *I am a priest; not just a man; a priest.* I have made certain grave commitments and renunciations. Yes. I know the full meaning of this. Yes yes yes. I do know—but I am a man, too, I have needs I have a right to— No. No. Not this. . . . Mark—you would do this to him? this? not this no no it will end here tomorrow we will be ourselves again; it happened—we couldn't help—but tomorrow we'll—we know better, yes; we are not irresponsible insensitive we know we both know we have obligations—my parish, he needs her—we both love him—would not hurt him—

I sat there shaken. Sick. I tried to pray. I could not pray but I tried; it was like climbing up a slick wall but I tried and I felt an echo of penitence, a faint—

But *she* needs someone too . . . wasn't she hurt as much as

he? or more? much more . . . of course she was—and none of
it her fault— He went in the store; she didn't, I didn't, he did.
He was there. Why did he ask me to do what he should have
been doing? didn't he know what would happen? he isn't naive
he knows of course he knows I'm a man, too; surely—maybe he
doesn't, maybe not maybe not maybe not . . . you are his
eunuch-friend, safe to leave her with me oh sure sure sure you
lose a leg and put on the vestments of a priest and that makes
you safe that makes you— Pity for myself crawled over me like
a horde of ants. I sat there letting it sting me crazy.

The phone rang. I answered it. Don't know who it was or
what I said.

All right: suppose you go back—she wants you to, you know
that. All right. Suppose you go back . . . what can come of it?
what? what? think of next week, next year, your commitment to
the Church, the work you love and believe in what can come of it
all? what? what? what? what?

The phone rang. I answered it.

I want her. And she wants me. She hasn't wanted anything for
so long and now she wants me. What else matters? I have a
right to something, haven't I? A little something, haven't I? Mark
. . . why think of him—is he thinking of her? is he? but—you
are thinking of her—yes yes—

And so: I sat in my study, tearing off shred after shred of my image
of myself, putting what I could back on, tearing it off again until
there was no image left. I was like a beetle who tears up another beetle—or that insect, whatever it is, that eats itself: something in me ate off my conscience, honor, my feeling for my
Church, common sense, and then it ate off my love for Mark
and then—I am beginning to see it now—it ate off my love for
her, too, and all that was left was a nub of a clamorous somebody at the center of me with whom I had never come to terms
and whom I actually knew little about.

This is hindsight. This is what I think after two years of tortured thinking. Then: I felt words racing through my mind
making brief sense canceling out words that had a moment be-

fore raced through making brief sense, too, each blowing the other around and around—

Suddenly I was quiet. I felt I had made a decision: I won't go over for two days, I told myself. By then, everything will be better. We'll both be in control of the situation, and ourselves. Now I can get back to work. It is high time. These two days I'll try to catch up on things; that sermon: where did I put it? in the drawer maybe where are those notes what was it I was going to say where did I put that piece of paper I jotted down something it was good I said it quite well extremely well where did it get to. . . .

I thought the storm was over. But I had, of course, just slipped into the eye of the hurricane.

Wind shifted:

All my life everything I've wanted cared for has slipped by me . . . this time I'm going to hold on . . . I won't let go. . . .

Wind shifted:

You cannot do it to Mark . . . you cannot do it to Mark . . . you can never live outside the Church you can never—

Four hours later, I went back. Like a sleepwalker I went across that street and opened the door and took that woman in my arms—

How easy it would be to lie. At this moment, the truth is not close: here but not here; a rope, swung down to a man who is at the bottom of a steep drop: it swings toward me, I reach for it—or do I? it swings away.

Perhaps only an old man tall with wisdom could grasp it. I don't know. Perhaps only an old man would want or could afford the truth. Someone who had pared his vanity down to the bone; and his shame; who had ground the agony smooth between conscience and heart and mind year after year after interminable year. Then, finally, he might see it: might look at it and its consequences as one, lying there motionless in the bottomless pool of his years, might look at it quietly—

But I am not that Old Man. An edge of my mind feels his

presence in me, of course; but only a thin edge feels it and only now and then. That Old Man . . . I've thought of him many times, lately; he may turn out to be a witless mumbling old fool; quite probably; how many old men are wise? but he has, nevertheless, a fabulous gift: he can, if he wants to, look back at my future; while I can only stare at the blind curve around which it may or may not come. If I could see what he can see: if I could put distance between that afternoon and me. . . .

Were he to tell what he knows, that Old Man I shall someday become, I wonder if he might say it like this: *You understand, don't you* (would he say?) *that it is not Mark's friend who is walking across that street, nor the priest of All Saints, nor is it the brother figure who has tried day after day to ease her trouble. No. Nor is it the man who knows he loves but has quietly renounced what he acknowledges is not his. No. None of these fine chaps you like to think of as You is walking toward that house. Nor is it the lover you feel yourself capable of becoming. No. It is the loser: the one you keep hidden away because you have never come to terms with him: the one who thinks he has lost and lost and lost: he'd tell you about losing his little playmate long ago, he wouldn't say it but he thinks his real childhood was stuffed away somewhere, maybe in that blue bowl—crazy? yes but things are, sometimes—and only its ghost was left playing tennis, football, swimming—winning those cups on his mother's sideboard; and then his girl—well, never mind: no need to name the losses; they exist all right; and the big gaping holes exist, too, and he is going to try to fill them: He thinks, This time he'll take; he's through losing, see? he's going to take. You could call him a compulsive thief, a starving greedy—*

I don't know. There are times, there are cruel moments when I see it this way. But not always. For my conscience is not inclined to lash me, to give me more than a tap or two, and my disposition is pretty easygoing—I always look around for a spot of sun somewhere when things turn chilly— I'd say this: Maybe that sleepwalker was something of a mixed-up confused sixteen-year-old somebody who had never grown up, say, who went across the street and took that woman in his arms and kissed her and pushed her with immense shyness and urgent rudeness into her bedroom. And maybe the woman knew it . . . and gave to that boy exactly what the man in him had to have and what she, too, had to have.

I'd like to settle for that. It is a view of myself I could live with; embarrassing, foolish, crazy but something a part of me could feel sympathetic toward, could incorporate—

But it would be only a shred of the truth. No more. For there was that hour: and it is that hour I keep twisting and turning, twisting and turning, seeing a sliver of it now and then, but not all of it, not yet understanding; a little, yes; but not— I see it this way, sometimes: it was as if we had been lost a long time in a blazing desert and in a kind of exhausted madness were demanding that each drink from a dry cup offered by the other—

No. I did the demanding; not she. I offered the empty cup—

After writing that sentence I laid away my papers. I could not put down another word.

I got in the car and drove out to the lake. There is a finger of wooded land that lies far out in the water. I knew no one would be there on so cold a night. I drove my car to the point. Walked along the edge of the water. It was a large night: clear, quiet, easy to see a million light-years away; easy to feel the earth's smallness, to know it as a shifty speck in the universe and at the same time to know it as something that holds an awesome importance for the universe; to think of one's self as too small for the human vocabulary to name and at the same time too vast a creation for a mind ever to encompass. Standing there, close to the water's edge, looking at that sky, it was easy to want to take flight into space and escape by swift dissolution into whirling planets and nebulae and burning stars and cold stars that died long ago . . . never to come back to this small earth, this small implacable Windsor Hills, this small haunted house across the street and the woman waiting there, even now, in my memory—

A jet plane went over: there was a dull trembling in the ears as it tore through the night. Now I was looking at the thin rim of sand. A log lay half in the water. The current sucked against it: There was a sigh. That was all. Again, it sucked against it, a sigh, then the world was still. The water was dark but somehow the luminous sky gave it a skin of light and you felt the light go deepdown in the water even though you could not see.

I thought of her: her stillness. I have never known a woman who could be so still and so alive: a body so compliant and so full of reservations. No. She had demanded nothing of me that afternoon. I did the demanding, I was the one who tried in my panic to take; but she gave nothing. So much compliance . . . and she gave nothing. And I had thought, It is because I am crippled; oh sure she is repelled even she even she cannot accept me as a real man she—

And then it came: the terror. Sweeping through me: fear, fury, panic, greed, lust— I don't know the names of the feelings, energies that drove me on on on on— And I don't want to know— All I know is I was caught up, driven by them and I began to compel her, to force, to lay my weight and strength. . . . I felt the bone in her shoulder give a little, I knew I was hurting her, crushing her but I kept on I kept on . . . I wanted to hurt she had to had to—and she gave me nothing—so compliant a body and she gave nothing nothing nothing and suddenly I was overcome by despair and shame. I—

I saw the log in the edge of the water. Heard the sigh as the current sucked past it. Kept looking at that log until it absorbed my awareness.

I had stopped remembering that afternoon. I could not claim that hour. Not yet.

Just stared at the log, the water, the sky. Now I had begun to think with intent concentration of what lay beneath the water, the soft sludgy mud, wet, full of slow-moving life— I remembered how I had wanted when I was a kid to walk into a pond or lake and keep walking keep walking until the water reached my waist until it reached my neck keep walking until it had covered my head keep walking on the bottom of it until I had seen all that—

I was once more remembering: the room: it seemed dark but
it could not have been dark in mid-afternoon but it seemed dark
—even now, as I write it down, I see it as a dark room. I was overcome, yes; and could not keep on— I turned to stone and lay
there and she was so still and all I was aware of was the pounding: two hearts pounding in a dark dimensionless world . . .
separated only by a thin band of rib and muscle and soft flesh
and yet as far apart as heaven and hell—and I could not bear the
sound; I turned away and buried my face in the pillow and nothing moved all was still until I heard someone sobbing and I
thought she's crying but I can't do anything about it she'll just
have to—she'll just have to—and then I knew with a shock that
it was me crying, those heavy dry gasps were coming out of my
throat and lungs and I could not do anything about that either it
was as if it would never stop I felt stripped of every control,
lost, disintegrating—

And then it happened. A voice said, Dave. . . .

The strangulating sounds continued—as if a machine made
them.

"Dave . . . I love you."

Like the voice of God. I was stunned. She said it again,
quietly, "Dave, I love you."

That was all. There was nothing more for a long time. Then
she said, "I want you to love me, too. I need you." She laid her
hand lightly on the side of my head, felt around until she found
my face, touched my eyelid, forehead, let her hand rest on my
hair. Even now, I feel the feather lightness of it, lying there.

After a long time, the voice said, "There is nothing to be
afraid of—if you love me." *if you love me*— The words were
soft, I was not sure I was hearing them, but they held a solid
weight and authority that seemed to come out of all the universe
has ever learned about itself.

I could not answer. I didn't love her. I didn't feel a thing.
Once I had loved her, a million years ago, but—something had
happened, something had— I didn't know what. I didn't know
anything so I didn't answer. I lay there mute and empty. And

she did not say more, just left her hand on my head. But I felt her filling the room . . . the whole world . . . and then, slowly slowly I felt her seeping into me into my loins my arms and muscles and—this is where words cannot say it—and finally I mumbled something, I put my hand on her face, hair, breast . . . clumsily I guess, but I tried to touch her gently, tried to tell her I loved her, too. I don't know what I said or did but she turned and was suddenly looking down in my eyes and I felt her all of her and her eyes were smiling and she laughed, she kissed me and then—well, we both laughed; we have always been able to laugh together at the ridiculous, the absurd, the sad grotesque things and so we laughed, we were hurting but we could laugh; and she kissed me again and I kissed her and then she put her breast on my mouth and then slowly slowly this woman who had years ago given me back my confidence as a person, gave me not what I had lost—how could she? or anyone?—but something I had never had and never known; and somewhere along the way she freed me from anger and guilt and the terror and when she did my love for her swept through me and into her binding us— How? I don't know. I may find out someday but now I don't know; all I know is the astounding truth that she loved me and her love did this.

Everything in the sky had tilted a little. It was late. I was numb with cold. I went to the car to go home but instead, just sat there. Lit a cigarette and sat there. Not wanting to give up this moment. Remembering her. She was so full of unexpected ways . . . some I had guessed, some I knew nothing about. She may have thought me awkward and clumsy, I don't know. All I know is her body was sweet and good and yielding and her mind and heart were sweet and good and she loved me: and I loved her.

Afterward, we talked. She had not talked since Andy's death. Now she talked. Not of that. Not of the present. Not of these six weeks. Not of her grown-up years. But of a strange mythic land she called her childhood, of ogres and kings and queens, the Bad Ones and the Good Ones who walk that land shrinking the

children they come near or causing them suddenly to grow too
tall— And I talked too. Not much. It is incredible what one
chooses to tell. I remember I told her how I had hated ginger-
bread when I was a kid and we had it every Wednesday and she
told me how she had feared an old dowdy neighbor who
caught her and two little friends playing doctor. Other things,
too; but this is all I remember.

I do not pretend to know why this swift journey was made back
to those musty memories. I suppose we could not deal with the
present, we dared not tangle with the months that had led up
to the present—so we skipped, we did a full regression and
landed in childish experiences which we could accept with ease.

After a time we hushed. I think we slept. And then, abruptly,
I awoke with a sense of cold certainty that she was lying dead
beside me and I had killed her; in my panic and madness I had
crushed the life out of her and all the other was the dream but the
dead body beside me was the reality. I was shaking with dread.
I dared not look at her lying there so quietly. And for a long
minute that even now can stretch into years I did not look. But
finally I turned and saw the faint rise and fall of her breathing.
Shadows were blue under her eyes and on her shoulder was a
red-black blotch where I had bruised her but her face was relaxed and curiously young. And then she eased, turning slightly,
and a little gas from her belly oozed out like a sigh; she was
alive, earthy, real—

I lay there trembling. I had come close to the edge of total
annihilation of all I cared for, believed in, loved, valued— I
wanted to wake her. I wanted her once more to lift the iron
weight off me as she had done, to free me from it as she had done,
and I reached out to touch her to say her name and then I saw
a smile on her mouth: she was dreaming a good dream . . . she
was no longer walking the snow in her sleep, she was dreaming a
good dream; and I lay there trying not to move. Praying for the
dream to continue. Praying God to rest this girl, a little. She
turned again, settled down in the bed, slipped to another level of
unconsciousness, breathing steadily, immersed now. I lay there

a long time, looking at her; then, when I saw how deep was her sleep, I got up, slipped out, left a note in the living room saying, *I did not want to disturb you,* and went back across the street to my study.

Then what? I don't know. I don't remember much about that evening. There must have been things to do, there always are, and I suppose I did them. Walked through them, anyway. But I don't find it easy to reconstruct that evening. I have tried. I can't get it back: there is too much now between me and it— and it doesn't matter.

It is that hour with her I need to understand. I keep thinking about it, keep trying to turn it around, to see it as it was then, as it has become now, turning it—

As if one could. You can't solidify an experience into an object and turn it—but one tries. One tries to find something analogous to it in the external world, it is natural to want to tie it up with the senses in order to be sure it happened at all, to find an image, two three four and say, It is like this, it is like that—

The old mountain up at Jane's place, thrusting its peak high above but close to the ridge where her cabin lies hidden in rhododendron tall as trees: In the morning as the sun comes up, that mountain is full of pockets of darkness, there is depth, there are levels on levels of depth, hidden planes, strata shelving strata crushing piling up smoothing out every million years or so, or hundred million, maybe; you think this once, twice, then you forget: your eye plunges into those bottomless caves of shadow, you stumble around in them, you think of small panting creatures living down there which you never see never hear only find a track of now and then— Two hours later, the mountain has lost its fathomless depth: it is thin glittering surface reflecting light like a million pieces of glass and one sees nothing but surface, nothing but light— And then, again, the rain comes: the peak is covered with clouds the whole mountain is swirling steaming twisting cloud, revealing a ghost of a tree, two three four trees maybe, for a moment, then hiding, then revealing, then slowly smoothing out to blank grayness— And you could say, if you came upon it for the first time, *There is no mountain here.*

The hour is like that: there is no hour for days at a time. For weeks it is blanked out. Then suddenly it opens up—

I sat in the car on that night at the lake losing it, finding it, feeling the terror as I felt myself forcing my brute strength on her, as I felt myself pushing her flesh and bone as if it were a *thing,* in my desperate attempt to wrest from her all I had missed hungered for longed for— Yes, that is it. I was determined to take what I wanted, to force it out of her—to force into her my fears and frustrations and loneliness: and take from her —to rape— That word had hung on a wall of my mind a long time. I had tried not to look. But I could no longer escape it. And now, I had a quick awful vision, insight I guess it was: It seemed to me that all Renie had dreamed, and S.K., and Dewey Snyder, all they and Nella and Miss Hortense and the rest of them had made up had broken through from my own depths and become a real thing: I was the criminal they had created in their collective fantasy. Not Mark, but *me.* I had acted it out for them: what they desired, dreamed, feared and dared not do. Sweat poured from my armpits. I saw this, knew it was possible, felt the truth of it but I shut it away quick. In Biblical times, in the Middle Ages, I could have said, A vision appeared and an Angel of the Lord came unto me— What I did say was, That is quite a theory, you must have read it somewhere; sounds a bit Jungian and mixed up; forget it. Anyway, I told myself, you didn't—kill her. You stopped. Yes, I stopped—or something stopped me. In time. In time. What was it? A man needs to know what pulls him back from the verge— Was it the mercy of God? was it my love for her which I had felt so long? did it prove itself stronger than fear, hate, lust—did it? did I hate her? him? or only myself? is it all the gentle good compassionate things in your life that coalesce into an iron hand and pull you back from that final act? is it? is it your love of God? what is it?

And now—things moved deep within me, rearranged themselves, and I was feeling only my love for her: only that. I knew my love was real and good. I had cared what happened to her. I knew this. I loved this girl and she had loved me, at least for a few days—and I knew this love was the most profound experience of my life, the most disturbing and the best. This, that I still call wrong and the world calls wrong for a priest, was right for me and her. I knew this. And then, as if she had returned to me, I felt her presence: I was feeling her that second time I had turned to her, and the other times, the next day and the next—her low laugh when . . . always that low laugh . . . sensuously feeling her, responding with glands heart mind, remembering the good hard pressure of body on body, the warm deep interlocking of rhythms, the tearing ecstasy, the slow ebbing, the quiet emptiness . . . remembering . . . her playful soft teasing, the tender relinquishment, the little push she always gives that says, Go away now . . . losing everything for a time, unable to think— Then, as suddenly, I felt her compassion: the miracle of it as it had wrapped around me and lifted me out of the horror of myself, redeeming the dark violence in me, the evil surging through me, the blind blind anger, transmuting it and me. *Redemption.* What do I know of it? what does it mean? this word: so bitter, humbling, transfiguring, holding within it the most difficult chapter in man's biography. I wonder how long a time passed before man learned how to accept forgiveness, how long before he learned to forgive. How long it will be before he learns that he cannot take by violence what can only be given freely. I have used those words so glibly. They have been on my tongue too much, until the meaning has been licked out of them by me and others like me who call ourselves men of God—and also by those who have listened to us. How we tossed them around in our discussions at the seminary: talking in fine theological terms about redemption, quoting this thinker and that; oh yes, we mastered it intellectually, we could quote the philosophers, we could quote the saints, we could quote the Scriptures, we could intone *I know that my Redeemer liveth*—ah, but do we ever? quite know? do we ever quite understand the alchemy, the spiritual chemistry, the ontogeny of forgiveness? There have been a few times when I have known it as a child knows it; and times when I have felt it dimly as one feels symbolic truth, as one feels the familiar contour of an ancient myth one has never heard before. But to make it one's own:

I don't know, I am not sure—how could I be? but it seems to me now, that one has to live it through the hard way, on level after level—child to parent, parent to child, brother to sister, playmate to playmate, man to man, and finally on that most difficult and complex of human terms: of man to woman, woman to man. Perhaps it is so hard to understand forgiveness because it is so hard for man and woman to forgive each other for being unchangeably different in body . . . function . . . tempo . . . purpose—and for needing each other so desperately. It is bitterhard to love what one needs and can never quite have; bitterhard to accept the rude fact that what one needs most is what is most different from one's self and farthest away, and closest. Perhaps that is why it is so hard to love God . . . we need Him too much, we have to have Him in order for each of us to save his own soul and for the human race to save its humanity. And because it is so hard, man makes it easier by creating his God in the image of his own sex: that makes it simpler, somehow—and more terrible.

This is what I write down now, in a quieter, more relaxed mood; the mood I used to be in when Mark and I would bat our ideas back and forth. But out at the lake that cold still night, it was not God that I thought about, nor that poor image of Him which man has whittled out of his loneliness and despair. No. It was my love for her and her love for me. I was remembering the minutes of that hour and the days that followed which now have crept back into it as if they belong there—remembering with mind and body— Even now, my hands are full of memories —even now if all the rest of me were gone my hands would tell me—

From where I sat in the car I could see the thin edge of trees on the other side of this point of land. It was narrow here where it jutted out into the lake and the moon was rising and the bare branches were outlined black against its pale disk. There had been a full moon that other night, too; that first evening after I left her. Yes, I remember now: a few slivers of memory are drifting back into my mind: I had gone outside: had stood a long time looking across at the house, knowing she was there, alone; wanting to go to her; knowing she was alone for he was at the lab, he stayed every night until midnight there was no reason to think he had come home; but knowing I must not go; seeing her in my mind walking around those rooms, maybe packing a little; maybe not; maybe she had come out of her deep sleep feeling rested and was now sitting there quietly thinking about what had happened; what she thought would not be what I thought, I knew that; what she had felt was not what I had felt—it couldn't be—for even in our deepest fusion two strangers lay in us watching each other, cold and unwilling to come closer—I knew. But I wondered what she thought, her thinking was important to me, will always be; I wanted her desperately, not simply her body but *her,* her thoughts, feelings, dreams, to come close to mine— I got up. I would go over again and take her in my arms; gently—I'd never let her feel the violence in me again never never— I knew I must not go. But I could no longer stay in that study. So I walked a mile or two down Arlington Road, past the quiet homes of my parishioners —and all I was aware of was that she loved me and I loved her and nothing else mattered.

The other—the conflict—I don't think I felt it again that first night, nor the next day nor the next. It came back later. And then, for a time, I felt nothing but the broken things: feelings shattered by conscience, conscience shattered by feelings, relationships tearing each other up— My mind was subjected to a saturation bombing from all sides of my nature. But it was later —after Charlie's death, yes, that all of it came together and began to pound me. I'd see it this way, I'd see it that way, I'd push it off and see, feel nothing. Sometimes it would appear as a relentless chain reaction of sin. I'd tell myself: One afternoon between five and six a little girl named Susan went skating and a scientist named Mark went to Matthews for some Cokes and they met on a strange journey in an ancient dark place; and Renie, like an evil soothsayer, took a festered desire out of her own heart and changed it into the first lie and let it loose and it found its mate in other minds, more and more minds, in all our minds— and a monster came forth from lies that had lain too close together and began to roam our community and our hearts— Was that it? No. That is easy to say but it is only half the truth, a splinter of the truth. Then what? what? And then I'd hear, *You have never acknowledged your capacity to sin—*

Sin. I had always heard in that word a morbid sound. This is the truth. It is not easy to acknowledge it. But sin was a word not used in my family—Mother saw everything in terms of sportsmanship and the game—Dad saw it in terms of law— how do I know this? I know nothing nothing about him— At church? of course . . . but somehow the litany was poetry it was remote it was like music— I had heard much about sin at the seminary, yes. Theoretically. But I don't believe I had ever consciously felt guilty of sin until that hour. Not guilty of the big sins we all commit either in deed or in fantasy; no; I had felt myself just a little above sin; guilty of mistakes, of course; hundreds of them and some pretty mean ones. I had weaknesses, plenty of them, and knew it; I was always too easygoing, always tended to take the nearest path out of a tangled mess as I did in that television affair with Dewey Snyder; I have done a lot of things for the sake of expediency, been guilty of gross stupidities, lack of awareness— And worried about them. But I suspect I had actually lived most of my life as complacently as a Pharisee—and am afraid I still do. The big sins, the tragic choice, the black bottomless evil that lurks in every one of us were always the Sins of the Others: when I looked down into the dark pool of human error, stared deep into it, the face I saw staring back at me I had never recognized as my own, no; it was always the stranger I saw there: the Other One. Until that hour—

A good guy—I thought the phrase, suddenly. People had always called me "a good guy." Ever since I could remember. I rather liked it and wore it, I'm afraid, like a rubber shield against the unchangeable lethal facts of the human condition. It was seductive—I suppose it might be to a lot of Americans: to be a priest and still be a good guy: that seemed on the plus side of things. But they had begun it long before I was grown: *Dave . . . he's a good guy*, they'd say at high school; they'd say on the football squad in college, *He's not morbid like most of those fellows going into the Church, he's OK, he's a good guy;* and they said it in the Air Force, *Go on over to the chaplain's quarters and spill it to him, he's a good guy, he's no piss-and-vinegar preacher, you can tell him anything he won't cut you down to size, he's OK*—and I'd laugh at the crazy idiots when it was repeated to me but secretly I sort of liked it. I did try to play straight with them. I thought I had—but now. . . . I don't know.

Funny—I try to think something through: and all I do is remember things and some of them don't seem to connect up too well, either. When Mark thinks, he takes his facts, scrutinizes them, throws out the phony ones, puts them in squads and marches them around and around in his mind until the weak ones fall out and the others come together in some kind of logical pattern that makes sense to him. While I sit here remembering—and call it thinking. Well, anyway:

There was a rummy little guy in our squadron, in the war, about as big as a tick; he was always upsetting somebody or something in his outfit, incessantly bragging about the time he fought some big stiff somewhere or how he plumb exhausted the last whore he was with, or telling in total recall how he had tricked a certain bitch somewhere—his language was vile and his body and heart seemed to match his words: a dirty little —— the others called him, and I must confess it was difficult to see him any other way. Then, one day, his plane—he was a gunner—cracked up as it came in, just as it touched ground, and he was burned badly, he was going to die and they sent for me. There he was: wrapped like a mummy where they could bandage him, most of him was too bad to bandage, and I went over to his bed and sat down by him with that sick-terrible-awed-praying-God-to-stay-near-and-help-us feeling. He turned when I spoke to him; he couldn't see but he could hear—he *tried* to turn, I should say, because he couldn't move—and he was crying and I thought, He's trying to say something, he wants to ask you to do something; so I kept saying, I'm listening I'm right here by you, tell me if you can. I'd identify myself now and then by saying, I'm Dave Landrum the chaplain. But he just lay there whimpering, it was that kind of crying. I tried again: I said, Your mother? you want me to write her? I'll write her, sure I will; I'll tell her just what you want me to. And then he managed it: he said, Naw, bud—all—wan—is—nice lil virg—no fun like lay'n nice lil virg —never got—chance—want—never got—didn't get—all want was—didn't get it— All the time crying, saying it, crying, saying it, kept saying it—

And I nodded at him; he couldn't see but I nodded, I said, I'm mighty sorry, I sure am sorry. And I was: sorry he didn't get what he wanted out of his brief life. Oh it was a cesspool I was looking in, all right, but a piece of every one of us was floating around in it, a dirty smelly little echo of that old anguished cry of man: *I didn't get it . . . what I wanted . . .*

A nurse was standing by his cot. She had a hypo, she was looking for a place to stick it in, one spot the flames had missed; and I helped her. She was cold and steady—I remember how blistered dry her eyes were as if burned by an intense light which she had looked at too long. We found a spot and she stuck the needle in but it wasn't needed, he was dead in a minute or two. She drew in a deep breath, stood there, holding the empty syringe. And I stood there, hearing that terrible echo. Finally, she said, "Aren't you going to say a prayer?" I felt her sarcasm, I didn't look at her, I knew there was some kind of twisted smile on her mind or her face, but it brought me back to my role, my duty, and I said a prayer and I hoped God heard. And she stood there and listened. Then she said, "He just wanted a chance to deflower a nice little virgin . . . that's all. Couldn't think of anything else in the whole world he wanted . . . the dirty, filthy—" her shining teeth were pressed hard together, "and you told him you were sorry."

"I am."

"Yes." And then she said it, too: "You're a good guy, you would be."

This time, I reacted. I wished she hadn't said it. A good guy wasn't enough and this time I knew it.

Before I could speak, she said, "Maybe I'm sorry, too. At least he knew he'd missed something. A lot of folks never catch on they've missed a thing."

Now she was talking without desire to communicate, I felt, almost as if under hypnosis. "When things get rough, I have something I think about, too; just like him; everybody has something, I guess." She stopped.

"I'd like to hear it if you want to tell me."

"Well, I don't want to but it looks like I'm going to." She was staring at what was left lying on that cot. "It's a memory I have. When I was a kid I used to tote a dirty little sock around; slept with it. Now I tote this around, and when things get rough, I concentrate on it. It's crazy." She stopped. Then she said, "It's a rainy day. I'm a little kid. My mother and father are edgy. She says something cruel and he says something cruel and she says something cruel and he says— And I listen. Then she turns to me and smiles real stiffly, her face doesn't have a thing in it, like a mask, it looks exactly as if a mask were painted on it, and she says, It's a nice rainy day—don't you want to make some fudge, dear? run in the kitchen and make you a nice big batch of candy. You'll like that, won't you?"

I can see that little girl holding on to her small rag of a memory hidden inside the grown-up nurse with the blistered eyes who stood, syringe in her hand, beside that wrapped-up mummy lying on the cot—beyond us, rows of other cots of wounded and sick, all of it full of sound, movement, smells, except around us: we are sucked into a vacuum somehow. Then she said, "I've got to see about him, find an orderly." She turned away. And I walked down the ward, stopping to speak to the men. Down at the other end a nurse I knew said I could help her if I would, and I did: she was rigging up the apparatus to give some plasma; I remember the softness and brightness of her as she did with quick efficiency what had to be done; and how the men's eyes followed her, drinking in her prettiness and her reassurance: she had seen everything the other nurse had seen in the war, she had somehow, by means of a miraculous spiritual metabolism, transmuted the horror into a warm merciful milk which she offered the hurt ones a drink of. And you felt she would always be able to do this. Drink it in remembrance—

It washes over you: the endless levels, the infinitude of human experience, the vacuum you are sucked into now and then, the spots where right and wrong seem irrelevant—not unimportant, they are never unimportant but at a certain spot just irrelevant; where pain and pleasure are irrelevant, too; where birth and death seem never to have existed, where there are no terminal points—

Next day came. And the next and the next and the next: no one else existed in my world; every relationship and commitment and obligation had slipped away; everything but this. I walked through my work, yes; I carried out my parish duties but it was an unreal world I worked in. A sleepwalker's world. We were surrounded and cut off by our amplified awareness of each other: voice, body, eyes, hair, hands, her words, my words, her memories, mine; what she believed and thought, what I believed and thought; her rhythms, mine; her tastes, mine; we had done what you cannot do: we had fused and become one and loneliness was gone. Was it love? I don't know. Obsession? I don't know. I don't know where the dim wavering line lies between *in love* and obsessional concern and pleasure. Love—every in-tense, intimate bond—is too delicately compounded of reason and irrationality, of the earthy rhythm and the nonexistent de-sign, of nerve endings and body heat and glands and pulse rate and the vague memory that seems to come out of the womb and the precise taste one writes down slowly in one's mind as the years go by: *she-he must be this and this and this*—it can be love, yes; but it can slip into something not love, not real—

She desperately needed what I gave her; and I needed what only she could give me. But what have I said when I say this? Only words that sound pompous and embarrassingly trite. We were collaborators in a dream; but so are murderers who carry through their orgastic crime; and creators who bring their play to the stage or their builded temple to the worshippers.

Even today, I don't know how to think about it: I know only how I felt and how she felt, and what her love did for me; I know only that I watched her strength coming back each day, knowing it would not have come without me; that she had found in me someone to whom she could give the love Andy no longer needed and Mark no longer seemed to want; but it was more than that—we loved each other because she was Grace and I was myself.

It might have gone on and on and on, I don't know. But on the fifth day, Charlie dropped in to the study to talk with me and afterward, I knew I must tell her, and I knew the telling would change everything.

Charlie said this: After choir practice, Billy had stayed behind. He came over to the organ console and asked Charlie a question about the stops; another question about the pedals. Then he got it out: Somebody named Gus Hestor had waited around, last Thursday, when the boys came out from choir practice and had called him and Jimmie off and told them he had a job for them.

—What kind of job? they asked him.

—Oh it didn't amount to anything much. Just something he wanted them to throw through a window.

—What was it?

—Oh, just a rock.

—Where did he want it throwed?

—Over there, through that big window.

—What big window?

—In that dirty scientist's house. Biggest window he'd ever seen. They'd seen it, hadn't they?

—Naw. Where was it?

—Around the corner from the church.

—No big window there; that's the Parish House.

—Dumb, huh? Across the street! Didn't they have eyes?

—What did he want to throw a rock for?

—They asked too many questions.

—But why?

—Well, there was something he wanted that scientist to read. On the paper.

—What paper?

—One the rock was wrapped in. It'd learn them a lesson all right; learn him and his wife people have to behave if they live in this city.

The choirboys told Gus they didn't want to.

Gus said he was organizing the Super Rockets, an affiliation of the Atom Smashers, and he'd see to it they got on the inside committee where they'd be running the outfit. He said he had two switchblades he didn't need, they could have them when they did the job.

They said they didn't want to.

—What you mean you don't want to! You sound like leaky pisspots—nobody but a dirty leaky pisspot would be caught singing in a church anyway and wearing skirts. Aint that something now!

They said they didn't wear no skirts, they wore cassocks.

He said it didn't matter if you call it a skirt or a nightgown whoever was inside it wasn't no man, men wear pants. Then he asked them if they was taking up for low-down folks who eat with niggers and dance with niggers?

They said they wasn't taking up for nobody, they just didn't want to break a window.

OK. He guessed what they wanted was to have their front teeth broke out, maybe that's what they wanted so they could sing on TV without no teeth.

He began to rough them up. There is a sycamore tree near the sidewalk and he pushed their heads against it and rubbed their faces into the bark—he was pushing pretty hard and might have completed the dental work had a police car not passed. It slowed down . . . Hestor slipped behind a clump of tall shrubs and into the driveway that led around the church and into the alley back of it.

The cops asked the boys what was wrong. They said nothing was wrong. Who was that guy talking to you? Oh, somebody—they didn't know exactly. Know his name? Don't think so. See him before? Guess so. Was he saying something he had no business saying to them? Naw! You're sure? They said they were sure; nothing was wrong.

The cops drove into Arlington Road and parked near the Parish House and the boys ran past them up Arlington to the shopping center to pick up their bus on the corner where the lights are bright and plenty of people around.

Billy had begun by asking Charlie what he thought about folks who broke windows in a house? when folks live in it?

Charlie laughed, looked at me, rubbed his chin. He said he told Billy he didn't believe he would break anybody's window whether folks were living there or not. After Billy had told him the rest of it, Charlie asked again who the man was and Billy said it was just somebody named Gus Hestor. "Have you heard of him, Dave?"

I told him I had heard the name but didn't know too much about the man except he was no good; a trouble maker. "Maybe a dangerous one, Charlie, I wouldn't tangle with him."

Then Charlie said he tried to find out what he looked like. Billy said he was just big, that's all he knew.

—Had he seen him before?

—Yeah, down in the Flats.

—Often?

—Guess so.

—What does he do?

—Oh he's just around.

Billy finally said he bossed one of the gangs down there, maybe two; he didn't know—he was just always around.

—Ever talked to him before?

—Oh sure.

—About breaking windows? or other things?

—Other things.

—You don't listen to him, do you, Bill?

—Naw!

As Charlie was saying this, I thought, When he finishes with it, I must tell him what Neel said. But I didn't. He was in a good state of mind; not thinking about his aches and pains and fears. He was deeply concerned about these choirboys. I didn't want him to get his mind on himself again—after all, I had no facts, only a warning and warnings were Charlie's trouble, had always been: warnings seeping up inside him, speaking a language he couldn't quite hear. No. I was not going to say something vague and ominous. His pattern of life was pretty simple: Work on the opera in his apartment half the day; organ practice and choir practice at the church; three or four hours a week at Paul Pottle's, sometimes just with Paul, sometimes with Katie and Sydney, talking about contemporary music, books, Japan, the theater. Now and then, he went to the Flats, as he had said, but how could he watch his step with a man he had never seen! I'll tell him more, sure; but not now; next time I see Neel, maybe I can get something explicit out of him about this Hestor—

I did say, "Keep out of his way, Charlie. He's no good. Likes to pick fights with people." Then I asked him how the third act was coming along. And when he finished telling me, I had to go for I was already late for the board meeting of the Mental Health Association.

The next morning, I talked to Grace. I did not tell her what Billy had told Charlie but I said enough for her to know the feeling in the Flats and some parts of Windsor Hills was not too good.

I began by asking when Mark was leaving the lab. I had not

mentioned his name, nor had she, during these days. Perhaps not since I began going over to see her when she came home. Now, as I said his name, her body tensed up. All of her was waiting.

And, in a curious way, I was waiting, too.

I said, "When is he due at his new post?"

"The first of the year."

"Are you going to Baltimore for Christmas?"

"No."

"There is no reason, then, for his staying here the rest of the month, is there?"

She swallowed hard.

"Did Mark tell you about that janitor and Miss Mabel letting the animals out?"

She nodded.

"I don't think it adds up to much, not on the surface. It wasn't good for the lab, of course, nor for those experiments. But the real harm is the talk. The more people talk the more scrambled their minds become. I think S. K. should have been arrested. It would have set a limit on things. But Neel thought it wiser not to push it and the Chief agreed with him and so did Mark. Since S. K. was fired he has been hanging around the Flats and here at the shopping center—at the filling stations, other places, talking about what goes on in the lab or what he thinks goes on. His interpretation is about as bizarre as—"

She didn't care in the least about S. K. Her face had turned white. I wanted to stop. But I continued saying the words that had to be said and I knew, as I said them, that they would change everything and yet I must say them.

"S. K. is telling people what the scientists are doing to the animals. The thing he talks about most is the hormone experiment: He interprets this experiment as a method of turning male mice into female mice; he tells folks the male mice are castrated and something put in them and suddenly they turn into females. Then he tells them Mark is in favor of mixing the races, too, and turning white folks into colored folks, that is why he is for integration; and then he says these scientists in the lab are mostly

Jews from Russia and all they do is carry out Communist orders and that's why the FBI sent men here asking questions—"

"The FBI?"

"You remember they were checking Mark's record last year when he was planning to go to Oak Ridge for that special project. He was cleared, of course." I told her briefly S. K. claimed the agents talked with him; and he had developed quite a story of what he told the agents and what they told him about Mark.

She was swallowing hard. She said, "You know what it would mean to him if he could stay long enough to complete *something!*"

"But he can't."

"He knows. But he keeps saying, One more week . . . one more. He was at the lab until one o'clock last night, the night before, the night before—up at six and back to the lab." She was looking through me now, "It is all he's got left, Dave—and he doesn't know how to let go."

Yes, I knew.

She walked to the window, looked out on the terrace where those tulip bulbs were planted, or beyond the terrace at the trees which stretched down to the bottom of the ravine, or maybe she was looking only inside herself. I don't know. She turned, looked at me a long time, said, "I'll talk to him."

I called her name. I don't think she even heard me. I took her in my arms: she was soft and unresponding, she let me kiss her and her lips were soft and her eyes were wide and dark and soft as she looked at me but she was not in my arms, she was not seeing me. I eased her away, patted her shoulder, said, "Can I help you do anything?" She said no. I said perhaps I should get back to my work, there were quite a few calls I should make, I needed to work on my sermon— She smiled gently. That was all. But she wanted me to leave, I was sure of that.

Next day, when I went over, the shoes, toilet things, cups, vases and the rest of the stuff had disappeared from chairs and tables. Four or five boxes were ready to be closed up. I closed them, nailed them, marked them. The paintings were off the living-room wall and piled on the floor. Those in her bedroom were down. I went in, stacked them. It was as if I had never been in that room before. No feeling was left there. I brought the paintings out. We had no boxes suitable for packing them. I went to the shopping center to see what I could pick up.

She was downstairs in Mark's workroom when I returned. His books were out of the shelves. She had sorted them with care: Cassirer, Whitehead, Hegel, Kant, Russell, Unamuno, and so on, in one pile; his technical studies on chemistry, biology, the cell, the blood, all kinds of monographs and technical journals whose names I don't remember were in another; in the third stack were his books on aeronautics, electronics.

The large Jackson Pollock painting she had given him years before Pollock had become well known was still hanging. Together, we eased it from the wall, let it lean against the paneling. She said she thought Mark might want to pack it. I looked at it, thinking now of Mark, of how we used to sit here batting our ideas back and forth: we'd stop talking now and then and smoke our pipes and he'd look at that painting. I had never been able to fit the painting and Mark's imagination together—that is, I was surprised that it held so much meaning for him—but she had known.

As we were packing his books, photographs, guns, camping gear, she'd say: *Mark used to like . . . Mark used to think . . . Once Mark told me . . . Once Mark and I . . . Mark once said. . . .* As if she had known a man named Mark, long ago, in a dim remote period of her life and now that dim remote time was sliding closer closer—

I knew, and I didn't know. On the surface, I refused to acknowledge it. As I write it down, now, I think I must have seen it coming from the moment I said his name. But I numbed up, I refused to acknowledge the consequences of my words, I knew only that I must say them, whatever honor and decency I had left in me compelled me— No. It was more than that. I, too, had known a man named Mark.

After we finished things down in his workroom, we went up to the first floor. We pulled everything out of the kitchen shelves:

dishes, silver, glassware, mats, linens and pots and pans, groceries—leaving just enough for them to do with for a few days. She'd say, This will be enough—as if she knew already the date of their departure.

The movers could have done all of it better, of course, as Mark had said long ago. But she seemed now to want to. She said she needed to separate things, send some to Baltimore to be stored, they would have only a small apartment in Illinois. We went back to the living room and packed the records, leaving the hi-fi for Mark and the movers. Back and forth, back and forth, past Andy's room. I knew his trunk and boxes from school were there, unopened. The things he had left at home were just as they had been, these months. But she did not mention that room nor did she even glance at the door as she passed it.

The next day I had things to do and did not go over to see her until mid-afternoon. When I walked in, she came to me quickly, and put her hands on my arms. She was with me, I felt it, but I pushed her off and looked at her: her eyes had those miraculous flecks of light in them, her mouth— She said, I love you, Dave. I knew she meant it: she was with me as I kissed her, touched her. . . . Everything a woman could give a man she gave me, that afternoon. She was tender and completely with me; teasing—and we were suddenly laughing; then, as suddenly, somber and urgent—then she lay quietly looking at me and her eyes were telling me things I tried not to hear. I am not sure a man ever listens when a woman talks that language. But I know now, she was saying one thing quite plainly: *This is all.* But I refused to listen. I had no intention of giving her up. I would not lose again. I said bluntly, foolishly, "Grace—we've got to talk about things. About you and me and Mark."

I think minutes must have passed. She had not answered. She was not going to answer. I took her hand. She let me but there was no response in it.

Slowly she sat up, pushed her hair back of her ears, said quite casually, "I am going to make you a chocolate cake."

I was too astounded to answer her.

She said, "If you will close up those boxes in the hall and address them to Mother, I'll have the cake done by the time you finish. Why not put on a record and we'll—" She rolled off the bed, caught herself on her hands, did a flip, landed on her toes. She had slipped into shorts and a shirt before I could think of a word to say. I finally came up with, "We've packed the records."

"Yes, of course. Then run over to your study and get one, won't you?" She said—and I must admit she looked it—"I feel wonderful! You do, too." We stared at each other. She whispered, "Be nice, Dave."

With those words she pushed me back to age six, stripped this terrible moment of its importance—she had suddenly turned into my mother, her mother everybody's mother— *Be nice!* I couldn't take it—whatever it was she was doing—I didn't know what she was doing! Feed the greedy thing a piece of his favorite cake and he won't notice he's lost all in the world he wants and must have and cannot give up— I was too angry and confused to speak. I left her. Went over to the study and sat down at my desk. I had no intention of going back.

I'd work on my sermon. Needed to, all right. Looked in the drawer, pulled out the folder, read words that had no meaning. None. None. What does she think she can—what on earth is she up to!

Your fault. You brought it up. You mentioned his name. You said he must go and you convinced her. You did it. You! Why? Because I had to. He is in trouble—in danger—I had to tell her but that doesn't mean we—

It is all he's got . . . Her words rolled over and over in my brain. Mark: I saw him in the kitchen that night at the Ryders'. My friend. Sitting there holding that newspaper clipping as if it were a stone. I was now beyond words: chunks of memories were moving through my mind like wreckage—reeling, colliding—

What had I done to him!

I don't know how long the questions, the confusion, the tearing memories lasted. Finally, there wasn't much left in me—except a resentment I didn't know I felt: *—they always do it to you always manage you always end up managing you—change your*

diapers sure send you to the toilet feed you pull you always train-
ing training you to be a big man and cutting you down to size if
you grow an inch—if you begin to mean something to have
power over them they'll show you quick who has the power
who—

Grace had disappeared. Nothing was left now but women
women women—all the women I had known and not known—
the managing planning outwitting petting tenderkind women always turning into the thing you dread most, always cutting you
down to size, cutting your dreams down to size, your agony. . . .

She slowly came back: as if she had quietly walked into the
room, and was waiting until I was willing to see her . . . that
shaggy black hair . . . those eyes . . . the easy movement of
her body . . . the small jokes . . . her voice full of depth—not
deep but full of her depth—her sudden passionate ways . . . always looking with you feeling with you never pushing never
pressing but always— I loved her and I knew it. And I knew she
was worth all the love I had given her and would always give
her— Whatever this is, whatever her silly idea, go along with it—
why not? She's trying to make it easier—she knows talking about
it won't help—she knows you know it won't help—she knows
you know Mark is her life and you are not her life, she knows you
know he needs her now and you don't, she knows your love
would destroy you both and him, you know that—

I picked up the first record I came to. Smetana's *The Moldau*.
Sort of odd—oh, it'll do anything will do! And I went back to her.

She had set up a small table. The cake was in the middle of it. A
gooey chocolate cake—exactly what I like. Her silver coffee pot:
she had dug it out of a box. Cups, plates, forks. She had gone out
on the terrace and broken off a piece of pyracantha heavy with
red berries and stuck it in a glass. She was smiling, teasing, gay.
When had she been gay! Months ago. It seemed years. Go along
with her. Think of the times she's gone along with you!

She cut the cake, put a big hunk of the stuff on my plate. I
took a bite. I suppose I hoped it would taste like sawdust. But it

was soft and moist and warm and delicious. She looked at me. Her eyes were saying a hundred things at one time. She was smiling, she was eating a piece, too, but now the eyes were full of tears. Not one tear fell, she just kept swallowing hard and eating and looking at me. Then we laughed—at the same time at the same absurdity, same anguish, helplessness, hurt, memories—

She said, Let's put on the record, please.

I put it on. We drank that coffee and ate that cake and talked about nothing against the sounds pouring out of the hi-fi and everything was rocking and surging and heaving as if that table were on a tumultuous sea and yet somehow we were managing to sit there and eat the cake and drink the coffee, defying currents, swells, undertow—

Then Jane rang the doorbell. In a moment she was seated with us and now the sea was growing calm and still. Everything was most pleasant: three friends were drinking coffee together and eating a rich chocolate cake. Jane was quietly asking if she could help do anything. Casual and relaxed about it as if this were a most ordinary moment. And it was now; it had turned into just that. Ordinary and inevitable.

When she left, I left with her. Outside, on the street, she said, "Grace looks much better." I said I thought so, too. She looked at me steadily and said, "I don't think she could have pulled through it without you, Dave. She was close to—" I said, "Yes, I know." Then she said, "She phoned me this morning to tell me they are leaving next week." So.

She got in her car. As I closed the door for her she said, "Have you seen Mark, lately?"

"No."

I waited while she pulled out from the curb, then I went to my study.

I worked with the church secretary the next day until noon. After lunch, I made two or three pastoral calls then finally went over to the house. Grace was sitting on the floor of the living room packing the books. There were empty boxes near her.

She looked up and smiled, said hi. I thought, This shouldn't be possible but it is. I spoke as casually to her. Then took over the job of pulling the books out of the shelves while she sat on the floor and packed them.

I handed her *Ulysses, Portrait of the Artist as a Young Man, Finnegans Wake.* I pulled out T. S. Eliot's books. Opened *Four Quartets,* read a few lines from "Burnt Norton." She stopped her packing, pushed her hair back of her ears, listened until I was done, resumed the packing. Not a muscle in her face had moved. I saw she was not going to respond on any level except the most casual.

Two boxes were filled. We began on the third: Dylan Thomas . . . Sean O'Casey . . . Auden . . . Viereck . . . Ezra Pound . . . Gertrude Stein . . . Proust . . . Valéry . . . Jeffers . . . Gide . . . Malraux . . . Perse . . . Sartre . . . Camus . . . Henry James . . . Kafka. . . .

Then I pulled out the Dostoevskys: behind *The Idiot* was a shawl and hidden in its folds was *The Possessed.* So she had not burned it, after all. She was concentrating on fitting tall and short books together and did not look up. Just as well. I slipped them into a box, put two Kierkegaards on top and three Henry James. Now I was pulling out Donne and a bright new copy of Dante—and now eight or ten of Freud's books and four or five of Jung's and one of Ferenczi's and two Ranks and Ernest Jones —now her art books, ten or twelve Skiras, *The Tao of Painting, The Art of Indian Painting*—

I began to feel we were packing up our own era: a stretched-out thinned-out double generation—

"What next? What next, Grace?"

She stopped. She stared at me. And then, instead of answering, she began to cry. Hard, tearing sobs.

I went into the kitchen and made some coffee. When I brought it in she was quiet. We drank the coffee without saying a word. I shall always remember: that hair pushed back behind her ears making her look like a young boy and very much a woman, too, and a fifteen-year-old girl, and the mother of a dead son, yes; these images, these faces piled on each other, transparent, over-lapping, pressing down, easing, pressing, easing.

She said, "Dave—when things happen, this that has happened

to us—" She stopped. She said, "I had been drinking so much
. . . I can scarcely remember it—and you let me?"

"I had nothing better to suggest." That was the truth. Until we
—I felt she was thinking it with me—until we, together, found
the strength— We looked at each other a long time.

She said, "It blurs . . . I don't remember much."

"You haven't wanted to, have you?"

This time, she was trying *not* to think with me, pulling back,
face paling out—

We packed a box. We began on another—

She said, "There is something you want me to do?"

"Yes." I hadn't realized it but there was. It was hard to say, but
she was listening— "I want you to go in Andy's room."

"No!"

Once, long ago, you succeeded in blacking out what you could
not understand and accept and could not, therefore, remember.
So you tried it again, didn't you? deliberately tried to lose all that
was good and alive because you could not accept the rest of it,
the obscenity, the death—

I did not intend to—I did not want to—but I was saying:

"Grace . . . You had a son whom you loved and were proud
of, whom Mark loved and needed desperately, and this son died.
And because you could not—"

"Don't!" She whispered it but it held such agony in it that I
could not go on. The good guy in me tried to stop the words—
don't hurt her you can't—

But something stern and old and inexorable that had to be said
was using me as its mouthpiece:

"I want you to listen. It is going to hurt you. You feel you can't
take more pain but you can, we all can; and I want you to listen:
Andy died a brave death while on a difficult and dangerous mission. He was only a child but he went out, one night, in search
of an image he had lost and was determined to find again.
There is nothing in the whole world more fragile than what he
was looking for, or more necessary to the human being. But most
of us would have given up, would have let our faith go without a
struggle and become trivial-minded afterward and cynical and

incapable of any real relationship even with ourselves. But Andy was different: you and Mark had made him so: through a lifetime of training you gave him courage: he was not afraid of the dark or of distance or difficulty. All he felt was: If he could just get to that cabin, the memory of his father, of their talks and trips together, would be there waiting: and all the evil that had rushed into his mind when he read that newspaper clipping, the obscenity and doubt, suspicion, all of it, would go away—and they would find each other again; and when that was done, the two of them would find you; and the trinity of your love for them and theirs for you and for each other would be re-established. He died on that search."

Her weeping—I couldn't bear the sound of it. I stopped. I thought, I can't say it. But the words came: "Because the loss of this image had come about through the hate and obscenity of people, of every one of us, because the sight of this evil is so hideous and terrifying, you have not looked at the glory of your son's death. Not once. He died with dignity—no matter what foulness forced him to do so. He died for something good, something men cannot live without. As young men die bravely in wars caused by the cowardice and stupidity and greed and blindness and power-lust of the rest of us, so Andy died. But we who love him have not honored him. We have pushed his death away as if it were as evil as the murderers who—"

She had covered her face.

I stopped. I took her hands and held them. I lifted her hair back. She was pale but she was listening. "Grace—he died *because* of human evil but he died *for* the best thing a human can die for: a good relationship."

I still feel those cold hands, the soft ebbing sobs, as if they were inside me. Finally, she whispered, "If you will leave me, Dave—for a little while. If I can be alone—"

And I left her. I stood at the door a long time. I finally said, "Are you sure you will be all right?" And she looked up and managed to say yes. But I couldn't leave like that. I went back and kissed her mouth and touched her hair and she let me, and that was the last time.

The rest of it came steadily, irresistibly. We had left our walled-in space, our walled-in hour. There was no going back. I suppose that is one way to say it.

The next night—I felt I had just dropped off to sleep—the telephone rang. When I picked it up, Grace was speaking. She said, "Dave, Mark has not come home. It is three o'clock. I have phoned his office. There's no answer."

I said, "He's in the lab, working; he's forgotten what time it is. I'll go see. It will take me only a few minutes. I'm sure he is all right."

She said, "I want to go with you." I felt she shouldn't, something might have—but her voice made me say, "I'll have the car in your driveway in five minutes."

As I drove down those empty dim streets, neither of us could manage a word. When we got to the lab the front door was locked. I rang for the night watchman. He recognized her and let us in. We got in the elevator, I pushed the fourth-floor button. When we stepped out, I asked her to wait while I went to his office. When I saw it was empty, I beckoned her and told her to go in and sit down, I would take a look in the lab; he wasn't aware of how late it was— The walk through that corridor to the lab cubicle where he usually worked was the longest journey I have ever taken. There is no use to say what was in my mind, what feelings and memories and beliefs and fears were pulling at each other. When I got there, the door was half open. Before going in, I said, "Mark: it is Dave." Mark was at the small desk, his head down on his arms. I hoped, I prayed he was asleep. I went to him and put my hand on his shoulder. I said, "Mark: it is Dave." And he looked up: I blank out here. I have tried not to remember that face. I think I said, "Grace is here, Mark. She wants you to come home. She needs you." He did not react. I wanted to say, I need you, too—for God knows, I did, but this was not the time. I said, "You are all she has, Mark, and she can't live without you." I left him and went back to his office. I said, "He's all right; he is just tired out. You go to him." She said, "Yes."

She did not even look at me. I watched her walk down that corridor . . . I heard her say "Mark . . ." I heard his stifled sob.

I got in the elevator and went down to my car.

They left Thursday morning.

The moving van came at six; by ten, it had pulled out of the driveway. I was there with them, of course, helping where I could. I said, once more, I'd turn the keys over to the real estate people today or tomorrow. I said I'd check and see that all the switches were pulled. Mark asked me if I would call the plumber and have the pipes drained. I asked if there was anything else I could see about. They said no. "Can you take time out for some coffee? can you come over to the study?" They said no.

The luggage was in the car. There was not much of a leave-taking. Quite casually, Mark said, Dave? looked hard at me, gripped my hand, got in the car. I put my hands on Grace's shoulders. She was trembling. I patted her and opened the car door. She was quickly settled inside, I closed the door. Mark looked at me again. There was a moment when I thought he was about to say something: his eyes lit up, there was that quick dilation of pupil which so characteristically precedes a sentence he has been trying to say a long time. But he did not say it. He turned the switch, started the engine. "Take care," I called. Grace put her hand on her mouth, she was looking at the house, through it beyond it— Mark backed down the drive, turned into Arlington . . . that blue car swung slowly around the corner and toward the highway. They were gone.

I'd like to say, This is it; this is all. But the rest of us were still here and what had happened was here with us:

to read the prayer—what prayer? *what was she thinking?* I
opened the Prayer Book, turned pages. . . .

I stopped. Made some coffee. Drank two cups, standing there.
Forced myself back to the desk. Managed three small decisions
that should have been made a week ago. Called the chairman of
the church finance committee, cleared up a small matter or two.
Called the president of the altar guild. Called the chairman of
the buildings and grounds committee. Called . . . called. . . .

That sermon: I pulled from my files a sermon I used last December; pulled out the one I used two years ago. Read both of
them. They were good sermons but a stranger had written them;
they had no relationship with me. Wait a bit. Your head will
clear, after an hour or so. Call the chairman of the committee on
physical rehabilitation, tell him about your idea—what idea? I
called the chairman; he had things on his mind about the campaign for the cerebral palsy school and I was glad to listen. He
suggested that I call the chairman of the finance committee; I
did; I caught up on that. Then I called two or three parishioners
who had not been well; I promised to bring one of them a record-
ing of Dino Lipatti's, her voice brightened, I was glad I had
suggested it. Such small things sometimes . . . I jotted it down
on my pad: *Lipatti record.* Brain seemed to be clicking along
now with fair efficiency. I had certainly cleared a small space in
front— But back of it, a shaky blurred pieced-together film had
begun to unreel: everything everything nothing everything fading flickering blazing without beginning without end—I slowly
became aware that I had come into the middle of a monstrously
sad parade winding through staid sensible avenues of my mind
trumpets blowing without permit, yet somehow not colliding with
the ordinary flow of the mind's traffic. On on: led by two small
boys on horses—and suddenly they were racing and suddenly
one fell and the horse stopped and the boy lay still and the parade faltered but only to catch its breath at the sight—then it
went steadily on on . . . led now by a boy in a football helmet
running down the line down the line the line as a little
lady cheered him on so ardently that she dropped her hot water
bottle but she didn't notice she cheered and cheered and once

more the parade paused while the little lady was awarded fifteen silver cups and that took time but soon it was on its way again and the trumpets were blowing and now there came a grave-faced young acolyte lighting the candles of an ancient church whose blue windows glowed with new light that had come out of his young dream of God, and an organ full-stopped and yet diminished in sound drowned out the trumpets and a priest in a black robe was reading the litany and voices were singing *Nunc Dimittis,* and then then then—the organ changed to the crash of sea waves and a girl and a boy were lying on the beach watching sea gulls and in an instant they were swimming side by side through rough surf in strong sure rhythm until a shark slipped his fin through that rhythm . . . and suddenly bombs were exploding and homes and cities were exploding and beliefs were exploding and dreams were exploding and a parachute was falling and dragging across a wet rough field, and the parade faltered on a hospital cot but only for a moment, only a moment; then a priest was heading the procession slowly and with a slight limp but it was moving with dignity when a small girl with pale stringy hair stepped up and took over, she picked up a trumpet with a giggle and S. K. picked up a trumpet, and Miss Hortense, and Renie, and Miss Mabel—

I got up. Opened the door into the hall. Opened the door leading into the street. Stood there, looking at the traffic, looking at the house across the street, the wet pavement. Went upstairs to the bathroom. Came down. Called Neel. I said, "Neel—how about our getting together the first of the week? Think we may be able to work out something about that recreation center, the Junior Chamber of Commerce is interested, et cetera." Neel suggested we ask the president of the Jaycees to join us at lunch. We made a date. Then he said, "I'd like to drop in tomorrow and talk to you about Gus Hestor. I've been checking on what you told me—by the way, did you ever talk to your organist?"

"No, there are reasons—I'll discuss it tomorrow." Afterward, I kept thinking about Charlie. Perhaps I should tell him. No need to alarm him but he should be told something. Made a note, *Talk to Charlie.*

I called two or three shut-ins and we discussed the bad weather; we compared it with the weather last December; we agreed it was worse than last December.

I had no more calls to make. Sat in that swivel chair, stacking papers in a neat pile. Stacking. Restacking. Somehow I felt better. Parade had gone away. I had come together, had focused on my work. Somewhere, in a small lost corner of my mind where time never enters and never leaves I know a horse immortally trembles and crops the grass and a crumpled up little friend keeps turning to fresh stone and a dark fin slides through the bright edge of the sea and a blue bowl falls but never breaks and a doll's face is shattered to dust and mends itself and a small boy is walking walking in the snow and the woman I love is saying *It is all he's got now* . . . and I reply, *Yes, I know, yes, I know, I know I know*—but pictures, words are always moving in the corners of the mind; one learns to pay no attention. And now I was all right, I had pushed it away.

Chores began to get done. I selected a prayer, read it twice: yes, it is right. I jotted down an idea for a sermon. It might do. Enlarged it into a paragraph; read it; yes, it will do. Someone called: a communicant whose mother was ill—would I drop in to see her? I made a note on my pad: *Go see Mrs. Askew in the morning.* Read the paragraph again. No, it wouldn't do, not for Christmas; be fine for Lent; better for the Pentecost season—well, anyway, it wouldn't do. I sketched out another idea. Began to work on it.

The servers—their surplices were wrinkled and dingy, last Sunday. Remind them to check their vestments ahead of time. Call Bill: tell him to remind the others. Call him at four, after school: I jotted his name down on the pad. Your own stole—does it need cleaning? how about your cassock? could take pressing, couldn't it? Better call the cleaners. Check the midnight music with Charlie. Someone said the church was cold last Sunday—

A tap on the door. The decorator walked in. He held some swatches of cloth in his hand. He had a color chart. Something I had to select, presumably. He asked me to choose one of five color tones. For a chair? Yes. What chair? Vaguely irritated. I did not like the idea of rattling around in that new rectory. These rooms in the Parish House suited me fine. Small, dark, cramped, yes; but I like them small and dark and cramped. Big responsibility, that rectory. Don't know about housekeeping; don't mind messing with a coffee pot here in my study or broiling steaks outdoors, but a kitchen big enough for fifty people— I could see the ladies of the church buzzing around in there. Taking over. Taking me over. Or Mother—would she think she owed it to me to come and keep house—

The decorator was saying things were about ready: paneling in breakfast room and study finished. Did I like it? I admitted reluctantly that I had not seen it, had not been able to get over to the rectory during the past few days. He was startled, covered his astonishment with a quick elastic smile, continued his report: the paint jobs were done, papering along stairwell done; floors waxed. Now: he was ready to hang things.

What things? Things—he smiled—window curtains, canopy over the walnut four-poster. Canopy? not in my— A reassuring smile. Charming, actually; the Young Women's Business Club had given it for the east guest room, the more feminine one, he stressed. Would I look over these swatches and select one? for a chair?

"I don't know about chairs," I said. Voice grumpy. Stubborn. "Shall I do it for you, sir?"

I told him I'd appreciate it if he would. And so on and on. There was a couch for the sun terrace. Would I just take a look at the photograph? I took a look. Did I approve? I said yes. I felt boorish. The Auxiliary and altar guild were pushing him, he said. They would be extremely disappointed if the housewarming did not take place on Christmas afternoon.

Of course. Why take it out on him? "Can you make it?" I asked, hoping my voice sounded sympathetic.

"Oh yes, surely—by working one or two nights."

And then he asked it: "Where do you want those superb Marins hung, sir?"

"Why not put them in the dining room?" Nice place. You can

forget they're there. You'll go in only when the bishop comes; or when Mother or Meg comes—

The decorator's voice was calm, tactful, persistent. "I believe, sir, Mr. Snyder expects them to be hung in your study."

"There's no room. My personal things will fill the place." Voice full of anger. It startled me. The voice had become unreliable, lately. I was ashamed. Said as quietly as I could manage it, "I have a great many books."

He pinched his nose, kept pinching it between thumb and first finger, looked down at the floor, sniffed, took out his handkerchief, delicately wiped each nostril, looked pointedly at my Marin prints in their simple frames hanging on the study wall. It was obvious what he was thinking. I opened a desk drawer, fumbled round in it, closed it; swished the papers on my desk, stacked them in a neat pile. He was examining the old swivel chair I was sitting in—not with scorn so much as with bright curiosity, the kind children have.

He said "Of course, if you want them in the dining room we'll hang them there." That was settled. We moved on to other decisions. I felt rigid; said to myself, You're dead tired, take it easy. He hasn't done anything to you. You're dishonest, too; making a big virtue out of your half rejection of Snyder's gift. *You*, of all people—you refused them for yourself, sure; but you accepted them for the rectory. As long as you are here they are yours— you can leave, of course.

More trivia: a mirror; something about it; it would look good upstairs, bad downstairs, I think he said. Something about a silver coffee service, that atrocious nightmare of Miss Hortense's: she was about to donate it to the rectory: what could they do? I said, Somebody will have to make her mad. I said it gravely and he laughed hysterically; there was something about the laugh that reminded me of Dewey Snyder; I wanted him to hush but I began to laugh, too. I asked if he would mind talking these matters over with Jane Houghton? she would know what to do. I noticed my voice had lost its percussive quality. He said he would, and left.

Charlie called. He invited me to the rehearsal that evening.

I couldn't make it, I told him. He said, "I wanted Billy to sing his solo for you. His voice is amazing in the Britten but he's pretty sure to get scared on TV. Of course—if you are busy—"

The last words I heard Charlie speak. I didn't know—how could I know! I felt irritated and I showed it. It is useless to stress this and yet, you cannot help but wish you had spoken differently. All I could see at the moment was: Charlie is too dependent on me. I knew it, he knew it, I think. I slowly put the receiver on the phone. Thought, We must talk this out and it isn't going to be easy for either of us. I am not wise enough, I don't know enough—but it can wait. Two hours later, I thought, There's something else I intended to say to Charlie, can't think what. It pushed around inside my brain but the connections didn't hook up. Left me feeling uncomfortable.

Mrs. Riley called. About flowers, of course. Afterward, I thought about her: It is not an easy thing to find the hidden source of someone's courage. Where had it come from? Why had she cared so much about human decency? She hardly knew the Channings. There was no reason of friendship. And yet she cared. Tucked away somewhere in that vague mind behind those watery eyes was a code, maybe as old-fashioned as a piece of parchment, but *there,* clearly worded, and she knew it by heart and the miracle was that she lived by it. As I thought about her, she became sort of incandescent: this little woman whose throat was always wrapped up as if it was sore and whose nose was red and whose eyes were dim and vague and who held her prayer book close to her eyes at church and was always arranging flowers and quoting poetry: I'd never forget that she believed in something enough to live by it.

The secretary of the altar guild called. The contractor called about air conditioning at the new rectory. Miss Hortense called. Her voice was stretched with excitement. They had found more Communists, she said. Not in the government this time, she said. This time, they were these people right here in the South who want to mix the races. Wasn't it awful how the country was infested? did I see Senator So-and-So on *Meet the Press?* wasn't he fine? what he said about states' rights and our sacred way of life? didn't I think we could do without a Supreme Court? what good was it? nobody she had asked could tell her one reason why we should have a Supreme Court. What could those stupid old judges do that our governors could not do far better? can't we get rid of them?

She lowered her voice. She said, "Are you listening?"

I assured her I was.

She whispered, "I know something *I* could do," and then she hushed.

There are times when she makes me think of absolutely fantastic possibilities. I said, easily, lightly, "Perhaps it is a good idea to keep them, Miss Hortense: you know—the way you hold on to your antiques."

She laughed with the shrill glee of a child at my feeble effort to appease her. Then she said, "But of course antiques *know when not to talk*, Father Landrum. You hadn't thought of that —now, had you?" She laughed again, peal after peal of absolutely gay laughter. She said she must tell Phelia what their dear priest said about those dreadful old judges, oh dear oh dear. Then she said, "These people who want race mixing are moral perverts, don't you think? Phelia prefers *moral* to *sex*. It *is* better bred, perhaps. Or should we just face it? I was telling Phelia last night—" Then she said in a low voice, "The dogs are barking so; do excuse me," and hung up. In thirty minutes she called back to say—and her voice was quietly modulated and delicate in its loneliness—that the reason she had phoned was to invite me for eggnog on New Year's Day. Would I come? I said I would.

The phone rang again. Jane. Inviting me for dinner. "Any time, Dave. I'm making a shrimp pilau, I remember you like it; you may leave as soon as you wish, afterward." I told her I could not manage it, I must work.

Then she said, "Did they get off—all right?"

I said, "Around ten. Not quite as early as they had planned."

She said call her if she could be of help and I thanked her, forgetting to tell her I had already sent that decorator to her.

In a few minutes, Paul Pottle telephoned to say my books had come. "What books, Paul?" He said, "The books you ordered for

Christmas gifts." I said, "Yes yes, of course; I'll drop by for them, Monday. OK?" And Paul said, "Certainly."

Then he said, "Have they gone?" and I said, "Yes, this morning." And after that, we were silent. Then he said, "I hope I haven't bothered you too much." I said, "Not at all." We hung up.

Then the director of the Laboratories called and said, "Did they get off all right, Mr. Landrum?" I said, "Yes, about ten." And he said, "Good: they should be in Illinois tomorrow night, don't you think?"

That sermon. I put a sheet of paper in the typewriter. I stared at it a long time, hoping my hands would do what my brain now seemed incapable of.

Not a word found its way there. My mind had begun to pile up again with faces, sounds, words. Concentration gone. Focus blurred. Then, as suddenly, everything cleared: *Renie flourishes.* Words big as road signs. She, alone, has escaped hurt. I had seen her yesterday, Wednesday; yes, the day before they left; I saw her down at the shopping center: in a new tweed suit, as usual looking casually smart, speaking pleasantly to everybody; swinging the station wagon skillfully, easily, into Arlington Road. Off —to lunch, perhaps, with her friends; or on her way to help at the blood bank or at the hospital as a Gray Lady. To her, Andy's death had no connection with Susan and the store. She would never tie the two events together. No. Their leaving, Susan's giant scissors snipping Mark off from his research, she would never tie them together, either. For she never tied events together. She said what she said, did what she did, and never looked back at where words and acts fell. She was a hit-and-run driver who never got caught, not even by her own conscience. She said—after Andy's death, when the story of the blizzard appeared in the *Advertiser*—voice soft, eyes soft, "I am so sorry; I suppose they never taught the child how to handle himself in snow. And they always let him have his own way too much, didn't they? My old Mammy down in Mississippi would say it just goes to show the Lord always punishes the transgressor. Of course, I don't think that—it would be too superstitious—it must have been simply a dreadful accident, don't you think?" I held on to Renie: grimly piling the blame on her—relieved to find *one* guilty person—sliding away from the truth that we were all guilty—

The phone. Nothing important. But I was compelled to answer it cheerfully, rationally; and afterward, I picked up a pencil and like an automaton wrote that sermon.

Words added up to sentences, to paragraphs, to pages. To meaning? How could it! I was deeply shaken; what I called my world view was trembling and gasping; for weeks I had lied and cheated in word and act and thought until I felt no longer sure I knew the true from the false. Perhaps my sense of truth had never had a keen edge; my values, my beliefs must have been pretty vague to begin with: no more than a handful of somebody else's intellectual assumptions; what I called "faith"—maybe Neel was right—was nothing but glandular euphoria. Why had I chosen the Church? why had I made so grave a commitment? why did I feel good enough, wise enough, brave enough, dedicated enough to think I could carry through a priest's responsibilities in this crazy upside-down lost world? I was close to despair. I was certainly not thinking in existential vocabulary— I think in the simple words of my youth when I hurt—but in mood I was close to those haunting agonized exclamations of Kierkegaard. I was full of sin and knew it . . . but even now, I dared not look at sin. I dared not measure the shadow it cast. Something in me I used to call "healthy-mindedness" kept nudging me, Don't be a masochist! Watch out! There's peculiar pleasure in self-flagellation, remember. Look at what is good in you— A little good, a little kindness, yes—but *where was the Center?* I was a long way from God . . . I felt the people of our town were a long way from God . . . God? Who are we to dream of God? we, who make mean hard images of ourselves and set them up in His name. The others are a shade better, maybe: they who declare there is no God because their nineteenth-century reason cannot prove God exists so they announce God is dead and build a tomb around their dead proof. They? we? you? me?

What could a man in this mood have to say?

This is what: A part of me, a facile, clever fellow, knowing a clergyman speaks every Sunday regardless of personal turmoil, regardless of pain and confusion, regardless of a mind in torment, wrote that sermon—paraphrasing old sermons and filching a few paragraphs from my betters. Now—there it was. And it would do. It was calm, hopeful, right: for this season of Advent. I thought, I'll close by quoting from "Das Marien-Leben." Let me see . . . I'll use the line that begins: *Hadst thou not simplicity, how should that happen to thee which now lights up the night?* Hadst thou not simplicity—

I went to the bookshelf, pulled out Rilke's *Collected Poems,* began to read the "Marien-Leben." I read it in German, although my German is a poor thing: then in Herter Norton's English translation:

> *Hattest du der Einfalt nicht, wie sollte*
> *dir geschehn, was jetzt die Nacht erhellt?*
> *Sieh, der Gott, der über Völker grollte,*
> *Macht sich mild und kommt in dir zur Welt.*

> *Hast du dir ihn grösser vorgestellt?*

> See, the God who rumbled over nations
> makes himself mild and in thee
> comes into the world.

> Hadst thou imagined him greater?

I read all of it. Went to the bookshelves, found the *Duino Elegies.* Read four of them. Slowly, as I read Rilke's words, something opened . . . something shut. All was as it had been, months ago. My mind had not answered one question; had not solved one problem; had not found new facts; nor reached new depths; nor climbed one step toward new insight—and yet, I felt at peace. I had not earned this quietude but it was given me. I could feel the afternoon falling away, light dimming . . . traffic on Arlington growing heavier . . . all of it I was aware of and not aware of. Slowly I was flooded with unwarranted certainty: some day it would come clear, not in answers but in a new feeling among men; some day there'd be understanding, and forgiveness. Some day this mad, obscene, ambiguous, anonymous hour in which we live will find its good name and its place in time, will slip into its small crevice and lie there diminished and tamed by love, and compassion, and the slow-growing knowledge of a truth beyond facts, an intelligence beyond our small logic, a love beyond the anguish. Now and then, as I read, I heard Charlie at the organ, playing a fragment of something I didn't recognize, again and again; to master it? no; to master himself. Charlie . . . maybe he would work it all out, somehow; he would go as far as he could with his thinking and then, somehow, he would hear the rest of it as he hears the uncreated music he creates, he would find his life not twisted and knotted in the senseless way he had thought and I had thought but unfolding, and it would begin to find its inherent form—he'd find beyond the dissonance, the harmonic ground—

—the cassock!

I had forgot to call the cleaners. I telephoned. It was too late, they'd pick it up on the early morning round.

I went upstairs for the cassock and stole—I'd get them now while they were on my mind. Went in the bathroom; stood there, staring down in the bowl, listening to the spatter of urine: now I was looking at the raised toilet seat, and Angela Finch was saying, *No gentleman would leave the toilet seat up, afterward; no gentleman would do that, that is why I am divorcing him, Mother says I'm right, Mother agrees, Mother. . . .* I wanted to say, But Angela all men—your father doesn't he leave— I said, "And what does Martin say?" She wiped her eyes, she said, "Martin says it is his prerogative, every man's prerogative to leave the seat up." The sound of her words swished across my mind. . . . And I saw her unhappy face, felt her pain, heard her ultimatum: *If Martin will promise to put the seat down afterward . . .* But Martin said *never!* And so Angela was leaving him, taking her child—

I flushed the toilet. Turned to wash my hands. Saw my face in the mirror over the washbowl. Haggard, worn, miserable. I had thought I was at peace. My face was not at peace. I went back to the bedroom. Walked to the window: The house. Their

house. Built with care and hope for the good years to come.
. . . Smudgy white in the late afternoon dimness. I had promised to see that the realtors listed it and put a *For Sale* sign on
the lawn. Must do it, tomorrow. Where were they now? Ken-
tucky? What route had they taken? I had not asked. The fresco
. . . I wished she had cut it out, had taken it with her—or given
it to me. It would have ruined the wall to do so, yes; but I didn't
like to think it would be stared at by real estate clients who
would ask, *What on earth does it mean, that painting?*

I picked up the bundle, came downstairs and laid it on the
table in the hallway for the cleaners' truck. Went to the front
door. It had been raining quite heavily but had stopped. Then I
went back to my study. I opened the door—

Susan: sitting in the green-striped chair. Pale stringy shining
hair. Yellow eyes shining. Susan: in her arms Ali Baba, sleek and
fat, his yellow eyes blinking into space. I looked at him; one ear
quivered; I knew he had recognized me.

She was staring at me; had turned the corners of her mouth
down, in a half-embarrassed, half-teasing way.

I said, "Hello."

She said, "I brought him back."

Nothing from me.

"I don't need him any more. I have a new cat my daddy gave
me. *His* name is Supersonic. You can have your old Ali Baba
now." She handed my old Ali Baba to me. I let him slip to the
floor.

She had been sitting prim and straight on the edge of the
chair. Now she settled back, scrunched her legs up. I don't think
I moved.

Ali Baba looked at me, then he pattered to the desk, peered
under it, pattered over to the cabinet where the coffee things
are, rubbed against it, pattered to the leather chair, rubbed
against it, walked with slow stalking movements toward the
window, tensed up to pounce on an invisible enemy, relaxed,
walked slowly toward us.

Susan looked at me. The seed of a face began to warm, to en-
large, to light up—

I prayed, Don't let her tell me another—

She said, "I don't suppose you have any chocolate cake?"

"No."

"Sure?" Eyes dancing. Teasing now.

"Sure."

"Well—I guess I better be going." She didn't move. I didn't move. Ali Baba didn't move. We stared solemnly at each other. Then she made a face, a clown face. And of course I laughed.

She said, "I go to a clinical psychologist. Once a week," she explained.

"Do you like him?"

She ignored the question. She said, "We play silly games. And afterward, he asks me silly questions."

"Do you answer them?"

"Sometimes. Sometimes I tease him and give him play answers. I tell him stories, too. He told me last time he didn't want me to tell him any more stories. Ever ever! I had a real good story and he wouldn't let me tell it. He's a bad man." She stared hard at Ali Baba. She looked up at me. Her eyes had turned dark and beady-smooth. She said, "He did something real bad, too." She waited for me to ask what. I didn't ask.

She uncurled and stood up. I said goodbye. She said goodbye —and started out the door. She stopped, she said, "Ali Baba does bad things, too." She closed the door behind her. I heard the hall door open and shut.

Five minutes later, I realized it was dark and I should have taken her home. I don't know what I thought or did during those next minutes. Suddenly I was at the door: I opened it, looked at Ali Baba, hissed, *get out!* He began to arch his back, he decided against arching it, he ran toward the door, turned, was immobilized for a second or two, then leaped into the striped chair and lay there blinking at me.

I made a sandwich and coffee and went on with my work.

Once, around nine-thirty (I am fairly sure of the time for I heard the choirboys practicing and thought, He's keeping them late), I went to the window and looked across the street at that dark house. I saw nothing out of the ordinary, saw no one on the lawn. There are two maples, the dogwood, four or five clumps of boxwood, the nandina, the pyracantha, the forsythia—it is possible that someone, or two, or three, or four, or twenty may have been hiding behind shrub and tree or walking on the side terrace, for a low fog obscured things, pulling house and landscape out of place and shape. And my attention was not on the exterior of the house: I was inside, groping my way through those dark bare rooms—the living room . . . Mark's workroom . . . the bedroom . . . Andy's—had she opened that trunk? did she and Mark open it together?—measuring my loss by their emptiness, beginning to feel it now, in the dull delayed way I always react to things that go hard with me. I lit a cigarette; let the realization slug me.

Finally, I turned back to my work.

Five minutes or twenty or thirty may have passed. I don't know.

Then—

It began with a small muffled explosion. Before I could interpret it, a blaze outside lit up the study. I turned off the desk lamp, went to the window. On the Channing lawn was a Cross, fringed with bluish flames which turned yellow-red and flared up larger larger larger, arms stretched wide . . . enormous against the fog . . . ten feet, twenty—such words are useless for measuring the monstrous image that struck my brain: a flaming Cross had leaped out of the blackness. That was all. No sight of living creature. The flames had thrown a thick yellow fuzz on the fog reducing visibility to near zero, and yet, I believed I saw people moving toward the Cross, away from it, toward it, away. . . . Slowly, the fog thinned; wispy strings of it floated up, out, leaving clear spaces illumined by the flames. And now, I saw six or eight shadows bending down, in genuflecting movement like the devout at prayer . . . a shadow raised its arms . . . another . . . fog closed in, new space cleared, there were shadows half-crouched and running toward the house. . . .

Dread was seeping through me: as if this were a thing I had been forbidden to look upon: this befouling of the symbol of

Atonement—ah, but those shadows—were they mine? were they everybody's? Look at them: they are celebrating, they are exulting; it has stood in their way so long: that old Sign of Man redeeming man, of the weak needing sacrifice from the strong and the strong needing to be sacrificed; words words: *compassion, mercy, forgiveness:* the shadows are wiping them out with a match, a few rags, a gallon of gasoline: just like that: burn them burn them—destroy everything you don't understand, cannot comprehend, dare not become: trample the symbols, burn them —then we can return to the animal kingdom: we can do evil and feel no guilt, we can sin and it will not be sin, we can die and will not know death—

Those phrases did not quite form for under pressure of that blazing image all the words I knew melted; I was trembling, I felt stripped of verbal sophistication, of mental garments that insulate one from contact with the awesome, the unknowable, the terror and the mystery beyond word and image—

I opened the window. Smelled the burning gasoline rags. It did something: restored the actual moment; reduced the image to its small literal implications; broke it out of its unmeasurable framework. I went to the phone, turned on the desk lamp, dialed the police station, told them hoodlums were burning a cross on the Channings' lawn. When I said the words the dread subsided, the images faded. It sounded quite ordinary for "hoodlums to burn a cross": two sticks of wood nailed tight, stuck in the ground, set on fire. That is all. Trespassing is a misdemeanor. Something the police are expected to deal with.

The desk sergeant asked where.

Arlington Road. I gave the number. Across from All Saints Parish House, I added. Got it?

Yep, the voice said. How many you think there?

Twenty, I told him. Maybe a hundred. Not sure. Maybe more. "I seem to hear a crowd back of the house."

I dialed the Windsor Hills fire station. As I was giving the address, I heard the noise: one thin long cracking sound. Another quick cracking sound. Silence. Another, another, another— a long one this time, like a rifle shot pulled out five times its normal duration. "Something else is happening," I said. "Don't know what."

I put the receiver on the phone; turned off the light, went to the window. The fog was lifting. Easier to see now. Three cars had stopped—on Arlington, toward the park. Six men got out—they were in pairs—they climbed the steep embankment at the edge of the trees. . . . I was seeing things clearly, counting, placing with precision. Two cars were moving slowly up Arlington from my left, from the direction of the lake. They stopped a hundred yards down the street. Eight men got out, walked toward the Channing lawn. As they moved under the street light, I saw they were high-school age, or near that. They ran up the front embankment of the lawn. Another car eased up slowly. Another. But I had a feeling the mob was coming up from the ravine. I was not sure. I was guessing—

I went to the phone, dialed Jane, asked her to call Neel and the Chief, told her hoodlums, etc. "They're breaking the windows, from the sound of it; seem to be at the rear of the house, most of them." She wanted to know how many. I told her my estimate. "Boys? men?" "Both," I said. "In cars?" "Not many cars; they're coming up through the trees, leaving their cars across the park, maybe; or down on the lower level. I'm guessing," I reminded her.

I slipped on a sweater, turned off the light, went into the hall, locked the study door. Seemed to know what I was doing; that is, my actions were quick, decisive, but I was not aware of where those actions were heading. I went outside, locked the entrance door to the Parish House, stepped into the street. Remember thinking, *Take it easy.*

From here on out, I am compelled to guess at what occurred. That is, what I shall say is elaboration, a reconstruction of events whose shape and sequence and scope I had, at the time, little idea of. For I was abruptly tipped over into it. The big things were happening behind the house but things were happening close to me, too, that I neither saw nor heard and have not to this day been able to pull together into a pattern that makes sense.

It began this way:

As I stepped off the sidewalk into the street, I saw the choir-boys running across Arlington up at the corner near the church—some twenty yards to the right of me. They were heading straight for the Channings' lawn: "going to the fire." I'd say there were ten; the others had left the church, probably, by the rear door; with no knowledge of the excitement on the Channings' lawn, they had cut through the alley, picked up their bus as usual on the boulevard two streets over to the east.

About the time I saw the kids, Gus Hestor saw them. He was on the lawn. He sidled down the steps to the sidewalk. That walk of his: he holds his legs close, swings his hip muscles later-ally. I had seen him only twice but I recognized it. There's a light near the sidewalk steps; otherwise, I might not have been so sure. The fog was lifting but not enough to give clear vision. I couldn't see faces well. With him was a stranger, tall, not too heavy. Four or five of Gus's gang were back of him, say ten feet back. I recognized Kipsie, the boy who had come home from State Training School six months before, on probation; I knew him because I had worked with Neel on the case and had helped find him a job. He's young, about seventeen, has a squat body, wide shoulders, big head. Easy to spot. The others looked older, twenty or twenty-two, maybe; I wasn't sure of identities; the stranger could have been my age; there was something curi-ously familiar about him—I knew I had never seen him before but felt that I had—I still feel it—with the vividness of a *déjà vu* experience.

Gus met those kids as they scrambled up the rock garden em-bankment. He seemed to be talking to them; he pushed one—in that playful, sadistic way some big men use with children; the boy fell, got up quick; they seemed to be breaking into two groups: three of the boys ran toward the cross, another followed them; the others moved slowly in the direction of the terrace that leads around the house. I had a feeling they didn't want to go where they were going; I thought, Gus is up to his nasty low-down tricks: he's giving them a job his gang is scared to do. But it was happening fast—

Next thing I saw—actually the two were occurring simultaneously—was Charlie running across the street toward the lawn.

What probably pulled Charlie in is this: he sent the boys away from choir practice, then closed up the church and left in his car. He must have driven to the corner of Arlington from the church before he saw the burning cross and the choirboys scrambling up on the lawn. Whether he saw Gus's gang, I don't know. But he knew those boys would be sucked into the mess. He stopped his car near the corner and headed into the mob.

I remember thinking, He's gone after the boys and Gus will kill him.

Now here, I have to push back a little: Gus had been edging closer and closer to Charlie. I knew this. Neel had warned me. Twice. But I had not warned Charlie—not because it had got lost in my mind, although it was lost for days, but because I didn't know how to deal with it, there was a lot involved, Charlie's own mood, attitude—so I kept pushing it off. I had known from what Billy had said, and other things, too, but in a fuzzy wordless way—that Gus was out to break up this choir project and pull those kids back to the Flats where he could dominate and use them. And he was out to get Charlie. Why? I didn't know. His bragging around the Flats—Neel had told me this, too—that he had a list of folks whose ways his gang didn't approve of and he was going to run them out of town; said *no place in this city for them artists and eggheads, and organ-players and rock 'n' rollers and fairies, Communists, nigger-lovers who talk about civil rights, and dirty perverts and traitors and Jews who pretend they're scientists—they're all one and the same,* he said; *they're un-American,* he said, *and we don't want none of them in this country and we're not going to have none of them in this city. I'll see to that.* And Neel and I had laughed. Why? Because it was so incredibly stupid. Because it made no sense, and too much. Because we hoped it wouldn't amount to anything, and knew it could build up into something we did not want to name. I had been able to repress it, to push it out of the probable into the dimly possible. Neel had been more obviously worried. I had seen Gus in front of All Saints Church, twice, since Billy talked to Charlie. Had stopped him, the last time, had asked pointedly if he was waiting for anyone; he said no and walked away. All this—which I had known and tried not to know—flooded my consciousness with a heavy spurt, the way your heart quickens, as I saw Charlie go up on the lawn. At that moment, I heard sirens coming from opposite directions, but at a distance.

I blank out here. Next thing I remember: I was on the lawn, in the middle of about a dozen of Gus's gang. The cross was blazing. Something was happening inside the house. There was a dull tramp tramp of feet on floors. I heard this but I could not see. Beyond me, two or three feet away, I saw Charlie's blond head; he towered above all of them and his hair picked up the light. I couldn't see the kids. I saw Gus pushing through: aiming for Charlie, sidling toward him, in no hurry, slow, sure of himself, coming close to me, intent on Charlie—I shifted my balance, turned an inch, easy; as he took a step forward I let go and Gus was on the ground and somebody was yelling, *My God it's the crippled preacher,* and I turned quick and swung, smacked him on the jaw, saw him stagger, turn away. Somebody took a step toward me, another—I gave him a punch, didn't think it had much muscle behind it but to my amazement he fell. I wasn't mad, felt cool and light-headed and curiously released—felt I'd like to keep slugging, like to slug a hundred, a thousand, felt I had been bound in elastic and suddenly it had snapped and I was free free free—then I saw Charlie's eyes, was close to him now, they were excited, alert—I felt a sudden terrific pressure behind me, someone or two or three were trying to throw me off balance, I was penned in, wasn't sure what they were up to and couldn't maneuver to see—something to the side of me flashed, arm shot across my face, caught another arm, two bodies clinched, saw one was Charlie—who hadn't taken a punch at anybody since he was five years old—saw the bodies bend, saw one giving, wasn't feeling now just watching as it slipped under the other, he's losing his balance, he can't make it, then I saw that blond hair easing easing around, a sudden quick twist—and Charlie came up with a switchblade he'd pulled away from the tall stranger. Stranger slid back in the crowd . . . my hand was feeling for Charlie's, closing over the knife, I was inching it into my pocket—

Charlie laughed. You hear a lot of sounds in a lifetime and only a few stay with you. I'll never forget that one. Somebody said, *I be damned if it aint that girlie who plays dat org*— Charlie's fist landed in the speaker's mouth, came out bloody, jabbed his belly and the guy doubled up. Something eased, somewhere; the pressure on us gave—not much but a little. It happened so quick I was thrown off my axis and had difficulty catching myself. Then I saw those organ arms of Charlie's, hard as steel, flailing out in all directions. Suddenly he lunged across me, I ducked to avoid getting my face smashed. I called, *Hit him coming in!* It wasn't necessary. Charlie had steadied. He did a full left swing at the guy in front of him, and laid it on his jawbone. Now he was making it count, punching with the speed and power-precision that had made him our city's most brilliant pianist and organist. And they moved away from him. It surprised me. I couldn't figure it out. Sirens were close now. Right at us. Things were happening in the street and back of us at the rear of the house; inside it, too. I heard a cop whistle insistently, heard somebody up at the house yell a warning; heard sirens in front; where we were, there was a deep pocket of silence, but it was about to be filled:

Gus had climbed off the ground. Was coming toward us. I got ready for him but he brushed past me, didn't give me a glance. He was after Charlie. Somehow, Charlie didn't catch on. He didn't know Gus, knew his name all right, but he'd never spoken to him or seen him, as far as I know. But Gus knew him, Gus's dream life was full of Charlie. I needed to warn him. It was a nightmare. I couldn't warn him. What I needed to say should have been said weeks before. I didn't make a sound. Just kept looking hard at Charlie. Hoping he'd turn and see what he needed to see on my face. But Charlie didn't look—it was too dark to see, anyway—and Gus came right up to him, slow and sidling, and said it: the foul slimy rotted words he'd raked together in his head for months—and then he punched Charlie on the jaw. It was a full swing, perfectly pivoted, perfectly timed. I believe I heard that bone crack. Maybe not. But Charlie couldn't take it; he staggered, he bent over, he almost fell. I wanted to help him; knew if I did and we lived through it, it would ruin him. This was his risk and his big chance. Maybe I rationalize it now; maybe I was plain paralyzed, but I don't think so; think I'm right about this. Everybody was still; it was like somebody was already dead; the words had drained the juice out of those who heard.

Then Gus made his mistake: He turned to the others and said, *See how easy it is with a slobby* —— —— —— *fairy?* walked over to Charlie and stroked his face. Once. Once did it. Charlie came to. With a lightning twist of body he turned on Gus, gave him one straight look and shot his fist into his mouth, then he did a left swing and caught Gus in the groin. Gus stumbled, he was about to right himself, he was moving fast, but Charlie lunged and hit him on the head, or the back of the neck, and then smacked him in the belly. I'm not sure about the next tenth of a second but somehow he got him down. Then those steel-muscled arms began to punch head chest neck belly face head chest neck belly face head chest neck—playing him like an organ, pounding out a score that had been written a long time ago on bleak lonely nights when Charlie's soul was shriveled with fear. And it was making fine music. Yes, I admit it: I never heard anything that sounded so grand. He beat Gus's face to pulp. We stood there listening to those blows and I knew he'd kill him—not because he wanted to kill but because he didn't know how to quit. I caught his arm, said it's enough, you've done enough, and he stared at me. He looked down at Gus, then he sort of smiled slow, and let go. I said, Let's get the boys out, Charlie—and he followed me through that crowd. Nobody ran interference. I wondered why they didn't kill us, right there. It would have been mighty easy to. We must have gone twenty steps before we saw the boys: huddled up close to the cross, as close as the flames permitted, wide-eyed and shaking-scared. Back of the house—I think it was happening as we moved toward those kids—there was a sudden thunderous roar thinning out to a few random yells. I had the impression people were stampeding. We didn't say a word—at least I don't remember a sound—but the boys saw us coming and ran to us and Charlie patted this small head and that one, and Billy said, We never done it, Charlie, we never done it, and grabbed Charlie's arm and just held on as if they were in deep water and he couldn't swim. Two grabbed me and it seemed like the rest of them were pushing into the small of my back and half under my legs and under Charlie's, and we started out with them and then we felt the ice-cold spray: they had turned the fire hose on us, full force. It cut to the bone and knocked one of them down. Charlie picked him up. The kids began to cry, three or four of them. The small crowd on the lawn broke up fast now and slipped away toward the ravine, and we walked straight out, with no blocking from anybody, pushing the boys in front of us toward the sidewalk.

It was like waking up after a prolonged dream. Street roped off and full of police cars, fire hose, fire engines; sidewalk on the Parish House side of the street crowded with spectators and more fire hose; cops everywhere, things organized, things under control, at least in front—and here we came, wet as rats, and the kids squalling. We must have been a sight to look at. I felt a sharp stabbing pain in my bad hip, stopped, took another step, slowed, thinking in panic, This is it, I'm going to fall. But I didn't, somehow. And there, suddenly, was Neel, face noncommittal, eyes—well, I don't know what he was thinking. I tried to grin, I said, "See that they get home safe, will you, Neel? they're freezing."

Neel called two of his men who put the boys in police cars and took them to the Flats. By this time, I had lost Charlie. He was there and then he wasn't there. Neel said, Can you make it to the study? I said, Oh sure. But he slipped his hand on my arm and we worked our way through the cars and staring people, most of whom I did not know, saw Johnny suddenly, he was grinning, he called Hi, Reverend, we were at the Parish House door now, I unlocked it or rather I gave Neel the key for I found I couldn't turn it, was trembling too much.

Seems kind of cold, I said. Neel laughed, said, Come in and sit down. Then he went up to my room and got a bathrobe and I stripped and got in it. I noticed there was blood, thought the stump was bleeding a little, not much; decided not to mention it; didn't seem to hurt much. Then Neel said, How about me making the coffee, this time? and I sat there dumb as a rabbit and shook, just shook, while he turned on the switch and got the kettle boiling. I was plain fogged up and did nothing but shake and stare, I'm afraid. Then he handed me a cup of black coffee and I gulped it. About that time two of his men stepped in, nodded at me, grinned, and one said to Neel, "We picked up five—the ones he and that organist beat up."

They kept looking at me. One of them said, "Father Landrum, you should have played football, way you broke through that crowd."

The other one said in a low voice, "He was All-American, crazy!" Then he said, "That organist fellow gave Gus Hestor the whipping of his life, broke two or three ribs, four teeth, bloodied his eye and I don't know what."

What crowd did I break through? I remembered only what I have set down here.

I was cold and the leg was in trouble and I was beginning to feel like something worse than a fool and I hoped they'd go away. But I asked, "Did you pick up the stranger?"

They had seen no stranger. I described him: tall, narrow-shouldered, no muscle much, black straight longish hair, blue eyes—unless I made it up, not sure about that—"Was with Gus Hestor, had a knife," I handed the switchblade to Neel, "Charlie caught it just before it went in my side."

Neel sent them back to check. "Find out who has seen him with Gus."

"May not be a stranger," I said to Neel. "But I think so. Cultivated accent; college man, I'd guess; never saw him in Windsor Hills before."

I drank another cup of coffee. Then I asked what happened. Neel summed it up:

Nobody knew who set the cross on fire; the big crowd, the

real mob had gathered at the rear of the house—and that is where the damage was done. Gus's gang had got hung up in front, on Charlie and me. The ones at the rear had been scattered, finally, with tear gas grenades. The police were about to toss in a few on us when somebody told them the choirboys were there and the preacher—Neel laughed, I laughed, too—so they turned the fire hose on us, instead. Neel said the mob had gone inside, had written all over the walls what you'd expect them to write, had cut Grace's painting to shreds, had urinated on the floors, broken the windows—

"—then they slipped into the trees and ran down the ravine, cut across to the road below." That is where the police picked up the handful they caught.

At this moment, the dynamite went off. Window shook, cups rattled, phone fell off the desk—we were not sure, for a moment, whether it was under the Parish House or across the street.

"I better go. You all right?"

"Oh sure."

Neel went out as Sydney and Katie appeared in the hall. "My God," I heard Sydney say, "it must have ruined the place. At the rear of the house. Everything blew as we stepped out of the car."

Katie walked in, face chalky, expressionless. Sydney followed her, almost grinning, saying, "Well, it's here—the back-alley revolution. The good old rural proletariat. The pygmie minds with their big sticks of dynamite. They're probably blowing up the lab now."

Katie's voice crossed his, sharp. "Stop it! He's hurt." She pointed to the floor at a small pool of blood. It surprised me.

"Where are you hurt?" Sydney asked.

"I don't know."

"The leg. Does it pain you?"

"Not that much."

Sydney went to the car for his bag. Katie was looking me over. She picked up the wet sweater, picked up my slacks, showed me the knife tear—a slit about ten inches long beginning above the hip pocket.

"Don't worry," I laughed it off, "the prosthesis got the brunt of it."

Apparently the switchblade had dug in above my hip pretty close to the kidney, had skittered along the flesh when Charlie caught it, and along the prosthetic leg.

Sydney examined the wound, said he'd have to take some stitches. He stretched me out on two chairs, shot a local anaesthetic in, cleaned it and gave me a shot of penicillin while he sent Katie up to my bedroom for pajamas and the crutches. Between them they did a neat job of it, then they helped me upstairs and into bed. Sydney insisted on a bit of sedation. Afterward, they sat there, apparently waiting for it to take effect. Katie's face a blank mask. "They're better at it than we are," I thought; "we show our feelings; they've learned not to show anything." I kept saying this to myself, over and over as if it were the most important of thoughts; until I slipped off under the sedative.

I suppose they left when I fell asleep.

Then suddenly, I was awake. I felt curiously quiet and passive. The exultation had left me, and the feeling-like-an-idiot reaction had left, too. The only thought in my head was awareness of a thin pain in my hip. It was not that it hurt much. It didn't. It was like a child's night light: something to focus on. And I held to it as long as I could: for in the darkness behind that pain were things I couldn't look at; if I could keep feeling the thin pain— But the sedative wore off after a time, and I began to feel beat and pulled down; every muscle in my body began to ache, bones— I began to remember the house—everything—Gus . . . the stranger . . . there I was: reverting to the technics of a half-back: slogging it out, punching heads like a roughneck and enjoying it, yes, enjoying it—I was smiling now in the dark, thinking, Man man! when I see him tomorrow what a time we'll have! Good old Charlie . . . good old— And then I was sobbing. I didn't know what it was all about, the sudden crackup—oh sure I knew, it was everything, it was— I lay there and let it wash through me: all that had happened—all I had felt . . . I was struggling in a swollen flood of wordless images and shame and despair and longing and a terrible knowledge of failure—and everywhere I saw Mark's face—and hers—

I was not capable of thinking, as I lay there that night. But now, I can find a few words for it. I think it was this: what was moral triumph for Charlie, what was a great thing for him, was a miserable failure for me, and I knew it and the knowing lay like a dead thing in me. He had gone ahead: I had turned back. As a man he had found the physical courage, or the love, yes, it was that, to do what he had to do: as priest I had not found the spiritual courage, or was it the desire, to do what I had to do— there was another way for me, and I had not found it . . . things to say and I had not said them . . . warnings to give and I had not given them . . . renunciations to make and I had not made them . . . always between me and the irrevocable commitment was the good guy: *me*, the good guy who didn't like to offend his friends, didn't like to stir up disunity in his congregation, didn't like to look at evil when it came too close—never wholly accepting the lonely stark uncharted mission that was mine . . . now and then showing a spurt of courage, catching a fleeting vision and finding a few words for it, now and then now and then—now and then carrying out one brief mission—but mission after mission after mission. . . .

I got control of myself, after a while, and lay there quietly in the dark thinking of the past thinking of the small present ashamed of my failures ashamed of my wavering cloudy vision praying God to speak words to me that I could understand, begging for certitude, begging for clarity, begging Him for what He, in His wisdom, has never yet given us: the human beings he created and left here on this small earth to work the rest of it out, themselves; their part, their role in the cosmic destiny; in His wisdom as Creator never telling us how; giving us only our vocation: to create the human destiny out of uncreated possibilities of evil and good, never asking us to separate evil and good—which in the nature of the human condition we cannot do—but giving us both, and out of both expecting us to find the truest form that our life can assume, never the ultimate form, no; but in the process of forming, to find an integrity of purpose, of commitment—

But this fragmentary glimpse which I had searched for during the years, and now and then felt I was about to see clearly, I held now only for a moment: Then, once more, I was seeing Charlie's face, hearing that laugh when he wrenched the knife from the stranger who had tried to kill me. I had not known before but I knew now: Charlie was aware that he had saved my life. And, in sudden realization of what I owed him, I felt his new strength, his new freedom: he had whipped it—that old nagging fear, that old infecting guilt which had crept through his whole life—except for his music. Now, he was on top of it. He had won. He had risked everything for his choirboys and he had won everything for himself, and my life for me. He'd never go back to the quicksands, never! . . . good old Charlie . . . good old Charlie. . . . I dropped off on that.

My sleep must have been pretty heavy, for that phone had been ringing a good while, I think, when I came to sufficiently to find it and mutter, Yes?

"Is this the Reverend Landrum?"

"Yes."

A crisp wide-awake voice said, "We dislike to disturb you, sir, but there has been a serious accident." She told me the organist, Charles Owens, had been badly injured: "We don't know his family." I told her there was no family but I was his friend and she could talk to me. He was in the County Hospital, Room 304, she said. His neck had been fractured, perhaps broken; there were contusions on his head; apparently he had been struck several times on the head.

"I take it, it is bad."

"Yes. We don't know the extent of the break or other injuries but he is in a critical condition."

"Unconscious?"

"Yes."

I told her I'd come down right away. Did she have any knowledge of how it had happened? Not much, she said. He had been found by the police lying on the pavement close to his car in front of his apartment. An iron pipe had been found near the curb.

I thanked her and hung up. I felt almost no surprise or shock. The feeling hadn't responded, as yet, to the fact. This sort of thing went through my mind: *So that's the way they did it. That is why they didn't do it in the open, why they didn't kill us both. Easier this way, sure.* Obvious, now. And yet, I hadn't thought of its possibility.

I couldn't manage that trip to the hospital by myself. I turned on the light. Saw Sydney had scribbled his phone number on a card where I couldn't miss it. I called him and he answered at once. I told him what I knew. He said, "I'll come for you, Dave." Then he said, "Wait—" Katie came to the phone. She said, "We're coming, Dave; don't attempt anything until we get there." I tried to disobey her but I couldn't manage the pull-up that was necessary to get out of bed.

When we got to the hospital Sydney and I went in to Charlie's room. Katie, silent and white-faced, stayed outside as Sydney had suggested she do. One look was enough for us to see what they had done to him. He was breathing with difficulty and seemed to me inert and close to death but of course I didn't know too much about these things.

Sydney said he wanted to talk to the head nurse and to the attending doctor, and then he'd call a neurologist he thought highly of and put him on the case. He went out and I was left with Charlie. I looked at that white swathed head and neck, the closed eyes. I took his hand. It was flaccid and cold. I said, *Charlie* . . . hoping he might, somewhere inside him, hear me: *Charlie, you were great! you were just great!* And then I prayed. I said the Lord's Prayer and I began, *O Father of mercies, and God of all comforts, our only help in time of need; We fly unto thee for succour in behalf of this thy servant* . . . and then, suddenly, I was praying as a small boy prays: begging God to let Charlie know in some way that he had done all right, begging Him to let him live the life he had just begun to live, even if it meant living it paralyzed; for I knew his spirit would never be paralyzed again— But as I prayed, I finally stopped asking for the small things we have no right to ask for, I asked only for the big thing: that God help me understand this—all of it—especially my part in it—asked Him to give me the strength to look at the evil that is in me, in all of us and surrounding us, and then I prayed for the extra strength to look at the good that is so close to the evil, and that we must see and acknowledge or perish.

Katie came in. She stood with her head bowed until I had finished my prayer and then she went to the bed and knelt and took Charlie's hand. When she felt that cold nerveless flesh and bone, she turned and looked at me and her eyes slowly filled with horror: there was no room for grief. Then she looked at that hand a long time and gently kissed it and walked out of the room.

I stayed on with Charlie until the neurologist came. I spoke to him and left him with Sydney and I went out and sat with Katie. Her face was cold and white and she was hunched up in the chair leaning her cheek against her hand and staring at the floor. I knew what was in her mind: I knew it was pulling and tearing and binding her and tearing and binding. . . . I knew the horror would stay in her eyes a long time: that an ignorant, stupid, hating mob, a stranger she knew nothing about, and so much about, could end and had ended the beauty and wonder of Charlie's music. And I knew there was nothing that could help her, just now. Without looking at me, she said, "I don't want him to live." I did not answer her. The two of us who loved him did not even agree on what we wanted for him: I wanted him to live; she wanted him to die. What would happen was completely out of our power, now. There were decisions we could have made but we failed to make them at the right time. This was not ours.

Dawn was breaking when the surgeon and Sydney came to us. They did not need to say it. We knew.

The three of us were silent as Sydney drove back to the Parish House. They helped me up the stairs and to bed. Sydney said, You should let your doctor see that hip in the morning. I said I would. Katie came to the bed. She began to say, I'll call Jane—she should— But in the middle of it she began to sob. It was a lonely sound. Sydney did not touch her. She could not be reached just now, and he loved her enough to know it. The sobs stopped as suddenly as they had begun. As unemotionally as if talking of the most trivial thing, she said, "He can't finish it now."

But he had finished it: Charlie had found his last scene. I wanted to say so: I wanted to tell her how the Coward had at last found his way to courage in Charlie's own life. But I knew she would have none of it: she would say, The opera was more important; it was the best of him, the unique, creative part of him: the mob won, it is no use to pretend otherwise, it won! And she was right to think this. But I was right, too. And this is the agony and the glory of human existence that we both were right.

I did not try to answer. We could not talk about Charlie in philosophical terms, that night: we could only show each other our hurt hearts. In a moment, she said, Take care, Dave—and they left.

For days, I have read again and again what I have written down here, pondering it, remembering so much that did not come back at the right moment but now hovers on the edge of my mind, echoing, echoing. . . . I said when I began that I wanted to find its meaning, its form. I see now that its meaning is still in the making, its form is still being shaped by the living: For the rest of us are still here and this experience lies, even now, only half formed in the hard rock of our awareness.

I am not sure what will come next for we are still changing it: each time we feel one small movement of compassion or mercy or fear or hate, each time we glimpse a deeper level or turn away from the new vision, each time we find our courage or lose it, we are forming this hour. Someday, Katie with her talent which Charlie thought more real and sure than his may cease her mourning for the loss of his music and begin to create her own. Someday, perhaps I— But this is guessing and hoping. I am not sure what is ahead: or where the next hour lies: except I know it is hidden somewhere in this one, among quiet and noisy and un-counted possibilities. And we, the living, will find it or fail to, as we continue to shape this small piece of time we call our own.